More praise for Colin Dexter and *The Remorseful Day*

"Dexter gives fans plenty of reasons to mourn the series' end, since this 13th volume about the grammatically correct, lovelorn, poetry-quoting Oxford police officer is as strong as any before."
—*Boston Herald*

"The finish to what has been for me the most nearly perfect series of detective works ... Dexter's prose and plotting have been models of concision and consistency."
—*The Raleigh News & Observer*

"Once again, Dexter has written a classy, clever mystery that wraps itself around realistic yet intriguing characters and has all the muddled trappings of real life."
—*San Jose Mercury News*

"A worthy conclusion to a fine series. Dexter, known for his extraordinarily literate prose and eye for detail, is at the top of his game."
—*Richmond Times-Dispatch*

Please turn the page for more reviews. . . .

By Colin Dexter

THE REMORSEFUL DAY

Colin Dexter

FAWCETT BOOKS • NEW YORK

A Fawcett Book
Published by The Ballantine Publishing Group
Copyright © 1999 by Colin Dexter

All rights reserved under International and Pan-American Copyright Conventions. Published in the United States by The Ballantine Publishing Group, a division of Random House, Inc., New
York. Originally published in Great Britain by Macmillan Publishers, Ltd., in 1999.

Fawcett is a registered trademark and the Fawcett colophon is a
trademark of Random House, Inc.

www.randomhouse.com/BB/

Library of Congress Catalog Card Number: 00-109767

ISBN 0-8041-1954-6

This edition published by arrangement with Crown Publishers, a
division of Random House, Inc.

Manufactured in the United States of America

First Ballantine Mass Market Edition: February 2001

10   9   8   7   6   5   4   3   2   1

For
George, Hilary, Maria, and Beverley
(Please note the Oxford comma)

Acknowledgments

My special thanks are due, imprimis to Terry Benczik from New Jersey, for sending me so many apposite quotations; to Cyndi Cook from Hawaii, for singing to me as I wrote these chapters; to Allison Dexter, for sharing with me her expertise on coronary care; to Eddie Andrews, one of my former pupils, for initiating me (at last!) into some of the mysteries of the SOCOs; and to Chris Burt, producer of so many Morse episodes on TV, for his constant support and encouragement.

The author and publishers wish to thank the following who have kindly given permission for use of copyright materials:

Extracts from *More Poems XLI*, *More Poems XVI*, and *A Shropshire Lad* by A. E. Housman are reproduced by permission of The Society of Authors as the literary representative of the Estate of A. E. Housman.

Extract from *On the Dole in Darlington* by David Mackenzie is reproduced by permission of the author.

Extract from translation of *An Die Musik* by Basil Swift is reproduced by permission of the author.

Extract from *I'm a Stranger Here Myself* by Ogden Nash (from the collection *Candy is Dandy*, Andre Deutsch Ltd, Copyright © 1938 by Ogden Nash, Renewed) is reprinted by permission of Curtis Brown

Ltd, Andre Deutsch Ltd, and Little, Brown and Company, Inc.

Extract from *Catch-22* by Joseph Heller is reproduced by permission of the author.

Extract from *The Fiddler of Dooney* by W. B. Yeats is reproduced by permission of A. P. Watt Ltd on behalf of Michael B. Yeats, and Simon & Schuster Inc.

Extract from *Come to Think of It* by G. K. Chesterton is reproduced by kind permission of A. P. Watt Limited on behalf of the Royal Literary Fund.

Extract from *Oxford* by Jan Morris is reproduced by permission of Oxford University Press.

Extract from *Lovelace Bleeding* by Roy Dean is reproduced by permission of the author.

Extract from *Nightwood* by Djuna Barnes is reproduced by permission of the author and Faber and Faber Ltd.

Every effort has been made to trace all copyright holders but if any has been inadvertently overlooked, the author and publishers will be pleased to make the necessary arrangement at the first opportunity.

Ensanguining the skies
How heavily it dies
  Into the west away;
Past touch and sight and sound
Not further to be found
How hopeless under ground
  Falls the remorseful day.
          (A. E. Housman,
          More Poems, XVI)

When I wrote my 1997 letter I thought I had little to look forward to in 1998, but it turns out that I was stupidly optimistic.

          (David Mackenzie,
          On the Dole in Darlington)

Prolegomenon

> *As o'er me now thou lean'st thy breast,*
> *With launder'd bodice crisply pressed,*
> *Lief I'd prolong my grievous ill—*
> *Wert thou my guardian angel still.*
> (Edmund Raikes, 1537–65, *The Nurse*)

"So I often hook my foot over the side of the mattress."

"You *what*?"

"Sort of anchors me to my side of the bed."

"Double bed?"

"Not unknown is it, for a married couple? People can share the same bed but not the same thoughts—old Chinese saying."

"Still makes me jealous."

"Idiot!"

"Everybody gets a bit jealous sometimes."

"Not everybody."

"Not you, nurse?"

"I've just learned not to show it, that's all. And it's none of your business in any case."

"Sorry."

"How I hate men who say 'sorry'!"

"I promise not to say it again, miss."

"And will you promise me something else? To be a bit more honest with yourself—and with me?"

"Scout's honor!"

"I can't believe you were ever in the Scouts."

"Well, no, but . . ."

"Shall I test you?"

"Test me?"

"Would you like me to jump into bed with you *now*?"

"Yes!"

1

"You're quick on the buzzer."

"Next question?"

"Do you think *I'd* like to jump into bed with *you*?"

"I'd like to think so."

"What about the other patients?"

"You could draw the curtains."

"What excuse. . . ?"

"You could always take my blood pressure."

"*Again?*"

"Why not?"

"We know all about your blood pressure. High—very high—especially when I'm around."

"It's those black stockings of yours."

"You're a stocking-tops man!"

"Nice word, isn't it—stocking-tops?"

"If only you weren't stuck in this bloody ward!"

"I can always discharge myself."

"Not a wise move, good sir—not in your case."

"What time are you off duty?"

"Half-eight."

"What'll you do then?"

"Off home. I'm expecting a phone call."

"You're trying to make me jealous again."

"After that, I suppose I'll just poke the thingummy, you know, around the four channels."

"Five, now."

"We don't get the new one."

"What about Sky?"

"In *our* village, satellite dishes are most *definitely* discouraged."

"You could always take a video home."

"No need. We've got lots of videos. You should see some of them—you know, the sex ones."

"You watch that sort of thing?"

"When I'm in the mood."

"When's that?"

"Most of the time."

"And even if you aren't in the mood?"

"Oh yes! They soon turn anybody on. Haven't you

seen some of these Amsterdam videos? All sorts of bizarre things they get up to."

"I haven't seen them, no."

"Would you like to?"

"I'm not quite sure I would, no."

"Not even if you watched them with me?"

"Please, nurse, am I allowed to change my mind?"

"We could arrange a joint viewing."

"How—how bizarre's bizarre?"

"Well, in one of 'em there's this woman—about my age—lovely figure—wrists tied to the top of the four-poster bed—ankles tied to the bottom . . ."

"Go on."

"Well, there's these two young studs—one black, one white—"

"No racial discrimination, then?"

"—and they just take turns, you know."

"Raping her . . ."

"You're so *naive*, aren't you? She wouldn't have *been* in the bloody video, would she, if she didn't want to be? There *are* some people like her, you know. The only real sexual thrill they get is from some sort of submission—you know, that sort of thing."

"Odd sort of women!"

"Odd? Unusual, perhaps, but . . ."

"How come you know so much about this?"

"When we were in Amsterdam, they invited me to do some porno filming. Frank didn't mind. They made a pretty good offer."

"So you negotiated a fee?"

"Hold on! I only said this particular woman was *about* my age—"

"—and had a lovely figure."

"Would you like to see if it *was* me?"

"One condition."

"What's that?"

"If I come, you mustn't hook your foot over the side of the mattress."

"Not much danger of that."

"Stay with me a bit longer!"

"No. You're not my only patient, and some of these poor devils'll be here long after *you've* gone."

"Will you come and give me a chaste little kiss before you go off duty?"

"No. I'm shooting straight back to Lower Swinstead. I told you: I'm expecting a phone call."

"From . . . your husband?"

"You must be kidding! Frank's in Switzerland for a few days. He's far too mean to call me from there—even on the cheap rates."

"Another man in your life?"

"Jesus! You don't take me for a dyke, do you?"

"You're an amazing girl."

"Girl? I'll be forty-eight this Thursday."

"Can I take you out? Make a birthday fuss of you?"

"No chance. According to your notes, you're going to be in at least till the end of the week."

"You know, in a way, I wish I *could* stay in. Indefinitely."

"Well, I promise one thing: as soon as you're out, I'll be in touch."

"Please! If you can."

"And you'll come and see me?"

"If you invite me."

"I'm inviting you now."

Chapter One

You holy Art, when all my hope is shaken,
And through life's raging tempest I am drawn,
You make my heart with warmest love to waken,
As if into a better world reborn.
  (From *An Die Musik*, translated by Basil Swift)

Apart (of course) from Wagner, apart from Mozart's compositions for the clarinet, Schubert was one of the select composers who could occasionally transport him to the frontier of tears. And it was Schubert's turn in the early evening of Wednesday, July 15, 1998, when—*The Archers* over—a bedroom-slippered Chief Inspector Morse was to be found in his North Oxford bachelor flat, sitting at his ease in Zion and listening to a Lieder recital on Radio 3, an amply filled tumbler of pale Glenfiddich beside him. And why not? He was on a few days' furlough that had so far proved quite unexpectedly pleasurable.

Morse had never enrolled in the itchy-footed regiment of truly adventurous souls, feeling (as he did) little temptation to explore the remoter corners even of his native land, and this principally because he could now imagine few if any places closer to his heart than Oxford—the city which, though not his natural mother, had for so many years performed the duties of a loving foster parent. As for foreign travel, long faded were his boyhood dreams that roamed the sands round Samarkand; and a lifelong pterophobia still precluded any airline bookings to Bayreuth, Salzburg, Vienna— the trio of cities he sometimes thought he ought to see.

Vienna . . .

The city Schubert had so rarely left; the city in which he'd gained so little recognition; where he'd died of typhoid fever—only thirty-one.

Not much of an innings, was it—thirty-one?

Morse leaned back, listened, and looked semicontentedly through the French window. In *The Ballad of Reading Gaol*, Oscar Wilde had spoken of that little patch of blue that prisoners call the sky; and Morse now contemplated that little patch of green that owners of North Oxford flats are wont to call the garden. Flowers had always meant something to Morse, even from his schooldays. Yet in truth it was more the nomenclature of the several species, and their context in the works of the great poets, that had compelled his imagination: fast-fading violets, the globèd peonies, the fields of asphodel . . . Indeed Morse was fully aware of the etymology and the mythological associations of the asphodel, although quite certainly he would never have recognized one of its kind had it flashed across a Technicolor screen.

It was still true though: as men grew older (so Morse told himself) the delights of the natural world grew ever more important. Not just the flowers, either. What about the birds?

Morse had reached the conclusion that if he were to be reincarnated (a prospect which seemed to him most blessedly remote), he would register as a part-time Quaker and devote a sizeable quota of his leisure hours to ornithology. This latter decision was consequent upon his realization, however late in the day, that life would be significantly impoverished should the birds no longer sing. And it was for this reason that, the previous week, he had taken out a year's subscription to *Birdwatching*; taken out a copy of the RSPB's *Birdwatchers' Guide* from the Summertown Library; and purchased a secondhand pair of 152/1000m binoculars (£9.90) that he'd spotted in the window of the Oxfam Shop just down the Banbury Road. And to complete his program he had called in at the Summertown Pet Store and taken home a small wired cylinder packed with peanuts—a cylinder now suspended from a branch overhanging his garden. From *the* branch overhanging his garden.

He reached for the binoculars now and focused on an interesting specimen pecking away at the grass below the peanuts: a small bird, with a greyish crown, dark-brown bars across the dingy russet of its back, and paler underparts. As he watched, he sought earnestly to memorize this remarkable bird's characteristics, so as to be able to match its variegated plumage against the appropriate illustration in the *Guide*.

Plenty of time for that though.

He leaned back once more and rejoiced in the radiant warmth of Schwarzkopf's voice, following the English text that lay open on his lap: "You holy Art, when all my hope is shaken . . ."

When, too, a few moments later, his mood of pleasurable melancholy was shaken by three confident bursts on a front-door bell that to several of his neighbors sounded considerably over-decibeled, even for the hard-of-hearing.

Chapter Two

When Napoleon's eagle eye flashed down the list of officers proposed for promotion, he was wont to scribble in the margin against any particular name: "Is he *lucky*, though?"
(Felix Kirkmarkham, *The Genius of Napoleon*)

"Not disturbing you?"

Morse made no direct reply, but his resigned look would have been sufficiently eloquent for most people.

Most people.

He opened the door widely—perforce needed so to do—in order to accommodate his unexpected visitor within the comparatively narrow entrance.

"I *am* disturbing you."

"No, no! It's just that . . ."

"Look, matey!" (Chief Superintendent Strange cocked an ear toward the lounge.) "I don't give a dam if I'm disturbing *you*; pity about disturbing old Schubert, though."

For the dozenth time in their acquaintance, Morse found himself quietly re-appraising the man who first beached and then readjusted his vast bulk in an armchair, with a series of expiratory grunts.

Morse had long known better than to ask Strange whether he wanted a drink, alcoholic or nonalcoholic. If Strange wanted a drink, of either variety, he would ask for it, immediately and unambiguously. But Morse did allow himself one question:

"You know you just said you didn't give a dam. Do you know how you spell 'dam'?"

"You spell it 'd—a—m.' Tiny Indian coin—that's what a dam is. Surely you knew that?"

For the thirteenth time in their acquaintance . . .

"Is that a single malt you're drinking there, Morse?"

It was only after Morse had filled, then refilled, his visitor's glass that Strange came to the point of his evening call.

"The papers—even the tabloids—have been doing me proud. You read *The Times* yesterday?"

"I never read *The Times*."

"What? The bloody paper's there—there!—on the coffee table."

"Just for the crossword—and the Letters page."

"You don't read the obituaries?"

"Well, perhaps just a glance sometimes."

"To see if you're there?"

"To see if some of them are younger than me."

"I don't follow you."

"If they *are* younger, so a statistician once told me, I've got a slightly better chance of living on beyond the norm."

"Mm." Strange nodded vaguely. "You frightened of death?"

"A bit."

Strange suddenly picked up his second half-full tumbler of Scotch and tossed it back at a draught like a visitor downing an initiatory vodka at the Russian Embassy.

"What about the telly, Morse? Did you watch *Newsroom South-East* last night?"

"I've got a TV—video as well. But I don't seem to get round to watching anything and I can't work the video very well."

"Really? And how do you expect to understand what's going on in the great big world out there? You're supposed to *know* what's going on. You're a police officer, Morse!"

"I listen to the wireless—"

"*Wireless?* Where've you got to in life, matey?

'Radio'—that's what they've been calling it these last thirty years."

It was Morse's turn to nod vaguely as Strange continued:

"Good job I got *this* done for you, then."

Sorry, sir. Perhaps I am a bit behind the times—as well as *The Times*.

But Morse gave no voice to these latter thoughts as he slowly read the photocopied article that Strange had handed to him. Morse always read slowly.

MURDER POLICE SEEK ANONYMOUS CALLER

A MAN HAS rung the police anonymously with information that could help identify the killer of Mrs. Yvonne Harrison who was found handcuffed and battered to death a year ago.

Detectives yesterday appealed for the caller to make contact again. No clear motive has ever been established for the murder of the 48-year-old nurse who was alone in her home in the Oxfordshire village of Lower Swinstead when her killer broke in through a ground-floor window.

Detective Chief Superintendent Strange of Thames Valley CID said that a man had rung twice: "We are very anxious to hear from this caller again as soon as possible. He can contact us in the strictest confidence. We don't believe the calls are a hoax and we don't believe the caller himself is the killer. But we think that he can give us more information to substantially further our inquiries into this brutal murder."

At the time of the murder Mrs. Harrison's husband Frank was in London where he works for the Swiss Helvetia Bank. Their son Simon works at the Daedalus Press in Oxford; their daughter Sarah is a junior consultant in the Diabetes Centre at the Radcliffe Infirmary in Oxford.

Had Morse's eyes narrowed slightly as he read the last few lines? If they had, he made no reference to whatever might have puzzled or interested him there.

"I trust it wasn't you who split the infinitive, sir?"

"You never suspected that, surely? We're all used to sloppy reporting, aren't we?"

Morse nodded as he handed back the photocopied article.

"No! Keep it, Morse—I've got the original."

"Very kind of you, sir, but . . ."

"But it interested you, perhaps?"

"Only the bit at the end, about the Radcliffe."

"Why's that?"

"Well, as you know, I was in there myself—after I was diagnosed."

"Christ! You make it sound as if you're the only one who's ever been bloody diagnosed!"

Morse held his peace, for his memory needed no jogging: Strange himself had been a patient in the self-same Radcliffe Infirmary a year or so before his own hospitalization. No one had known much about Strange's troubles. There had been hushed rumors about "endocrinological dysfunction"; but not everyone at Police HQ was happy about spelling or pronouncing or identifying such a polysyllabic ailment.

"You know why I brought that cutting, Morse?"

"No! And to be honest with you, I don't much care. I'm on furlough, you know that. The quack tells me I'm run down—blood sugar far too high—blood pressure far too high. Says I need to have a quiet little rest-cure and try to forget the great big world out there, as you call it."

"Some of us can't forget it though, can we?" Strange spoke the words very softly, and Morse got to his feet and turned off the CD player.

"Not one of your greatest triumphs that case, was it?"

"One of the few—very few, Morse—I got no-bloody-where with. And it wasn't exactly mine, either, as you know. But it was my responsibility, that's all. Still is."

"What's all this got to do with me?"

Strange further expanded his gargantuan girth as he further expounded:

"I thought, you know, with the wife . . . and all that . . . I thought it'd help to stay in the Force another year. But . . ."

Morse nodded sympathetically. Strange's wife had died very suddenly a year previously, victim of a coronary thrombosis which should surely never have afflicted one so slim, so cautious, so physically fit. She'd been an unlovely woman, Mrs. Strange—outwardly timid and inwardly bullying; yet a woman to whom by all accounts Strange had been deeply attached. Friends had spoken of a "tight" marriage; and most agreed that the widower would have been wholly lost on his own, at least for some while, had he jacked things in (as he'd intended) the previous September. And in the end he'd been persuaded to reconsider his position—and to continue for a further year. But he'd been uneasy back at HQ: a sort of supernumerary Super, feeling like a retired schoolmaster returning to a Common Room. A mistake. Morse knew it. Strange knew it.

"I still don't see what it's got to do with me, sir."

"I want the case reopened—not that it's ever been closed, of course. It worries me, you see. We should have got further than we did."

"I still—"

"I'd like you to look at the case again. If anyone can crack it, *you* can. Know why? Because you're just plain bloody lucky, Morse, that's why! *And I want this case solved.*"

Chapter Three

Which of you shall have a friend and shall go unto him
at midnight and say unto him, Friend, lend me three loaves.
And he from within shall answer and say, Trouble me not:
the door is now shut; I cannot rise and give thee. I
say unto you, though he will not rise and give him,
because he is his friend, yet because of his importunity
he will rise and give him as many as he needeth.

(*St. Luke*, ch. XI, vv. 5–8)

Lucky?

Morse had always believed that luck played a bigger part in life than was acknowledged by many people—

certainly by those distinguished personages who saw their personal merit as the only cause of their appropriate eminence. Yet as he looked back over his own life and career Morse had never considered his own lot a particularly lucky one, not at least in what folk referred to as the affairs of the heart. Strange may have had a point though, for without doubt his record with the Thames Valley CID was the envy of most of his colleagues—his success rate the result, as Morse analyzed the matter, of all sorts of factors: a curious combination of hard thinking, hard drinking (the two, for Morse, being synonymous), hard work (usually undertaken by Sergeant Lewis), and, yes, a sprinkling here and there of good fortune. The Romans had poured their libations not only to Jupiter and Venus and their associate deities in the Pantheon, but also to Fortuna, the goddess of good luck.

Lucky, then?

Well, a bit.

It was high time Morse said something:

"Why the Lower Swinstead murder? What's wrong with the Hampton Poyle murder, the Cowley murder . . . ?"

"Nothing to do with me, either of 'em."

"That's the only reason then? Just to leave a clean slate behind you?"

For a few moments Strange appeared uncomfortable: "It's partly that, yes, but . . . ."

"The Chief Constable wouldn't look at any new investigation—not a serious investigation."

"Not unless we had some new evidence."

"Which in our case, as the poet said, we have not got."

"This fellow that rang—"

"No end of people ring. We both know that, sir."

"—rang twice. He knows something. I'm sure of it."

"Did you speak to him yourself?"

"No. He spoke to the girl on the switchboard. Didn't want to be put through to anybody, he said. Just wanted to leave a message."

"For you?"

"Yes."

"A 'he,' you say?"

"Not much doubt about that."

"Surely from the recordings. . . ?"

"We can't record every crazy sod who rings up and asks what the bloody time is, you know that!"

"Not much to go on."

"*Twice*, Morse? The first time on the anniversary of the murder? Come off it! We've got a moral duty to re-open the case. Can't you understand that?"

Morse shook his head. "Two anonymous phone calls? Just isn't worth the candle."

And suddenly—why was this?—Strange seemed at ease again as he sank back even further in his chair:

"You're right, of course you are. The case wouldn't be worth re-opening—*unless*" (Strange paused for effect, his voice now affable and bland) "unless our caller—identity cloaked in anonymity, Morse—had presented us with some . . . some new *evidence. And,* after my appeal, my nationally reported appeal, we're going to get some more! I'm not just thinking of another telephone call from our friend either, though I'm hopeful about that. I'm thinking of information from members of the public, people who thought the case was forgotten, people whose memories have had a jog, people who were a bit reluctant, a bit afraid, to come forward earlier on."

"It happens," conceded Morse.

The armchair creaked as Strange leaned forward once more, smiling semibenignly, and holding out his empty tumbler: "Lovely!"

After refilling the glasses, Morse asked the obvious question:

"Tell me this, sir. You had two DIs on the case originally—"

"Three."

"—several DSs, God knows how many DCs and PCs and WPCs—"

"No such thing now. All the women are PCs—no sex

discrimination these days. By the way, you were never guilty of sexual harassment, were you?"

"Seldom. The other way round, if anything."

Strange grinned as he sipped his Scotch. "Go on!"

"As I say, you had all those people on the case. They studied it. They lived with it. They—"

"Got nowhere with it."

"Perhaps it wasn't altogether their fault. We're never going to solve everything. It's taken these mathematicians over three hundred years to solve Fermat's Last Theorem."

"Mm." Strange waggled his tumbler in front of him, holding it up toward the light, like a judge at the Beer Festival at Olympia.

"Just like the color of my urine specimens at the Radcliffe."

"Tastes better, though."

"Listen. I'm not a crossword wizard like you. Sometimes I can't even finish the *Mirror* coffee-break thing. But I know one thing for sure. If you get stuck over a clue—"

"As occasionally even the best of us do."

"—there's only one way to solve it. You go away, you leave it, you forget it, you think of the teenage Brigitte Bardot, and then you go back to it and—Eureka! It's like trying to remember a name: the more you think about it the more the bloody thing sinks below the horizon. But once you forget about it, once you come to it a second time, fresh—"

"I've never come to it a *first* time, apart from those early couple of days—you know that. I was on another case! And not particularly in the pink either, was I? Not all that long out of hospital myself."

"Morse! I've *got* to reopen this case. You know why."

"Try someone else!"

"I want you to think about it."

"Look." A note of exasperation had crept into Morse's voice. "I'm on furlough—I'm tired—I'm sleeping badly—I drink too much—I'm beholden to no one—I've no relatives left—I can't see all that much purpose in life—"

"You'll have me in tears in a minute."

"I'm only trying to say one thing, sir. Count me out!"

"You won't even *think* about it?"

"No."

"You do realize that I don't *need* to plead with you about this? I don't want to pull rank on you, Morse, but just remember that I *can*. All right?"

"Try someone else, sir, as I say."

"OK. Forget what I just said. Let's put it this way. It's a favor I'm asking, Morse—a personal favor."

"What makes you think I'll still be here?"

"What's that supposed to mean?"

But Morse, it appeared, was barely listening as he stared out of the window on to his little patch of greenery where a small bird with a grey crown and darkish-brown bars across its back had settled beneath the diminishing column of peanuts.

"Look!" (He handed the binoculars to Strange.) "Few nuts—and some of these rare species decide to take up special residence. I shall have to check up on the plumage but . . ."

Strange had already focused the binoculars with, as it seemed to Morse, a practiced familiarity.

"Know anything about bird-watching, sir?"

"More than you, I shouldn't wonder."

"Beautiful little fellow, isn't he?"

"She!"

"Pardon?"

"Immature female of the species."

"*What* species?"

"*Passer domesticus,* Morse. Can't you recognize a bloody house sparrow when you see one?"

For the fourteenth time Morse found himself reappraising the quirkily contradictory character that was Chief Superintendent Strange.

"And you'll at least *think* about things? You can promise me that, surely?"

Morse nodded weakly.

And Strange smiled comfortably. "I'm glad about that. And you'll be pleased about one thing. You'll have Sergeant Lewis along with you. I . . . did have a word with him, just before I came here, and he's—"

"You mean you've already . . ."

Strange flicked a stubby finger against his empty, expensive, cut-glass tumbler: "A little celebration, perhaps?"

Chapter Four

> He and the sombre, silent Spirit met—
>   They knew each other both for good and ill;
> Such was their power, that neither could forget
>   His former friend and future foe; but still
> There was a high, immortal, proud regret
>   In either's eye, as if 'twere less their will
> Than destiny to make the eternal years
> Their date of war, and their "Champ Clos" the spheres.
>   (Byron, *The Vision of Judgment*, XXXII)

It is possible for persons to be friendly toward each other without being friends. It is also possible for persons to be friends without being friendly toward each other. The relationship between Morse and Strange had always been in the latter category.

"Read through this as well!" Strange's tone was semiperemptory as he thrust a folded sheet of ruled A4 across at Morse, in the process knocking his glass on to the parquet flooring. Where it broke into many pieces.

"Ah! Sorry about that!"

Morse rose reluctantly to fetch brush and pan from the kitchen.

"Could have been worse, though," continued Strange. "Could have been full, eh?"

As Morse carefully swept up the slivers of the cut-glass tumbler—originally one of a set of six (now three) which his mother had left him—he experienced an irrational anger and hatred wholly disproportionate to the small accident which had occurred. But he counted up to twenty and was gradually feeling better, even as Strange extolled the bargain he'd seen in the Covered Market recently: glasses for only 50p apiece.

"Better not have any more Scotch, I suppose."

"Not if you're driving, sir."

"Which I'm bloody *not*. I'm being driven. And if I may say so, it's a bit rich expecting me to take lessons in drink-driving from you! But you're right, we've had enough."

A further count, though this time only to ten, prolonged Morse's invariably slow reading of the two handwritten paragraphs, and he said nothing as he finally put the sheet aside.

It was Strange who spoke:

"Perhaps, you know, on second thoughts, we might, er . . . anither wee dram?"

"Not for me, sir."

"That was meant to be the 'royal we,' Morse."

Morse decided that a U-turn was merely a rational readjustment of a previously mistaken course, and he obliged accordingly—for both of them, with Strange's measure poured into one of the cheap-looking wineglasses he'd bought a few weeks earlier from the Covered Market, for only 50p apiece.

"Is this" (Morse pointed to the paper) "what our dutiful duty sergeant transcribed from the phone calls?"

"Well, not quite, no." (Strange seemed curiously hesitant.) "That's what *I* wrote down, as far as I—we—could fix the exact words. Very difficult business when you get things secondhand, garbled—"

Morse interrupted. "No problem, surely? We *do* record everything that comes into HQ."

"Not so easy as that. Some of these recordings are poor-quality reception; and when, you know, when somebody's speaking quietly, muffled sort of voice . . ."

Morse smiled thinly as he looked directly across at his

superior officer. "What you're telling me is that the recording equipment packed up, and there's no trace."

"Anything mechanical packs up occasionally."

"*Both* occasions?"

"Both occasions."

"So all you've got to rely on is the duty sergeant."

"Right."

"Atkinson, was that?"

"Er, yes."

"Isn't he the one who's been taken off active duties?"

"Er, yes."

"Because he's become half-deaf, I heard."

"It's not a *joke*, Morse! Terrible affliction, deafness."

"Would you like me to have a word with him myself?" For some reason Morse's smile was broader now.

"I've already, er . . ."

"Were you at home, sir, when this anonymous caller rang you?"

Strange shifted uncomfortably in the chair, finally nodding slowly.

"I thought you were ex-directory, sir."

"You thought right."

"How did he know your number then?"

" 'ow the 'ell do I know!"

"The only people who'd know would be your close friends, family. . . ?"

"And people at HQ," added Strange.

"What are you suggesting?"

"Well, for starters . . . have *you* got my telephone number?"

Morse walked out into the entrance hall and returned with a white-plastic telephone index, on which he pressed the letter "S," then pushed the list of names and numbers there under the half-lenses now perched on Strange's nose.

"Not changed, has it?"

"Got an extra 'five' in front of it. But you'd know that, wouldn't you?" The eyes over the top of the lenses looked shrewdly and steadily up at Morse.

"Yes. It's just the same with my number."

"Do you think I should get a tap on my phone?"

"Wouldn't do any harm, if he rings again."

"*When* he rings again."

"Hoaxer! Sure to be."

"Well-informed hoaxer, then." Strange pointed to the paper still on the arm of Morse's chair. "A bit in the know, wouldn't you say? Someone on the inside, perhaps? You couldn't have found one or two things referred to there in any of the press reports. Only the police'd know."

"And the murderer," added Morse.

"And the murderer," repeated Strange.

Morse looked down once more at the notes Strange had made in his appropriately outsized, spidery handwriting:

Call One

That Lower Swinstead woman—nickers up and down like a yo-yo—a lot of paying clients and a few non-paying clients like me. Got nowhere much with the case did you—incompetant lot. For starters you wondered if it was one of the locals, didn't you? Then for the main course you wasted most of your time with the husband. Then you didn't have any sweet because you'd run out of money. Am I right? Idiots, the lot of you. No! Don't interrupt!
(Line suddenly dead.)

Call Two

Now *don't* interrupt this time, see? Don't say a dicky-bird! Like I said, that woman had more pricks than a secondhand dart-board, mine included, but it's not me who had anything to do with it. Want a clue? There's somebody coming out of the clammer in a fortnight—listen! He's one of your locals, isn't he? See what I mean? You cocked it all up before and you're lucky bastards to have another chance.
(Line suddenly dead.)

Morse looked up to find himself the object of Strange's steady gaze.

"It's incompet*ent*, sir, with an 'e'."

"Thank you very much!"

"And most people put a 'k' on 'knickers.'"

Strange smiled grimly. "And Yvonne Harrison put an embargo on knickers, however you spell 'em!"

He struggled to his feet. "My office Monday morning— first thing!"

"Eight o'clock?"

"Nine-thirty?"

"Nine-thirty."

"Now get back to your Schubert—though I'm surprised you weren't listening to Wagner. Just the job, *The Ring,* for a long holiday, you know. Especially the Solti recording."

Morse watched his visitor waddling somewhat unsteadily toward the police car parked confidently in the "Resident's Only" parking area. (Yes! Morse had mentioned the apostrophe to the Chairman of the Residents' Welfare Committee.)

He closed the front door and for a few moments stood there motionless, acknowledging with a series of almost imperceptible nods the simple truth about the latest encounter between two men who knew each other well, both for good and ill:

Game, Set, Match, to Strange.

Or was it?

For there was something about what he had just learned, something he had not yet even begun to analyze, that was perplexing him slightly.

The following Sunday was a pleasant summer's day; and along with three-quarters of the population of Hampshire, Morse decided to go down to Bournemouth. It took him over an hour to park the Jaguar; and it was a further half-hour before he reached the seafront where carloads and busloads of formidable families were negotiating rights to a couple of square meters of Lebensraum. But moving away from the ice-cream emporia,

Morse found progressively fewer and fewer day-trippers as he walked toward the further reaches of the shore-line. He'd always told himself he enjoyed the chang-ing moods of Homer's deep-sounding sea. And he did so now.

Soon, he found himself standing alongside the slowly lapping water, debating with himself whether the tide was just coming in or just going out, and staring down at the glasslike circular configuration of a jellyfish.

"Is it dead?"

Until she spoke, Morse had been unaware of the auburn-haired young woman who now stood beside him, almost wearing a bikini.

"I don't know. But in the absence of anything better to do, I'm going to stand here till the tide comes in and find out."

"But the tide's going *out*, surely?"

Morse nodded somewhat wistfully. "You may be right."

"Poor jellyfish!"

"Mm!" Morse looked down again at the apparently doomed, transparent creature at his feet: "How very sad to be a jellyfish!"

He'd sounded a comparatively interesting man, and the woman would have liked to stay there awhile. But she forced herself to forget the intensely blue eyes which momentarily had held her own and walked away with-out a further word, for she felt a sudden, slight suspi-cion concerning the sanity of the man who stood there staring at the ground.

Chapter Five

In the country of the blind, the one-eyed man is King.
(Afghan proverb)

It was on Tuesday the 14th, the day *before* Strange's visit to Morse, that Lewis had presented himself at the Chief Superintendent's office in Thames Valley Police HQ, in punctual obedience to the internal phone call.

"Something for you, Lewis. Remember the Lower Swinstead murder?"

"Well, vaguely, yes. And I've seen the bits in the paper, you know, about the calls. I was never really on the case myself though. We were on another—"

"Well, you're on it now—from next Monday morning, that is—once Morse gets back from Bermuda."

"He hasn't left Oxford, has he?"

"*Joke*, Lewis." Strange beamed with bonhomie, settling his chin into his others.

"The Chief Inspector's agreed?"

"Not much option, had he? And you enjoy working with the old sod. I know you do."

"Not always."

"Well, he always enjoys working with *you*."

A strangely gratified Lewis made no reply.

"So?"

"Well, if it's OK with Morse . . ."

"Which it is."

"I'll give him a ring."

"No, you won't. He's tired, isn't he? Needs a rest. Give him a bit of time to himself—you know, crosswords, booze . . ."

"Wagner, sir. Don't forget his precious Wagner. He's

just bought *another* recording of that *Ring Cycle* stuff, so he told me."

"Which recording's that?"

"Conductor called 'Sholty,' I think."

"Mm . . ." Strange pointed to three bulging green box-files stacked on the side of his desk. "Little bit of reading there. All right? Chance for you to get a few moves ahead of Morse."

Lewis got to his feet, picked up the files, and held them awkwardly in front of him, his chin clamping the top one firm.

"I've never been even *one* move in front of him, sir."

"No? Don't you underestimate yourself, Lewis! Let others do it for you."

Lewis managed a good-natured grin. "Not many people manage to get a move ahead of Morse."

"Oh, really? Just a minute! Let me hold the door for you . . . And you're not quite right about what you just said, you know. There *are* one or two people who just occasionally manage it."

"Perhaps you're right, sir. I've just not met one of 'em, that's all."

"You have though," said Strange quietly.

Lewis's eyes turned quizzically as he maneuvered his triple burden through the door.

That same evening, Lewis had just finished his eggs and chips, had trawled the last slice of brown bread across the residual HP sauce, and was swallowing the last mouthful of full-cream cold milk, when he heard the call from above:

"Dad? Da—ad?"

Lewis looked down at the (presumably problematical) first sentence of his son's A-level French Prose Composition: "Another bottle of this excellent wine, waiter!"

"Easy enough, that, isn't it?"

"What gender's 'bottle'?"

"How am I supposed to know? What do you think I bought you that dictionary for?"

"Left it at school, didn't I!"

"So?"

"So you mean you don't know?"

"You're brighter than I thought, son."

"Can't you guess?"

"Either masculine or feminine, sure to be."

"That's *great.*"

"Feminine, say? So it's, er, *'Garçon! Une autre bouteille de cette—'* "

"No! You're useless, Dad! If you say *'Une autre bouteille,'* you mean a *different* bottle of wine."

"Oh."

"You say *'Encore une bouteille de'* whatever it is."

"Why do you ever ask me to help you?"

"Agh! Forget it! Like I say, you're bloody useless."

Lewis had never himself read *Bleak House* and, unlike Morse, would not have known the soothing secret of counting up to however-many. And in truth he felt angry and belittled as he walked silently down the stairs, picked up the box-files from the table in the entrance hall, walked past the living room, where Mrs. Lewis sat deeply submerged in a TV soap, and settled himself down at the kitchen table, where he began to acquaint himself with the strangely assorted members of the Harrison family—wife, husband, daughter, son—four of the principal players in the Lower Swinstead case.

He concentrated as well as he could, in spite of those cruel words still echoing in his brain. And after a while he found himself progressively engaged in the earlier, more grievous agonies of other people: of Frank, the husband; of Sarah, the daughter; of Simon, the son; and of Yvonne, the mother, who had been murdered so brutally in the Cotswold village of Lower Swinstead, Oxon.

Chapter Six

> The English country gentleman galloping after a fox—the unspeakable in full pursuit of the uneatable.
>
> (Oscar Wilde)

At first he'd felt some reluctance about an immediate interview with her. But finally he decided that earlier rather than later was probably best; and in tones considerably less peremptory than those in which Strange had summoned Lewis three days earlier, he called her to his office at 4:30 P.M.

At which time she stood silent and still for a few seconds at the door before knocking softly, feeling like a schoolgirl outside the headmistress's study.

"Come in!"

She entered and sat, as directed, in the chair opposite him, across the desk.

Professor Turner was a fair-complexioned, mild-mannered medic, in his early sixties—the internationally renowned chief-guru of the Radcliffe Infirmary's Diabetes Centre in Oxford.

"You wanted to see me, sir?"

Yes, he wanted to see her; but he also wanted to put her rather more at ease.

"Look, we're probably going to be together at lots of do's these next few months—years, perhaps—so, please, let's forget this 'Sir' business, shall we? Please call me 'Robert.'"

Sarah Harrison, a slimly attractive, brown-eyed brunette in her late twenties, felt her shoulder muscles relax a little.

Not for long.

"I've sat in with you once or twice, haven't I?"

"Three times."

"And I think you're going to be good, going to be up to it, you know what I mean?"

"Thank you."

"But you're not quite good enough yet."

"I'd hoped I was improving."

"Certainly. But you're still strangely naive, I'm sorry to say. You seem to believe everything your patients tell you!"

"There's not much else to go on, is there?"

"Oh, but there is! There's a certain healthy and necessary skepticism; and then there's experience. You'll soon realize all this. What I'm saying is that you might as well learn it now rather than later."

"Is there anything particular. . . ?"

"Things, plural. I'm thinking of what they tell you about their blood-sugar records, about their sexual competence, about their diet, about their alcohol intake. You see, the only thing they can't fool you about is their *weight*."

"And their blood pressure."

Turner smiled gently at his pupil. "I haven't got *quite* as much faith as you in our measurements of blood pressure."

"But they don't all of them make their answers up."

"Not *all* of them, no. It's just that we all like to pretend a bit. We all tend to say we're fine, even if we're feeling lousy. Don't we?"

"I suppose so."

"And *our* main job" (Turner spoke with a quiet authority) "is to give *information*—and to exert some sort of *influence*—about the way our patients cope with what, as you know, is potentially a very serious illness."

Sarah said nothing. Just sat there. A little humiliated.

And he continued: "There are a good many patients here who are professional liars. Some of them I've known for years, and they've known me. We tell each other lies, all right. But it doesn't matter—because we *know* we're telling each other lies ... Anyway, that's enough about that." (Turner looked down at her folder.) "I see you've got Mr. David Mackenzie on your list next Monday. I'll sit in with you on him. I think he did once tell me his date of birth correctly, but he makes everything else up as he goes along. You'll enjoy him!"

Again Sarah said nothing. And she was preparing to leave when Turner changed the subject abruptly, and in an unexpected direction.

Or *was* it unexpected?

"I couldn't help seeing the articles in the newspapers . . . and the department was talking about them."

Sarah nodded.

"Would it mean a lot to you if they found who murdered your mother?"

"What do *you* think?" The tone of her voice bordered almost on the insolent, but Turner interpreted her reply tolerantly, for it was (he knew) hardly the most intelligent question he'd ever formulated.

"Let's just wish them better luck," he said.

"Better brains, too!"

"Perhaps they'll put Morse on to it this time."

Sarah's eyes locked steadily on his.

"Morse?"

"You don't know him?"

"No."

"Heard of him, perhaps?" Turner's eyes grew suddenly shrewd on hers, and she hesitated before answering:

"Didn't my mother mention she'd nursed him somewhere?"

"Would you like to meet him, next time he comes in?"

"Pardon?"

"You didn't know he was diabetic?"

"We've got an awful lot of diabetics here."

"Not too many like him, thank the Lord! Four hefty injections a day, and he informs me that he's devised a carefully calibrated dosage that exactly counterbalances his considerable daily intake of alcohol. And when I say considerable . . . Quite a dab hand, too, is Morse, at extrapolating his blood-sugar readings—backwards!"

"Isn't he worried about . . . about what he's doing to himself?"

"Why not ask him? I'll put him on your list."

"Only if you promise to come along to monitor me."

"With *you* around? Oh, no! Morse wouldn't like that."

"How old is he?"

"Too old for you."

"Single."

"Gracious, yes! Far too independent a spirit for marriage ... Anyway, have a good weekend! Anything exciting on?"

"Important, perhaps, rather than exciting. We've got a meeting up at Hook Norton tomorrow at the Pear Tree Inn. We're organizing another Countryside March."

"That's the 'rural pursuits' thing, isn't it? Fox-hunting—"

"Among other things."

"The 'toffs and the serfs.'"

Sarah shook her head with annoyance. "That's just the sort of comment we get from the urban chattering-classes!"

"Sorry!" Turner held up his right hand in surrender. "You're quite right. I know next to nothing about fox-hunting, and I'm sure there must be things to be said in favor of it. But—please!—don't go and tell Morse about them. We just happened to be talking about fox-hunting the last time he was here—it was in the news—and I can't help remembering what he said."

"Which was?" she asked coldly.

"First, he said he'd never thought much of the argument that the fox enjoys being chased and being pulled to little pieces by the hounds."

"Does he think the chickens enjoy being pulled to little pieces by the fox?"

"Second, that the sort of people who hunt do considerably more harm to themselves than they do to the animals they hunt. He said they run a big risk of brutalizing themselves ... dehumanizing themselves."

The two of them, master and pupil, looked at each other over the desk for an awkward while; and the Professor of Diabetes Studies thought he may have seen a flash of something approaching fury in the dark-brown eyes of his probationary consultant.

It was the latter who spoke first:

"Mind if I say something?"

"Of course not."

"I'm surprised, that's all. I fully, *almost* fully, accept your criticisms of my professional manner and my strategy with patients. But from what you've just said *you* sometimes seem to talk to your patients about other things than diabetes."

"Touché."

"But you're right . . . Robert. I've been getting too chatty, I realize that. And I promise that when I see Mr. Morse I'll try very hard, as you suggest, to instill some sort of disciplined regimen into his daily life."

Turner said nothing in reply. It was a good thing for her to have the last word: she'd feel so much better when she came to think back on the interview. As she would, he knew that. Many times. But he allowed himself a few quietly spoken words after the door had closed behind her:

"Oh Lady in Pink—Oh lovely Lady in Pink! There is very, very little chance of a disciplined regimen in Morse's life."

Chapter Seven

> Whoever could possibly confuse "Traffic Lights" and "Driving Licence?" *You* could! Just stand in front of your mirror tonight and mouth those two phrases silently to yourself.
> (Lynne Dubin, *The Limitations of Lip-reading*)

Disabilities, like many sad concomitants of life, are often cloaked in euphemism. Thus it is that the "blind" and the "impotent" and the "deaf" are happily no longer amongst us. Instead, in their respective clinics, we know our fellow outpatients as those affected by impaired vision; as victims of chronic erectile dysfunction; as citizens with a serious hearing impediment. The individual members of such groups, however, know perfectly well what their troubles are. And in the latter category, they tend to prefer the monosyllabic "deaf," although they realize that there are varying degrees of deafness; realize that some are very deaf indeed.

Like Simon Harrison.

He had been a six-year-old (it was 1978) attending a village school in Gloucestershire when an inexplicably localized outbreak of meningitis had given cause for most serious concern in the immediate vicinity. And in particular to two families there: to the Palmer family in High Street, whose only daughter had tragically died; and to the Harrison family in Church Lane, whose son had slowly recovered in hospital after three weeks of intensive care, but with irreversible long-term deafness: twenty-five percent residual hearing in the left ear; and almost nothing in the right.

Thereafter, for Simon, social and academic progress had been seriously curtailed and compromised: like an athlete being timed for the hundred-meters sprint over sand dunes wearing army boots; like a pupil, with thick wadges of cotton-wool in each ear, seeking to follow instructions vouchsafed by a tutor from behind a thickly paneled door.

Oh God! Being deaf was such a dispiriting business.

But Simon was a fighter, and he'd tried hard to make the best of things. Tried so hard to master the skills of lip reading; to learn the complementary language of "signing" with movements of fingers and hands; to present a wholly bogus facial expression of comprehension in the company of others; above all, to come to terms with the fact that silence, for those who are deaf, is not merely an absence of noise, but is a wholly *passive* silence, in which the potential vibrancy of active silence can never again be appreciated. Deafness is not the brief pregnant silence on the radio when the listener awaits the Greenwich time-signal; deafness is a radio set that is defunct, its batteries dead and nonrenewable.

Few people in Simon's life had understood such things; and in his early teens, when the audiographical readings had begun to dip even more alarmingly, fewer and fewer people had been overly sympathetic.

Except his mother, perhaps.

And the reason for such lack of interest in the boy had not been difficult to fathom. He was an unattractive, skinny-limbed lad, with rather protuberant ears, and a whiny, nasal manner of enunciating his words, as though his disability were not so much one of hearing as one of speaking.

Yet it would be an exaggeration to portray the young Harrison as a hapless adolescent, so often mishearing, so often misunderstood. His school fellows were not a gang of unmitigated bullies; nor were his teachers an uncaring crew. No. It was just that no one seemed to like him much; certainly no one seemed to love him.

Except his mother, perhaps.

But Simon did have some residual hearing, as we have seen; and the powerful hearing aids he wore were themselves far more valuable than any sympathy the world could ever offer. And when, after many a struggle, he left school with two A-level certificates (a C in English and a D in History) he very soon had a job.

Still had a job.

In the early 1990s, Oxfordshire's potential facilities for business and industry had attracted many leading national and international companies. During those years, for example, the county could boast the largest concentration of printing and publishing companies outside the metropolis; and it was to one of these, the Daedalus Press in North Oxford, that on leaving school Simon had applied for the post of apprentice proofreader. And had been successful, principally (let it be admitted) because of the employers' legal obligation to appoint a small percentage of semidisabled applicants. Yet the "apprentice" appellation was very soon to be deleted from Simon's job description, for he was prov-

ing to be surprisingly and encouragingly competent:
accurate, careful, neat—a fair combination of qualities
required in a proofreader. And with any luck (so it was
thought) experience would gradually bring with it that
needful extra dimension of tedious pedanticism.

On the morning of Friday, July 17, he found on his
desk a photocopied extract from some unspecified
tabloid which some unspecified colleague had left, and
which he read through with keen attention; then read
through a second time, with less interest in its content,
it appeared, than in its form, since his proofreading pen
applied itself at five points in the article.

NEW CLUE TO OLD MURDER

Information received by Thames Valley Police seems likely to prompt renewed enquiries into the bizarre murder of Mrs. Yvonne Harrison just over a year ago.

Residents of the small hamlet of Lower Swinstead in Oxfordshire are bracing themselves for further statements and a fresh upsurge of media interest in the ghastley murder of their former neighbour.

Tom Biffen, landlord of the Maidens Arms, remains philosophical however 'You can't blame people, can you? Exactly the same as Jack the Ripper. Nobody knows who he was. That's why he's so interesting. Same with who done Mrs. Harrison in. Nobody knows who he was. Or she was.'

It's difficult to disagree. Would we still be reading about the Ripper if we knew who it was who murdered and mutilated a succession of prostitutes in the East End of London in the 1870s? As it is, his identity remains unknown, just like that of Yvonne's murderer.

The villagers themselves are less than forthcoming, and seem dubious about any new breakthrough in the case. 'Let's just wish the police a bit better luck this time round,' says Mrs. May Kennedy, who runs the surprisingly well-stocked village shop.

And so say all of us. All of us, that is, except the murderer.

Chief Inspector Morse had not as yet encountered
Simon Harrison, but he would have been reasonably
impressed by the proofreader's competence. Only reasonably, of course, since he himself was a man who
somewhere, somehow, had acquired the aforemen-

tioned dimension of "tedious pedanticism," and would have made three further amendments. *And,* of course, would have corrected that gross anachronism, since historical accuracy had engaged him from the age of ten, when he had taken it upon himself to memorize the sequence of the American presidents, and the dates of the kings and queens of England.

Chapter Eight

> *Bankers are just like anybody else,*
> *Except richer.*
> (Ogden Nash, *I'm a Stranger Here Myself*)

The London offices of the Swiss Helvetia Bank are tucked away discreetly just behind Sloane Square. The brass plaque pinpointing visitors to these premises, albeit highly polished, is perhaps disproportionately small. Yet in truth the Bank has little need to impress its potential clients. On the contrary. Such clients have every need to impress the Bank.

Just after 4 P.M. on Friday, July 17, a smartly suited man in his late forties waved farewell to the uniformed guard at the security desk and walked out into the sunshine of a glorious summer's day. Traffic was already heavy; but that was of no concern to Frank Harrison, one of six portfolio and investment managers of SHB (London). His company flat was only a few minutes' walk away in Pavilion Road.

Earlier in the day he'd been very much what they paid him so handsomely for being—shrewd, superior, trustworthy—when his secretary had poured coffee for a small, grey-haired man and for his larger, much younger, cosmetically exquisite wife.

"You realize that SHB deals principally with portfolio investments of, well, let's say, over a million dollars? Is that, er. . . ?"

The self-made citizen from South Carolina nodded. "I think you can feel assured, sir, that we shall be able to meet that figure—ah!—*fairly* easily, shan't we, honey?"

He'd taken his wife's heavily diamonded left hand in his own and smiled, smiled rather sweetly, as Harrison thought.

And he himself had smiled, too—rather sweetly, as he hoped—as mentally he calculated the likely commission from his latest client.

Almost managed a smile again now, as he stopped outside Sloane Square Underground Station and bought a copy of the *Evening Standard*, flicking through the sheets, almost immediately finding the only item that appeared to interest him, then swiftly scanning the brief article before depositing the paper in the nearest litter bin. Had he been at all interested in horse-racing, he might have noticed that Carolina Cutie was running in the 4:30 at Kempton Park. But it had been many years since he had placed a bet with any bookie—instead now spending many hours of each working day studying on his office's computer screens the odds displayed from the London, New York, and Tokyo stock exchanges.

Considerably safer.

And recently he'd been rather lucky in the management of his clients' investments.

And the bonuses were good.

He let himself into his flat, tapped in the numbers on the burglar alarm, and walked into the kitchen, where he poured himself a large gin with a good deal of ice and very little tonic. But he'd never had any drinking problem himself. Unlike his wife. His murdered wife.

Lauren had promised to be along about 6 P.M., and she'd never been late. He would call a taxi . . . well, perhaps they'd spend an hour or so between the sheets first, although (if truth were told) he was not quite so keenly aware of her sexual magnetism as he had been a few months earlier. Passion was coming off the boil. It usually happened. On both sides, too. It had happened with

Yvonne, with whom he'd scaled the heights of sexual ecstasy, especially in the first few months of their marriage. Yet even during those kingfisher days he had been intermittently unfaithful to her; had woken with heartaching guilt in the small hours of so many worryful nights—until, that is, he had discovered what he *had* discovered about her; and until he had fallen in love with a woman who was living so invitingly close to him in Lower Swinstead.

The front doorbell rang at 5:50 P.M. Ten minutes early. Good sign! He felt sexually ready for her now; tossed back the last mouthful of his second gin; and went to greet her.

"You're in the paper again!" she blurted, almost accusingly, brandishing the relevant page of the *Evening Standard* in front of his face after the door was closed behind them.

"Really?"

For the second time Harrison looked down at the headline, NEW CLUE TO OLD MURDER; and pretended to read the article through.

"Well?" she asked.

"Well, what?"

"What have you got to tell me?"

"I'm going to take you out for a meal and then I'm going to take you upstairs to bed—or maybe the other way round."

"I didn't mean that. You know I didn't."

"What are you talking about?"

"I want you to tell me what *happened*. You've never spoken about it, have you? Not to me. And I want to know!" Her upper lip was suddenly tremulous. "So before we do anything else, you'd better—"

"Better what?" He snapped the words and his voice seemed that of a different man. "Listen, my sweetheart! The day you tell me what to do, that's the day we finish, OK? And if you don't get that message loud and clear" (paradoxically the voice had dropped to a whisper) "you'd better bugger off and forget we ever met."

There were no tears in her eyes as she replied: "I can't

do that, Frank. But there's one thing I *can* do: I'm going, as you so delicately put it, to bugger off!"

In full control of herself she turned the catch on the Yale lock, and the door closed quietly behind her.

Chapter Nine

> *He looked at me with eyes I thought*
> *I was not like to find.*
> (A. E. Housman, *More Poems*, XLI)

It had been the previous day, Thursday, when after collecting her boss's mail Barbara Dean had walked along the corridor, white blouse as ever perfectly pressed, flicking through the eleven envelopes held in her left hand. And looking with particular attention (again!) at the one addressed with a scarlet felt-pen, in outsize capital letters, to:

> STRANGE (SUPER!)
> POLICE
> KIDLINGTON
> OXFORD

The execution of this lettering gave her the impression of its being neither the work of a particularly educated nor of a particularly uneducated correspondent. Yet the lowercase legend along the top-left of the envelope—"Private and Confidencial" (*sic*)—would perhaps suggest the latter. Whatever the case though, the envelope was always going to be *noticed*—by whomsoever. It was like someone entering a lucky-dip postal competition with multicolored sketches adorning the periphery of the envelope; or like a lover mailing off a vastly outsize Valentine.

What would her boss make of it?

Barbara had been working at Police HQ for almost six years now and had enjoyed her time there—especially these past three years working as the personal secretary of Chief Superintendent Strange; and she was very sad that he would be leaving at the end of the summer. "Strange by name and strange by nature"—that's what she often said when friends had asked about him: an oddly contradictory man, that was for sure. He was a heavyweight, in every sense of the word; yet there were times when he handled things with a lightness of touch which was as pleasing as it was unexpected. His was the reputation of a blunt, no-nonsense copper who had not been born with quite the IQ of an Aristotle or an Isaac Newton; yet (in Barbara's experience) he could on occasion exhibit a remarkably compassionate insight into personal problems, including her own. All right (yes!) he was a big, blundering, awkward teddy bear of a man: a bit (a lot?) henpecked at home—until recently of course; a man much respected, if not particularly liked, by his fellow officers; and (from Barbara's point of view) a man who had never, hardly ever, sought to take the slightest advantage of her . . . well, of her woman-hood. Just that once, perhaps?

It had been at the height of the summer heat wave of 1995. One day when she had been wearing the skimpiest outfit the Force could ever officially tolerate, she had seen in Strange's eyes what she thought (and almost hoped?) were the signs of some mild, erotic fantasy.

"You look very desirable, my girl!"

That's all he'd said.

Was that what people meant by "sexual harassment"?

Not that she'd mentioned it to anyone; but the phrase was much in the headlines that long, hot summer, and she'd heard some of the girls talking in the canteen about it.

"*I* could do with a bi' o' that sexual harássment!" confessed Sharon, the latest and youngest tyro in the typing pool.

That was the occasion when one of the senior CID officers seated at the far end of the table had got to his

feet, drained his coffee, and come across to lay a gentle
hand on Sharon's suntanned shoulder.

"You mean sexual hárassment, I think. As you know,
we usually exercise the recessive accent in English; and
much as I admire our American friends, we shouldn't let
them prostitute our pronunciation, young lady!"

He had spoken quietly but a little cruelly; and the
uncomprehending Sharon was visibly hurt.

"Pompous prick! Who the hell does he think he is?"
she'd asked when he was gone.

So Barbara told her.

Not that she knew him personally, although his blue
eyes invariably smiled into hers, a little wearily sometimes but ever interestedly, whenever the two of them
passed each other in the corridors; and when she sometimes fancied that he looked at her as though he knew
what she was thinking.

God forbid!

It was not of Morse, though, but of Strange that she
was thinking that morning when she tapped the customary twice on his office door and entered. Sometimes,
when he sat there behind his desk—tie slightly askew, a
light shower of dandruff over the shoulders of his
jacket, hairs growing a little too prominently from his
ears and from his nostrils, white shirt rather less than
white and less than smoothly ironed—it was then, yes,
that she wished to mother him. She—Barbara!—less
than half his age.

That he'd never had such a complicated effect on
other women, she felt completely convinced.

Well, no; not *completely* convinced . . .

Chapter Ten

> He was a self-made man who owed his lack of success to nobody.
>
> (Joseph Heller, *Catch-22*)

"Probably some nutter!" growled Strange as he slipped a paper knife inside the top of the envelope and unfolded the single, thin sheet of paper contained therein. And for a while frowned mightily; then smiled.

"Have a look at that, Babs!" he said proudly, making as if to hand the sheet across the desk. "May well be what we've been waiting for—from my appeal, you know."

"Won't there be some fingerprints on it?" she asked tentatively.

"Ah!"

"You can *get* fingerprints from paper?"

"Get almost anything from anything these days," mumbled Strange. "And what with DNA, forensics, psychological profiling—soon be no need for us detectives any more!"

But in truth he appeared a little abashed as he held the top of the sheet between his thumb and forefinger and leaned forward over the desk; and Barbara Dean leaned forward herself and read the undated letter, typed on a patently antiquated machine through a red/black ribbon long past its operative sell-by date, with each keyed character unpredictably produced in either color.

"Bit illiterate?" suggested Strange.

"I wonder if he really is," said Barbara, replacing her spectacles in their case.

"You should wear 'em more often. You've got just the

face for specs, you know. Hasn't anyone ever told you that?"

You got it right when you said the calls wsan't from the person that done it because that wsa me, see! I made them calls. But you got it wrong when you didn't look a bit longer in the village, Mister Strange. So you want some help so there's a fellow due out of Bullingdon Friday next week 24th OK. WATCH HIM CAREFULLY!

The Ringer.

PS You can buy me a pint of Bass in the Maidens if you recognize me.

No one ever had, and Barbara hoped she wasn't blushing.

"Thank you."

"Well?"

"I'm not in the Crime Squad, sir."

"But you don't think he'd last long in the typing pool?"

"You fairly sure it's a 'he'?"

"Sounds like it to me."

Barbara nodded.

"Not much of a typist, like I say."

"Spelling's OK—'recognize,' and so on."

"Can't spell 'was.' "

"That's not really spelling though, is it? You sometimes get typists who are sort of dyslexic with some words. They try to type 'was,' say, and they hit the 's' before the 'a.' Do things like that regularly but they don't seem to notice."

"Ah!"

"Grammar's not so hot, I agree. Probably good enough to pass GCSE, I suppose, sir."

"Does anyone ever *fail* GCSE?"

"Could do with a bit more punctuation too, couldn't it?"

"Dunno. Not as much as Morse'd put in."

"Who do you think 'The Ringer' is?"

"Ringer? One who rings, isn't it? Chap who's been ringing us up, like as not."

"Does the postmark help?"

"Oxford. Not that that means anything. It could have been posted anywhere in our patch of the Cotswolds . . . Carterton! Yes. That's where they take the collections and do the sorting before bringing everything to Oxford."

"Scores of villages though, sir."

"Go and fetch Sergeant Dixon!"

"Know where he is?"

"Give you three guesses."

"In the canteen?"

"In the canteen."

"Eating a doughnut?"

"Doughnuts, plural."

It was like some of the responses she'd learned so well from the Litany.

"I'll go and find him."

"And send him straight to me."

"The Lord be with you."

"And with thy spirit."

"You *do* go to church, sir!"

"Only for funerals."

Sergeant Dixon was not so corpulent as Chief Superintendent Strange. But there was not all that much in it; and the pair of them would have made uncomfortable copassengers in economy-class seating on an airline. Plenty of room, though, as Dixon drove out alone to Carterton in a marked police car. He'd arranged a meeting with the manager of the sorting office there. A manageress, as it happened, who quickly and competently answered his questions about the system operating in West Oxfordshire.

Yes, since the Burford office had been closed, Carterton had assumed postal responsibility for a pretty wide area. Dixon was handed a printed list of the Oxon districts now covered; was informed how many postmen were involved; where the collection points were, and how frequently the boxes were emptied; how and when the accumulated bags of mail were brought back to Carterton, and how they were there duly sorted and categorized—but not franked—before being sent on to Oxford.

"Any way a particular letter can be traced to a particular post-box?"

"No, none."

"Traced to a particular village?"

"No."

Dixon was not an officer of any great intellectual capacity; indeed Morse had once cruelly described him as "the lowest-watt bulb in the Thames Valley Force." He had only five years to go before retirement, and he knew that his recent elevation to the rank of sergeant was as high as he could ever hope to climb. Not too bad, though, for a man who had been given little encouragement either from home or from school: if he'd made something of himself he'd made something of himself *himself*, as he'd once put things. Not the most elegant of sentences. But "elegance" had never been a word associated with Sergeant Dixon.

And yet, as he looked down at his outsize black boots, buffed and bulled, he was thinking as hard as he'd thought for many a moon. He was fully aware of the importance of his present inquiries, and he felt gratified to have been given the job. How good it would be if he could impress his superiors—something (he knew) he'd seldom done in his heretofore somewhat nondescript career.

So he took his time as he sat in that small postal office; took his time as he wrote down a few words in his black notebook; then another few words; then asked another question; then another . . .

When finally he drove back to Oxford, Sergeant Dixon was feeling rather pleased with himself.

That letter-cum-envelope was still exercising Strange's mind to its limits; but there seemed no cause for excitement. In late morning he had driven down to the Fingerprint Department at St. Aldate's in Oxford—only to learn that there was little prospect of further enlightenment. The faint, oversmeared prints offered no hope: the envelope itself must have been handled by the original correspondent, by the collecting postman, by the sorter, by the delivering postman, by a member of the HQ post department, by Strange's secretary, by Strange himself—and probably by a few extra intermediary persons to boot. How many fingers there, pray?

Forget it?

Forget it!

Handwriting? Only those red-felt capitals on the cover. Was it worth getting in some underemployed graphologist to estimate the correspondent's potential criminality? To seek possible signs of his (?) childhood neglect, parental abuse, sexual perversion, drugs. . . ?

Forget it?

Forget it!

The typewriter? God! How many typewriters were there to be found in Oxfordshire? In any case, Strange held the view that in the early years of the new millennium the streets of the UK's major cities would be lined with past-sell-by-date typewriters and VDUs and computers and the rest. And how was he to find an obviously *ancient* typewriter for God's sake, one with a tired and overworked ribbon of red and black? He might as well try to trace the animal inventory from the Ark.

Forget it?

Forget it!

What Strange needed now was new ideas.

What Strange needed now was Morse to be around.

Chapter Eleven

> *Take notice, lords, he has a loyal breast,*
> *For you have seen him open 't. Read o'er this;*
> *And after, this: and then to breakfast with*
> *What appetite you have.*
>
> (Shakespeare, *Henry VIII*)

Detective Sergeant Lewis of the Thames Valley CID kept himself pretty fit—very fit, really—in spite of a diet clogged daily with cholesterol. Quite simply, he had long held the view that some things went with other things. He had often heard, for example, that caviar was best washed down with iced champagne, although in truth his personal experience had occurred somewhat lower down the culinary ladder—with fried eggs necessarily complemented with chips and HP sauce; and (at breakfast time) with bacon, buttered mushrooms, well-grilled tomatoes, and soft fried bread. And, indeed, such was the breakfast that Mrs. Lewis had prepared at 7:15 A.M. on Monday, July 20, 1998.

It will be of no surprise, therefore, for the reader to learn that Sergeant Lewis felt pleasingly replete when, just before 8 A.M., he drove from Headington down the Ring Road to the Cutteslowe roundabout, where he turned north up to Police HQ at Kidlington. No problems. All the traffic was going the other way, down to Oxford City.

He was looking forward to the day.

He'd known that working with Morse was never going to be easy, but he couldn't disguise the fact that his own service in the CID had been enriched immeasurably because of his close association, over so many years now, with his curmudgeonly, miserly, oddly vulnerable chief.

And now? There was the prospect of another case: a

big, fat, juicy puzzle—like the first page of an Agatha Christie novel.

Most conscientiously, therefore (after Strange had spoken to him), Lewis had read through as much of the archive material as he could profitably assimilate; and as he drove along that bright summer's morning he had a reasonably clear picture of the facts of the case, and of the hitherto ineffectual glosses put upon those facts by the CID's former investigating officers.

From the very start (as Lewis learned) several theories, including of course burglary, had been entertained, although none of such theories had made anywhere near complete sense. There had been no observable signs of any struggle, for example. And although Yvonne Harrison was found naked, handcuffed, and gagged, she had apparently not been raped or tortured. In addition, it appeared most unlikely that she had been forcibly stripped of the clothes she'd been wearing, since the skimpy lace bra, the equally skimpy lace knickers, the black blouse, and the minimal white skirt were found neatly folded beside her bed.

Had she been lying there completely unclothed when some intruder had disturbed her? Surely it was an unusually early hour for her to be abed; and if she *had* been abed then, and if she had heard the front doorbell, or heard something, it seemed quite improbable that she would have confronted any burglar or (unknown?) caller without first putting something on to cover a body fully acknowledged to be beautiful. Such considerations had led the police to speculate on the likelihood of the murderer being well known to Mrs. Harrison; and indeed to speculate on the possibility of the murderer living in the immediate and very circumscribed vicinity, and of being rather *too* well known to Mrs. Harrison. Her husband was away from home a good deal, and few of the (strangely uncooperative?) villagers would have been too surprised, it seemed, if his wife conveniently forgot her marriage vows occasionally. In fact it had not been difficult to guess that most of the villagers, though loath to be signatories to any specific allegations, were fairly strongly in favor of some sort of "lover theory." Yet although the Harrisons often appeared more than merely geographically distanced, no evidence was found of likely divorce proceedings.

Once Mr. Frank Harrison, with a very solid (if very unusual) alibi, had been eliminated from the inquiries, painstakingly strenuous investigations had produced (as one of the final reports admitted) no sustainable line of positive inquiry . . .

As he pulled off right, into Thames Valley Police HQ, Lewis was smiling quietly to himself. Morse would very soon have established some "sustainable line of positive inquiry." Even if it was a wrong line.

So what?

Morse was very often wrong—at the start.

So what?

Morse was almost always right—at the finish.

Chapter Twelve

Yet ev'n these bones from insult to protect
   Some frail memorial still erected nigh,
With uncouth rhimes and shapeless sculpture deck'd,
   Implores the passing tribute of a sigh.
      (Thomas Gray, *Elegy Written in a Country Churchyard*)

The following is an extract from *The Times*, Monday, July 20, 1998:

A VILLAGE MURDER

Two PSYCHICS AND a hypnotist have already been involved in the case. It has caught the attention of the *Still a Mystery* series on ITV, although it has yet to be promoted to the Premier Division of such classical unsolved cases as the disappearance of Lord Lucan, the fate of the racehorse Shergar, or the quest for the Holy Grail itself.

Although the murder of Yvonne Harrison has long been out of the immediate headlines, we are led to believe that the box-files concerning the case, stacked on the shelves at Thames Valley Police HQ, are definitely not accumulating layer upon layer of undisturbed dust. After all it is only just over a year since the body of Mrs. Harrison was discovered in the living room of her Grade-II-listed Georgian house, set in four acres of wooded ground in the Cotswold village of Lower Swinstead. The home, "The Windhovers," was sold for £350,000 fairly soon after the murder, and the family have long since left the quiet leafy village—all except Yvonne, of course, who is buried in the small, neatly mown churchyard of St. Mary's, where, in the form of a Christian cross, a low, wooden stake is the only memorial to the body reposing beneath it:

R.I.P.

YVONNE HARISON

1947-1997

Perhaps, when the ground is sufficiently settled, the murdered woman will have some worthier monument. But for the present the grave shows little if any sign of tender loving care, and flowers no longer adorn this semi-neglected spot.

Yvonne Harrison, a fully qualified nurse, had resumed work in Oxford after her two children had left home, and on the evening of her murder had returned to an empty house, her husband Frank, as normally during the week, spending his time in his London apartment. "The Windhovers" had been broken into a few years earlier, when TV sets, video-equipment, radios, a computer, and sundry electrical items had been stolen. As a result, the Harrisons had installed a fairly sophisticated burglar alarm, with "panic-buttons" in the main bedroom and beside the main entrance door; had enlisted in the local Neighbourhood Watch group; and had acquired a Rottweiler puppy, christened Rodney, who had subsequently displayed a healthier taste for Walkers Crisps than for any unwelcome visitors, and who had sadly been run over a few months previously.

With the smashed rear window, the burglary theory was at first the favourite, although there was no apparent theft of several readily displayed items of silverware and non-too-subtly concealed pieces of jewellery. What was far more obvious to those who entered the house later that night was a body—the body of Yvonne Harrison, lying on the bed in the main bedroom: naked, handcuffed, and gagged. And dead.

What immediately caught public interest was the fact that the man who discovered the body was none other than the murdered woman's husband.

A somewhat delayed post-mortem established that Yvonne Harrison had probably been murdered by some sort of "tubular metal rod" two or three hours before her body was discovered at 11:20 P.M., and fairly certainly not after 9:30 P.M. Independent evidence corroborated the pathologist's findings. A local builder, Mr. John Barron, had rung Mrs. Harrison at 9 P.M.—on the dot, as instructed. But he had heard only the "engaged" signal. At about 9:30 P.M. he had rung again; but although he had persisted there had been no reply. The phone was quite certainly ringing at the other end. Either the Ansaphone had not been activated...or else the lady of the house was not alive to take the call.

Another call however had been made more successfully that evening. An extraordinarily puzzling call. At just after 9 P.M. Yvonne's husband picked up his phone in Pavilion Road, London, to hear a man's voice informing him that his wife was in trouble and that he ought to get out there immediately. Normally he would have driven home post-haste in his BMW. But with the car in for repairs, he took a taxi to Paddington where he caught the 9:48 train to Oxford, arriving at 10:50, where he took another taxi for the ten-mile journey out to Lower Swinstead.

Late-night traffic was thin, and when Mr. Patrick Flynn braked his Radio Taxi outside "The Windhovers" at 11:20 P.M. he saw a village mansion ablaze with lights turned on in almost every room, and the burglar-alarm box emitting sharp blue flashes and a continuous ringing. The front door stood open...and the rest is history.

Or it **was** history until a fortnight ago, when two anonymous phone calls were received at Thames Valley Police HQ, where it is the view of Chief Superintendent Strange that promising new lines of enquiry may soon be opened.

It is surely universally to be hoped that the identity of Yvonne Harrison's murderer will finally be revealed; and that on some more

permanent memorial in St. Mary's churchyard the name of the murdered woman will be spelt correctly.

Chapter Thirteen

Ponderanda sunt testimonia, non numeranda.
(All testimonies aggregate
Not by their number, but their weight.)
> (Latin proverb)

Most of the Thames Valley Police personnel were ever
wont to pounce quickly upon any newspaper clipping
concerning their competence, or alleged lack of competence. And that morning Lewis had been almost immediately apprised of the article in *The Times*—which he'd
read and assimilated swiftly; far more swiftly (he suspected) than Morse would read it when he took it along
at 8:30 A.M. The Chief was a notoriously slow reader,
except of crossword clues.

Lewis remembered the case well enough; certainly
remembered the frustration and disappointment that
many of his CID colleagues had felt when lead after lead
had appeared to peter out. Yes, he'd often experienced
frustration himself, but seldom any prolonged disappointment; for which he was grateful—profoundly
grateful—to Morse.

Most usually (Lewis knew it well) a murder investigation revolved around corroborated suspicion. A clue
was pursued; a suspect targeted; an alibi checked; a
motive weighed in the balances; a response to questioning interpreted as surly, cocky, devious, frightened . . .
It was all cumulative—that was the word!—a series of
pieces in the jigsaw that seemed to form a coherent pattern sufficiently convincing for a formal charge to be
brought; for a dossier to be sent to the DPP; for a period

of remand, further questioning, sometimes further evidence, with nothing cropping up in the interim to vitiate the central police hypothesis: that in all probability the arrested suspect was guilty as hell.

That was the usual pattern.

Not with Morse though.

For some reason Morse often shunned the standard heap-of-evidence approach. In fact Lewis had seldom if ever observed him, through distaste or idleness perhaps, riffle through any heap of dutifully transcribed statements, claiming (as Morse did) that since he could seldom remember what he'd been doing himself the previous evening, he found it difficult to give much credence to people who claimed to recall anything from a week last Wednesday—unless, of course, it was watching *Coronation Street* or listening to *The Archers*, or some similar regularly timetabled ritual.

No, Morse seldom worked that way.

The opposite, more often than not.

With most prime suspects, if female, youngish, and even moderately attractive, Morse normally managed to fall in love, sometimes only for a brief term, yet sometimes throughout Michaelmas and Hilary and Trinity. Toward some other prime suspects, if men, Morse occasionally appeared surprisingly sympathetic, especially if he suspected that the quality of their lives had hardly been enhanced by getting hitched to some potential tart who had temporarily managed to camouflage her basic bitchiness . . .

Lewis had a quick look at the *Mirror*, drained his coffee, and looked at his watch: 8:25 A.M. Time he got moving.

As he walked out of the canteen, he (literally) bumped into the stout figure of Sergeant Dixon—"Dixon-delighting-in-doughnuts" as Homer would have dubbed him.

"You see the thing on the Lower Swinstead thing?" (Variety was not a feature of Dixon's vocabulary.)

Lewis nodded, and Dixon continued:

"I was with him on that for a while. Poor ol' Strange.

He thought he knew who done it, but he couldn't prove it, could he? Poor ol' Strange. Like I say, I was with him on that thing."

Lewis nodded again, then climbed the stairs, wondering how that Monday morning would turn out—knowing how Morse hated holidays; how little he normally enjoyed the company of others; how very much he enjoyed a very regular allotment of alcohol; how he avoided almost all forms of physical exercise. And knowing such things, Lewis realized that in all probability he would fairly soon be driving Morse out to the Muzak-free pub at Thrupp where a couple of pints of real ale would leave the Chief marginally mellower and where a couple of orange juices would leave the chauffeur (him!) unexcitedly unintoxicated.

Chapter Fourteen

The man who says to one, go, and he goeth, and to another, come, and he cometh, has, in most cases, more sense of restraint and difficulty than the man who obeys him.

(John Ruskin, *The Stones of Venice*)

Lewis knocked deferentially on Morse's door before entering.

"Welcome home, sir! Nice break?"

"No!"

"You don't sound very—"

"Sh!"

So Lewis sat down obediently in the chair opposite, as his chief contemplated the last clue: "Stiff examination (7)" A—T—P—Y; then immediately wrote in the answer and consulted his wristwatch.

"Not bad, Lewis. Ten and a half minutes. Still it's usually a bit easier on Mondays."

"Well done."

"Have you done it, by the way?"

"Pardon?"

"That *is* a copy of today's *Times* you've got with you?"

"They showed it to me in the canteen—"

"Does Mrs. Lewis know that the first place you head for after breakfast is the canteen?"

"Only for a coffee."

"Not a crime, I suppose."

"It's this article, sir—about the Harrison case."

"So?"

"So you're not interested?"

"No!"

"But we're supposed to be reopening the case, sir—you and me."

"You and *I*, Lewis. And we are not."

"But the Super said you'd agreed."

"*When* am I supposed to have agreed?"

"Last week—Tuesday."

"Last week—Wednesday! He came to see me on *Wednesday*."

"You mean . . . he hadn't seen you *before* he saw me?"

"You're bright as a button this morning, Lewis."

"But you must have agreed, surely?"

"In a way."

"So what's biting you?"

Morse's blue eyes flashed across the desk. "I'd had too much Scotch, that's what! I'd been trying to enjoy myself. I was on a week's furlough, remember?"

"But why start the week off in such a foul mood?"

"Why *not*, pray?"

"I don't know. It's just that, you know—another case for us to solve perhaps? Gives you a good feeling, that."

Morse nodded reluctantly.

"So why agree to it, if you've no stomach for it?"

Morse looked down at the threadbare carpet—a carpet stopping regularly six inches from the skirting boards. "I'll tell you why. Strange's carpet goes right up to the wall—you've noticed that? So if you ever get up to Super status, which I very much doubt, you just make sure you get a carpet that covers the whole floor—and a personal parking space while you're at it!"

"At least you've got your name on the door."

"Remember that fellow in Holy Writ, Lewis? 'I also am a man set under authority.' I'm just like him—*under* authority. Strange doesn't *ask* me to do something: he tells me."

"You could always have said no."

"Stop sermonizing me! That case stinks of duplicity and corruption: the family, the locals, the police—shifty and thrifty with the truth, the whole bloody lot of them."

"You sound as if you know quite a bit about it already."

"Why shouldn't I? About a local murder like that? I do occasionally pick up a few things from my fellow officers, all right? And if you remember I *was* on the case right at the beginning, if only for a very short while. And why was that? Because we were on *another* case. Were we not?"

Lewis nodded. "Another murder case."

"Murder's always been our business."

"So why—?"

"Because the case is old and tired, that's why."

"Who'll take it on if we don't?"

"They'll find another pair of idiots."

"So you're going to tell the Super. . . ?"

"I've already *told* you. Give it a rest!"

"Why are you so sharp about it all?"

"Because I'm like the case, Lewis. I'm old and tired myself."

The ringing of the telephone on Morse's desk cut across the tetchy stichomythia.

"Morse?"

"Sir?"

"You ready?"

"Half-past nine, you said."

"So what?"

"It's only—"

"So what?"

"Shall I bring Sergeant Lewis along?"

"Please yourself."

The phone was dead.

"That was Strange."

"I could hear."

"I'd like you to come along. All right with you?"

Lewis nodded. "I'm a man under authority too."

"*Lew*-is! Quote it accurately: 'a man *set* under authority.'"

"Sorry!"

But Morse was continuing with the text, as if the well-remembered words brought some momentary respite to his peevishness: " 'Having under me soldiers, and I say unto one, Go and he goeth; and to another, Come and he cometh'."

"Lewis cometh," said Lewis quietly.

Chapter Fifteen

I have received no more than one or two letters in my life that were worth the postage.

(Henry Thoreau)

"C'm in! C'm in!"

It was 8:45 A.M.

"Ah! Morse. Lewis."

Perhaps, in all good faith, Strange had intended to sound brisk rather than brusque; yet, judging from Morse's silence as he sat down, the Chief Superintendent had not effected a particularly good start. He contrived to beam expansively at his two subordinates, and especially at Morse.

"What does 'The Ringer' mean to you?"

"Story by Edgar Wallace. I read it in my youth."

Morse had spoken in clipped, formal tones; and

Lewis, with a millimeter rise of the eyebrows, glanced quickly at his impassive face.

Something was wrong.

"What about you, Sergeant? You ever read Edgar Wallace?"

"Me?" Lewis grinned weakly. "No, sir. I was a *Beano*-boy myself."

"Anything else, Morse?"

"A campanologist?"

"Could be."

Morse sat silently on.

"Anything else?"

"It's a horse that's raced under the name of a different horse—a practice, so they tell me, occasionally employed by unscrupulous owners."

"How does it work?"

Morse shook his head. "I've seldom donated any money to the bookmakers."

"Or anyone else for that matter."

Morse sat silently on.

"Anything else?"

"I can think of nothing else."

"Well, let me tell you something. In Oz, it's what you call the quickest fellow in a sheep-shearing competition. What about that?"

"Useful thing to know, sir."

"What about a 'dead ringer'?"

"Somebody almost identical with somebody else."

"Good! You're coming on nicely, Morse."

"No, I'm not. I've stopped."

Strange shook his massive head and smiled bleakly. "You're an odd sod. You never seem to see anything that's staring you in the face. You have to look round half a dozen corners first, when all you've really got to do is to look straight up the bloody street in front of you!"

Lewis, as he sat beside his chief, knew that such a criticism was marginally undeserved, and he would have wished to set the record aright. But he didn't, or couldn't. As for Morse, he seemed quietly unconcerned

about the situation: in fact (or was Lewis misunder-
standing things?) even a little pleased.

"What about this, then?" Suddenly, confidently,
Strange thrust the letter across the desk; and after what
seemed to both the other men an unnecessarily prolonged perusal, the slow-reading Morse handed it back.
Without comment.

"Well?"

"'The Ringer', you mean? You think it's the fellow
who decided to ring you—"

"Ring me *twice*!"

"It's a possibility."

"Where do you think it was posted?"

"Dunno. You'll have to show me the envelope."

"Guess!"

"You're expecting me to say Lower Swinstead."

"No. Just waiting for your answer."

"Lower Swinstead."

"Explain *that*, then!" Strange produced a white envelope on which, above the lurid red capitals, the pewter-
gold first-class stamp was canceled with a circular
franking:

OXFORD M.L.O.
7.15 pm
15 JULY
1998

"All right," conceded Morse. "I'll try another guess.
What about Oxford?"

"Hm! What about the writing on the envelope?"

"Probably an A-level examiner using up one of his
red pens. His scripts were sending him bananas and he
happened to see your invitation in one of the newspapers. He just wondered why it was only the candidates who were allowed to make things up, so he
decided to have a go for himself. He's a nutter, sir. A
harmless nutter. We always get them—you know that."

"Oh, thank you, Morse!"

"No fingerprints, sir?" asked Lewis diffidently.

"Ah, no. No fingerprints. Good question, though!"

"Best forget it, then," counseled Morse.

"Rea-lly?" Strange allowed the disyllable to linger ominously. "When I was a lad, Morse, I once wrote off an entry for a Walt Disney competition and I drew a picture of Mickey Mouse on the front of the envelope."

"Did you win?"

"No, I didn't. But let me just tell you one thing, matey: I'd like to bet you that somebody noticed it! That's the whole point, isn't it?"

"You've lost me, sir."

Strange leaned back expansively. "When I asked Sergeant Dixon where *he* thought the letter was posted, he agreed with you: Lower Swinstead. And when I showed him the postmark he said it might *still* have been posted there, because he knew that some of the letters from that part of the Cotswolds were brought to Oxford for franking. So he went out and did a bit of legwork, and he traced the fellow who did the collections last week; and the postman remembered the envelope! There'd only been three letters that day in the box, and he'd noticed one of 'em in particular. Not surprising, eh? So Dixon decided to test things, just for his own satisfaction. He addressed an envelope to himself and posted it at Lower Swinstead."

Strange now produced a white unopened envelope and passed it across the desk. It was addressed in red Biro to Sergeant Dixon at Police HQ Kidlington, the pewter-gold first-class stamp canceled with the same circular franking:

Strange paused for effect. "Perhaps you ought to start eating doughnuts, Morse."

"They won't let me have any sugar these days, sir."

"There's no sugar in beer, you're saying?"

Lewis was expecting some semiflippant, semiprepared answer from his chief—something about balancing his intake of alcohol with his intake of insulin. But Morse said nothing, just sat there staring at the intricate design upon the carpet.

"One of these days, perhaps," persisted Strange quietly, "you might revise your opinion of Dixon."

"Why not put him in charge of the case? If you're still determined—"

"Steady on, Morse! That's enough of that. Just remember who you're talking to. And I'll tell you exactly why I'm not putting that idiot Dixon in charge. Because I've already put somebody else in charge—you and Lewis! Remember?"

"Lewis maybe, sir, but I can't do it."

Feeling most uncomfortable during these exchanges, Lewis watched the color rise in Strange's cheeks as several times his mouth opened and closed like that of a stranded goldfish.

"You do realize you've got little say in this matter, Chief Inspector? I am *not* pleading with you to undertake an investigation for Thames Valley CID. What I *am* doing, as your superior officer, is telling you that you've been assigned to a particular duty. That's all. And that's enough."

"No. It's not enough."

For several minutes the conversation continued in a similar vein before Strange delivered his diktat:

"I see . . . Well, in that case . . . you give me no option, do you? I shall have to report this interview to the Chief Constable. And you know what that'll mean."

Morse rose slowly to his feet, signaling Lewis to do the same. "I don't think you're going to report this interview to the Chief Constable or to the Assistant Chief Constable or to anyone else, for that matter, are you, Superintendent Strange?"

Chapter Sixteen

> The vilest deeds like poison weeds
> Bloom well in prison-air,
> It is only what is good in Man
> That wastes and withers there:
> Pale Anguish keeps the heavy gate,
> And the warder is Despair.
> (Oscar Wilde, *The Ballad of Reading Gaol*)

Until comparatively recently, Harry Repp had associated the word "porridge" chiefly with the title of the TV comedy series and not with oatmeal stirred in boiling water. For as long as he could remember, his breakfasts had consisted of Corn Flakes covered successively (as his beer gut had ballooned) with full, semiskimmed, and finally the thinly insipid fully skimmed varieties of milk. It was his common-law wife, Debbie, who'd insisted: "You keep pouring booze into your belly every night and it's low-fat milk for breakfast! Understood?" So there'd been little choice, had there? Until almost a year ago, when he had come to realize that the TV title was wholly appropriate, with porridge (occasionally ill-stirred in lukewarm water) providing the basic breakfast diet for prison inmates.

Normally Repp would have accepted the proffered dollop of porridge; but he asked only for two sausages and a spoonful of baked beans as he and his coprisoners from A Wing stood queuing at the food counter at 8 A.M. He had read that prisoners in the condemned cell were always given the breakfast of their choice; but he felt he could himself have eaten little in such circumstances—with the twin specters of death and terror so very close behind him. And even now, back in his cell, he managed only one mouthful of beans before pushing his plate away from him. He felt agitated and apprehensive, although he found it difficult to account for such emotions. After all, he wasn't awaiting the Governor and the flunkey from the Home Office and the Prison Chaplain . . . and the Hangman. Far from it. It was that day, Friday, July 24, that was set for his release from HM Prison, Bullingdon.

At 8:35 A.M., still in his prison clothing, he heard steps outside the cell, heard his name called, and was on his feet immediately, picking up the carrier bag in which he'd already placed his personal belongings: a battered-looking radio, a few letters still in their grubby envelopes, and a "sexy-western" paperback that had clearly commanded regular rereading. "Let's hope we don't meet again, mate!" one of the prison officers had volunteered as the double doors were unlocked and Repp was escorted for the last time from the spur of A Wing.

At 8:50 A.M., after changing into his personal civvies, he was admitted into a bench-lined holding cell, where another prisoner, a thin sallow-faced man in his forties, was already seated. Their exchange of conversation was brief and unmemorable:

"Not much more o' this shit, mate."

"No," said Repp.

At 9:05 A.M. his name was again called, and he was taken along to a reception desk where one of the Principal Officers took him through the forms pertaining to his release: identity check, behavior and health records, details of destination and accommodation. It seemed to Repp somewhat reminiscent of a check-in at Heathrow or Gatwick. Except that this, as he kept reminding himself, wasn't a check-in at all. It was a check-out.

He signed his name to several documents without bothering too much what they were. But before signing one form he was asked to read some relevant words aloud: "I understand that I am not allowed to possess or have anything to do with firearms or ammunition of any description . . ." It didn't matter anyway. In all probability there'd be no need to use the gun; and apart from himself only Debbie knew its whereabouts.

Almost finished now.

He took possession of an order issued under the Criminal Justice Act re Supervision in the Community, specifying the Oxford Probation Service in Park End Street as the office to which he was required to report regularly. Then he completed the Discharge Certificate itself, with a series of initials against Travel Warrant (Bullingdon to Oxford), Personal Property (as itemized), Personal Cash (£24.50), Discharge Grant (£45), Discharge Clothing (offered but not issued). And, finally, one further full signature, dated and countersigned by the Principal Officer, underneath the unambiguous assertion: I HAVE NO OUTSTANDING COMPLAINTS. And indeed Harry Repp had nothing much to complain about. At least, not about Bullingdon—except perhaps that any residual good in him had wasted and had withered there.

He was escorted across the prison yard to the main gates, where he reported to the Senior Officer, citing his full name and prison number to be checked against the Discharge List. And that was it. The heavy gates were opened, and Harry Repp stepped out of prison. A free man.

He looked at his wristwatch, repeatedly glancing around him as if he might be expecting someone to meet him. But there seemed to be no one. According to the bus timetable they'd given him, there would be a wait of ten minutes or so; and he walked slowly down the paved path which led from the Central Reception Area to the road. There he turned and looked back at the high concreted walls, lightish beige with perhaps a hint of some pinkish coloration, lampposts stationed at regular intervals in front of them, sturdily vertical until, at their tops, they leaned toward the prison, like guardsmen inclining their heads around a catafalque.

Harry Repp turned his back on the prison for the last time, and walked more briskly toward the bus stop and toward freedom.

Chapter Seventeen

> *What is it that roareth thus?*
> *Can it be a Motor Bus?*
> *All this noise and hideous hum*
> *Indicat Motorem Bum.*
>
> (Anon.)

Seated at the front window of the Central Reception Area, Sergeant Lewis had been a vigilant observer of the final events recorded in the previous chapter, immediately ducking down when the newly released man had turned to look back at the prison complex. Needlessly so, for the two men were quite unknown to each other.

This was hardly the trickiest assignment he'd ever been given, Lewis knew that; and in truth he could see little justification for the trouble being taken. Except in Superintendent Strange's (not usually fanciful) imagination, there seemed only a tenuous connection between the Harrison murder and Harry Repp—the latter sentenced to fifteen months' imprisonment, and now released early on parole on grounds of exemplary behavior. And in any case, Strange's instructions (not Morse's) had been vague in the extreme: "Keep an eye on him, see where he goes, who he meets, and, er, generally, you know . . . well, no need to tell an experienced officer like you."

And yet (Lewis considered the point afresh) had Strange's motivation been *all* that fanciful? Repp was known to have been active in the vicinity at the relevant period, and had in fact been under limited police surveillance for some time, although not of course on the night of the murder. And then there was the letter to Strange—a letter which, whilst pointing a finger only vaguely at the general locality of Lower Swinstead, had quite specifically pointed toward the man now being released from prison.

As Repp walked away Lewis got to his feet and shook hands with the prison officer who had communicated to him as much as anyone at Bullingdon was ever likely to know about the man just released: aged 37; height 5' 10''; weight 13 stone 4 pounds; hair dark brown, balding; complexion medium; tattoo (naval design) covering left forearm; sentenced for the receipt and sale of stolen goods; at the time of arrest cohabiting with Debbie Richardson, of 15 Chaucer Lane, Burford.

After driving the unmarked police car from the crowded staff car park, Lewis stopped on the main road, moving round the car as he slowly checked his tire pressures, all the while keeping watch on the bus stop, only fifty yards away, where two men, Repp and a slimmer ferrety-looking fellow, stood waiting; from where Lewis could hear so very clearly the frequently vociferated plaints from the ferret: "Where the fuckin' 'ell's the fuckin' bus got to?"

In fact, the fuckin' bus was well on its way; and a few minutes later the two men boarded a virtually empty bus and uncommunicatively took their separate seats.

Lewis moved smoothly into gear and followed discreetly, not at all unhappy when another (rather posh) car interposed itself between him and the bus. (Another posh car behind him, for that matter.) Any minor worry that Repp might unexpectedly get off at some stage between Bullingdon and Bicester was taking care of itself very nicely, since the bus made no stop whatsoever until reaching the Bure Place bus station in Bicester, where the ferret straightaway alighted (and straightaway disappeared); and where Repp, the immediate quarry, walked up the line of bus shelters to the 27 OXFORD (Direct) bay, promptly boarding the bus already standing there.

Repp was not the only one who had done his homework on the Bicester–Oxford timetable. For Lewis, knowing there would be a full ten-minute wait before departure, and leaving his car in the capacious car park

opposite, walked quickly through the short passageway to Sheep Street, passing the public toilets on his
left, where at Forbuoys Newsagent's he bought the *Mirror*. Even if there was a bit of a queue, so what? He
would rather enjoy not following but chasing the 27 to
Oxford. But the bus was still there, filling up quite
quickly, as he got back into his car.

After the implementation of the Beeching Report of
the mid-sixties, passengers between Oxford and Bicester
had perforce to use their own cars. But the former railway line had now been re-opened; and the deregulated
bus companies were trying their best, and sometimes
succeeding, in tempting passengers back to public transport. There were no traffic jams on the rail, and a newly
designated bus lane from Kidlington gave a comparatively fast-track entry into Oxford. So perhaps (Lewis
pondered the matter) it was hardly surprising that Repp
had not been picked up at Bullingdon by a friend, or by
a relative, or by his common-law wife. Yet it would
surely have been so much easier, quicker, more convenient that way?

At 10:10 A.M. the 27 pulled out of the bus station
and headed toward Oxford, in due course crossing over
the M40 junction and making appropriately good speed
along the A34, before turning off through Kidlington
and then over the A40 down toward Oxford City
Centre.

And again Lewis was fortunate, for no one had got
off the bus along the route until the upper reaches of the
Banbury Road.

Easy!

Driving at a safe and courteous distance behind the
bus, Lewis had ample opportunity for reflecting once
more on the slightly disturbing developments of the previous few days . . .

Morse had been as good as his word that Monday
morning, when the latter part of their audience with
Strange had turned almost inexplicably bitter. No,
Morse could not agree to any involvement in the re-
opening of the Harrison inquiries. Yes, Morse realized

("Fully, sir!") the possible implications of his non-compliance with the decision of a superior officer. Yet oddly enough, it had been Strange who had seemed the more unsure of himself during those final exchanges; and Lewis had found himself puzzled, and suspecting that there were certain aspects of the case of which he himself was wholly unaware.

Could it be. . . ?

Could it be perhaps. . . ?

Could it be perhaps that Morse had some reason for keeping his head above the turbid waters still swirling around the unsolved murder of Yvonne Harrison? Some *personal* reason, say? Some connection with the major participants in the case? Some connection (Lewis was thinking the unthinkable) with *the* major participant: with the murdered woman herself? For there must be *some* reason . . .

Some reason, too, for Morse's (virtually unprecedented) absence from HQ on those two following days, the Tuesday and the Wednesday? To be fair, he had rung Lewis (at home) early on the Tuesday morning, saying that he was feeling unwell, and in truth *sounding* unwell. He'd be grateful, he'd said, if Lewis could apologize to all concerned; perhaps for the following day as well. Lewis had rung Morse that Tuesday evening, but there was no answer; had rung again on the Wednesday evening—again with no answer.

Was Morse ill?

Not all that ill, anyway, because he'd appeared on the Thursday morning at his usual, comparatively early hour. And said nothing about his absence. Or about his row with Strange. Or about his health, for that matter. But Morse seldom mentioned his health . . .

Just below the Cutteslowe roundabout, the bus stopped and four passengers alighted—but not Repp.

At the Martyrs' Memorial, the majority of the passengers alighted—but not Repp.

At the Gloucester Green terminus, the last few passengers alighted—but not Repp.

The 27 bus was now empty.

Chapter Eighteen

> Any fool can tell the truth; but it requires a man of some sense to know how to lie well.
>
> (Samuel Butler)

Lewis knew what he must do as soon as he saw Morse's maroon Jaguar parked in its wonted place.

"Still feeling better, sir?"

"Better than what?"

"Can you spare a minute?"

"Si' down!"

Seated opposite, in his own wonted place, Lewis said his piece.

"You're in a bit of a mess," said Morse, at the end of the sorry story.

"That's not much help, is it?"

"Remember the Sherlock Holmes story, *Case of Identity*? A fellow gets in one side of a hansom cab and gets out through the opposite side."

"Doors on buses are always on the *same* side."

"Really?"

"You never go on a bus."

"But you weren't watching *either* side. You were queuing for coffee."

"Buying a paper."

"Listen!" Morse looked and sounded strained and weary. "I thought you were asking for my advice. Do you want to hear it?"

There was a brief silence before Morse continued: "It's not really a question of your own competence or incompetence—probably the latter, I'm afraid. The main concern is what's happened to your man, Repp. Agreed?"

Lewis nodded joylessly.

"Well, the situation's fairly simple. You just lost contact with him in the middle of things, that's all. No great shakes, is it? He's fine, believe me! Absolutely fine. At this very second he's probably got his bottom on the top sheet with that common-law missus of his. She picked him up somewhere—that's for certain. Most of these people released from the nick have somebody to pick 'em up."

"Except she doesn't drive a car."

"All right. She arranged for somebody *else* to pick him up."

"Why did he ask for a travel warrant, then?"

Morse looked less than happy. "He got on the bus at Bicester and while he was sitting there somebody saw him and tapped on the window and offered him a lift to Oxford or wherever he was going—and we know where that is, don't we? *Home.* Which is exactly where he is now, you can put your bank balance on that! It's a racing certainty. And if you don't believe me, go and see for yourself!"

Lewis considered what he had just heard. "It must have been somebody unexpected, sir. Like I say, he'd asked for a warrant."

"You're right, yes. Well, partly right. Either unexpected—or not really expected ... Perhaps not really welcome, either," added Morse slowly, a weak smile playing on his lips as though for the first time that morning his brain was possibly engaged in some serious thinking.

"You reckon that's what happened?"

"Lewis! *Something* happened, didn't it? If you think your man decided to dematerialize, you've been watching too many space videos."

"I don't watch—"

"Look! Remember what I've always told you when we've been on a case together—unlike this one! There's always, without exception, some wholly explicable, wholly logical causation for any chain of events, in any situation. In this case, you've just got to ask yourself where the link broke, then how it broke, then why it broke—and nothing in that sequence of events is going to be anything but simple and commonplace."

Lewis looked the troubled man he was. "I just can't see how . . ."

Morse's question was quietly spoken. "You remember that car, the one you said somehow squeezed in between you and the bus from Bullingdon?"

Lewis looked across the desk in pained surprise. "You don't think . . ."

"What do you remember about it?"

"Dark color—black, I think—pretty recent Reg—one person in it—man, I think—pretty sure it was a man."

"Not very observant—"

"I was looking at the *bus* all the time, for God's sake!"

"—and not much help, if you want the truth."

No, it wasn't, Lewis knew that. "What do I tell the Super, though?"

"If I were you? I certainly wouldn't tell him the truth. Not a very wise thing, you know, going through life telling nothing but the truth. So in this case, I'd tell him I'd followed the bus to Bicester, then followed the bus to Oxford, then seen Repp get off outside The Randolph, get picked up there in a car, and get driven off in the general direction of Chaucer Lane, Burford. Easy!"

Uneasy, however, was Lewis's minimal nod.

"But I'm *not* you, Lewis, am I? I'm a very accomplished liar myself, but I've never rated you too highly in that department."

A puzzled look suddenly came over Lewis's brow. "How come you know where Repp lives?"

"Great man, Chaucer, born in 1343, it's thought—"

"You're not answering my question!"

"I know a lot of things, Lewis—far more than you think."

"You've still not told me what I'm supposed to say to the Super."

"Cut your losses and tell him the truth."

"He'll tear me apart."

"You may well be surprised."

But, as he rose to his feet, Lewis appeared far from convinced.

"Well, I suppose I'd better—"

"Hold your horses!" (Morse looked at his wristwatch.) "It may just be that I can help you."

Lewis's eyebrows lifted a little as Morse continued:

"*You* promise to buy me a couple of drinks, and *I'll* promise to give you a big, fat juicy clue."

"If you say so, sir."

"Off we go then."

"What's this big, fat—?"

"I'll give you the Registration Number of the car that you followed from Bullingdon to Bicester! Bargain, is it?"

Lewis's eyebrows lifted a lot. "No kidding?"

Morse rechecked his wristwatch. "First things first, though. They've already been open five minutes."

Chapter Nineteen

It's good to hope; it's the waiting that spoils it.
(Yiddish proverb)

With increasing impatience and with incipient disquiet, lighting one cigarette from another, drinking cup after cup of instant coffee, Deborah Richardson had been watching from the front-room window, on and off from 10:30 A.M., on and off from 11:30 A.M., and virtually on and on from midday and thereafter—at first with that curiously pleasing *expectation* of happy events which Jane Austen would have swapped for happiness itself. Not that Debbie had ever read Jane Austen. Heard of her, though, most recently from that elderly Oxford don (well, wasn't fifty-eight elderly?) with whom she'd spent the night at the Cotswold Hotel in Burford . . .

It wasn't that she was keenly anticipating any renewal of sexual congress with her newly liberated partner. Although she felt gratified that physically he'd always been so demanding of her, it had often occurred to her that he was probably enjoying the sex more for its own sake than because he was having it with *her*. And perhaps that was why only occasionally did she experience that "intercrural effusion" of which she'd read in one of the women's magazines . . .

Nor was she looking forward to the regular resumption of cooking and washing and ironing that had monopolized her time in the years prior to his arrest . . .

Nor—she ought to be honest with herself!—was she at all anxious to witness his eating habits again, especially at breakfast, when he would regularly offer some trite and ill-informed commentary on whatever article he was reading in the *Sun*, and openly displaying thereby a semimasticated mouthful of whatever . . .

And—oh, most definitely!—she would never never ever tolerate again the demands his erstwhile criminal dealings had made upon the space, *her* space, in the quite unpleasantly appointed little semi he'd bought three years earlier at rock-bottom price during the slump in the housing market. After which, at almost any given time, every conceivable square foot of space had been jam-packed with crates of gin and whiskey, cartons of cigarettes, car radios, video recorders, cameras, computers, and hi-fi equipment. No! There'd have to be an end to all that stolen-property lark; and surely (now!) there'd be little further risk of Harry himself taking part in any of the actual burglaries. For he *had* taken part occasionally, Debbie knew that, although the police hadn't seemed to know, or perhaps just couldn't find sufficient evidence to prosecute. Certainly Harry had never asked for any further offenses to be taken into consideration. He'd made only the one plea in mitigation of his sentence: he might have known the possible provenance of the miscellaneous merchandise he'd acquired; *might* have known, if only he'd asked— but he'd just never asked. He was in business, that was all. He knew a few clients who wanted to buy things at less than market price. Who didn't? "Just like yer duty-frees, innit? Everybody's always looking round for a bargain, officer" . . .

So?

So why was she still standing there at the window, staring up and down the quiet road? The answer was simple: she just wanted a man *around* the place. Without Harry she felt isolated, lonely, unshared. She'd lost her man; and there was no man there to talk to, to talk to others about, to grumble at, to argue with, even to walk out on—because you couldn't walk out on a man who wasn't there to start with, now could you?

Where was he? What had happened? . . .

Not that her grass-widowhood had been entirely minus men. There'd been that nice little affair with the young plasterer who'd come in to patch up a crack in the kitchen wall. And that civilized little liaison with the Oxford don (so undemanding, so appreciative) she'd met in a Burford pub. But in each case, and on every occasion, she'd been so very, very careful . . .

Only once had she had *that* dreadful worry, after buying a Home Pregnancy Kit from Boots, when she'd just had to tell Harry, and when he'd been surprisingly sympathetic. If they did have a kid, it'd be good for him (him!) to have a mum *and* a dad. Yeah! He'd hated both his mum and his dad—but he'd hated his mum *less*, and it was proper to have a choice. Something else too: you know, when the poor little bugger went to school and one of the other kids said what's your name or what's your dad do—well, it was probably old-fashioned to think like that but, yeah!, better to have two of them, two parents. So she ought to change her name to his, but no need for any of all that nuptial stuff! Just for the kid's sake, mind—nothing to do with any social worker!

But she'd be "Debbie Repp," then; and that would be too close to "demirep" (a word she'd met in the "inter-crural" article), which she'd looked up in the biggest dictionary she could find in the Burford Public Library: "a person, esp. a woman, of dubious and libidinous disposition." Her name, she'd decided, would henceforth remain "Richardson." And in any case the subsequent messy miscarriage had settled *that* domestic crisis.

At 12:50 P.M. she left her vigil for the kitchen, where she felt the neck of the champagne bottle, standing beside two glasses on the table there. Inappropriately *chambré* she decided (another recent addition to her vocabulary), and she put it back in the fridge. Not Premier Division stuff: £8.99 from the supermarket, although in truth she'd begrudged even that. Money! God, how important that was in life! They had enough money— what's more, money temporarily held in her own name. But that was Harry's money, and she would never dare to touch more of it than the reasonably generous allowance he'd authorized.

She'd taken some occasional office-cleaning jobs in Burford, usually from 6 P.M. to 8 P.M. But £4.75 per hour was hardly the rate of remuneration to support any reasonable lifestyle; certainly not the style she'd begun to get accustomed to with Harry. So did she find herself *almost* hoping that he might pick up again on some of those very shady but very profitable activities?

No! No! No!

At 1:15 P.M. she rang Bullingdon Prison, learning that Harry Repp had left on schedule that morning with a bus warrant for Oxford. Nothing further they could tell her: no longer their responsibility, was he? She could ring the Probation Office in Oxford—that might have been his first port-of-call. Which number she was about to dial when she noticed a car pulling up outside—an R-Reg., dark blue, expensive-looking model; and a man she'd never seen before getting out of it, and walking toward her up the narrow, amateurishly cemented front path.

Chapter Twenty

Then said the Jews unto him, Thou art not yet fifty years old, and hast thou seen Abraham? Jesus said unto them, Verily, verily, I say unto you, Before Abraham was, I am.
(*The Gospel according to St. John,* ch. VIII, vv. 57, 58)

Already, an hour or so before driving out to see Debbie Richardson, it had been an unusual morning for Sergeant Lewis.

Morse had insisted on buying the second round in the Woodstock Arms, albeit one consisting only of one pint of Morrell's Best Bitter for himself, since as yet Lewis was only halfway down his obligatory orange juice.

Unusual? Yes. And quite certainly surprising.

"Do you really mean it—about the car number, sir?"

"Just be patient!"

"What do you think I *am* being?"

"You say the car was darkish, newish, toppish range?"

"Like I said, I was really concentrating on the bus."

"Be more *specific*, man! Go for it. Back your hunches!"

"All right: black; R-Reg.; twenty thou."

"That's better."

Lewis smiled dubiously. "Thank you."

"And how many people in that car of yours? One? Two? Three?"

"Certainly one, sir."

"We'll make a detective of you yet," mumbled Morse, leaning forward as he buried his nose in the froth.

"Could've been two, I suppose. I can't really remember but . . . you know, it was a bit like one of those cars going off on a family holiday, you know what I mean?"

"No."

"Well, you know—"

"For Christ's sake stop saying 'you know'!"

"Well, you've got things packed everywhere, haven't you? Not just cases and things but nappies, bedding, towels, boots, wellingtons, thermoses, carrier bags—all piled up so you can hardly see out of the back window."

"What sort of bags?"

Lewis was trying hard to revisualize the scene, and fortunately Morse had picked on the one thing that finally jogged his fading memory. Bags! Yes, there'd been bags in the back of that car: bags you could stick all sorts of things inside. And suddenly the picture had grown clearer:

"Black bags!"

"You think he was off to the rubbish dump?"

"Could've been. 'Waste Reception Area,' by the way, sir."

"Where's the biggest rubbish dump in Oxfordshire?"

"Or in Oxford, perhaps?" Lewis's face had brightened. "Redbridge. People go there from all over the county—straight down the A34—then turn off—" But Lewis stopped. "Forget it, sir. From Bullingdon you'd turn on to the A41, and then straight on to the A34. You wouldn't go into Bicester at all."

"And you're quite sure the car went into Bicester?"

"That's one thing I am sure about."

"If only you'd concentrated on that car, Lewis, and forgotten all about the bus!"

"I just don't understand why you're so interested in the car. Repp was on the *bus*."

"So you keep saying," said Morse quietly. "But you're not right, are you? Repp *wasn't* on the bus."

"Not when he got to Oxford, no."

"You lost him. You might as well face it."

Lewis drained his orange juice. "Yep! I agree. I lost him. And that's exactly why I need a bit of help."

"Like the number of that car, you mean?"

"I think you're having me on about that."

"Oh no. And if you think it'll help . . ."

Morse took out his pen and pushed his empty glass across the table: "Your round! And pass me your notebook."

A minute later, Lewis stared down at Morse's small, neat handwriting:

R456 LJB

And incredulity vied with amazement in his face as Morse continued quietly: "You know, you weren't your usual sharp self this morning, were you? You failed to observe the car in *front* of you—and you failed to observe the car *behind* you."

"You—you don't mean. . . ?"

"I do mean, yes. *I* was right behind you this morning. But being the law-abiding citizen I am, I instructed my driver to keep an appropriately safe distance from the vehicle in front."

"I just don't believe this. I just don't understand."

"Easy, really. I thought it wouldn't be a bad idea to keep an eye on our Mr. Repp, just like Strange did. So I rang up the prison Governor, an old friend of mine, and told him what I was intending to do; and he said there was no need because he'd had a call from Strange setting up *your* surveillance. So I just told him to forget it—told him we'd got some crossed wires—came out in an unmarked car, like you did—parked in the visitors' area—listened to Mahler's Eighth—and watched and waited. *And* took a flask of coffee—yes, *coffee*, Lewis— and the rest is history."

"You're having me on!"

"Oh no! How the hell do you think I could give you that car number unless I'd *seen* the bloody thing? You don't think I'm psychic or something, do you?"

Lewis reflected on this extraordinary new development. Then slowly formulated his thoughts aloud. "You saw the car in front of me. You saw who was in it and what was in it—"

"Black plastic bags, yes. You were right."

"—and you saw the Registration Number."

"Only just. You know, I'll have to see an optician soon."

"You told me off for saying 'you know'," snapped Lewis.

Morse curled his right hand lovingly round his beer glass. "Sometimes, you don't fully appreciate my help, you know."

Lewis let it go. "And you knew the car went into Bicester, to the bus station. You knew it all the time."

"Yes."

"So when I went to get a paper you saw Repp get out of the bus and get into the car. But you didn't tell *me*— oh no! You just left me to go on a wild goose chase after the bus. Well, thank you very much."

For a while Morse was silent. Then: "How many times have I been to the Gents this morning?"

"Twice since you've been here."

"Six times in all, Lewis! And the reason for such embarrassingly frequent retirements is not any lack of bladder control. It's those diuretic pills they've put me on."

The light slowly dawned; and Sergeant Lewis suddenly looked a happy man. "The thermos, sir? Three cups of coffee in that, say?"

Morse nodded. Not a happy man.

"So when you got to Bicester bus station you were dying for a leak and you saw the Gents' loo there, and when you came out—the car was gone. Right?"

Reluctantly Morse nodded once more. "And we followed you, you and the bus, back to Oxford."

A gleeful Lewis looked as if he'd won the Lottery. "You really should have kept your eyes on that car, sir!"

"You mean the black R-reg Peugeot, Lewis? You were right, by the way: £19,950 licensed and on the road, so they inform me. Not far off, were you?"

"And the owner?"

"Some insurance broker in Gerrard's Cross reported it missing two days ago."

Chapter Twenty-one

BURMA (Be Undressed Ready My Angel)
(An acronym frequently printed on the backs of envelopes
posted to sweethearts by servicemen about to go on leave, or
by prisoners about to be released.)

Unlike the (equally unknown) man who had called
upon her the previous evening, he held up his ID for several seconds in front of her face, like a conjurer holding
up a playing card toward an audience.

But she didn't really look at it; didn't even notice his
name. He seemed a decent, honest-looking sort of fellow—
not one of those spooky pseuds who occasionally sought
her company. And she was hardly too bothered if he
wasn't one of those decent, honest-looking sort of fellows.

"Deborah Richardson?" (He sounded rather shy.)

"Yes."

"Sergeant Lewis, Thames Valley CID."

"He's not here, yet. It *was* Harry you wanted?"

"Can I come in?"

"Be my guest!"

As she sat opposite him at the Formica-topped table,
Lewis saw a woman in her midthirties, of medium
build, with short blonde hair, and wearing a white
dress, polka-dotted in a gaudy green, that reached
halfway down (or was it halfway up?) a pair of thighs
now comfortably crossed in that uncomfortable kitchen.
She was not by any standards a beautiful woman; certainly not a pretty one. Yet Lewis had little doubt that
many men, including Morse perhaps, would have called
her quietly (or loudly) attractive.

She lit a cigarette and smiled rather nervously, the
pleasingly regular teeth unpleasingly coated with nicotine.

"He's OK, isn't he?"

"I'm sure he is, yes."

"It's just—well, I was expectin' him a bit before now."

"You didn't arrange to meet him at the prison?"

"No. We've got a car, in the garage, but I never got on too well with drivin'."

"Perhaps one of his mates. . . ?"

"Dunno, really. Expect so. He just said he'd be here as soon as he could."

"He might have rung you."

"Havin' a few beers, I should think. Only natural, innit? The champagne's back in the fridge anyway."

Lewis looked at his watch, surprised how quickly the latter part of the morning had sped by. "Only half-past one."

"So? So why have you called then, Sergeant?"

Lewis played his less than promising hand with some care. "It's just that we've received some . . . information, unconfirmed information, that Harry might have . . . well, there might be some slight connection between him and the murder of Mrs. Harrison."

"Harry never had nothin' to do with that murder!"

"You obviously remember the case."

"Course I do! Everybody does. Biggest thing ever happened round here."

"So as far as you know Harry had nothing—"

"You reckon I'd be tellin' you if he *had*?"

"But you say he hadn't?"

"Course he hadn't!"

"You see, all I'm saying is that Harry's a burglar—"

"*Was* a burglar."

"—and there was some evidence that there could have been a burglary that night that might have gone a bit wrong perhaps."

"What? Her lyin' on the bed there with her legs wide open? Funny bloody burglary!"

"How did you know that? How she was found?"

"Come off it! How the hell do any of us know anythin'? Common knowledge, wasn't it? Common gossip, anyway."

"Where did you hear it?"

"Pub, I should think."

"Maiden's Arms?"

"Shouldn't be surprised. Everybody talks about everythin' there. The landlord, 'specially. Still, that's what landlords—"

"Is he still there?"

"Tom? Oh, yes. Tom Biffen. Keeps about the best pint of bitter in Oxfordshire, so Harry said." (Lewis made a mental note, for Morse would be interested.)

"You know him fairly well, the landlord?"

She lit another cigarette, her eyes widening as she leaned forward a little. "*Fairly* well, yes, Sergeant."

Lewis changed tack. "You saw Harry pretty regularly while he was inside?"

"Once a week, usually."

"How did you get there?"

"Friends, mostly."

"Awkward place to get to."

"Yep."

"When did you last see him?"

"Week ago."

"What did you take him?"

"Bit o' cake. Few cigs. No booze, no drugs—nothin' like that. You can't get away with much there."

"Can you get away with *anything* there?"

She leaned forward again and smiled as she drew deeply on her cigarette. "Perhaps I could have done if I'd tried."

"Could he give *you* anything? To take out?"

"Well, nothin' he shouldn't. Just as strict about that as the other way round. We all sat at tables, you know, and they were watchin' us all the time—all the screws. You'd be lucky to get away with anythin'."

But Lewis knew that it was all a little too pat, this easy interchange. Things got in, and things got out—every prison was the same; and everybody knew it. Including this woman. And for the first time Lewis sensed that Strange was probably right: that the letter received by Thames Valley Police had been written by

Harry Repp at Bullingdon Prison, handed to one of his visitors, and posted somewhere outside—at Lower Swinstead, say.

For whatever reason.

But as yet Lewis couldn't identify such a reason.

"*Did* Harry ever ask you to take anything out of prison?"

"Come off it! What'd he got in there to take *out*?"

"Letters perhaps?" suggested Lewis quietly.

"If he'd forgotten some address. Not often, though."

"To some of his old cronies?"

"Crooks, you mean?"

"That's what I'm asking you, I suppose."

"Few letters, yes. He didn't want them people in there lookin' through everythin' he wrote. Nobody would."

"So you occasionally took one away?"

"Not difficult, was it? Just slip it in your handbag."

"What was the last one you took out?"

"Can't remember."

"I think you can." Lewis was surprised with the firm tone of his own voice.

"No, I can't. Just told you, didn't I?" (Yet another cigarette.)

"Please don't lie to me. You see, I *know* you posted a letter at Lower Swinstead. Harry'd asked you to post it there because he thought—he was wrong as it turned out—that it would be postmarked from there."

For the first time in the interview, Debbie Richardson seemed unsure of herself, and Lewis pressed home his perceptible advantages.

"How did you get to Lower Swinstead, by the way?"

"Only three or four miles—"

"You walked?"

"No, I drove—" She stopped herself. But the words, in Homeric phrase, had escaped the barrier of her teeth.

"Didn't you say you couldn't drive?"

"Lied to you, didn't I?"

"Why? Why lie to me?"

"I get used to it, that's why." She leaned forward across the table. And Lewis saw for certain what he had already suspected for semicertain—that she wore no bra beneath her dress; probably no knickers, either.

"How often do you go to the pub there, the Maiden's Arms?"

"Often as I can."

"Not in the car, I hope?"

"Sometimes get a lift there—you know, if somebody rings."

"When were you there last?"

"When I posted the letter."

"Open all day, is it?"

"What's all this quizzin' about?"

"Just that my boss'll be interested, that's all."

"You're all alike, you bloody coppers!"

It seemed a strange reply, and Lewis looked puzzled. "Pardon?"

"What you just asked me—about the pub bein' open all day. Exactly what the other fellow asked."

"What other fellow?"

"Can't remember his name. So what? Can't remember yours, come to that."

"When was this?"

"Last night. Asked me out for a drink, didn't he? I reckon he fancied me a little bit. But I was already—"

"From the *police*, you say?"

"That's what he said."

"You didn't check?"

Debbie Richardson shrugged her shoulders. "Nice he was—sort o' well educated. Know what I mean?"

"You can't recall his name?"

"No, sorry. Tell you one thing though, Sergeant, er . . ."

"Lewis."

"Had a lovely car, he did. Been nice it would—ridin' round in that. A Jag—maroon-colored Jag."

Chapter Twenty-two

> . . . a mountain range of Rubbish, like an old volcano, and its geological foundation was Dust. Coal-dust, vegetable-dust, bone-dust, crockery-dust, rough dust, and sifted dust—all manner of Dust in the accumulated Rubbish.
>
> (Dickens, *Our Mutual Friend*)

"Not for scrap, is she?" Stan Cox nodded toward the Jag parked in the no-parking area outside his office window in the Redbridge Waste Disposal Centre.

"Getting on a bit," conceded Morse, "like all of us. You know, windscreen wipers packing up, gearbox starting to jam, no heat . . ."

"Sounds a bit like the missus!"

"Pardon?"

"Joke, sir."

"Ah, yes." Morse's smile was even weaker than the witticism as he looked round the cramped office, his eyes catching a girlie calendar in the corner, from which a provocatively bare-breasted bimbo, with short blonde hair, stared back at him.

"Nice, ain't she!"

Morse nodded. "Past her sell-by date, though. She's the May girl."

"Remember the ol' song, sir—'From May to September'?"

"You just like having her around."

It was Cox's turn to nod: "Drives me mad, she does. Keeps me sane at the same time though, if you follows me meaning."

Morse wasn't at all sure that he did, but he was conscious that he'd drunk too much beer that lunchtime; that he should never have driven himself out to Redbridge; that what he'd earlier seen as a clear-cut outline had now grown blurred around the periphery. In the pub, with Lewis, he'd felt convinced he could see a cause, a sequence, a structure, to the crime.

Perhaps two crimes now.

It was the same old tantalizing challenge to puzzles that had faced him ever since he was a boy. It was the certain knowledge that something *had* happened in the past—happened in an ordered, logical, very specific way. And the challenge had been, and still was, to gather the disparate elements of the puzzle together and to try to reconstruct that "very specific way."

Not too successfully now, though. For here, at Redbridge, there seemed a great gulf fixed between the fanciful hypothesis he'd so recently formulated, and the humdrum reality of a rubbish dump.

Is that what Cox was trying to say?

"How d'you mean? Keeps you sane?"

"Well, it's not exactly your Botanical Gardens here, is it? Just all the filth and useless stuff people want shut of. So there's not much good to look at, 'cept her, bless her heart! Pearl in a pigsty—that's what she is."

"Why don't you write her a fan letter?"

"Think she'd read it?"

"No."

"So what can we do for you, Chief?"

Morse told him, making most of it up as he went along.

And when he'd finished, Cox nodded. "No problem. We'd better just let the County Authorities know."

"Already done," lied Morse. And refusing a cup of coffee, he left the office and walked unaccompanied around the site, only a few hundred yards from the southern stretch of Oxford's Ring Road, thinking about the things he'd learned from Cox . . .

"Do you reckon," he'd asked, "you could dispose of a body here, in one of your, er. . . ?"

"Only in one of the compactor bins—that'd be the best bet. You'll be able to see for yourself, though. The others are a bit too open, really."

"Black bag, say? Put a body in it? Just chuck it in?"

"You'd need a big bag."

"Well, let's say we've got a big bag."

"Heavy things, bodies. Ten, twelve stone, say? You couldn't just . . . well, unless you had two people, I suppose."

"Or cut the body in half, perhaps."

"Mm. Still a bit awkward, wouldn't you think? Unless it were stiff, of course."

"Yes . . ."

"*Was* it stiff, this body of yours?"

"Er, no. No, I don't think it was."

"Or unless it was a pretty small body. *Was* it small, this body of yours?"

"Er, no. No. I don't think it was."

"Well, as I say . . ."

"How would *you* get rid of a body here?"

"Well, if it were a littl'un, like I said, I'd go for a compactor bin. They got ramps that go back and forrard reg'lar like, and everything soon gets pushed through into the back o' the bin. Doubt anybody'd notice it really—not *this* end, anyway."

"There's *another* end?"

"Sutton Courtenay, yes, out near Didcot. The bins get driven out there, to the landfill site. Somebody might notice summat there, I suppose."

"Funny, isn't it? Dustmen always seem to notice some things, don't they?"

"You mean our Waste Disposal Operatives."

"They refused to take my little bag of grass cuttings last week."

"Ah, now you're talking business, sir."

"Put a human head in the bottom of the bag though—"

"—and you'd probably get away with it? Right! But I shouldn't try your grass cuttings again, Inspector."

As he walked around, Morse was impressed by the layout and the management of the large area designated there to the various categories of Oxford's disposable debris: car batteries; can bank; engine-oil cans; paper bank; clothing bank; tools; bottles (green, brown, white); bulky items; scrap metal; fridges and freezers; garden waste (green); garden waste (other) . . .

Only the vast "Bulky Items" bins seemed to offer any scope so far; and even there a body would have lain uncomfortably and conspicuously amid the jagged edges of broken tables, awkwardly angled cupboards, tilted mattresses.

Then Morse stood still for many minutes inspecting what he'd been waiting to see: the compactor bins— twelve of them in a row. Each bin (Morse attempted a non-too-scientific analysis) was a 12-ton, 6 feet x 20 feet, white-bodied metal container, a broad green stripe painted horizontally along its middle, with a grilled covering at the receiving end which customers could easily lift before depositing their car-booted detritus there; and where a ramp was ever moving forward and back, forward and back, and pushing the divers deposits from the bin's mouth through into some unseen, unsavory interior. On the side of each bin were "start/stop" and "red/green" buttons and switches which appeared to control the complex operation; and even as Morse watched, a site workman came alongside, somehow interpreting the evidence and (presumably?) deciding whether any particular bin was sufficiently stuffed to get lifted on to one of the great lorries lumbering around, and to get carted off to—where was it?—Sutton Courtenay.

Morse tackled the young ponytailed operative as he was tapping one of the bins, rather like a man tapping the upturned hull of some stricken submarine to see if there were any signs of life.

"How long's it take to fill one of these things?"

"Depends. Holidays and weekends? Pretty quick— only a day, sometimes. Usually though? Two, three days. Depends, like I said."

"How many bins have gone today?"

"Two? No, three, I think."

"You didn't, er, notice anything unusual about . . . about anything?"

"What sort o' thing, mate?"

"Forget it, son! And, by the way, I wasn't aware I *was* one of your mates."

"An' I wasn't aware you was me fuckin' father, neither!" spat the spotty-faced youth, as an outsmarted Morse walked unhappily away.

It had not been a particularly productive afternoon. Morse hadn't even had the nous to bring his little bag of grass cuttings along, to be tossed, with full official blessing, into the garden waste (green) depository.

Back in Cox's office Morse was (for him) comparatively generous with his gratitude for the help he'd been provided with. And before leaving, he took a last look at the month of May's lascivious self-offering to all who looked and longed and lusted after her. People like Stanley Cox; like Cox's fellow Waste Disposal Operatives; like Chief Inspector Morse, who stood in front of her again and thought she reminded him of another woman—a woman he'd met so very recently.

Reminded him of Debbie Richardson.

Chapter Twenty-three

A novel, like a beggar, should always be kept "moving on." Nobody knew this better than Fielding, whose novels, like most good ones, are full of inns.

(Augustine Birrell, *The Office of Literature*)

It was still only 2:30 P.M. that same day when Lewis pulled into the small car park of the Maiden's Arms, a low-roofed building of Cotswold stone which was Lower Swinstead's only public house. A notice beside the entrance announced the opening hours for Friday as 12 noon–3 P.M., 6:30–11 P.M.

At a table by the sole window of the small bar sat two aged villagers drinking beer from straight pint glasses, smoking Woodbines, and playing cribbage. Only one other customer: a pale-faced, ear-pierced, greasy-haired youth, who stood feeding coin after coin into an unresponsive fruit machine. When Lewis asked for the landlord, the man behind the bar introduced himself as no less a personage.

"What can I get you, sir?"

Lewis showed his ID. "Can we talk?"

Tom Biffen was a square of a man, small of stature and wide of body, his weather-beaten features framed with a grizzly beard, a pair of humorous eyes, and a single earring in the left lobe. A dark-blue T-shirt paraded "The Maidens Arms" across a deep chest.

Lewis came to the point without preamble: "You know a woman called Deborah—Deborah Richardson?"

"Debbie? Oh yeah. Everybody knows Debbie." He spoke with a West Country burr, and clearly neither of the cardplayers was hard-of-hearing, for had Lewis had occasion to turn round at that moment he would have noted a half-smiling nod of agreement on each of their faces.

Lewis continued: "Her partner's been released from prison this morning. You know Harry Repp?"

"Harry? Oh yeah! Everybody knows Harry." (The fingers of the cardplayers froze momentarily, and each had stopped smiling.)

"He's not been in this morning?"

"I'd've seen him if he had, wouldn't I?"

"It's just that he's not been home yet, that's all. And we want to make sure he's OK."

"Having a noggin or two somewhere, I shouldn't wonder. That's what I'd be doing."

"How long have you been landlord here?"

"Let's see now . . ."

"Seven year come September, Biff," came an answer from behind.

"Thank you, Bert!" Biff turned his attention back to Lewis as he held a proprietorially polished glass up to the light like a radiographer examining an X ray. "You're going to ask me about the murder—I know that. There's been things in the papers, and we're all interested. Can't pretend we're not. Biggest thing ever happened round here."

"Lots of rumors, weren't there? You know, about Mrs. Harrison. Having a bit on the side, perhaps?"

"Well, it weren't me! And Alf and Bert here, they're both a bit past it now."

("Speak for yourself!"—from one of the septuagenarians.)

"Did she ever come in here with any men?"

Biff shook his head indeterminately: "Simon, the boy? Only occasionally though. Deaf, see! I 'spect it was a bit dull for him—not being able to hear the sparkling repartee of my regulars, like Alf and Bert here."

("Used to drink Coca-Cola—" from Alf, or was it Bert?)

"What about the daughter?"

"Sarah? Nice pair o' legs, Sarah."

("Not the only nice pair o' things!"—*sotto voce* from behind.)

"With a boyfriend in tow, was it?"

"Sometimes."

"With her mum?"

"Nah! Wouldn't have wanted *her* around, would she?"

"Why not?"

"Well . . . attractive, wasn't she, Sarah? It was her mum had the real sex appeal, though. Could have had most fellahs round here, if they'd had a jar or two."

("Even if they hadn't!"—from Bert, or was it Alf?)

"Did you ever come up with any names?"

"Names? Nah! Like I said . . ."

"Must have been rumors though?"

"Never heard any meself." Biff looked over Lewis's shoulder: "You ever hear any rumors, lads?"

"Not me," said Bert.

"Nor me," said Alf.

Lewis felt certain that all three of them were lying. And, according to the report, the police on the original inquiry had felt very much the same: that the villagers were quite willing to hint that Yvonne Harrison had not exactly been the high priestess of marital fidelity; but that when it came to naming names, they'd decided to clamp up. En bloc.

"Drink on the house, sir?"

Lewis declined, and bade his farewell, nodding to the cardplayers as he walked to the door, where he stopped and turned back toward the landlord, pointing to the T-shirt:

"Shouldn't there be an apostrophe before the 's'?"

Biff grinned. "Funny you should say that. Fellow in here last night asked me exactly the same thing!"

Lewis walked slowly round to the car park, noting the plaque on the sidewall:

> Parking strictly for customers.
> Other vehicles will be clamped.
> Release fee £25

Need more than that, thought Lewis, to unclamp a small community which was so clearly still maintaining its conspiracy of silence.

But Lewis was wrong.

As he took out his car keys, he saw the youth who had just been feeding the fruits of his labors into the fruit machine. Waiting for him. Beside the car.

"Police, aincha?"

"Yes?"

"You was asking about things in there."

"I'm always asking about things."

"Just that somebody else was asking them same sort o' questions, see? Couldn't help hearing, could I? And this fellah—he was asking *me* a few things. About Mrs. Harrison. About if I'd ever seen her with any fellah in the pub. But I couldn't quite remember. Not at the time."

"You remember now, though?"

"Right on the nail, copper. Told me to give 'im a buzz if I suddenly remembered something. Said, you know, it might be worthwhile like."

"Why didn't you ring him?"

"That's just it, though. I'd seen her with the fellah that *asked* me, see? Same bleedin fellah!"

"You mean ... it was *him* you'd seen with Mrs. Harrison?"

"Right on the nail, copper."

"What did he look like, this fellow?"

"Well, sort of ... I can't really ..."

"He gave you his name?"

"No. Gave me 'is phone number though, like I said."

The youth produced a circular beer-mat from his pocket.

Lewis looked down at a telephone number written above the red *Bass* triangle, written in the small, neat hand he knew so well: the personal ex-directory telephone number of Chief Inspector Morse.

Chapter Twenty-four

In many an Oxfordshire Ale-house the horseshoe is hung upside-down, in the form that is of an Arch or an Omega. This age-old custom (I have been convincingly informed) is not to allow the Luck to run out but to prevent the Devil building up a nest therein.

(D. Small, *A Most Complete Guide to the Hostelries of the Cotswolds*)

As he stood amid the wilderness of waste, a High Viz jacket over his summer shirt and a red safety helmet on his head, Chief Inspector Morse realized that he had miscalculated rather badly. But he'd had to check it up.

It had always been the same with him. Whenever as a young boy reading under his bedside lamp he'd come across an unfamiliar word, he'd known with certainty that he could never look forward to sleep until he'd traced the newcomer's credentials and etymology in

Chambers' Dictionary, the book that stood alongside *The Family Doctor* (1910), *A Pictorial History of the First World War*, and *The Life of Captain Cook*, on the single short shelf that comprised his parents' library.

His father (sadly, almost tragically) had been a clandestine gambler. And Morse was fully aware that this time he himself had put his money on a rank outsider: the possibility that someone had murdered Harry Repp; had disposed of his body in the Redbridge Waste Disposal Centre; had disposed of this hypothetical body in a particular part of that Centre—specifically in one of the compactor bins perhaps: further, that the said and equally hypothetical bin had been, was being, or was about to be, driven out in a hypothetical black bag to Sutton Courtenay. And, above all, that somebody might have *observed* such a hypothetical deposit. Ridiculous! William Hill or Ladbrokes would probably have offered odds of 1,000,000–1 against any such eventuality.

On impulse Morse had driven down the A34, thence along the A4130, to the landfill site on the outskirts of Sutton Courtenay. Where, after a series of telephone calls from the temporary (permanent) Portakabins, the management had finally acknowledged the *bona fides* of their dubious visitor.

It was in a Landrover that (finally) Morse had been driven out to the tipping area, where virtually continuous convoys of lorries from the whole of Oxfordshire were raising the telescopic legs of container-cargoes to some 45 degrees as they began to tip their loads, moving forward in disjunctive jerks as they ensured the contents were fully discharged, and leaving behind a distinctive trail of their own particular type of rubbish. As a rather dispirited Morse watched these operations, he imagined that perhaps when viewed from some hovering helicopter each truck would seem like an artist's brush, with the trail of the gradually extending rubbish like a stroke of variegated paint being smeared across the canvas of the landscape. But Morse accepted the more prosaic truth of the situation immediately: the truck drivers themselves would very seldom, if ever, have occasion to notice, let alone to examine, the contents of the loads they were emptying.

He voiced his thoughts. "If a driver dumped a body . . . well, he wouldn't really know much about it, would he?"

Colin Rice, the site manager, hesitated awhile before replying—not because he had the slightest doubt about the answer to this question, but because he felt reluctant immediately to disappoint his somewhat melancholic inquisitor.

"No."

"How many of those compactor bins do you get from Redbridge every day?"

"Depends."

"Today?"

"Four or five? I could check."

"No. No need."

Morse watched as the yellow-painted BOMAG tractors were once again setting about their dismal business, the metal teeth of their giant wheels compacting the recently deposited mounds; and then, with a fair-weather frontage reminiscent of a snowplow, pushing forward the leveled rubbish toward its burial ground.

For the moment Morse said nothing more, suddenly and strangely aware that, if he half-closed his eyes, the piles of refuse around him could almost appear like some wondrously woven multicolored quilt, black and white mostly, but interspersed with vivid little patches of blue and red and yellow.

It was Rice who spoke: "If anybody'd see anything it'd be those chaps on the levelers. They're looking forward at all the rubbish, see? Your normal truck driver, he's not even looking backward at it."

"You wouldn't be able to pinpoint the place where any lorry loads from Redbridge. . . ?"

The site manager shook his head. "No chance."

"If you had enough personnel though?"

"How many?"

"Five or six?"

"Five or six hundred, you mean?"

Morse decided to quit the unequal struggle. He

kicked a hole in one of the black plastic bags at his feet, and briefly surveyed the nauseating mixture of spaghetti and tomatoes that oozed therefrom, like the innards of a road-squashed rabbit.

"If you'd like to stay?" suggested Rice, without enthusiasm. "You never know. We had a load of brand-new cameras dumped here once."

"I've never had a camera myself," admitted Morse. "I just hope you appropriated one for yourself."

Rice smiled, forgivingly. "You don't really know much about the rules in a place like this, do you, sir?"

Morse lifted his eyes from the ground toward the giant cooling-towers of Didcot Power Station which stood sentinel on the immediate landscape, only a few hundred yards away.

"No, I don't," he said quietly.

As he drove back along the A34 into Oxford, Morse doubted he'd expressed adequate thanks to Greenways Waste Management. He was (he acknowledged the fact) never a man renowned for voicing much gratitude. He'd even dismissed, and that cursorily, Rice's thoughtful offer of issuing a memo to everyone working either permanently or temporarily on the site, acquainting them with the situation.

But Morse felt unable to feel too self-critical, because he knew there *was* no "situation." And he repeated to himself this recently corroborated conviction as he turned on the car radio, and listened again to the slow movement of Bruckner's Seventh.

When later that same afternoon Lewis arrived back at Kidlington HQ, he felt more pleased, more excited, and (yes!) more confident in himself than he'd been for a long, long while. In almost all previous cases he'd usually reached first base only to find that Morse was already sprinting off to second base; and so on, and so on, all round the baseball pitch. So now he decided to do a little sprinting for himself.

First, he rang Redbridge—only to discover that Morse had already visited the site.

Second, he rang Sutton Courtenay—only to discover that Morse had already visited the site, and where he'd pronounced that any search of said site was quite certainly foredoomed to failure.

So Lewis had coolly countermanded these instructions. It was as if he—Lewis—was taking charge of the case. Well, he was, wasn't he?

Chapter Twenty-five

> Sometimes it is that searchers spot
> The kind of thing they'd rather not.
> (Lessing, *Nathan der Weise*)

During "Jammie" Jarnold's twenty-two years' service on the Sutton Courtenay site, he'd seen most things. Not everything. For example, he'd never caught a glimpse of that sack of notes the Metropolitan Police were certain had been deposited in one of the trucks on that long train which arrived in the early hours of each morning from Brentford, via a branchline from Didcot, with its thousands of tons of the capital's refuse. Four hundred and fifty thousand pounds, they'd said, in fivers and tenners. Yes, Jammie had kept his eyes wide open on that occasion; had occasionally climbed down from his cab to prod anything that seemed even minimally promising.

If, on balance, it was a steady old job, it was also a job that was unmemorable and predictably monotonous. For this reason, neither Jammie nor his colleagues in the team of BOMAC tractor operators had dismissed as so much negligible bumf the single Xeroxed sheet which had been handed out that Saturday morning, both to permanent on-site personnel and to every dump truck driver entering the site from the far quarters of Oxfordshire.

(Morse himself would have been pleased to write such a succinct note—though inserting, of course, an apostrophe in the humorous parenthesis.)

MEMO FROM SITE MANAGER

Thames Valley Police have advised of the possibility of a human body, probably bagged, being recently conveyed from the Redbridge Centre in Oxford. Everyone is asked to be extra vigilant and to report anything unusual (or usual, provided its a body).

Just after the start of the shift, a colleague shouted across at Jammie, waving a copy of the memo.

"Better keep your eyes open!"

"What's the reward?"

"Night with Sophia Loren in the Savoy."

"Bit young for me."

"I still reckon you'll keep your eyes open."

"Yeah! I reckon."

"Like looking for a needle in an 'aystack though."

"Like finding a shadow in the blackout, as me ol' mum used to say."

"I like that, Jammie. Sort o' poetic, like."

Jarnold braked his tractor at 10:05 A.M. and jumped down from his cab on to the semileveled, semicompacted mound of recently deposited rubbish. It was not that the specific item he'd spotted was unusual in any way. In fact, any pair of shoes was a very common sight: thousands of pairs were ever to be observed on every part of the site, worn down, worn out, worn beyond any possible repair. But there were unusual aspects about this particular pair of shoes. For a start, they looked comparatively new and were clearly of good quality; then, they were the only objects sticking out of a large black bag; what's more, they seemed strangely reluctant to drop *out* of that large black bag, as if (perhaps?) they might be attached, permanently, to something *inside* that large black bag.

Jarnold shouted over to a colleague.

"Come over 'ere a sec!"

But already he had half-torn one side of the plastic.

"Christ!"

He turned away to vomit full-throatedly over a piece of conveniently positioned carpeting.

Had he been dining with Miss Loren at the Savoy, this would have caused considerable consternation. Not here, though. Not at the landfill site at Sutton Courtenay in Oxfordshire.

Chapter Twenty-six

UNDERGRADUATE:	But you're blowing up the wrong tyre, sir. It's the back one that's flat.
DON:	Goodness me! You mean the two of them are not connected?
	(Freshman seeking to assist his tutor outside Trinity College, Oxford)

Morse (for some reason) was in that Saturday morning when Lewis knocked on his office door just after ten.

"Spare a few minutes, sir?"

"C'm in! I've finished the crossword."

"How long?"

"Let's just say the brain is deteriorating."

"Thirty thousand brain cells a day we lose after thirty, so you told me once."

Morse nodded morosely. "I just thought I was the exception, that's all. Si' down!"

Lewis did so, and took a deep breath. "I've been following you, sir."

Morse looked across at his sergeant uncomprehendingly.

"You were at Debbie Richardson's house—before me;

you were at the Maiden's Arms—before me; you were at Bullingdon—before me; you were at Redbridge—before me; you were out at Sutton Courtenay—before me. You've been one move ahead of me all the time."

"Only *one*?"

"Why couldn't you just *tell* me?"

"Tell you what?" asked Morse. "And don't forget that time when it was *me* following *you*: from Bullingdon. At exactly the distance recommended in the Highway Code."

"Which is?"

"Next question?"

"You will be taking on the case, won't you?"

"Next question?"

"Why not?"

"Pass."

"You're getting people's backs up here, you know that?"

"Nothing new about that."

"But surely—?"

"Listen!" Unblinking blue eyes glared across the desk. "I am not taking on the Harrison case."

"I was just hoping you'd help me, that's all."

"Yes?"

"Well, do you mind me asking you if . . . if you've got any personal interest in all of this?"

"Nil." If there had been a quick flicker of unease in Morse's eyes, it was as quickly gone.

"But you know a lot about it, don't you? So you must have some idea about what happened on the night she was murdered?"

"Ideas—plural."

"There was a logical sequence of events, as you would say."

"There was a concatenation of events, yes, with each link of the chain causally connected to its predecessor."

"What do you think happened that night?"

"Not much argument about that, is there?"

"You'd agree with this, then?" Lewis produced a sheet of A4 on which he had typed a timetable for the day of the murder:

7 A.M.–1 P.M.	Yvonne on early shift at JR2 Ward 7C
1:15–2 P.M.	Lunches in staff canteen
2:15–4 P.M.	(?)Drives down to Oxford shopping at M&S and Austin Reed
4:00(?)–4:30 P.M.	Drives home avoiding main traffic exodus
6–7 P.M.	Evening meal of mushroom omelette
9:00 P.M.	Local builder rings—number engaged or phone off hook
9:10 P.M.	Frank H gets phone call and catches 21.48 Paddington to Oxford train
9:30 P.M.	Builder rings again—ringing-tone but no reply
11:00 P.M.	F H gets taxi to Lower Swinstead
11:20 P.M.	Discovers wife naked, gagged, handcuffed and dead

Morse glanced at the sheet in perfunctory fashion.

"You ought to use the Oxford comma more."

"Pardon?"

"The presumption was—is—that somewhere between nine and half-past . . ."

"Pathologist's report seemed to confirm that."

"Would I had your faith in pathologists!"

"Not just that though, is it? The whole thing hangs together. Pretty well everything there's confirmed: statements from the hospital; receipts from the two shops; postmortem details on the meal; phone calls checked out—"

"Nonsense! The builder? First time the number's engaged? Second time nobody answers? How the hell do you check that?"

"You can't check absolutely everything—"

"What about the husband? Odd sort of call, wasn't it? Drop whatever you're doing and get here double-quick! So who was it who rang him?"

"That's what I'm asking you, sir."

"His number couldn't have been too well known. He was renting a flat, wasn't he?"

"Still is."

"But somebody knew it—and rang him. Did we check the phone records of the suspects?"

"What suspects?"

"The two children?"

"They *weren't* suspects. And if they were, why shouldn't they ring their dad occasionally?"

"How did he pay for his train journey?"

"No credit card record—must have paid cash. *And* for the taxi ride. Anyway, he'd got the best alibi of any-body: taxi driver remembers the time exactly. He was just listening to the 11 o'clock news headlines."

"Was the train a bit late that night? If it's the one I sometimes catch, it's due in at 22:53."

"Too late to find out, sir."

"Rubbish! Too difficult, possibly. But they keep all these times of arrivals: they make statistical tables out of 'em, for heaven's sake."

"Must've been on time, surely?"

"What? Seven minutes for somebody in one helluva rush? From Platform 2 to the taxi-rank? It'd only take a geriatric like me a couple of minutes."

"Perhaps there was a queue."

"*Was* there a queue?"

"Dunno. Perhaps he nipped into the snack bar."

"Closed."

"I don't quite see what you're getting at."

"What is essential, Lewis, is usually invisible to the outward eye."

"Which doesn't help *me* much, does it?"

"All right. Get back to your facts."

"She was burgled. At some point that evening the back patio window was smashed in from the outside and somebody was after something. The TV was unplugged—"

"But not taken."

"—so he was probably disturbed. He must have thought the place was empty. Probably none of the lights would have been on—not then anyway. Midsum-mer, wasn't it? Sunset was about a quarter-past nine—I looked it up." (Morse nodded approvingly.) "I know some people always leave one or two lights on anyway when they go out—"

"But she *didn't* go out."

"No. So as I say the burglar must have thought the coast was clear, and must have been prepared for the alarm to ring—it's quite a way to the next house—while he grabbed a few of the valuables, smartish like."

"The alarm was ringing when Harrison got there, wasn't it? Twenty-past eleven."

Lewis nodded. "Two hours or so after she was murdered."

"And the alarm would cut out automatically after twenty minutes' ringing?"

"Yes."

"So?"

"I dunno, sir. But it seems we didn't discount the theory that the murderer might have set it off himself."

"You mean two hours *later*?"

"I don't know what I mean."

"Pretty little puzzle."

"You're not trying to help me, are you? You've usually got some theory or other of your own."

Morse smiled amiably. "The obvious one. Mrs. H. surprised a burglar and the burglar panicked and murdered her. Or perhaps . . ." (the smile had faded) ". . . perhaps she was entertaining one of her lovers that night and things went wrong—things went sadly wrong. That's all I've got to offer: the burglar theory and the lover theory. What else is there?"

"Maybe a bit of both, sir? Say she was in bed with some fellow when she heard the window being smashed in and . . ."

"Could well be."

"You see, she'd *not* had sex that night, sir—certainly not been raped or tortured or physically assaulted. Clothes all neatly folded by the side of the bed."

"Couldn't the murderer have folded them? Doesn't take me long to fold a pair of pajamas."

Lewis shook his head slowly. "Naked, gagged, handcuffed . . ."

"Yes," agreed Morse. "Don't forget the handcuffs."

"Not much good remembering them, either."

"No. I recall they were, er, not to be found later on."

"But all the proper procedures were gone through. Left on her wrists till the PM, and the path people did all the usual checks—blood, fibers, hairs. Couldn't come up with anything though, could they? *And* they checked them for prints—job they'd normally leave to the SOCOs. Bit of a muddle, by the sound of it. Probably that's how they came to be lost."

"Temporarily misplaced, Lewis."

"Not the only things that went missing, were they? There was a file of personal letters . . ."

"I doubt they'd ever have been much help."

"We still didn't do a very good job."

"Bloody awful job."

"If only we knew who rang Frank Harrison in London that night!"

"One of his children, the builder, the burglar, the lover, the candlestick-maker? I'm like you: I don't know. But unlike you I'm not concerned with the case."

Lewis looked shrewdly into Morse's face. "You're *interested* though, I think."

Morse got to his feet. "Just give me a lift down to Oddbins. I'm out of Glenfiddich."

The phone rang as they were leaving.

"Morse?" (Strange's unmistakable voice.)

"Sir?"

"Listen to this!"

"Not me, sir. It just so happens that Sergeant Lewis—"

"MORSE!" But the receiver had already been transferred; and although aware of the explosions at the other end of the line, Morse walked out into the corridor and along to the Gentlemen's loo.

On his return, the telephone conversation had concluded.

"They've found a body. Out at Sutton Courtenay."

"Just like I said."

"No, sir. Not just like you said. *You* told the people there not to worry any more. It was *me* who told them to keep looking."

"Well done! You were right and I was wrong. I

thought Repp was due for his comeuppance, and probably he thought so too. But I just didn't follow it through. That letter he wrote from prison was a cry for help in a way, asking us to keep a protective eye on him. Which we did, of course. Or rather which we didn't."

Suddenly he gave his chest a vigorous massage with his right hand.

"OK, sir?"

"Bit of indigestion."

"You sure?"

"They've found the body, you say?"

"Half an hour ago."

"You'd better get off then."

"Will you come along?"

"Certainly not. I'm not worried about him any longer. He was a cheap crook, a part-time burglar, a nasty piece of work—should have been rumbled years ago. Good riddance, Harry Repp!"

Chapter Twenty-seven

> *In the afternoon they came unto a land*
> *In which it seemèd always afternoon,*
> *All round the coast the languid air did swoon,*
> *Breathing like one that hath a weary dream.*
> (Tennyson, *The Lotus-eaters*)

After an excited, if somewhat dispirited, Lewis had dropped him off at Oddbins, Morse picked up two bottles of single-malt Glenfiddich ("£4 Off When Two Are Purchased"); then walked further down the Summertown shops to Boots, where he bought two large boxes of Alka-Seltzer (sixty tablets in all) and two packets of extra-strength BiSoDoL (sixty tablets in all), reckoning that such additional medicaments might keep him comparatively fit for a further fortnight. But in truth his acid indigestion and heartburn were getting even worse. All right, it was a family affliction; but it gave little comfort to know that father and paternal grandfather had both endured agonies from hiatal hernia—a condition not desperately serious perhaps, but certainly far more painful than it sounded. The cure—so simple!—had been repeatedly advocated by his GP: "Just pack up the booze!" And indeed Morse had occasionally followed such advice for a couple of days or so; only to assume, upon the temporary disappearance of the symptoms, that a permanent cure had been effected; and that a resumption of his erstwhile modus vivendi was thenceforth justified.

He would try again soon.

Not today, though.

He walked down South Parade to the Woodstock Road, turned right, and soon found himself at the Woodstock Arms, where the landlord rightly prided himself on a particularly fine pint of Morrell's Bitter—of which Morse took liberal advantage that early Saturday lunchtime. The printed menu and the chalked-up specials on the board were strong temptations to many a man. But not to Morse. These past two decades he had almost invariably taken his lunchtime calories in liquid form; and he did so now. Most of the habitués he knew by sight, if not by name; but after a few perfunctory nods he settled himself in a corner of the wall-seating, and thought of many things . . .

Instinctively (or so he told himself) he'd known that Harry Repp was doomed to die from the moment he'd left Bullingdon. Harry had known too much. Harry had been a bit player—a bit more than a bit player in the drama that had been enacted on the evening Yvonne Harrison was murdered. But Harry had decided to remain silent. And the reason for such silence was probably the reason for many a silence—money. Someone had ensured that Harry's discreet silence had been profitably rewarded. On his release Harry had probably decided that the goose could soon be persuaded to change the golden eggs from medium to large. But he'd miscalculated: something had happened—probably there'd been some communication during the last few weeks of his imprisonment—that had cast a cloud of fear over his impending release; justifiable fear, since he now lay stiff and cold amidst the trash and the filth of Sutton Courtenay.

It seemed a predictable outcome though far from an inevitable one, and Morse felt no real cause for any self-recrimination. Lewis would go along there—was probably there already; would join the SOCOs and supervise the necessary procedures; would draw a few tentative, temporary conclusions; would report to Strange; and all in all would probably do as good a job as any other member of the Thames Valley CID in seeking the motive for Repp's murder.

He ordered himself a third pint, conscious that the world seemed a considerably kindlier place than heretofore. He even found himself listening to the topics of conversation around him: darts, bar-billiards, Aunt Sally, push-penny . . . and perhaps (he thought) his own life might have been marginally enriched by such innocent divertissements.

Perhaps not, though.

Leaving the Woodstock Arms, he slowly walked the few hundred yards north to Squitchey Lane, where he turned right toward his bachelor flat.

No messages on the Ansafone; no letters or notes pushed through the letter-box. A free afternoon!—for which, in his believing days, he would have given thanks to the Almighty. His dark-blue Oxford University diary was beside the phone, and he looked through the following week's engagements. Not much there either, really: just that diabetes review at the Radcliffe Infirmary at 9 A.M. on Monday morning. Only an hour or so that; but the imminent appointment disturbed him slightly. He had promised his consultant, and promised himself, that he would present a faithful record of his blood-sugar measurements over the previous fortnight. But he had failed to do so, and there was little he could now do to remedy the situation except to take half a dozen such measurements in the remaining interval of thirty-six hours and to extrapolate backward therefrom, in order to present a neatly tabulated series of satisfactory readings. He'd done it before and he would do it again.

Kein Problem.

He half-filled a tumbler with Glenfiddich, then topped it up with commensurate tap water. Such dilution (a recent innovation) would, as Morse knew, mark him out in the eyes of many a Scot as a sacrilegious Sassenach. But according to his GP, the liver preferred things that way; and Morse's liver (according to the same source) was in need of a bit of tender loving care, along with his heart, kidneys, stomach, pancreas, lungs.

Lungs . . .

Well, at least he'd finally managed to pack up smoking, a filthy habit, as he now recognized; but one which had given him almost as much pleasure as any other vice in life. And he knew that were he privy to the date and time of an early Judgment Day (the following Monday, say) he would set off immediately to the nearest newsagent's to buy in a store of cigarettes. And he almost did so now, as if he could already hear the trumpets sounding on the other side.

In the living room, he selected Bruno Walter's early recording of *Die Walküre*, with Lauritz Melchior and Lotte Lehmann singing the roles of Siegmund and Sieglinde. Wonderful! So Morse turned the volume control to maximum as he listened to the anagnorisis at the end of Act I, and heard neither of the telephone calls made to his ex-directory number that afternoon, conscious only that he was falling deliciously asleep as the benighted brother and sister rushed off into the forest to beget Siegfried . . .

It was coming up to 2:45 P.M. when Morse jerked abruptly awake, disappointed that his semi-erotic dream was prematurely terminated: a dream of a woman seated intimately close to him—a dream of Debbie Richardson, with legs provocatively crossed, the texture of the cheap black stockings tautly stretched along her upper thighs.

Wonderful!

But even as she'd leaned toward him, he'd voiced his deep anxiety: "Aren't you frightened someone will come in?"

"No one'll come in. Harry won't be comin' back. Ever. I'll get you another drink. Just—stay—where—you—are."

So Morse had stayed where he was, awaiting her return with impatience, and with an empty glass beside him. And when he awoke, he was still sitting there alone, awaiting her return with impatience, and with an empty glass beside him.

Wagner had long since run his course, and finally Morse got to his feet and turned off the CD player. He felt tired, hot, thirsty—and a sharp pain in his chest betokened another bout of indigestion. In the bathroom, he cleaned his teeth and dropped three Alka-Seltzer tablets into a glass of water; then he filled up the washbasin and thrice dipped his head into the cold water. The tablets had fizzed and dissolved and he downed the dosage at a single draught. Thence to his bedroom, where he took his blood-sugar level: 24.8—almost off the scale. His own fault, since he'd forgotten to inject himself at lunchtime—making up for it now, though, with an extra four units of Actrapid insulin. Just to be on the safe side. Back in the bathroom, he drank two further glasses of cold water, acknowledging how surprisingly pleasing was its taste, since water had seldom figured prominently in his drinking habits. Finally he decided that a couple of Paracetamol would be appropriate. So he shook out the tablets on to his palm; shook out three in fact—and decided to take the three. Just to be on the safe side.

Suddenly he was feeling much better, his faith in this curious combination of assorted medicaments seemingly justified once more. Suddenly, too, he decided to follow his consultant's somewhat despairing exhortation to take a bit of exercise occasionally. Why not? It was a warm and gentle summer's day.

In the small entrance hall, he noticed the figure "2"

on the window of his Ansafone. Pressing "Play" he listened to the first message:

> *Morse? Janet! Ten-past one Saturday afternoon.*
> *Good news! I hope to be back in Oxford on the 14th.*
> *So you'll be able to take me somewhere? To bed per-*
> *haps? Give me a ring—soon. Bye!*

Any semiremembrance of Debbie Richardson was lingering no longer, and Morse smiled happily to himself.
He would ring immediately. But the second message had
followed without a pause, and he was destined not to
ring Sister McQueen that afternoon.

Instead he dialed HQ and finally got through to the
young PC who had driven him out to Bullingdon the
previous morning in an unmarked police car.

"Get the same car, Kershaw—nice, comfy seats—and
pick me up from home *quam celerrime*."

"Pardon?"

"Smartish!"

"Sir, I was just going off duty when you rang and
I've—"

"Make it five minutes!"

Deeply puzzled, Morse walked back into the sitting
room where he sat in the black-leather armchair; and
where his right hand reached for whiskey once more as
mentally he rehearsed that second, quite extraordinary
message on the Ansafone:

> *Sir? Lewis here—half-past one, nearly—I'm out at*
> *Sutton Courtenay. Please come along as soon as you*
> *can—for my sake if nobody else's. I think you should*
> *get here before we move the body. You see, sir, it isn't*
> *the body of Harry Repp.*

Chapter Twenty-eight

> *Alas, poor Yorick!—I knew him, Horatio.*
> (Shakespeare, *Hamlet*)

It was just after 4 P.M. that same Saturday afternoon when Morse and Lewis finally sat down together in the requisitioned office of the site manager.

"Straightaway I knew it wasn't him, sir, when I saw his arms. Harry Repp had this tattoo: all twisted chains and anchors, you know—a sort of . . ." Lewis undulated his hands vertically, as if tracing a woman's willowy figure.

"Convoluted involvement," suggested Morse gently.

"Well, this fellow's not got any, has he? Anyway he's much smaller, only—what?—five-four, five-five. Doesn't weigh much either—eight, nine stone? No more."

Morse nodded. "And he's got different colored hair, and he's got a port-wine stain on his neck, and he's not wearing Repp's clothes, and his shoes are three sizes smaller—"

"All right. I wasn't expecting the Queen's Medal!"

At which Eddie Andrews, the 2i/c senior SOCO, knocked on the door and entered the office, at once uncertain whether to address himself to Morse or to Lewis. He decided on the former:

"Safe, I reckon, to move him now? Dr. Hobson says there's not much else she can do here."

Morse shrugged. "You'd better ask Sergeant Lewis. He's in charge."

And Lewis rose to the occasion. "Yes, move him. Thank you."

As he was about to leave, Andrews noticed the TV set.

"Mind if I just see how Northants are getting on in the cricket?"

"Important to you, is it?" queried Morse mildly.

Andrews was digitally discovering Sport (Cricket) on Ceefax when the office door burst open to admit a florid-faced Chief Superintendent Strange, an officer resolutely determined to retain the appellation "Chief," whatever most of his collateral colleagues in the Force were doing.

"You've ruined my afternoon's golf, Lewis! You know that?"

Surprisingly, the words were spoken with little sign of animus. But before Lewis could respond in any way, Strange was addressing Morse in considerably sharper tones:

"And how exactly do *you* come to be here?"

"Same as you really, sir. Ruined my day, too. I was just indulging in a little Egyptian PT—"

"After indulging in a lot of Scottish whiskey by the smell of it!"

"—when Lewis here rang and asked me to come along. Well, he's been a faithful soul most of the time, so . . ."

"So you just came along as a sort of personal favor?"

"That's about it." (Andrews sidled silently from the room.)

"Well let me tell you one thing, matey. You won't be staying *on* as a personal favor—is that clear? You'll be staying on because you're in charge of *this* case—because that's an *order*. You may have had some excuse as far as the Harrison case was concerned: I could just about understand that." (Strange's voice had momentarily dropped to a semisympathetic register.) "But you've no bloody excuse now. And if you decide to get on your high horse again and start arguing the toss with me, you'll be up before the Chief Constable first thing Monday morning!"

"The Chief's on furlough," interposed a brave Lewis.

"Shut up, Lewis! And he'll have your guts for garters, Morse. So that's settled. All you've got to do is sober up and put your thinking cap on."

"I usually think better when—" But Morse's disquisition on his personal style of ratiocination was cut short by a further knock, with Dr. Hobson's pretty head appearing round the door.

"Oh, sorry! It's just—"

"Come in!" growled Strange, his jowls still wobbling.

"Just thought I'd check. We've got him outside and Andrews says it's OK if—"

"Who *is* he?" asked Strange.

"Don't know. I had a tentative feel round his pockets. No wallet, though, no cards—"

"He's pretty easily recognizable though?"

"Oh, yes. His face is fine. It's his stomach that's all a gory mess where the knife or whatever it was went in."

"At least we've got a good mug shot of him then."

"Probably identify him straightaway. I got this from his trouser pocket."

Strange looked down at a white "Cardholder's Copy" receipt from Oddbins of Banbury Road, itemizing the purchase of a crate of Guinness, the number of the Visa credit card printed below in a faded indigo.

"There we are, Lewis! Shouldn't be too difficult, should it?" He handed over the receipt with an unconvincing smile. "Unless you manage to lose *that*, of course."

It was a hurtful dig. But the patient Lewis briefly examined the evidence himself and sought to put a finger on the fairly obvious:

"Not much chance this afternoon, sir. Saturday? The banks'll all be shut."

"What? For Christ's sake, man! We've put someone on the moon, remember? And you say we can't trace a credit-card number because it's a bloody *Saturday*! Is that what you're telling me?"

Morse had remained silent during these exchanges; and remained so now, his brain already galloping several furlongs ahead of the field. And Lewis, after such a withering rebuke, also remained silent, holding the receipt tightly, like a punter clutching a winning betting slip. Only Strange, it appeared, was willing to break the awkward silence as he turned again to Dr. Hobson.

"They're just carting him off, you say?"

"Yes."

"Well, let us know—let Chief Inspector Morse know—what you come up with. Sooner the quicker. Understood?"

"Of course."

The assembled personages rose to their feet; and matters at Sutton Courtenay were seemingly now at an end.

But not so; not quite.

It was Morse, at last, who made his brief though extraordinarily significant contribution to the afternoon's developments.

"Sir, I think you ought to have a look at him."

"I don't like dead bodies any more than you do, Morse."

"I know that, but . . ."

"But *what*?"

". . . but you ought to have a look at him." Morse spoke his words slowly and quietly. "You see, I think it's quite possible that you'll recognize him."

Frequently afterward, in the post-Morse years, would Sergeant Lewis recall that afternoon at the fill-in site in Oxfordshire: when Chief Superintendent Strange had looked at the bloodless face of a murdered man; and when his erstwhile ruddy cheeks had paled to chalky white.

"Bloody 'ell! I knew him, Morse. I interviewed him twice in the Harrison murder inquiry."

When the top brass had finally dispersed, Eddie Andrews let himself back into the now deserted office, turned on the TV, found Sport (Cricket) on Ceefax and noted with quiet satisfaction that Northamptonshire were really doing rather well that day.

Chapter Twenty-nine

CALIPH:	And now how shall we employ the time of waiting for our deliverance?
JAFAR:	I shall meditate upon the mutability of human affairs.
MASRUR:	And I shall sharpen my sword upon my thigh.
HASSAN:	And I shall study the pattern of this carpet.
CALIPH:	Hassan, I will join thee: Thou art a man of taste.

(James Elroy Flecker, *Hassan*)

Most patiently—no, most impatiently—had PC Kershaw been waiting for his passenger to emerge from the closeted consultations. Like some starry-eyed teenager he had been looking forward so much to his first date with Susan Ho, a delightful, delicately featured Chinese girl, a researcher at Oxford's Criminological Department; and although he had been able to contact her after Morse's diktat, neither he nor she had been particularly pleased.

He opened the passenger door as Morse approached.

"It's all right, Kershaw. Sergeant Lewis'll be taking me back to Oxford."

"You mean—?"

"I mean you can bugger off, yes."

"Couldn't you have told me earlier, sir? I've been ..."

But his voice trailed off as he found Morse's blue eyes looking straight at him; uncomprehending, cold.

Lewis was grinning wryly as he pushed the police car into first gear. "You never treated even me as bad as that."

"Cocky young sod! University graduate, God help us!"

"What's he doing with us?"

"Dunno. Learning how to make a cup o' tea, I shouldn't wonder."

"Exactly where I started."

"I hope he's better than you were."

"Isn't it about time you told—"

"I just don't believe this!" said Morse as he picked up the single cassette that lay in the tray beside the gear lever, inserted it into the player, and subsequently sank back into his seat with the look of a man sublimely satisfied with life.

"Just find out who usually drives this car, Lewis. He's a man after my own heart. I never realized we had such sensitivity in the Force. There's not much of it out there, you know."

For a moment it seemed that Lewis was going to speak. But clearly he thought better of it; and as he drove way above the speed limit down the A34 to Oxford, he listened, with considerable enjoyment himself, to the Prelude to Wagner's *Parsifal*, convinced that Morse was soundly albeit unsnoringly asleep.

"Turn off here, Lewis."

"Next exit's best, sir—avoid the city traffic that way."

"Turn off *here*!"

So Lewis turned off there, driving sedately now, up the Abingdon Road, past Christ Church, straight over through Cornmarket and Magdalen Street, where (as bidden) he turned left at the lights by the Martyrs' Memorial and duly stopped (as bidden) on the double-yellows beneath the canopy of the Randolph, above which the Union Jack and the flag of the EC drooped languorously that late afternoon.

Lewis was still in brave mood. "Like the Super said, don't you think you ought—"

"*Think*? That's exactly why I'm here—to think! I can't think unless I'm given the chance to think. You don't imagine I drink just for the *pleasure* of it, do you?"

*   *   *

Morse sat back with his pint of bitter and stared serenely at the Ashmolean Museum just opposite in Beaumont Street. "If there's a bar anywhere in Britain with a better view than this . . ."

Lewis hesitated awhile over his orange juice. "You ready to tell me how you knew it was Paddy Flynn?"

"I didn't really *know*. Just that I always wondered about him a bit. Key witness, agreed? Picked up Frank Harrison from the railway station, then parked outside the house just when the burglar alarm was ringing."

Lewis nodded. "Only person to give Harrison a convincing alibi."

It was Morse's turn to nod. "That's why Strange interviewed him."

"Interviewed him twice."

"Suspicious mind, that man's got!"

"But you're still not telling me how you guessed it was *him*."

"Full of guesses, what we do, isn't it? After the first couple of days, I only read about the case at second hand—"

"Like me."

"—but I remember thinking I'd have put an each-way bet on some of the outsiders in the race: the builder—he gave himself and several others an alibi; the landlord at the Maiden's Arms—he's got the testosterone level of a randy billy goat; and then there was the taxi driver . . ."

"Why *him*, though?"

"Put yourself in his position. You pick up your fare outside the station and drive him out to Lower Swinstead; and there you're asked if you want to earn a bit—a lot—of extra money. You don't really have to do much at all. Fellow says he's going into the house—*his* house, anyway—and the burglar alarm is going to ring. All you've got to do is to say, if you're questioned about things, that you heard the alarm ringing while you were parked outside. Not too difficult? The alarm *was* ringing by then. And you're offered—what? I dunno—twenty or thirty quid, two or three hundred quid? But the key point is that Flynn never fully realized how vital his testimony was going to be."

"Are you making it all up?"

"Yes! So allow me to continue making it all up. Flynn's got little idea of why he's getting such a bonus for doing virtually bugger-all. But then he starts to read a few press reports; and unlike our boys he puts two and two together, and he smiles to himself because he knows the answer. And pretty soon he realizes he's sold himself stupidly cheap, and he decides he'll balance the books a bit better."

"Are you saying what I think you're saying? He's been trying to blackmail Frank Harrison?"

Morse drained his pint. "Not sure. But I'd like to bet that someone that night was more than ready to pay his way out of trouble."

"Or her way."

"Could be, yes." Morse contemplated an empty glass. "Is it your round or mine, by the way?"

"Yours."

Morse consulted his wristwatch. "Good gracious me! Time you drove me home. I need a shot of insulin, Lewis. You should've reminded me."

"You still haven't told me why you thought it was Flynn," complained Lewis as he drove north through the Summertown shopping area.

"Small man—that's why."

"So's the landlord of the Maiden's Arms."

"Ah, but Flynn was very fond of Guinness."

"What the hell's *that* got to do with anything?"

"I forget. I'm, er, I'm getting muddled."

Lewis pulled up outside Morse's flat.

"Anything . . . anything I can do for you, sir?"

"Certainly not. It's just that I'm beginning to feel exquisitely sleepy, that's all. The day's still comparatively young, I grant you. But don't ring me—not tonight—not unless anything dramatic happens."

"You mean" (Lewis's heart rose within him) "you mean you *are* going to take on the case?"

"Different ball game, isn't it? As they say in Chicago or somewhere."

"Shall I let the Super know?"

"I've already told him—when we were at the rubbish tip."

Lewis shook his head in benign bewilderment as Morse made to get out of the car.

"And I'll take possession of this—just temporarily, of course. And if you can find out whose it is . . ."

He pocketed the *Parsifal* cassette and was walking toward his front door when Lewis wound down the car window.

"You can keep it as long as you like, sir. But let me have it back when you've finished with it. They said at Blackwell's it's the top recording—by a fellow called Napperbush."

"You mean . . . ?"

Lewis nodded happily.

"Thou art a man of taste."

"I thought you'd be pleased, sir."

"By the way, Lewis, we pronounce him 'K-napper-t-s-busch'," amended the Chief Inspector, pedantically separating the consonantal clusters.

Chapter Thirty

Often would the deaf man know the answers had he but the faculty of hearing the questions. Likewise would the unimaginative man guess wisely at the answers had he but the wit of posing to himself the appropriate questions.

(Viscount Mumbles, from *Essays on the Imagination*)

As Lewis drove up to HQ, one particular thought was troubling him—as it often had: the marked inferiority of his own mental processes compared with those of the man he had just left; the man who was doubtless now sleeping off the effects of what had been (even for Morse) a hyper-alcoholic afternoon. It wasn't that his own processes were necessarily all that much slower; just that they seemed always to leave the starting blocks way after Morse had sprinted on ahead. Obviously (Lewis knew it!) innate intelligence was a big factor in everything: the speed of perception and understanding, the analysis of data, the linkage of things. But there was something else: the knack of *prospective* thinking, of looking ahead and asking oneself the right questions, as well as the wrong questions, about what was likely to happen in the future; and then of coming up with some answers, be they right or wrong.

So frequently in previous cases had Morse led him along, and by prompting the right questions evinced the right sort of answers. "Socratic dialectic," Morse had called it, recounting how Socrates had managed to elicit from a totally untutored slave boy the basic principles of plane geometry—just by asking the right questions.

So.

So, in his office that early evening, Lewis visualized himself seated opposite Morse—opposite Socrates, rather.

You've got to find the car, haven't you? The car that dumped the body? Where will you find it?

I don't know.

Where would you have driven that car?

I don't know. Anywhere, I suppose.

Isn't there blood everywhere? Blood all over your clothes?

Yes.

Haven't you got to change your clothes then?

Yes.

So you couldn't just leave the car anywhere, could you? You couldn't walk too far all covered in blood?

No.

So where would you go?

I'd go home, like as not.

Before, or after, you'd ditched the car?

Before, probably, although . . .
Go on!
Might be a bit risky. Neighbors would probably notice the strange car. Might even notice the blood-stained clothes.
What's the alternative for you?
Well, get someone to meet me somewhere and bring me a full change of clothes.
Where would you meet?
Anywhere. How do I know. Except . . .
Go on!
If we met in a lay-by, say, I'd have to leave the car there, wouldn't I? I couldn't get back in and get the new clothes almost as bloodstained as the old. And the car would pretty certainly get reported **almost** immediately. So . . .
So?
So I'd have somebody to meet me. Friend? Wife, perhaps?
Where do you meet?
I don't know.
You do know. You know the Chesterton story—I've often mentioned it.
Remind me.
Where do you hide a leaf?
Ah, yes. In the forest.
Where do you hide a pebble?
On the shore.
Where do you hide a corpse?
On the battlefield.
And where do you hide a car?
In a car park.
Which car park?
I don't know.
The bigger the better?
Yes.
In Oxford?
Probably.
How many car parks are there in Oxford?
Dozens.

If you'd committed a murder near Oxford, what would you want to do above all?

Get the hell out of the place.

How?

Drive away.

You haven't got a car now, have you?

Bus?

Where's the bus station?

Gloucester Green.

Isn't there a car park opposite?

Yes.

And you could catch a train?

Yes.

Isn't there a station car park opposite?

Yes . . .

As he drove down toward Oxford, Lewis felt pleased with himself, and just after he'd negotiated the Cutteslowe roundabout he was tempted to call in on Morse. But he put the temptation behind him. He felt fairly certain that the great man would be asleep.

And on this occasion he was right.

Instead, he decided to continue the Socratic dialogue, though this time installing *himself* as Chief Inquisitor and making the far bolder hypothesis that if only the blurred outlines of the anonymous murderer could be adjusted more sharply, it was Harry Repp who would come into focus.

Don't you think it would be easier, sir, for Debbie Richardson to take a change of clothes to *him*? Wouldn't it be dangerous for him to go out to Lower Swinstead?

I don't know, Lewis.

I asked you *two* questions.

I don't know. I don't know.

What do *you* think Harry Repp did?

I just don't know.

What about the car? Where's that? Come on! Back your hunch!

The car? Oh, I know where the car is, Lewis. It's parked at the back of Oxford Railway Station.

Chapter Thirty-one

His voice was angry: "What time do you call *this*?"

She stood penitently on the doorstep: "Sorry!"

"Where've you parked?" (It was the decade's commonest question in Oxford.)

"Exactly. I just couldn't find a parking space anywhere."

(Terry Benczik, *Still Life with Absinthe*)

Lucky Lewis!

He was walking up the steps to the station when the automatic doors opened in front of him, and Sergeant Dick Evans of the British Transport Police came toward him. Old friends, they greeted each other with appropriate cordiality.

"Know anything about a stolen car—R456 LJB?"

"Parked here?"

"Dunno," Lewis admitted.

"Well, not as far as I know. I've been in Reading all day, though. Just got back. Bob Mitchell'd know, perhaps. He's on duty here."

"I'd better go and wake him up then."

"He's not in the office. I looked in a couple of minutes ago—door's locked. Probably called out on some trouble somewhere. Saturday! Football yobos and all that."

"But it's not the football season," protested Lewis.

"What's that got to do with it?"

"You straight off home?"

"Well, yes. It's getting late. If I can do anything to help an old mucker though . . . What's the trouble?"

Lewis told him, and the two men walked down the steps and across to the station car park.

It had been more than a year since Lewis had visited the station complex, and he was immediately surprised to find that the previously fairly extensive car-parking space had been drastically reduced: the northern section had been taken over by "Another Prestigious Development"—a series of Victorian-style town houses, built in attractive terra-cotta bricks, with white stuccoed lower stories; "spacious and luxurious" as the site board guaranteed.

"Year or two back," volunteered Evans, "I'd've parked up there if I'd wanted to keep out of sight for a while. Used to be a bit dark and creepy late at night, if you got back late from Paddington on the milk float."

Lewis nodded, but without comment. Late-night returns from concerts and operas in the capital had never figured large in the lifestyle of the Lewises. But now, in sunny daylight, the area seemed wholly benign, and still almost packed with cars marshaled there in semilegitimate rows.

"What if you come," asked Lewis, "and you just can't find a space?"

"Not easy, is it? You can always try Gloucester Green" (Evans pointed vaguely across toward Hythe Bridge Street) "or one of the side roads."

The two sergeants walked together to the northern area of the park, away from the main road where, with any choice in the matter, any murderous villain (as well as Sergeant Evans) would surely have headed with an incriminating car. But things had changed. Parading the site, tall stanchions now stood there, topped with video cameras and floodlights. No guarantee of complete security perhaps, but a sufficient deterrent for casual car thieves.

"You could still squeeze one or two more cars in?" suggested Lewis (himself a wizard at vehicular maneuvering), pointing to a few square meters amid heaps of sand and piles of jagged half-bricks and broken tiles.

"Not if you're worried about your suspension."

"Which he wasn't, Dick."

"No sign of it though, is there?"

They walked systematically through the lines of cars down to the southern end of the car park, bounded by the Botley Road.

Again, nothing.

And the questions that had already worried Morse were worrying his sergeant now. *Was* there any sign of criminal activity here? Were they on some profitless pursuit of a questionable quarry?

Morse!

Top-of-the-head Morse!

Things just didn't happen like that.

At bottom, any police investigation was a matter of pretty firm facts; of accumulating such facts; and of aggregating them into a hard core of evidence, on which suspicion could be progressively corroborated, until an arrest could be made, a charge brought, a prosecution formulated, and finally a case heard in a court of law. That's how things happened.

A dispirited Lewis stood with Evans for only a few seconds longer before walking up to the exit booth, where a red-and-white-striped barrier was being intermittently raised as a few patrons returning early to Oxford inserted their parking tokens, and where a uniformed Transport Policeman, clearly not at the peak of physical condition, came running toward them:

"What the 'ell are you doing here, Dick?"

"Just back from Reading, Bob. And what the 'ell's up with you? You know Sergeant Lewis here from HQ?"

Mitchell had regained some of his breath. "HQ? Huh! That's exactly what's up. Chap who said he was from HQ. Rang about a car—said it was parked here at the station . . ."

Evans finished the sentence for him. "But it wasn't."

"No. But I thought I'd look around a bit. This chap'd sounded pretty positive, like. So I went over to Gloucester Green—and Bingo! Just behind the Irish pub there."

"You've got this chap's number?" asked Lewis.

"In the office, yes. He said he couldn't get here himself. Said he was tired. Huh!"

"He must have given his name?"

" 'Moss,' I think it was. Look, I'll just . . ."

A temporarily rejuvenated Mitchell was bounding up the station steps three at a time as Evans turned to Lewis:

"Reckon he misheard a bit."

"Just a bit," said Lewis, with quiet resignation.

Chapter Thirty-two

Should any young or old officer experience incipient or actual signs of vomiting at the sight of some particularly harrowing scene of crime the said person should not necessarily attribute such nausea to some psychological vulnerability, but rather to the virtually universal reflex-reactions of the upper intestine.

(*The SOCO Handbook*, Revised 1999)

Barry Edwards was another of the SOCO personnel called out that busy Saturday. In fact, simply because he lived only a short distance away along the Botley Road, he was the first of the team to arrive at the scene of the crime. A well-set, dark-haired man in his late twenties, he had a pair of diffident brown eyes that seemed to some of his colleagues strangely naive, as if he would ever be surprised by the scenes that would inevitably confront him in his new career.

His SOCO training had been completed only a few months previously, and now he was a full-fledged (civilian) officer, employed by the Thames Valley Police. Furthermore, thus far, he was enjoying his job. After leaving school, with a comparatively successful performance in the comparatively undemanding field of GCSE, he had worked as a supermarket shelf-filler, hospital porter, barman, and ironmonger's shop assistant, before finally completing a police recruitment questionnaire and duly learning of the opportunities in his present profession.

He had taken his chance; and he was enjoying his choice. He felt quite important sometimes, especially when he dealt off his own bat with some fairly minor affair, when (as he knew) he *was* important. And he'd looked forward to the time when he would be called out to a big job, to some major incident. Like murder. Like now—as he sensed immediately when he drove his van into the Gloucester Green Car Park. The full complement of the team would have been called in, and almost certainly he would witness, for the first time, the operation of those basic principles—preservation of the scene, continuity and noncontamination of evidence—which had guided his training in photography, fingerprinting, forensic labeling, and the meticulous procedure vital to all in situ investigations.

Edwards had introduced himself immediately to the plainclothed Sergeant Lewis, obviously the man in charge: yet perhaps only temporarily in charge, since (as Edwards guessed) it would only be a matter of time before some more senior-ranking officer would put in an appearance—just as he himself was awaiting Bill Flowers, the senior SOCO, a man who had seen everything in life. As he, Barry Edwards, hadn't. Not yet. For the moment, however, the appropriate procedure had been applied, with blue-and-white police ribbon cordoning off an area containing three cars, noses all to the wall: R 456 LJB; to its left, a grey H-Reg. Citroën; to its right a dark-blue P-Reg. Rover—the owner of the latter (just arrived) making a statement to one of two uniformed PCs summoned from the St. Aldate's Station. No effort had as yet been made to disperse the growing band of curious onlookers who stood in silent, hopeful expectation of some gruesome discovery. Things were happening, though. Flowers arrived just before the other two SOCOs; and soon everything would be ready, once they got the word from someone. Doubtless the same someone awaited by Sergeant Lewis, the latter a man with "under authority" written all over his honest and slightly worried features.

But there was a frustrating twenty-minute wait before

the "authority" put in his appearance, stepping from the back of a marked police car with a marked unsuppleness of limb, the slate-grey suit decidedly rumpled, the telltale crease around the waistband betokening an increase in girth over recent months. A white-haired man, of medium height, his face of a pale-olive color, as if perhaps he had spent a holiday of less than uninterrupted sunshine in Torremolinos, or was suffering from incipient jaundice. But his voice was that of someone who demanded immediate attention—like another voice that Edwards once had known, that of his old Latin master.

Vox auctoritatis.

Lewis had approached the newcomer, and the two were in brief conversation before coming over to the others. Chief Inspector Morse (for such was he) appeared to recognize the other SOCOs, and nodded briefly as he was introduced to the youngest member of the team.

"Hello, Edwards!" He'd said nothing more, and Edwards gathered that the Chief Inspector was not a convert to the currently widespread practice of everyone addressing everyone—superiors, equals, and subordinates alike—by their Christian names. Yet he seemed a pleasant enough fellow, now surveying the scene with a keen if somewhat melancholy eye, while the SOCO team began to put on their green boilersuits and overboots.

"Anyone touched anything?"

"No more than we needed to, sir." (It was Lewis who replied.)

Morse looked again at the car for some lingering while—the car he'd followed when Harry Repp had turned his back on Bullingdon. Then he lifted his eyes and looked, again for some lingering while, at the pub sign of the Rosie O'Grady.

Bill Flowers was standing beside him.

"All yours!" pronounced Morse.

"Car's locked."

"How do you know?"

"Door catches all in the locked position."

Morse pressed a hand down on the nearside front handle.

"Don't—!" But Flowers checked his admonition in midvoice.

"You're right. Any of your lads here ever a juvenile car thief?"

"I know somebody who was."

"Where's he live?"

"Silverstone."

Morse turned to Lewis. "Give Johnson a ring."

"Know his number?"

"Saturday afternoon? He'll be in the Summertown bookie's."

"It's long gone afternoon, sir."

"Ah!"

"There'll be a Local Directory in the pub."

"You won't find him listed. They've cut his phone off."

"So how—?"

"He'll be in the Dew Drop if he's won a few quid."

"Perhaps he's not won a few quid."

"He'll still be in the Dew Drop."

"Do you know the number?"

"Get me a mobile!" snapped Morse.

Edwards watched as Morse turned his back on his colleagues, tapped out a number, and spoke *sotto voce* into the mouthpiece for a while, before blasting out *fortissimo*:

"Well, just tell him to get here on the bloody *bus* and get here bloody *quick*!"

Yet this order was not obeyed with either accuracy or immediacy, since there was a further twenty-minute wait before a rusting A-Reg. Ford pulled up on the main road outside the Rosie O'Grady, whence emerged from the passenger seat a sparely built, nondescript man, in his late forties, a self-rolled cigarette dangling from a thin mouth that even from a few yards exuded the reek of strong, excessive alcohol.

"Mr. Morse?"

The latter pointed to the car.

"Fee, is there?"

"Just open it, Malcolm!" (Edwards was surprised with the Christian-name address.)

The key wizard made no further remonstration as he winched a bunch of skeleton keys and bits of wire from his right-hand trouser pocket. Then, turning his back on his expectant audience, he surveyed the problem synoptically. Like Capablanca contemplating his next move in the World Chess Championship.

"It's central-locking," volunteered Flowers.

But Johnson said nothing, responding only for a semisecond with a look of contemptuous ingratitude.

As far as Edwards could make out, Morse had enjoyed that moment, since more than a semismile formed around his mouth when fifteen seconds later there was a quiet "clunk" as the catches on the four doors sprang upward in simultaneous freedom.

R456 LJB was open for inspection.

After pulling on a pair of green latex gloves, Flowers now opened the two offside doors; and Morse glanced over the front seats, before contemplating for a good deal longer the darkly glutinous covering of blood that stained the seats and flooring in the back. With a softly spoken "OK," he was walking away toward the Rosie O'Grady when Johnson tapped him on the shoulder.

"You mentioned expenses, Mr. Morse?"

"I did. You're right."

"Well, there's that taxi I came in—eight quid—two-quid tip—ten quid—here and back. Twenny, I make that."

"Since when's Snotty Joe been running a taxi business?"

"Well, you know, more a sort of . . . private hire, like."

Morse felt in his pockets and pulled out a handful of coins. "85p, isn't it, the bus fare to St. Giles? And, you're right, you've got to get back."

He handed Johnson two £1 coins. "Keep the change. You can buy a copy of *The Times* to read on the ride back."

"Wrong, aincha, Mr. Morse! *Times* is 50p Sat'days."

Unsmiling, Morse handed over a further 20p, and the pair parted without any further word. And Edwards, who had witnessed the brief scene, found himself wondering what exactly were the favors each had bestowed upon the other in the prosecution and pursuance of crime in North Oxford over recent years.

Morse was a few steps ahead of Lewis as he made his way to the pub entrance. "We'd better leave 'em for half an hour or so. They won't want us breathing down their necks . . . By the way, you'd better lend me a fiver, Lewis. I've just parted with the only—"

Morse stopped. Turned round. Stepped back to the scene of the crime. Ordered Flowers to open the boot.

Not himself knowing the identity of the body he now saw curled up in fetal configuration there, young Edwards was to remember that particular moment with an oddly inappropriate sense of gratitude, for he saw the color of Morse's cheeks fade by swiftly developing degrees from dingy yellow to sickly white, and watched as of a sudden the great man turned away and vomited violently over the recently renovated tarmac. It was like a fledgling actor appearing on stage with Sir John Gielgud and seeing *that* great man fluffing the friendliest of lines in rehearsal, and thereby giving some unexpected encouragement to the rest of the cast, all of them now less terrified of fluffing their own.

Chapter Thirty-three

> *For the good are always the merry,*
> *Save by an evil chance,*
> *And the merry love the fiddle,*
> *And the merry love to dance:*
>
> *And when the folk there spy me,*
> *They will all come up to me,*
> *With "Here is the fiddler of Dooney!"*
> *And dance like a wave of the sea.*
> (W. B. Yeats, *The Fiddler of Dooney*)

Morse, after disappearing into the Gents for several long minutes, now sat looking slightly more his wonted self as he sank his nose into the deep head on the Guinness.

"Just the stuff if you've got a foul taste in the throat!"

Giving his chief a little while to recover some measure of dignity, Lewis gazed around him. Everything was wooden there: the bar, the wall-settles, the floor, the table at which they sat—all good solid if somewhat battered wood, with any once-applied stain long since worn off. The walls and ceilings had originally been painted in yellow and orange, but now were coated over with the nicotine of countless cigarettes. The friezes of the walls were adorned with the dicta of several great Irishmen, their words attractively set in black-lettered Gaelic script. One in particular had already caught Lewis's eye:

> *Where is the use of calling it a lend*
> *when I know I will never see it again?*

Good question! But a question not so pressing as the one he now put to Morse:

"Was it a surprise to you?"

"Was *what* a surprise?"

"Finding Harry Repp's body in the boot?"

Morse nodded as he wiped away a white moustache.

"This morning I thought I had a fair idea about what we were dealing with. But now that I'm perfectly sure that I've none . . ." He pointed up at the wall to their right. "Bit like Oscar Wilde, really."

Lewis looked up at the words written there:

I was working on the proof of my poems all this morning and took out a comma. In the afternoon I put it back again.

For Lewis it was a somber moment and he sipped his orange juice with little joy; even less joy as he saw the outline of Chief Superintendent Strange looming large in the doorway, then waddling awkwardly to their table, where he sat down, wiping his moistened brow with a vast handkerchief.

"Pretty kettle o' fish you've got us into now, Morse!"

Then, turning to Lewis: "You in the chair?"

"Well—"

"Good! Good man! I'll have the same as the Chief Inspector here."

"Pint, sir?"

"The *same* as the Chief Inspector—that's what I said, Sergeant."

Lewis repaired to the bar once more and listened to the comparatively quiet background music that was as Irish as the pub was Irish, all flutes and fiddles, and wondered how long Morse would stick the noise before calling for a few less decibels.

After taking a deep draught, Strange turned to Morse. "You do realize, don't you, that you and Lewis have dragged me away from the golf course twice!"

"I'd've thought you'd be glad, especially if you were losing."

Strange grinned wryly. "I don't often win these days, you're right."

"None of us gets much better as we get older."

"Only two things we can be sure of, Morse—death and taxes. Some U.S. President said that."

"Benjamin Franklin," supplied Lewis, to whom each of the two senior officers turned with some surprise, though without inquiry into the provenance of such splendid knowledge.

"What do you make of all this?" continued Strange quietly.

Morse shook his head. "You may have been having a lousy round of golf. I was having a lovely sleep myself."

"That's no answer."

"Dr. Hobson'll be here soon."

"Already here."

"Nothing we can do till we get some reports, results of the postmortems—"

"Somebody once told me the plural should be post-mortes."

"Bloody pedant!"

"It was *you* actually, Morse."

"Ah!"

"You've got a good team of SOCOs."

Morse nodded. "So we'll wait to hear about all the bits and bobs they'll be bagging up and labeling and sending off to forensics. And all the fingerprints they'll be taking from windows and side mirrors and body work and seat belt buckles and cassettes and . . ." Morse had run out of potential surfaces.

"That's it!" Strange sounded somewhat heartened. "All you've got to do is eliminate ninety-five percent of the dabs, and then you've got your man."

"Unless he was wearing gloves," suggested Lewis.

"It's all tied up with that bloody Lower Swinstead business!" blurted out Strange.

"You're probably right," said Morse.

"And don't forget the simplest answer is usually the correct answer! Spur o' the moment stuff, most homicides. You know that."

"Perhaps so," admitted Morse, beckoning the landlord over. "Open all day?"

"All night too should you wish it, sorr."

And yes, of course, the police could make use of one of the bars for the evening; of course the police could make use of whatever the Rosie O'Grady had to offer: telephone, washing and toilet facilities, bar facilities . . .

"And perhaps . . . ?" The landlord pointed to the two empty glasses. "On the house—the pleasure's all mine."

"Well, perhaps, er . . ." said Strange.

"You're twisting my arm," said Morse.

"Make it *three* pints of Guinness," said Lewis.

Morse glanced across at his sergeant with a look of astonishment; the landlord departed; and Strange got down to business.

"Logistics, Morse. Let's talk logistics. How many men do you want?"

"If you gave me a hundred, I wouldn't know what to do with one of them—not yet."

"Now come off it, matey! Couldn't you perhaps have a look at when and how and what and why your bloody corpses were doing? See their relatives, friends, enemies, wives, for God's sake?"

"Flynn hadn't got a wife," interposed Lewis.

"*Repp* had!"

"No, sir," corrected Lewis bravely. "He'd got a partner—"

"Well go and see *her*!" snapped Strange.

"No," said Morse. "I'll go to see her myself."

"Why's that?"

"I have my reasons."

The landlord had returned with the drinks. "As I said—on the house, gentlemen!"

Morse thanked him and made a request: "You know this, er, music you're playing here—this Irish music . . . ?"

"Perhaps you'd like it . . . ?"

"Yes. If you could turn it up just a bit?"

Lewis glanced across at the Chief Inspector with a look of astonishment; the landlord departed; and Strange leaned back with an expression of contentment. "You know, Morse, I'm glad you said that. The missus

... we had a couple of days in Cork and we did a bit of Irish dancing together ... me and the missus ... or I suppose you'd say the missus and me."

"The missus and I, sir."

But further grammatical preferences were curtailed by the arrival of Dr. Laura Hobson.

"Everything all right, Doctor?" shouted Strange, above the background music that had suddenly lunged to the foreground.

"No, everything's all wrong! I cannot cope with things as they are out there. I want the car moved out to the lab with the body kept in the boot. How on earth you think—?"

"Done!" Strange held up the great slab that was his right hand. "Lewis will arrange it immediately, once he's finished his drink. Si' down, Doctor. Just give me a minute or two." He sat back in his chair, beaming like a benign old uncle.

"Takes you back, Morse, doesn't it?"

"Remember the old poem, sir?

'When I play on my fiddle in Dooney,
Folk dance like a wave of the sea ...' "

"Yes! Yes, I do," said Strange gently.

And for a while Sergeant Lewis and Dr. Hobson remained silent, as if they knew they should be treading softly; as if they might be treading on other people's dreams.

Chapter Thirty-four

> *Sunt lacrimae rerum et mentem mortalia tangunt.*
> (Always in life are there tears being shed for things, and
> human suffering ever touches the heart.)
>
> (Virgil, *Aeneid*, I, I. 462)

As she opened the door, the recently reapplied blonde
dye showed little or no trace of the hair's brunette
inheritance.

"Oh, hullo." The greeting was less than enthusiastic.

"May I come in?" asked Morse.

Apart from the minimal towel held in front of her
body, she was naked: "Just wait there a sec—I'll
just . . ."

She reclosed the door and Morse stood, as she had
bidden, on the threshold. Stood there for a couple of
minutes. And when she reopened the door and reap-
peared, it puzzled him that in such a comparatively long
time she had done little other than to exchange the
white towel for an equally minimal white dressing gown.

They sat opposite each other in the kitchen.

"Drink?" she ventured.

"No. I've had a busy day on the drink."

"That good or bad?"

"Bit of both."

"Mind if I have one?"

"Can you wait? Just a minute?"

"It's about Harry, isn't it?"

"Yes."

"He's dead, isn't he?"

"He's been murdered," said Morse flatly.

Debbie Richardson leaned forward on her elbows,
the long fingers with their crimson nails vertically veil-
ing her features. Then after a while she got to her feet

and turned to the sink, where she molded her hands into a shallow receptacle under the cold tap.

As they had spoken at the kitchen table, Morse had observed (how otherwise?) that whatever else Debbie Richardson had done behind the closed front door she had certainly not been searching for a bra; and now, as she leaned forward and held her face in the water, he observed (how otherwise?) that she'd had no thought for any knickers either. A provocative prick-teaser, that was what she was. Morse knew it; had known it when they'd met that once before. But for the moment his mind was many furlongs from fornication . . .

He felt fairly sure that she'd been upstairs when he'd rung the bell, for the light had been on in the front bedroom with the night now drawing in. Yet she'd answered the door very quickly, almost immediately in fact. Whoever the caller was, had she wished to give the impression to someone that she'd been downstairs all the while? It seemed a bit odd. After all, he could well have been a Jehovah's Witness or an equally dreaded member of the Mormons or a charity worker bearing an envelope. Quite certainly though she hadn't rushed down the stairs from a bath, since about her was none of that freshly scented aura of a woman recently risen from her toilet. Rather perhaps (although Morse was no connoisseur in such matters) it was the musky odor of sex that lingered around her.

Whilst she had stood silently at the sink, he had strained his ears as acutely as any astronomer waiting for the faintest bleep from outer space. But of any other presence in the house there had been no sound at all; no sight at all either, except for the two unwashed wine-glasses that stood on the draining board, a heel-tap of red in each of them. And Morse guessed that Debbie Richardson would never have taken the slightest risk of Claret and intercourse that day with anyone—unless it were with Harry Repp. And it *couldn't* have been with Harry Repp . . . Yet she may well have been tempted, this flaunting, raunchy woman who now dried her face and turned back to Morse; could certainly have been tempted if one of her admirers had called that evening for whatever reason—and if she had already known that Harry Repp was dead.

Morse watched her almost disinterestedly as she returned to the table.

"Shall I pour you that drink now?" he asked.

"Only if you'll join me."

Quite extraordinarily, Morse gave the impression that he was quite extraordinarily sober; and he poured their drinks—gin (hers), whiskey (his)—with only a carefully camouflaged shake of the right hand.

Quietly, as gently as he could, he told her almost as much as he knew of what had happened that day; and of the help that immediately awaited her should she so need it: advice, comfort, counseling . . .

But she shook her head. She'd be better off with sleepin' pills than with all that stuff. She needed nothin' of that. She'd be copin' OK, given a chance. Independent, see? Never wanted to share any worryin' with anyone. Loner most of her life, she'd been, ever since she'd been a teenager . . .

A tear ran hurriedly down her right cheek, and Morse handed her a handkerchief he'd washed and ironed himself.

"We ought to ring your GP: it's the usual thing."

She blew her nose noisily and wiped the moisture from her eyes. "You go now. I'll be fine."

"We'll need a statement from you soon."

"Course."

"You'll stay here . . . ?"

Before she could reply the phone rang, and she moved into the hallway to answer it.

"Hello?"

. . .

"You've got the wrong number."

. . .

"You've got the *wrong number*."

Had she replaced the receiver with needless haste? Morse didn't know.

"Not one of those obscene calls?"

"No."

"Best to be on the safe side, though." Giving her no chance to obstruct his sudden move, Morse picked up the receiver, dialed 1471, and duly noted the number given.

She had said nothing during this brief interlude, but now proceeded to give her views on one of the most recent developments in telephonic technology: "It'll soon be a tricky ol' thing conductin' some illicit liaison over the phone."

Morse smiled, feeling delight and surprise in such elegant vocabulary. "As I was saying, you'll stay here?"

She looked at him unblinking, eye to eye. "You could always call occasionally to make sure, Inspector."

For some little while they stood together on the inner side of the front door.

"You know . . . It doesn't hit you for a start, does it? You just don't take it in. But it's true, isn't it? He's dead. Harry's *dead*."

Morse nodded. "You'll be all right, though. Like you said, you can cope. You're a tough girl."

"Oh God! He kept talkin' and talkin' about gettin' in bed with me again. Been a long time for him—and for me."

"I understand."

"You really think you *do*?"

Her cheeks were dry now, unfurrowed by a single tear. Yet Morse knew that she probably understood as much as he did about those Virgilian "tears of things." And for that moment he felt a deep compassion, as with the gentlest touch he laid his right hand briefly on her shoulder, before walking slowly along that amateurishly concreted path that led toward the road.

Once in the car, Morse turned to Sergeant Dixon:

"Well?"

"Light went off upstairs soon as you rung the bell, sir."

"Sure of that?"

"Gospel."

"Anyone leave, do you think?"

"Must a' been out the back if they did."

"What about the cars parked here?"

"I took a list, like you said. Mostly local residents. I've checked with HQ."

"Mostly?"

"There was an old D-Reg. Volvo parked at the far end there. Not there any longer though."

"*And?*"

Dixon grinned as happily as if he were contemplating a plate of doughnuts. "Car owned by someone from Lower Swinstead. You'll never guess who. Landlord o' the Maiden's Arms!"

Morse, appearing to assimilate this new intelligence without undue surprise, handed over the telephone number of the (hitherto) untraced caller who had just rung Debbie Richardson; and could hear each end of the conversation perfectly clearly as Dixon spoke with HQ once more.

The call had been made from Lower Swinstead.

From the Maiden's Arms.

Chapter Thirty-five

The trouble about always trying to preserve the health of the body is that it is so difficult to do without destroying the health of the mind.

(G. K. Chesterton)

At 9:20 A.M. on Monday, July 27, as he sat in the out-patients' lounge at the Oxford Diabetes Centre at the Radcliffe Infirmary, Morse reflected on the uncoordinated, hectic inquiries which had occupied many of his colleagues for the whole of the previous day. He had himself made no contribution whatsoever to the accumulating data thus garnered, suffering as he was from one long horrendous hangover. Because of this, he had most solemnly abjured all alcohol for the rest of his life; and indeed had made a splendid start to such long-term abstinence until early evening, when his brain told him that he was never going to cope with the present case without recourse, in moderate quantities, to his faithful Glenfiddich.

Several key facts now seemed reasonably settled. Paddy Flynn had been knifed to death at around noon the previous Friday; Harry Repp had died in very similar fashion about two or three hours later. Flynn had probably died instantaneously. Repp had met a slower end, almost certainly dying from the outpouring of blood that so copiously had covered the earlier blood in the back of the car, and quite certainly had been dead when someone, somewhere, had lugged the messy corpse into the boot of the same car. No sign of any weapon; only blood blood blood. And, of course, prints galore—far too many of them—subimposed, imposed, and superimposed everywhere. The vehicle's owner had allowed his second wife and his three stepchildren regular access to his latest supercharged model, and fingerprint elimination was going to be a lengthy business. Even lengthier perhaps would be the analysis by boffins back at Forensics of the hairs and threads collected on the sticky strips the SOCOs had taped over every square centimeter of the vehicle's upholstery.

Yet in spite of so many potential leads, Morse felt dubious (as did Dr. Hobson) about their actual value. Too many cooks could spoil the broth, and too many crooks could easily spoil an investigation. For the moment, it was a question of waiting.

As Morse was waiting in the waiting room now . . .

On the day before, the Sunday, Morse had woken up, literally and metaphorically, to the fact that he should have been keeping an accurate record of his blood-sugar levels for the previous month. Thus it was that he had taken four such readings that day: 12.2; 9.9; 22.6; 16.4.

Although realizing that he could never hope for an average anywhere near the 4–5 range normal for nondiabetic people, he was nevertheless somewhat disturbed by his findings, and immediately halved that very high third reading to 11.3. Then he'd extrapolated backward as intelligently as he could for the previous six days, with the result that a reasonably satisfactory set of readings, neatly tabulated in his small handwriting, was now folded inside his blue appointment card.

He was ready.

He had finally managed to produce a "specimen," although inaccuracy of aim had resulted in a puddle on the unisexloo's floor; and the dreaded weighing-in was over.

And so was the waiting.

"Mr. Morse?"

The white-coated, slimly attractive brunette led the way to a consulting room, her name, black lettering on a white card, on the door: DR. SARAH HARRISON.

"You knew my mother a bit, I believe," she said as she opened a buff-colored folder.

Morse nodded, but made no comment.

A quarter of an hour later the medical side of matters was over. Morse had not attempted to be overly clever. Just short and reasonably honest in his replies.

"These readings—are they genuine?"

"Partly, yes."

"You could lose a stone or two, you know."

"I agree."

"But you won't."

"Probably not."

"How's the drink going?"

"Rather too quickly."

"It's *your* liver, you know."

"Yes."

"Any problems with sex?"

"I've always had problems with sex."

"You know what I mean—sex drive . . . ?"

"I'm a bachelor."

"What's that got to do with it?"

"Just that I lead a reasonably celibate life."

"It *is* my job to *ask* these questions, you understand that."

The dark-brown eyes were growing progressively less angry as she examined his feet, and then his eyes. She had in fact virtually finished with him when a nurse knocked and entered the room, explaining swiftly that an outpatient had just fainted in Reception; and since for the minute Dr. Harrison was the only consultant there . . .

After she had left, Morse stepped quickly over to the desk and opened his own folder. On top lay a brief handwritten note:

> Don't be intimidated, Sarah! He's hugely
> economical with the truth, but he's really a
> softie at heart (I think). Robert (sic!)

And underneath it, a copy of a letter (Strictly Confidential) sent to the Summertown Health Centre and dated May 18, 1998.

Re Annual Review: E. Morse.

Dear Dr. Roblin,

Hemoglobin A lc (as you'll see) is higher than we would like at 11.5%. I've instructed him to increase each of his four daily insulin doses by 2 units—up to 10, 6, 12, 36. In addition, his cholesterol level is getting rather worrying. It's pointless to ask him to cut his intake of alcohol, so please add to his prescribed medicines Atorvastatin 10 mg tablets nocte.

Eyes are remarkably good. Blood pressure is still too high. No problems with feet.

His general condition gives me no real cause for immediate anxiety, but I shall be glad if you can insist on a regular monthly review, at least for the rest of the year. I enclose the relevant clinical data.

Regards to your family.

With best wishes,

Professor R. C. Turner

Honorary Consultant Physician

P.S. He tells me he's stopped smoking! And he's certainly stopped listening to me.

Morse was sitting, slowly pulling on his socks, when Sarah Harrison returned.

"I'll tell you one thing: you've got quite nice feet."

"I'm glad bits of me are OK."

While tying his shoelaces, Morse had missed the look of quick intelligence in the large brown eyes.

"Bit sneaky, wasn't it?" She held up the file.

Morse nodded. "Don't worry, though. Professor Turner sent me a copy of that last letter."

"Well, in that case, there's not really much more . . ." She got to her feet.

"Please!" Morse signaled to the chair, and obediently she sat down again. "Why haven't you mentioned the murders, Doctor? They're all over the national papers."

"I bought *six* of them yesterday, if you must know."

"Your father? Your brother—Simon, isn't it? Do they know?"

"I've not seen Simon recently."

"You could have phoned him."

"Simon is *not* the sort of person you phone. He's deaf, *very* deaf—as you probably know anyway."

"And your father?" repeated Morse.

"I . . . whether or not . . . Oddly enough I saw him last week. He came to stay with me for a couple of nights."

"Which nights?"

"Wednesday and Thursday. He went back to London on Friday."

"What time?"

"Is this the Inquisition?"

"It *is* my job to *ask* these questions, you understand that."

"Touché! He caught the train—I'm not sure which one. He didn't bring the car—nowhere to park in Oxford, is there?"

"Why didn't you see him off?"

"I couldn't."

"Were you working?"

"No. I'd arranged to have Thursday and Friday off myself. Like Dad, I'd a few days' holiday to make up."

"So why not see him off?"

The eyes were fiery now. "I'll tell you why. Because he took me out the previous night to Le Petit Blanc in Walton Street and we had a super meal *and* we had far too much booze—before, during, and after, all right? And I got as pissed as a tailed amphibian and tried to sleep things off with enough pills to frighten even you! And when I finally staggered downstairs—eleven? half-eleven?—I saw this note on the kitchen table: 'Off back to London. Didn't want to wake you. Love Dad'—something like that."

"Any time on the note?"

"Don't think so."

"Have you kept it?"

"Course I've not kept it! Hardly a specimen of purple prose, was it?"

"Don't be cross with me," said Morse gently as he got to his feet and left the consulting room—with two blue cards for more immediate and urgent blood tests, and with instructions to fix up a further appointment for eight weeks' time.

After the door had closed behind him, Sarah dialed 9 for an outside line on the phone there; then called a number.

"Hullo? Hullo? Could you put me through to Simon Harrison, please?"

Chapter Thirty-six

Dr. Franklin shewed me that the flames of two candles joined give a much stronger light than both of them separate; as is made very evident by a person holding the two candles near his face, first separate, and then joined in one.

(Joseph Priestley, *Optiks*)

As he sat awaiting his turn outside the cubicle reserved for blood testing, Morse found himself wondering whether, wondering *how*, if at all, Sarah Harrison could have had any role to play in the appalling events of the weekend just passed. There *were* possibilities, of course (there were always possibilities in Morse's mind), and for a few minutes his brain accelerated sweetly and swiftly into that extra fifth gear. But stop a while! Strange had surely been right to remind him that the easiest answer was more often than not the correct one. What *was* the easiest answer, though? Lewis would know, of course; and it was at times like these that Morse needed Lewis's cautious 30 mph approach to life, if not to any stretch of road in front of him. Two heads were better than one, even though one of them was Lewis's. Yet what a cruel thought that was! And so unworthy . . .

"Mr. Morse?"

A nurse led him behind the blood-letting curtain; and as she wiped the inside of his right arm with a sterilizing swab of cotton wool before inserting a needle, Morse found himself thinking of Dr. Sarah Harrison . . . wondering exactly what she was thinking (doing?) at that very moment.

"Hullo? Simon Harrison here."

"Simon? Sarah! Are you hearing OK?"

"Where else? Course I'm here in the UK."

"Are you *hearing* me all right?"

"Oh, sorry! Yes. Fantastic this new phone system. You know that."

"Are you on your own, Simon?" She was speaking softly.

"Yes. But you can never count on it, sis. You know that."

"Now listen! I've only got a minute or so. I've just been talking to Chief Inspector Morse—"

"Who?"

"Morse! He's with the Thames Valley Police and he's just become one of my patients."

"He wasn't on Mum's case."

"Well, he's on *this* one."

"So?"

"So we've got to be careful, Simon."

"You told him Dad was here?"

"Had to! He'd have soon found out."

"What's *wrong*, sis?"

"*Nothing*'s wrong. But I'm a bit frightened of him, and when he sees you—"

"Seizure? What? Say it again."

"If he *sees* you, Simon, you did *not* come round last Wednesday. *You did not come*—"

"I *heard* you! I stayed at home and watched the telly. What was on, by the way?"

"Look it up in the *Radio Times*! And stop being—!"

A knock on the consulting-room door caused Sarah to replace the receiver hurriedly, almost hoping that another outpatient had passed out in Reception. But the knock was only a polite reminder that Dr. Harrison's A.M. schedule was now running over half an hour late.

Yet even as the next outpatient was ushered in, Dr. Sarah Harrison found herself wondering exactly what Chief Inspector Morse was thinking (doing?) at that very moment.

Turning right from the front entrance of the Radcliffe Infirmary, Morse began walking slowly down toward

St. Giles, noting that the time was 10:40—twenty minutes before the pubs were due to open. Yet since drink
was now definitely out for the duration, such an observation was of little moment.

The Oratory was on his right, a building he'd seldom
paid attention to before, although he must have walked
past it so many, many times. But apart from that wonderful line of cathedrals down the eastern side of
England—Durham, York, Lincoln, Peterborough, Ely—
the architecture of ecclesiastical edifices had never
meant as much as they should have to Morse; and the
reason why he now checked his step remains inexplicable.

He entered and looked around him: all surprisingly
large and imposing, with a faint, seductive smell of
incense, and statues of assorted saints around him, with
tiers of candles lit beside their sandaled, holy feet.

A youngish woman had come in behind him, a Marks
& Spencer carrier bag in her left hand. She dipped her
right hand into the little font of blessed water there,
then crossed herself and knelt in one of the rear pews.
Morse envied her, for she looked so much at home
there: looked as if she knew herself and her Lord so
well, and was wholly familiar with all the trappings of
prayer and the promises of forgiveness. She didn't stay
long, and Morse guessed that the cause of her brief
sojourn was probably the paucity of any sins worthy of
confession. As she left, Morse could see some of the
contents of the carrier bag: a Hovis loaf and a bottle of
red plonk.

Bread and wine.

The door clicked to behind her, and Morse stepped
over to meet St. Anthony, wondering whence had
sprung that oddly intrusive "h." According to the tex-
tual blurb at the base of the statue, this great and good
man was clearly capable of performing quite incredible
miracles for those who almost had sufficient faith.
Morse picked up a candle from the box there and stuck
it in an empty socket on the top row. At which point (it
appeared) most worshipers would have prayed fervently

for a miracle. But Morse wasn't at all sure what miracle he wanted. Nevertheless the elegant, elongated candle was of importance to him; and on some semi-irrational impulse he took a second candle and placed it beside the first. Together, side by side, they seemed to give a much stronger light than both of them separate.

A notice suggested an appropriate donation per candle, and Morse pushed a £1 coin into the slot in the wall behind St. Anthony. Half of bitter. Then, remembering that he'd doubled his investment, the reluctant hagio-later pushed in a second £1 coin. A whole pint.

As he walked down to St. Giles, the man who had vir-tually no faith in the Almighty and even less in miracles noted that the past few minutes had slipped by quickly. It was now just after 11 A.M.; and when he came in sight of the Bird and Baby on his right, he saw that the front door was open.

He went in.

Chapter Thirty-seven

Careless talk costs lives.

(Second World War slogan)

I think men who have a pierced ear are better prepared for marriage. They've experienced pain and bought jewelry.

(Rita Rudner)

Five days after Morse had declined the free draw for a miracle at the Oratory, at noon, at Lower Swinstead, at the bar of the Maiden's Arms, Tom Biffen stood leaning forward on his tattooed arms. Very quiet so far for a Saturday. Just the two hardy perennials, horns already locked over their continuous cribbage; and the pale-faced, ear-pierced, greasy-haired youth already squaring up to the fruit machine.

It was twenty minutes later that the fourth customer arrived.

"Usual?"

The newcomer nodded and placed the requisite monies on the counter. The white van in the car park economically proclaimed the newcomer's profession: "J. Barron, Builder."

"Not out at Debbie's today, John?"

"What do you think? The day after the funeral?"

"No. Have you seen her since Harry. . . ?"

"No. Well, I wouldn't have gone last weekend anyway, would I? Thought they'd like being on their own, like—you know, the day after they'd let him out and all that."

"No."

The youth was standing beside them, a £10 note folded lengthways between the index and middle fingers of his right hand.

"You're taking all me change," complained Biffen as he exchanged the note for ten £1 coins from the till.

"You'll have bugger all left for the honeymoon," ventured the builder; but the youth, unhearing or uncaring, had already walked back to what was perhaps the first great love of his life.

At the bar a few low-voiced confidences were being exchanged.

"When's the wedding, Biff?"

"Five weeks today."

"Nice bit o' skirt?"

"Yeah. Dental receptionist down in Oxford somewhere."

"Glad *one* of 'em's earning!" The builder half-turned toward the unremunerative machine. "Nobody earns much of a living on them things."

"Except the Company," corrected the landlord.

"Except Tom Biffen," corrected one of the cribbagers.

The landlord grunted.

Odd really. Most men in their latish seventies would ever have been susceptible to deafness, arthritis, baldness, sciatica, hemorrhoids, incontinence, impotence, cataracts, dementia, and all the rest. And perhaps (for all the landlord knew) the two old codgers suffered from every single one of them—except quite certainly the first.

Biffen lowered his voice: "Did you get to the crematorium?"

"No. *Family*, wasn't it? I wasn't exactly a friend of the family."

"I thought you builders and plumbers were friends of everybody, especially a strapping young fellow like you?"

"Young?"

But the landlord had a point. John Barron, tall and well built, with dark close-cropped hair and clean-cut features, certainly looked younger than his forty-one years; and what appeared a genuinely open smile appealed to all the local ladies—except his wife, who had been known occasionally to feel jealous.

"What exactly are you doing for Debbie?"

"In the back passage, off the kitchen—you know, the old coal shed and the old loo. Knocking 'em into one so she can get her washing machine in—retiling the floor—replastering the walls—new electrical sockets—usual sort of thing."

"Just at weekends?"

"Yeah, well . . ."

"Bit o' moonlighting? Cash payment?"

For a second or two Barron's mouth tightened distastefully, but he made no direct reply. "I was hoping to finish it off before Harry was out."

"Poor sod! Bet he was looking forward . . . you know. Attractive woman, our Debbie!"

"Yeah." The builder took a deep draught of his bitter. "Did you go—to the crem?"

"No. Like you said . . ."

"Have you seen her at all since. . . ?"

"No. Like you said . . ."

"The police've been round, they tell me."

"Yeah. Came in—when was it?—Tuesday."

"What'd they want?"

Doubtless the builder would have been enlightened immediately had not two further customers entered at that point: an elderly, backpacking, stoutly booted couple.

"Two glasses of orange juice, please!"

"Coming up, sir."

"Beautiful little village you've got here. So quiet. So peaceful. 'Far from the madding crowd'—you'll know the quotation?"

The landlord nodded unconvincingly as he passed over the drinks.

"And you serve meals as well!"

The couple walked over to the corner farthest from the fruit machine: she consulting the hostelry's menu; he plotting a possible P.M. itinerary from *Family Walks in the Cotswolds*.

"Quiet and peaceful!" mumbled the landlord, as one of the elders stepped forward with two empty straight glasses. Words were clearly superfluous.

"You were saying?" resumed the builder.

"Saying what?"

"About the police?"

"Ah, yes. That sergeant came in and asked some of us about Harry and Debbie."

"But you hadn't seen either of them?"

"Right! But, I would've done, see—would've seen *her*, anyway, if it hadn't been for them—for the police. That Sat'day night I thought I'd just nip over and take 'em a bottle o' Shampers, like—give 'em both a bit of a celebration. Well, I'd just parked the car and I was just walking along when I saw this police car driving slowly round and the fellow inside making notes of Reg numbers by the look of it."

"What'd you say?"

"Didn't say nothing, did I? Just waited till the coast was clear, then buggered off back here smartish. They'd seen the number, though. So not much point in . . ."

"Good story!"

"Bloody *true* story, mate!"

The builder finished his pint. "Beer's in good nick, Biff."

"Always in good nick!"

("Is it fuck!" came *sotto voce* from the region of the cribbage board.)

"Summat else too," continued the landlord as he pulled the builder a second pint. "The police tell me there was a phone call for Debbie that Sat'day night—from the pay phone here."

"Could have been anybody."

"Yeah."

"Any ideas?"

"Sat'day nights? Come off it! Full up to the rafters, ain't we?"

The elderly lady now came to the bar and ordered gammon-and-pineapple with chips for two; and during this transaction the builder turned round and, with a fascination that is universal, watched the unequal struggle at the fruit machine.

From outside came the jingle of an ice-cream van—as happy a noise as any to the youngsters of Lower Swinstead that sunny lunchtime; almost as happy a noise as that clunk-clunk-clunk of coins falling into the winnings tray of a fruit machine.

Conversation at the bar was temporarily suspended, since several noisy customers were now arriving, including three members of the highly unsuccessful Lower Swinstead Cricket Club. There was therefore a comparatively large audience for the seemingly endless music of the machine: clunk—clunk - clunk - clunk - clunk - clunk - clunk - clunk - clunk - clunk - clunk - clunk-clunk-clunk-clunk-clunk-clunk-clunk-clunk; and an even larger audience as the impassively faced youth pressed the "Repeat" button—successfully—with a further twenty £1 coins duly clanking into the winnings tray.

"Nearly enough for that honeymoon," said the builder.

"Nonsense! He'll be putting it all back," said one of the cricketers.

But he wasn't.

With a temporary lull in business, the landlord

resumed the conversation. "Business still pretty good, John?"

"Plenty o' work, yeah. Having to turn some things down."

"What you got on at the minute?"

"Job in Burford in Sheep Street: bit o' roofing, bit o' pointing, bit o' painting."

"High up, is it?"

"High enough. I'll need a coupla extensions on the ladder."

Biffen screwed up his face and closed his eyes. "You'd never get me up there."

"You're OK, so long as things are firm."

"Not if you get vertigo as bad as me."

The coins bulged proudly in his trouser pocket as the bridegroom designate walked out of the bar. Once in the passage that led to the toilets, he lifted the receiver from the pay phone there, inserted 20p, and dialed a number.

But what he said, or to whom he spoke, not even the keen-eared elders could have known.

Chapter Thirty-eight

> *All persons are puzzles until at last we find in some word or act the key to the man, to the woman; straightway all their past words and actions lie in light before us.*
>
> (Emerson, *Journals*)

For much of the week Lewis had been working three-quarters of the way round the clock; but on Sunday, the day following the events described in the previous chapter, he felt refreshed after a good sleep and arrived at Kidlington Police HQ at 8:45 A.M. No sign of Morse. But that mattered little. It had been facts that were required. Not fancies. Not yet, anyway. And as he sat taking stock of the past week's activities, Lewis felt solidly satisfied—both with himself and with the performance of the personnel readily allocated to the case. There had been so much to cover . . .

Lewis had personally supervised the Monday and Tuesday inquiries into the activities of Paddy Flynn in the years, months, days—and morning—before his murder; and if the net result was perhaps somewhat disappointing, at least it had been thorough. Flynn had been living in an upstairs flat (converted a few years previously) on Morrell Avenue. He had been there for just over five months, paying £375 per calendar month for the privilege, and having virtually nothing to do with the tenant of the downstairs flat—a middle-aged accountant who, rain or shine, would walk each day down to St. Clements, across Magdalen Bridge, and up the High to his firm's offices in King Alfred Street. He knew Flynn by sight, of course, but only exchanged words when occasionally they encountered each other in the narrow entrance hall. Of Flynn's lifestyle, he had no knowledge at all: no ideas about the activities in which his fellow tenant might have been engaged. Well, just one little observation, perhaps, since not infrequently there was a car parked outside the semi—always a different car, and almost always gone the following morning. Lewis's notes had read: "Has no knowledge of F's professional or leizure time activities." But he'd consulted his dictionary, ever kept beside him, in case Morse decided to look at his notes, and quickly corrected the antepenultimate word.

By all accounts Flynn had led a pretty private, almost secretive life. He was quite frequently spotted in the local hostelries, quite frequently spotted in the local bookmakers, though never, apparently, the worse for excessive liquor or for excessive losses. His name figured nowhere in police records as even the pettiest of crooks, although he was mentioned in dispatches several times as the taxi driver who had picked up Frank Harrison from Oxford Railway Station on the night of Yvonne's murder. Radio Taxis had been his employer at the time, but he had been suspected of (possibly) fabricating fares for his own aggrandisement and duly dismissed— without rancor, it appeared, and certainly without recourse to any industrial tribunal. Dismissed too, subsequently, by the proprietors of Maxim Removals, a firm of middle-distance haulers, "for attempted trickery with the tachometer." (Lewis had spelled the last word correctly, having checked it earlier.) Since that time, five months previously, Flynn had reported regularly to the DSS office at the bottom of George Street. But lacking any testimonials to his competence and integrity, his attempts to secure further employment in any field of motor transport had been unsuccessful, his completed application forms seldom reaching even the slush pile. It was all rather sad, as the woman regularly dealing with the Flynn file had testified.

He'd been thirty-two when, seven years earlier, he'd married Josie Newton, and duly fathered two daughters upon that lady—although (this the testimony of a brother in Belfast) the offspring had appeared so dissimilar in temperament, coloration, and mental ability, that there had been many doubts about their common paternity.

Josie Flynn had been unable or unwilling to offer much in the way of "character profiling" of her late husband (they'd never divorced); had scant interest in the manner of his murder; and, quite certainly, no interest in attending his "last rites," whatever form these latter might take. Although he had treated her with ever-increasing indifference and contempt, he had never (she acknowledged it) abused her physically or sexually. In fact sex, even in the early months of their relationship, had never been a dominant factor in his life; nor, for that matter, had power or success or social acceptability or drink or even happiness. Just plain *money*. She'd not seen him for over two years; nor had her daughters—*she'd* seen to that. It was (again) all rather sad, according to Sergeant Dixon's report. Mr. Paddy Flynn may not have been the ideal husband, but perhaps Ms. Josephine Newton (now her preferred appellation) was hardly a paragon of rectitude in the marital relationship. "Not exacly a saint herself?" as Dixon's handwritten addendum had suggested. And Lewis smiled to himself again, feeling a little superior.

It had been Lewis himself (no Morse beside him) who had visited Flynn's upstairs flat: smell of cigarette smoke everywhere; sheets on the single bed rather grubby; dirty cutlery and plates in the kitchen sink, but not too many of them; the top surface of the cooker in sore need of Mrs. Lewis; soiled shirts, underpants, socks, handkerchiefs, in a neat pile behind the bathroom door; a minimal assemblage of trousers, jackets, shirts, underclothes, in a heavy wardrobe; a Corby trouser-press; eleven cans of Guinness in the otherwise sparsely stocked refrigerator; not a single book anywhere; two copies of the *Mirror* opened at the Racing pages; a TV set, but not even the statutory hard-core video; one CD, *Great Arias from Puccini,* but no CD player for Flynn to have gauged their magnitude; no pictures on the walls; no personal correspondence; and very little in the way of official communications, apart from Social Security forms; no sign of any bank account or credit facility.

Nothing much to go on.

And yet Lewis had sensed from the start that there was something missing. Sensed that he knew where that "something missing" might well be.

And it was.

Most petty crooks had little in the way of imagination, having two or three favoured niches wherein to conceal their ill-gotten gains. And Paddy Flynn proved no exception. The small, brown-leather case was on the top shelf of the old mahogany wardrobe, tucked away on the far left, beneath a pair of faded-green blankets.

It took one DC just under twenty minutes to itemize the contents; a second DC just over thirty minutes to check the original itemization—a cache of legitimate banknotes, in fifties, twenties, tens, and fives. The confirmed tally was £17,465 and Lewis knew that Morse would be interested.

And Morse, on being told, most decidedly *had* been interested.

A similarly painstaking review of Repp and Richardson had taken up the whole of the Wednesday. Little new had come to light except for the unexpected (?) discovery that an account with the Burford and Cheltenham Building Society showed a robust balance of £14,350 held in the name of Deborah Richardson, with regular monthly deposits (as was confidentially ascertained) always made in cash. Debbie Richardson had smilingly refused to answer Lewis's questions concerning the provenance of such comparatively substantial income, stating her belief that everybody—bishops, barmaids, presidents, prostitutes—all deserved some measure of privacy. Yes, Lewis had agreed; but he knew that Morse would be interested.

And Morse, on being told, most decidedly *had* been interested.

The Thursday and Friday had been taken up largely with a preliminary scrutiny and analysis of the scores of reports and statements taken from prison officers, bus drivers, rubbish-dump employees, car-park attendants, forensic boffins, and so on and so on—as well as from those members of the public who had responded to appeals for information. But so far there'd been little to show for the methodical police routine that Lewis had supervised. Vital, though! Criminal investigation was all about motives and relationships, about times and dates and alibis. It was all about building up a pattern from the pieces of a jigsaw. So many pieces, though. Some of them blue for the sky and the sea; some of them green and brown for the trees and the land; and sometimes, somewhere, one or two pieces of quirky coloration that seemed to fit in nowhere. And that, as Lewis knew, was where Morse would come in—as he invariably did. It was almost as if the Chief Inspector had the ability to cheat: to have sneaked some quick glimpse of the finished picture even before picking up the individual pieces.

Frequently when Lewis had seen him that week, Morse had been sitting in HQ, immobile and apparently immovable (apart from an hour or so over lunchtimes), occasionally and almost casually abstracting a page or two of a report, of a statement, of a letter, from one of the bulging box-files on his desk, YVONNE HARRISON written large in black felt-tipped pen down each of the spines. Clearly (whatever else) Morse had come round to Strange's conviction that some causal connection between the cases had become overwhelmingly probable.

But that was no surprise to Lewis.

What had occasioned him puzzlement was the *number* of green box-files there, since he had himself earlier studied the same material when (he could swear it!) there had only been three.

Chapter Thirty-nine

Q: Doctor, how many autopsies have you performed on dead people?
A: *All* of my autopsies are performed on dead people.
    (Reported in the *Massachusetts Lawyers' Journal*)

After (for him) an unprecedented early hour of retirement that same Sunday evening, at 9:30 P.M., Morse had awoken with a troublous headache. Assuming that the dawn was already breaking, he had confidently consulted his watch, to discover that it was still only 11:30 P.M. Thereafter he had woken up at regular ninety-minute intervals, in spite of equally regular doses of Alka-Seltzer and Paracetamol—his mind, even in the periods of intermittent slumber, riding the merry-go-round of disturbing dreams; his blood sugar ridiculously high; his feet suddenly hot and just as suddenly icy cold; an indigestion pain that was occasionally excruciating.

Ovid (now almost becoming Morse's favorite Latin poet) had once begged the horses of the night to gallop slowly whenever some delightfully compliant mistress was lying beside him. But Morse had no such mistress beside him; and even if he had, he would still have wished those horses of the night to complete their course as quickly as they could possibly manage it.

He finally rose from the creased and crumpled sheets, and was shaving, just as rosy-fingered Dawn herself was rising over the Cutteslowe Council Estate.

At 6 A.M. he once more measured his blood-sugar level, now dipped dramatically from 24.4 at 1 A.M. to 2.8. Some decent breakfast was evidently required, and a lightly boiled egg with toast would fit the bill nicely. But Morse had no eggs; no slices of bread either. So, perforce, it had to be cereal. But Morse could find no milk, and there seemed no option but to resort to the solitary king-sized Mars bar which he always kept somewhere in the flat. For an emergency. *In rebus extremis,* like now. But he couldn't find it. Then—bless you St. Anthony!— he discovered that the Co-op milkman had already called; and he had a great bowl of Corn Flakes, with a pleasingly cold pint of milk and several liberally heaped spoonsful of sugar. He felt wonderful.

Sometimes life was very good to him.

At 6:45 A.M. he considered (not too seriously) the possibility of walking up from his North Oxford flat to the A40 Ring Road, and thence down the gentle hill to Kidlington. About—what?—thirty-five to forty minutes to the HQ building. Not that he'd ever timed himself, for he'd never as yet attempted the walk.

Didn't attempt the walk that morning.

After administering his first insulin dosage of the day, he drove up to Police HQ in the Jaguar.

Far quicker.

In his office, as he reread the final findings of the two postmortems *(sic),* Morse decided, as he usually did, that there was no point whatsoever in his trying to unjumble the physiological details of the lacerations inflicted on the visceral organs of each body. He had little interest in the stomach; had no stomach for the stomach. In fact he was more familiar with the ninefold stomach of the bovine ilk (this because of crossword puzzles) than with its mono-chambered human counterpart. Did it really matter much to know exactly how Messrs. Flynn and Repp had met their ends? But yes, of course it did! If the tech-nicalities pointed to a particular type of weapon; if the weapon could be accurately identified and then found; and if, finally, it could be traced to someone who was known to have had such a weapon and who had the opportunity of wielding it on the day of the murders ...

Hold on though, Morse! Be fair! Amid a plethora of caveats,

> The knife was quite probably not all that long, maybe no
> more than 6"–9", since in each case the lacerations seem
> the result of forceful twisting, as if the murderer had
> gripped a handle that was short and firm, say perhaps not
> much more than 1"–1¹/₂" in width. The knife-blade was
> fairly certainly short too (? 1¹/₂"), but very sharp, with its
> end shaped in triangular fashion (◺). It could have been
> something like a Stanley knife, the sort of thing commonly
> used in DIY household jobs, carpentry, building, that sort of
> thing.

Dr. Hobson *had* pointed to a fairly specific type of weapon, had she not? And he read again the paragraph headed "Tentative Conclusions."

Morse suddenly stopped reading, sat back in his chair, and placed his hands on his head, fingers inter-linked, as he'd done so often at his teacher's bequest in his infant class. And what had been a faraway look in his eyes now gradually focused into an intense gaze as he considered the implications of the extraordinary idea which had suddenly occurred to him ...

Very soon he was rereading the whole report from Forensics, where almost all the earlier findings had been confirmed, although there remained much checking to be done. Prints of Flynn, prints of Repp, prints of the car owner, and several other prints as yet to be identified. Doubtless some of these latter would turn out to be those of the car owner's family. But (Morse read the last sentence of the report again): "One set of fingerprints, repeated and fairly firm, may well prove to be of considerable interest."

He leaned back again in his chair, pleasingly weary and really quite pleased with himself, because he knew whose fingerprints they were.

Oh yes!

Chapter Forty

> Odd instances of strange coincidence are really not all that odd perhaps.
>
> (Queen Caroline's advocate, speaking in the House of Lords)

Morse jerked awake as Lewis entered the office just before 8 A.M., wondering where he was, what time it was, what day it was. Yet it had been a wonderful little sleep, the deep and dreamless sleep that Socrates anticipated after swallowing the hemlock.

"No crossword this morning, sir?"

"Shop wasn't open."

"Why don't you pay a paperboy?"

"Because, Lewis, a little occasional exercise . . ."

Lewis sat down. "Do you mind if I ask you something?"

Morse pointed to the reports laid out on the desk. "You've read these?"

Lewis nodded. "But, like I say, I've got something to ask you."

"And I've got something to *tell* you. Is that all right, Lewis?" The voice was suddenly harsh. "You'll remember from all our times together how coincidence occurs in life far more frequently than anyone—except me—is prepared to accept. Coincidence isn't unusual at all. It's the norm. Just like those consecutive numbers cropping up in the National Lottery every week. But in this case the coincidence is even odder than usual."

(Lewis raised his eyebrows a little.)

"Let's go back to Yvonne Harrison's murder. She was a woman with exceptional sex drive, but she certainly wasn't just the deaf-and-dumb nymphomaniac with a bedroom just above the public bar that many a man has fantasized about. Oh, no. She was highly intelligent, highly desirable, like the woman in the Larkin poem with the "lash-wide stare," who in turn was attracted by a variety of men. A lot of men. So many men that over the years she inevitably came across a few paying clients with kinky preferences. I doubt she ever went in for S and M, but it looks very likely that a bit of bondage was on her list of services, probably with a hefty surcharge. It's well known that some men only find sexual satisfaction with women who put on a show of being utterly submissive and powerless. It gives these men the only sense of real power they're ever likely to experience in life, because the object of their desire is lying there defenseless, unstruggling, sometimes unspeaking, too. Not uncommon, that, Lewis. And you can read all about it in Krafft-Ebing's case studies . . ."

(Lewis's eyebrows rose significantly.)

". . . although, as you know, I'm no great expert in such matters. In fact, come to think of it, I can't even remember whether he's got one or two 'b's in his name. But it means there's a pretty obvious explanation of two of the items that puzzled our previous colleagues: a pair of handcuffs, and a gag not all that tightly tied. The woman offering such a specialist service is never going to answer back, never going to scratch your eyes out—and Yvonne Harrison had just about the longest fingernails . . ."

(Lewis's eyebrows rose a lot.)

"On the night of the murder she had a client in bed with her, and if ever there was a *locus classicus* for what

they call *coitus interruptus*, this was it, because someone interrupted the proceedings. Or at the very least,
someone saw them there in bed together."

"Harry Repp?"

"Repp was certainly there at some point. But I think he
kept his cool and kept his distance that night. I think
he realized there could well be something in it for himself. He was right, too. Because what he saw that
night—what he later kept from the police—was going
to prove very profitable, as you discovered, Lewis. Five
hundred pounds a month *from someone* just for exercising his professional skills as a burglar in staying well
out of sight and keeping his eyes wide open. Exactly
what he saw, we shan't know, shall we? Unless he told
Debbie Richardson, which I doubt."

"What do *you* think he saw?"

"Pretty obvious, isn't it?"

"You mean he saw who murdered Mrs. Harrison?"
Morse nodded.

"And you think you know who. . . ?"
Morse nodded.

But Lewis shook his head. "It's all so wishy-washy,
what you've just said. I don't know where to start.
When was she murdered? *Who* rang her husband? *Who*
set off the burglar alarm? *Who*—?"

"Lewis! We, remember, are investigating something
else. But if any study of the first case facilitates the solving of the second? So be it! And it does, as you'll agree."

"I will?"

Morse nodded again. "Three people were coinciden-
tally involved in a clever and profitable deception that
night, each of them able and willing to throw his individual spanner into any reconstruction the CID could
reasonably come up with. First, there was Flynn, our
corpus primum, who told as many lies as anybody: both
about the time he picked Frank Harrison up from
Oxford Station, and about what he noticed—or more
probably the person he saw—when he got to Lower
Swinstead. Second, there was Repp, our *corpus secun-*

dum, who told us no lies at all, but only because he told us nothing at all. Third . . ."

Morse hesitated, and Lewis looked across the desk expectantly.

"There's this third man of ours, and a man most unlikely to become our *corpus tertium*. Once Repp was out of jail, the three of them—Repp himself, Flynn, and this third man—they all arranged to meet together. They'd done pretty well so far out of their conspiracy of silence, and they were all keen on continuing to squeeze the milk cow even drier. So they *did* meet—a meeting where things went tragically wrong. Greed . . . jealousy . . . personal antipathies . . . whatever! Two of them had an almighty row in the car in which they were traveling together. And one of them, probably in a lay-by somewhere, knifed one of the others: one of them knifed Flynn. And the remaining two disposed of the body neatly enough at Redbridge—the rubbish bags proving very handy, I should think. So any profits no longer needed to be split three ways. And now the talk between the two of them must have been all about a fifty-fifty share of the spoils, and how it could be effected. But somewhere in the discussion there was one further almighty row; and this time it was Repp who had his innards ripped open."

"You know who this 'third' man was, you're saying?"

"So do you. We mentioned him when you produced that admirable schema of yours for the night of Yvonne's murder."

"You're saying there was somebody else there that night?"

"There was *always* somebody else, Lewis, wasn't there? The man in bed with Yvonne Harrison."

"If you say so, sir."

"You see, the major problem our lads had was the *timing* of the murder. Her body wasn't examined until several hours later, and all the pathological guesswork had to be married with the evidence gleaned at the time, or gleaned later. For example, with the fact that *someone* was in bed with Yvonne at some specific time that night, although nobody really tried to discover who that person was—until I did. For example, again, with the fact that *someone* had tried to ring her twice that night, at 9 P.M. when the line was engaged, and again half an hour later when the phone rang unanswered. And if you add all this together, you'll find that the person who sorely misled the police, the person who was in bed with her, and the person who murdered both Paddy Flynn and Harry Repp—*was one and the same man.*"

There fell a silence between the two of them, broken finally by Lewis. "You're *sure* about all this?"

"Only ninety-five percent sure."

"We'd better get our skates on then."

"Hold your horses! One or two things I'd like you to check first, just to make it one hundred percent."

"So we've got a little while?"

"Oh, yes. No danger of anyone murdering *him*—not today, anyway. So this afternoon'll be fine. Get out to Lower Swinstead—take someone with you, mind!—and bring him back here. OK?"

"Fine. Only one thing, sir. You forgot to tell me his name."

"Did I? Well, you've guessed it anyway. He's got a little business out there, hasn't he? A little building business. 'J. Barron, Builder,' as it says on his van."

Chapter Forty-one

> But when he once attains the utmost round,
> He then unto the ladder turns his back,
> Looks in the clouds, scorning the base degrees
> By which he did ascend.
> (Shakespeare, *Julius Caesar*)

Twenty miles west of Oxford, twenty miles east of Cheltenham, lies the little Cotswold town of Burford. It

owes its architectural attractiveness to the wealth of the
wool merchants in the fifteenth and sixteenth centuries;
and up until the end of the eighteenth century the small
community there continued to thrive, especially the coach-
ing inns which regularly served the E–W travel. But the
town was no longer expanding, with the final blow
delivered in 1812, when the main London road, which
crossed the High Street (the present-day Sheep Street
and Witney Street), was rerouted to the southern side
of the town (the present-day A40). But Burford remains
an enchanting place, as summer tourists will happily
testify as they turn off at the A40 roundabout. Pic-
turesque tea shops, craft shops, public houses—all built
in the locally quarried, pale-honey-colored limestone—
line the steeply curving sweep of the High Street that
leads to the bridge at the bottom of the hill, under
which runs the River Windrush, with all the birds and
the bright meadows and cornfields around Oxfordshire.

Mrs. Patricia Bayley, aged seventy, had lived for only
three years in Sheep Street *(vide supra)*, a pleasingly
peaceful, tree-lined road, first left as one descended the
hill. The house-date, 1687, had been carved (now almost
illegibly) in the greyish and pitted stone above the front
door of the three-storied, mullion-windowed building.
Her husband, a distinguished anthropologist from University College, Oxford, had died (aged sixty-seven)
only two months after his retirement, and only four
months after buying the Sheep Street property. Often,
since then, she had considered leaving the house and
buying one of the older persons' flats that had been
springing up for the last decade all over North Oxford,
for her present house was unnecessarily extensive and
inappropriate for her solitary needs. Yet the children
and the grandchildren (especially the latter) loved to
stay there with her and to find themselves lost amid
the random rooms. Only one real problem: she'd have
to do something about the windows. There could be no
Council permission for replacement windows, but the
casements were quite literally falling apart. And the
whole of the exterior just had to be repainted, from

the gutterings along the top to the front door at the bottom. Should she get it all done? Three weeks earlier she'd stood and surveyed the scene. Could she ever find anywhere else so pleasingly attractive as this?

No! She'd stay.

She'd consulted the Yellow Pages and found *Barron, J., Builder and Decorator*; not so far away, either—at Lower Swinstead. She'd rung him and he'd called round to survey the job. He'd seemed a personable sort of fellow; and when he'd quoted a reasonable (if slightly steep) estimate for both the restructuring and the repainting, she'd accepted.

He'd promised to be with her at 7:30 A.M. on Monday, August 3. And it was precisely at that time that he knocked in civilized manner on the front door of "Collingwood," again admiring as he did so the dripstone molding above it.

Born in North Oxford, Mrs. Bayley spoke her mind unapologetically: "You look as if you've just come straight from the abattoir, Mr. Barron!"

The builder (rather a handsome man, she thought) grinned wryly as he looked down at overalls bespattered with scarlet paint. "Not my choice, Mrs. B. I'm with *you*, all the way. If there's a better combination of color than black and white and yellow, I don't know it."

Mrs. B. felt gratified. "Well, I'll let you get on then. I won't bother you—no one will bother you. It's all very quiet round here. Would you like some coffee later?"

"Tea, if you don't mind, Mrs. B. Milk and two teaspoons of sugar, please. About ten? Smashing!"

From the ground-floor window she watched him as he removed the aluminum ladders from the top of the van, stood there for a few seconds looking up at the dormer window, then shaking out the first extension and, by means of a rope and pulley at the bottom, elongating the ladder to its fullest extent with a second, smaller extension. For a few seconds he stood there, holding the loftily assembled structure at right angles to the ground; then easing the pointed top of the third stage—most carefully, lovingly almost—into place against the casement of the dormer window some thirty feet above, before finally firming the bottom of the ladder on the compacted gravel of the pathway which divided the front of the houses there from the wide stretch of grass leading to the edge of Sheep Street, some four or five feet below.

For several minutes Mrs. B. stood by her front window on the ground floor, looking out a little anxiously to observe her builder's varied skills. Across the road, a solitary jogger in red trainers was running reasonably briskly past the Bay Tree Hotel, his tracksuit hood over his head, as if he were trying to work up a sweat; or just perhaps to keep his ears warm, since there was an unseasonal nip in the air that morning. Mrs. B thought jogging a silly and dangerous way of keeping fit, though. She'd known the young North Oxford don who had written the hugely popular *Joys of Jogging*, and who had died aged twenty-seven, whilst on an early-morning not-so-joyful jog.

Jogging was a dangerous business.

Like climbing ladders.

And Mrs. B.'s nerves could stand things no longer.

She would repair to the second-floor back bedroom to continue with her quilting—as well as to quell the acute fear she felt for a man who (as she saw it) was risking his life at every second of his working day. But before doing so, she knew she had the moral duty to impart a few cautionary words of advice. And she opened the front door just as the builder was beginning his ascent, his left hand on a shoulder-high rung, his right hand grasping a narrowly serrated saw, a long chisel, and a red, short-handled Stanley knife.

"You *will* be careful, won't you? Please!"

The builder nodded, successively grasping each rung (each "round" as the firemen say) at a point just above his shoulders as he climbed with measured step, professionally, confidently, to the top of the triple-length ladder. He'd always enjoyed being up high, ever since the vicar of St. John the Baptist's in Burford had taken him and his fellow choirboys up to the top of the church. It was the first time in his young life he'd felt superior, felt powerful, as he traversed his way along the high places there with a strangely happy confidence, whilst the others inched their cautious way along the narrow ledges.

It was just the same now.

Once he had reached the top rung but three, he looked up and immediately decided he would be able to work at the top of the dormer without any trouble. Then he looked down, and saw that the ladder(s) beneath him, though sagging slightly in the middle (that was good), seemed perfectly straight and secure. Funny, really! Most people thought you were all right on heights just so long as you didn't look up or down. Rubbish! The only thing to avoid was looking laterally to left or right, when there really *was* the risk (at least for him) of losing all sense of the vertical and the horizontal. He dug his red Stanley knife into the upper lintel, then the lower sill; in each case, as he twisted the blade, finding the wooden texture crumble with ominous ease. Not surprising though, really, for he'd noticed the date above the door. He secured the top of the ladder to the gutterings—his normal practice—and began work.

At the appointed hour Mrs. B. boiled the kettle in the second-floor front (as her husband had called it); squeezed a Typhoo bag with the kitchen tongs; and stirred in two heaped spoonsful of sugar. Then, with the steaming cup and two digestive biscuits on a circular tray, she was about to make her way downstairs when something quite extraordinary flashed across her vision: she saw a pair of oblique parallel lines passing almost in slow motion across the oblong frame of the second-floor window. So sharply was that momentary configuration imprinted upon her retina that she was able to describe it so very precisely later that same afternoon; was able to recall that earsplitting, skin-tingling shriek of terror as the man whose skull was about to be smashed to pieces fell headfirst on to the compacted pathway below, so very few yards from her own front door.

"Dead," the senior paramedic had told her quietly,

six minutes only after her panic-stricken call on 999. Incontrovertibly dead.

For the next hour or so Mrs. Bayley wept almost uncontrollably. Partly from shock. Partly, too, from guilt, because (as she repeatedly reminded herself) it was *her* fault that he'd appeared upon the scene in the first place. She'd found his name among the local builders and house renovators listed alphabetically in the telephone directory. In the Yellow Pages, in fact. Exactly where Sergeant Lewis, also, had discovered the address of J. Barron, Builder, together with a telephone number in Lower Swinstead.

Chapter Forty-two

> And what is the use of a book without pictures or conversations?
> (Lewis Carroll, *Alice in Wonderland*)

Had he been left to himself, had he been without any knowledge of the context in which the apparent "accident" had occurred, Lewis would not have suspected that it all amounted to murder. But it *had* been murder, he felt sure of that; and four hours earlier he had taken personal responsibility for initiating the whole apparatus of yet another murder inquiry. Same SOCOs as in the Sutton Courtenay murder, same pathologist, same everything; but with almost every sign of immediate activity over when, just before 3 P.M., Morse finally put in an appearance, very soon to be seating himself in Mrs. Bayley's north-facing sitting room on the ground floor.

"Northamptonshire faring any better?" he asked the senior SOCO.

"Next year, perhaps," said Eddie Andrews pessimistically.

"You'd be out of a job without me," continued Morse. "Just like Dr. Hobson here."

But the unsmiling pathologist could find little place in her heart for any banter and ignored the comment. As did Edwards.

The gloomy room was suddenly empty, apart from Sergeant Lewis. "You said there wasn't any danger of *him* being murdered, sir."

Morse could find no satisfactory answer and stared silently out of the window until Mrs. Bayley came in with (for Morse) wholly unwelcome cups of coffee and the same two digestive biscuits that Barron would have eaten with his oversugared tea.

"You mentioned to Sergeant Lewis what you saw from the window? The one above this, wasn't it?"

She nodded. "It made such a vivid imprint on the, er . . ."

"Retina?" suggested Lewis.

"Thank you, Sergeant. I *did* myself once work in the Oxford Eye Hospital." She turned to Morse. "You'll think me a silly old woman, but it reminded me of something I saw quite a few years ago now in one of the Sundays. There were these outline drawings sent in by readers and you had to guess what they were; and one of them always stuck in my, er . . ." (This time Lewis desisted.) She took a pencil and without permission made a quick little drawing in Lewis's notebook:

"Can't you guess, Inspector?" Her eyes twinkled.

Morse frowned, about to suggest something wildly inappropriate when the undeterred Lewis intervened:

"Giraffe walking past a window?"

"You clever man."

"No!" Lewis smiled deprecatingly. "I'd seen it before."

He took a pencil and made an equally quick little drawing underneath:

"Aristocratic sardine in a tin!" she cried triumphantly.

"You clever woman!"

She shook her head. "I'd seen it before."

Morse sounded wearily impatient. "I'm very sorry to interrupt the fun, Mrs. Bayley, but . . ."

"Of course. Forgive me!"

"Which way was your, er, giraffe walking? Left to right? Right to left?"

"Left to right—exactly like I've drawn it, Inspector."

"So if the ladder fell across the window from left to right, the bottom of the ladder must have slipped from right to left—that is, from your point of view here in the house, Mrs. Bayley?"

"I'm not quite sure I follow you."

"I mean, if someone had come along and given the ladder a hefty kick at the bottom, he'd probably have been coming from" (Morse pointed to the right) "the center of Burford, say, to" (Morse pointed vaguely to the left) "wherever this road leads to?"

"Bourton on the Water."

"Thank you, Lewis!"

"But we know that, sir—about the ladder, I mean. They found him six or seven yards to the right of the front door. That's from Mrs. Bayley's point of view of course," he added mischievously.

"Yes!" whispered the lady of the household, as so vividly she recalled that terrible sight, with the red Stanley knife lying there beside the shattered skull.

Morse was looking far from pleased. Even less so when a further cup of coffee was suggested. The room had become chillier, and he shivered slightly as he got to his feet. It was time for the clichés:

"If you *do* remember anything else—anything odd—anything unusual—anything at all . . ."

And suddenly she *had* remembered something. It was Morse's involuntarily shivering shoulders that had jogged—yes, *jogged*—her memory.

The jogger.

"There *was* something a bit unusual. We don't get many people jogging here—we're all a bit too old. But there was one this morning, about a quarter-to-eight. He'd pulled the hood of his tracksuit over his head as if he was feeling the cold a bit."

"Or wasn't anxious to be recognized," added Morse quietly.

"Perhaps *you* could recognize him though, Inspector. You see, he was wearing a very distinctive pair of training shoes. *Red,* they were."

The two policemen left with appropriate expressions of gratitude; and with the two digestive biscuits still untouched on the circular tray, beside two cups, one of them full, of stone-cold coffee.

Chapter Forty-three

For coping with even one quarter of that running course known as "Marathon"—for coping without frequent halts for refreshment or periodic bouts of vomiting—a man has to dedicate one half of his youthful years to quite intolerable training and endurance. Such dedication is not for me.

(Diogenes Small, 1797–1805,
The Joys of Occasional Idleness)

After Lewis had turned right at the junction of Sheep Street and High Street and slipped the marked police car into the queue up to the A40 roundabout, Morse pointed peremptorily to the right, to the Cotswold Gateway Hotel.

Seated at a wall-settle in the bar, Morse tasted his pint of cask-conditioned ale and proclaimed it "not so bad." And Lewis, seated opposite, sipped his iced orange juice and said nothing.

Morse looked sourly out of sorts.

"Just nip and get me a packet of cigarettes, Lewis. Dunhill, if they've got them. I don't seem to . . ." In time-honored fashion, he patted his trouser pockets with little prospect, as it seemed, of finding any funds therein.

"I thought you'd stopped," ventured Lewis, as minutes later Morse peeled off the cellophane.

"First today!" said Morse as with obvious gratification he inhaled deeply.

In turn, Lewis took a deep breath himself:

"You mustn't get cross with me if—"

"Certainly not." Morse pushed his empty glass across the table.

Waiting at the bar, Lewis was rehearsing his carefully formulated sentence; was ready with it once he took his seat again.

"You mustn't be cross with me, sir, but—"

"Someone's been round to Mrs. Barron? You've seen to that?"

"Dixon, yes. With WPC Towle—she's an experienced officer."

"PC Towle, you mean. They're all PCs now, whatever the sex. Stands for Politically Correct."

For the umpteenth time in his working life with Morse, Lewis knew that any potentially favorable wind had suddenly stopped blowing for him; and that it would be Morse who would now be sailing serenely on, whatever the state of the weather. As he did now:

"Something worrying you, Lewis?"

"Yes. Something *is*. We started off with two murders and you said you knew who the murderer was. And now this murderer of yours gets murdered himself and . . ."

"And there's not all that much point in sitting around

in a pub all day just thinking about things. Is that what you're saying?"

"Yes! Why don't we sit back and look at what we've *got*—look at the *evidence*?"

"You're talking to me in italics, Lewis."

"All right! But don't you think it *is* time—to start again—at the *beginning*?"

"No," said Morse (no italics). "Let's start with those red trainers."

"All right. Good news that. There can't be more than a dozen people in Oxfordshire who've got a pair like that. Give us a few days. We'll find him. Guaranteed!"

"Let's hope you're right. Bit odd, though. Quarter to eight? And still running when Barron fell at ten past ten?"

"We're not all as unfit as you."

"What? I could have run a marathon in that time. Once."

Lewis smiled quietly to himself as Morse continued: "You know, what worried me about the murders of Flynn and Repp was how anyone could have got away from that car without people noticing all the blood on his clothes. Then it struck me. Barron could have got away with it easily. His overalls were already covered in red—covered in the maroon paint from Debbie Richardson's outhouse—*before* the murders. Nobody's going to worry about what he looks like, not in Lower Swinstead anyway. It's not exactly like spilling a bottle of Claret over your white tuxedo on the *QE2*. Is it now?"

"I wouldn't know, sir."

"Being too clever, am I?"

"Perhaps."

"You see, I thought *he* was clever, Barron. And in spite of what some of these criminologists say, some criminals *are* clever."

Lewis agreed. "Pretty clever of our murderer to knock him off his ladder: no weapon, no fingerprints . . ."

"Mm." Morse drained his beer and stood up. "You will be glad to know that the brain is now considerably clearer, although I am still, if it's of interest to you, exceedingly puzzled as to why our murderer should decide to draw almost inevitable attention to himself by wearing such a conspicuous pair of plimsolls and running around Burford for two and a half hours."

"Truth is, sir, some of 'em *aren't* all that clever. We both know that."

By the time they were back at Kidlington HQ, the strangely disturbing news was already beginning to filter through.

Not that Morse himself was to be in his office that late Monday afternoon, for he had instructed Lewis to drop him off at his flat in North Oxford. He longed for some music: some Mozart (though not *Eine Kleine Nachtmusik*), some Wagner (though not the *Ride of the Valkyries*), some Vivaldi even (though not *The Four Seasons*), or some Vaughan Williams (though not *The Lark Ascending*).

Most especially not *The Lark Ascending*, since Morse (as we have seen) had already spent enough of his time with the dawn that day.

Chapter Forty-four

CLINTON WINS ON BUDGET, BUT MORE LIES AHEAD
(From *USA's Best Newspaper Headlines*, 1997)

Sergeant Dixon swallowed the last of the jam-filled, sugar-coated doughnut: "I'm beginning to think he's losing his marbles. First he says we go and bring Barron in—and the next thing is we're telling his missus he's croaked it."

Sergeant Lewis looked up. "How did she take it?"

"Not very well. Kate was very good with her but . . ."

"Her GP knows?"

"Yep. And she's got her mum and sister there, so . . .

The kids though, innit? Poor little buggers: six and four."

"Easier for them, I suppose."

"Perhaps so. I just had the feeling though, you know, the marriage wasn't all that . . ." Dixon held out a shaky right hand, like that of a man with delirium tremens.

"What gave you that impression?"

Dixon tapped his right temple with a firmer finger. "Experience, mate."

He got up, walked over to the canteen counter, and looked hopefully along the glass shelves.

Lewis was summoned to Caesar's tent just after 5:30 P.M.

"Sorry state of affairs, Lewis, when a man can't even get a round of golf in on a Monday afternoon!"

"I just thought you ought to—"

"Winning I was. Two up at the turn. The swing really in the groove. And then . . ."

"I'm sorry, sir. But as I say I thought—"

"Where's Morse?"

"He, er, just went back home for a while."

"Best place for him. Nothing but disaster since he took over things."

"It was *you* wanted him," said Lewis gently.

"Too clever—that's Morse's trouble! Time he jacked it in—like me. Make way for these bright young buggers checking in through the fast track. It's all degrees these days, Lewis, and DNA, and . . ."

"Clipboards?"

Strange smiled sympathetically. "Old Morse doesn't like clipboards much, does he?"

"No."

"You'll miss him when he goes, won't you?"

"Is he going?"

"You'll be a richer man, for certain."

Lewis made no reply.

"Did he have a couple of beers out at Burford?"

"Just the one."

"Remarkable! And who paid for that, pray?"

"Oddly enough, *he* did."

Strange looked across the desk shrewdly. "Know something, Lewis? You're nearly as big a liar as that American president."

For the next ten minutes, and with no further lies, Lewis told the Chief Superintendent as much as he or anyone else (including Morse?) could know about the deliberate murder of J. Barron, Builder (and increasingly, as it appeared, Decorator) of Lower Swinstead.

"Mm!"

Strange contemplated the phone awhile, then rang Morse. But the ex-directory number was engaged. A minute later, he rang again; and, a minute later, again. Still engaged.

"Taken his phone off the bloody hook. Typical! He's supposed to be solving an assortment of murders."

"He's a bit tired, sir. I don't think he's been sleeping very well."

"Hardly surprising, is it? Having to get up for a pee every half hour?"

"I don't think it's *just* that."

"What d'you mean?" Strange's voice was sharper.

"Well, nothing really."

"*Out* with it, Lewis."

"Just that sometimes perhaps it almost seems as if he doesn't really care all that much . . ."

"Interesting!"

For a while Strange pondered matters. Then decided: "Go and knock him up!"

"Couldn't we give him a rest, just for today?" suggested a diffident Lewis. "Not much *he* can do for the minute, is there? Not much *you* can do, either."

"Mm. You could be right."

"Why not get back to the golf course?"

"Because, Lewis—*because* I've let him off the hook. Three up at the turn . . ."

"I thought you said it was *two* up, sir."

"Did I?"

Strange reached for the phone and rang Morse's number yet again.

Still engaged.

He stood up and repeated Lewis's words: "Not much *you* can do, either. Why don't you just bugger off home. Eggs and chips, what?"

For a good deal of these exchanges between Strange and Lewis, Deborah Richardson had been standing, head tilted, in the narrow passageway at the back of the property, wondering whether she'd been sensible in choosing that particular shade of maroon for the newly established outhouse. Two of the re-plastered walls had received their first coat—several weekends ago now—and they reminded her, according to the light, either of black currant jam or of blood.

She thought she'd probably change things.

The phone rang.

She reached it at the sixth ring.

The arrangements, unusually involved, took a little while to get sorted out.

Once they were, she felt almost unprecedentedly excited.

Chapter Forty-five

> *Nunquam ubi sub ubi!*

After he had locked the door behind them she immediately, albeit a little nervously, commented upon the civilized appearance of the bachelor flat, listening with half an ear to a love duet from one of the operas, although she had no idea which one; standing appreciatively for a while in front of a reproduction of *The Milkmaid*, although she had only just heard of Vermeer; looking wide-eyed along the shelves and shelves and shelves of books that lined three of the walls there; noticing too, although not herself a particularly houseproud woman, the thin layer of dust on the CD player and the thicker layer along the top of the skirting boards.

On the glass-topped coffee table there stood a chilled bottle of champagne, with two sparklingly bright glasses on their coasters beside it.

As quietly bidden, she sat down, the hem of the minidress riding more than halfway up her black-stockinged thighs as languidly she crossed her lengthy legs. Then, as he untwisted the wire at the top of the bottle, she turned away, holding the palms of her hands over her ears.

"No need for that," he said. "I'm an expert."

Tilting the bottle to 45 degrees, he turned the cork sharply, pulling only slightly—and that was it. Out! He filled the two glasses, sat opposite her, raised his glass, and said, "Cheerio!"

It seemed to her a strange thing to say. "Hello!" would surely have been more appropriate? It was obviously something he'd stored away in his verbal baggage from a period at least twenty-five years (she decided) earlier than her own.

Not that *that* mattered.

She sipped the champagne; sipped it again; and concluded, although she knew nothing whatever of Bruts and Crus, that it might well be fairly expensive stuff.

"Specially bought for the occasion?"

"No. I won it in a raffle."

She took a further sip, then drank off the rest in a single draught. "Lovely!"

He leaned forward and refilled her glass.

"Are you trying to get me drunk?"

"It might even things up a bit."

"Mind if I smoke?"

"No. I'll join you."

"You took a lot of trouble about gettin' me here—"

"Don't you like taxis?"

"—and I've never been told exactly what to wear before."

He surveyed her vertically striped brown-and-white dress, and counted the buttonholes: seven of them, the top three straining across her breasts.

"I like buttons. I've read that 'unbuttoning' was Philip Larkin's favorite present participle."

She let it go, fairly certain that she understood, and slowly unfastened the top button of her dress. "I shall expect a fee, you know that."

"Fee? You mean as well as the taxi and the champagne?"

She nodded and pointed to the bottle. "Will one be enough, do you think?"

"I won *two* in the raffle. The other one's cooling in the fridge."

She drained her second glass, and sat back in the deeply comfortable settee, unfastening the second button as he again refilled her glass.

She patted the cushion beside her. "Come and sit next to me."

"In a little while. It's just that I'd like to get my fill of sitting here and lusting after you."

She smiled. "I wonder how we would have been together?"

"Know something? You've just quoted T. S. Eliot, virtually verbatim."

She let it go, fairly certain that Eliot was a poet. But there wasn't much poetry out there—not in the world in which she moved. It all made her feel pleasingly important and decidedly sexy. Something more, too. As she tilted the third glass of champagne into her lipstick-moistened mouth; as she worked the third button of her dress loose; as she looked down at her braless breasts now almost fully exposed, she felt an animal sense of her own power—and she felt *good*.

He was right, though. She was enjoying teasing him, and he was enjoying being teased. No need for that rush to sexual congress the great majority of men (she knew full well) preferred.

"You know," she said, "I thought first of all when you rang that you wanted to ask me about the murders."

"Afterward, don't you think?"

She uncrossed her legs and leaned forward to light another cigarette. "No. Let's get the inquisition over. Where's the bedroom, by the way?"

He pointed to a door on his left. "Top sheet turned back in a very neat hypotenuse."

She let it go, for her own mathematics had stopped well short of Pythagoras.

"I didn't ask you here for any grilling—you know that. But there *is* one thing I'd like you to tell me."

"Fire away."

"I think you've got a good idea who murdered Harry. And if you *have*, I'd like you to tell me."

"But I don't—not for certain, I don't." She recrossed the legs that a little earlier had been provocatively open.

"Go on!"

"It's just . . . well, I reckon perhaps it was Johnnie— *might* have been, anyway."

"Why do you think that?"

"Somethin' he said and . . . well, you get the vibes sometimes."

He seemed to know nothing of "vibes"—interested only in strictly verbal significations.

"What exactly *did* he say?"

"Nothin' really. Nothin' I'm going to tell you, anyway."

"When was this?"

"Sat'day night."

"He was with you then?"

"Yes."

"Did he often call round?"

"Quite often."

"He'd been taking his time with your building alter-ations?" He drank the rest of the only glass of cham-pagne he'd allowed himself—drank it swiftly, like a man in a pub who knows that if he stays any longer the next round will surely be his, and who therefore decides to depart.

"And you went to bed—quite often—with Barron?"

What the hell! If this fellow just so happened to be

more gentle, more interesting, more articulate than some of her occasional partners—so bloody what!

"Yes!" She said it defiantly. "Pretty good in bed he was, too!"

"I'm sorry," he said slowly, "but Mr. Barron's dead."

"You thought I didn't know?"

"How *did* you know?"

"Come off it! I wasn't born yesterday."

He got to his feet and stepped over to sit beside her. For a while he held her right hand lightly in his; then, with his own right hand he refastened the top three buttons of the dress he'd specifically requested her to wear above no underwear.

Then he left the room and she heard his voice on the telephone: "Radio Taxis? . . . One of your drivers, as soon as you can . . . to Burford . . . on my account, please . . . Morse."

The two recently refilled glasses of champagne—the one for her, and the one for him—remained untasted on the top of the coffee table that had been polished so carefully before the arrival of Miss Debbie Richardson.

Chapter Forty-six

For the clash between the Classical and the Gothic revivals, visitors might go to the top end of Beaumont Street and compare the Greek glory of the Ashmolean on the left with the Gothic push of the Randolph Hotel on the right.

(Jan Morris, *Oxford*)

The Spires Restaurant in the Randolph Hotel is an impressively elegant affair. A full complement of Oxford College crests is mounted in a frieze around the room, the regal ambience of the place relieved by the soft lighting of flambeaux on the brown-papered walls, and by two central chandeliers, holding similar flambeaux, that hang from the high-beamed ceiling. Twenty or so tables are spaciously arranged there, cross-draped with maroon tablecloths, and laid with gleaming silverware, sparkling wineglasses, and linen serviettes of a pale-ochre color. The chairs, of uniform style, are upholstered in a material of bottle-green; and the color combination of the room *in toto* has appealed to many (if not to all) as an unusually happy one. Two large windows on the room's northern side overlook Beaumont Street, with the Ashmolean Museum and the Taylorian Institute just across the way; whilst those seated beside three equally large windows on the eastern side look out on to the Martyrs' Memorial, with St. John's and Balliol Colleges beyond it, sharing with their fellow diners a vista of St. Giles, the widest street in Oxford and visually one of the most attractive avenues in England.

At 7:15 that same evening, a man in the company of a much younger woman appeared to have eschewed either of these splendid views, for they had chosen a table (set for three) on the restaurant's west and windowless side, and now sat with their backs partly turned on the sprinkling of other early diners—like people who had no real objections to being seen, perhaps, but equally had no wish to draw attention to themselves.

At 7:25 P.M., the man was again consulting his wristwatch when a black-tied waiter asked if they would like a further drink while they waited.

Though expensive, the cocktail they had each been drinking was, in the young woman's judgment, "absolutely yummy"—Cognac, Kümmel, Fraise Liqueur, topped with chilled champagne—and she nodded. Might just as well be happy about something.

"Same again," said Frank Harrison. "Ailish cocktails." And when the waiter was gone: "Where the hell's he got to? I've not got all bloody evening."

"You've got to get back tonight, Dad?"

"That's got nothing to do with it. Seven-fifteen is seven-fifteen!"

"His hearing's not getting any better, you know. He probably thought you said seven-fifty."

"Who's ever ordered a dinner for seven-fifty, for Christ's sake?"

For the moment Sarah said nothing further, looking around her and enjoying the regal dignity of the restaurant. And in truth her father's tetchy impatience with Simon was not wholly displeasing to her. There had ever been a closer bond between herself and her father than with her mother; and, in turn, a very much closer bond between Simon and his mother than with his father. But such things were not spoken of freely in families; and it was better that way. Quite why she had always felt possessive about her father, she could not explain well even to herself. But she remembered clearly when she'd first been conscious of it: when she had crept silently downstairs late one night with a party in full swing below; and when, unseen herself, she'd watched her father kissing a young woman in the kitchen. She had cried herself to sleep that night. Only six, she'd been, but she could have murdered the woman. Disbelief? Shock? Outrage? All three mixed together, like a cocktail . . . like a cocktail topped up with a little chilled jealousy.

Simon appeared at 7:48. Like his father, not looking particularly in love with life.

"You're both early?" he ventured, as he took his seat. "Seven-fifty, wasn't it?"

"Forget it!" His father passed over a menu.

"I could do with a drink first, Dad."

"Just read the question-paper!"

Simon looked down at the succulent-sounding selections: *To Start . . . To Continue . . . Dessert . . . Beverages*—and felt a little happier, until Harrison père, brusquely ruling out starters, called over the waiter and put in their order for the main courses: Guinea Fowl; Calves' Liver; Steak (medium). "And a bottle of some decent Claret."

"Just one?" queried Simon. "Three of us?"

"Sarah's driving."

"Aren't *you* driving, Dad?" asked Sarah.

"I don't really need my daughter to tell me what I can drink, thank you very much."

Sarah put down her menu and stood up slowly. "Excuse me a minute! I'm just off to . . ."

But before making her way to the Ladies' Powder Room, Sarah Harrison stopped at Reception.

"Can I ring one of your guests from here?"

"Of course." The young girl smiled. "Just ring the room number." She pointed to the phone at the side of the desk.

"The name's Harrison—F. Harrison."

The receptionist tapped a few keys and looked at her video-screen.

"Yes. That's right."

"Can you just give me the room number?"

"I'm sorry. I can't do that. It's strict company policy—"

"I'm his daughter, for God's sake!"

"Just a minute!" The girl moved away and the phone on the desk sprang to life when she returned: "All yours."

Sarah picked up the phone and listened, wondering what on earth she was going to say. But she needn't have bothered.

"Hellóho." It was a female, husky, transatlantic voice.

Sarah put down the phone, a sudden glint of fury in her eyes.

She returned to the table to find father and brother, heads close together, in what seemed a significant conversation. But there the exchanges stopped—whether because of her own return or the contemporaneous arrival of the main courses, Sarah was uncertain.

Thereafter the food was appreciatively consumed, the few transmensal exchanges wholly mundane and perfunctory, the bottle of Claret rapidly going and going and soon wholly gone.

"Another bottle, Dad?" suggested Simon.

"No!"

"I came on the *bus*—I'm going *back* on the bus."

"But Dad's got to drive back to London, remember? Anyway I thought we were all supposed to keep sober tonight. Isn't that why we're here?"

"It *was*, yes. Just keep your voice down, will you? And read this. Simon's already seen it. Pretty quick off the mark, some of these local reporters."

Sarah looked down at the copy of the *Oxford Mail* passed across to her, the lower half of the back page folded over to show the LATEST NEWS column:

> Thousands of families evacuated as Hurricane Georges lashes Florida Keys with torrential downpours and winds of over 120 m.p.h.
>
> Huge traffic jam on A40 as lorry carrying thousands of gallons of cows' blood overturns near Eynsham
>
> Local builder John Barron of Lower Swinstead pronounced dead on arrival at JR2 after falling from ladder in Sheep Street, Burford

Chapter Forty-seven

> Different things can add up in different ways whilst reaching an identical solution, just as "eleven plus two" forms an anagram of "twelve plus one."
>
> (Margot Gleave, *A Classical Education*)

A wealth of police personnel and well-targeted inquiries had borne swift if, here and there, unexpected evidence—evidence which Sergeant Lewis (alone in his office late that Monday evening) was able to shift and to categorize at his own pace. Thus far, the facts, and the glosses on the facts, formulated themselves as follows in Lewis's mind:

First. The shiny orange-red Stanley knife had been purchased, together with other items, from a hardware shop in Burford on the Saturday of the previous week (receipt unearthed in Barron's Expenses File). Barron could still have been a murderer—of course, he could!—but quite certainly *not* with the knife he'd used that same morning as he stood almost atop the topmost section of the ladder and twisted the blade into the rotting, unresisting sill of the dormer window in Sheep Street.

Second. The stains on the overalls Barron had been wearing that morning had quite certainly *not* been human blood; but almost certainly smears of paint patented under the brand name Cremosin, two-pint tins of which were found in Barron's garage, a space now used exclusively for building and decorating materials.

Third. On the morning of the Friday when Flynn and Repp had been murdered, Barron had left home around his usual time to spend some of the morning in Thame, where two properties were inviting tenders for renovation, for which Barron had been keen to submit his own estimates. Necessarily, of course, this evidence had been taken from Barron's wife, Linda; and yet (already) a dated parking ticket for four hours that morning (South Oxon DC, Cattle Market) had been found in Barron's van—evidence, if anything, to substantiate the claim that the builder had paid for a fairly extensive stay in the center of Thame on July 24.

Fourth. There appeared, as yet, no evidence whatever that Barron had received any monies from anywhere to match the payments so regularly stashed into the balances of both Flynn and Repp. In short, *if* Barron had been the third man—*if* he had duly received his own share of the spoils for the conspiracy of silence—there was no sign of it, so far.

They were not in any way decisive, these findings and non-findings. The trouble was they all seemed to be pointing in the same direction.

Or were they?

For example (thought Lewis), it was surely to be expected that Barron would have got rid of the murder weapon and bought himself a new knife if in fact he *had* used the former for the murders.

For example (thought Lewis), it was most unlikely that Barron had only one pair of overalls. And if someone with an extravagantly fanciful mind (Morse!) could entertain the idea that a pair of white overalls covered with red paint was a good disguise for a soaking of blood . . . well, it *could* be, perhaps.

For example (thought Lewis), why buy a four-hour parking ticket in Thame on the day of the murders unless to create an alibi? Builders would usually have little difficulty in parking outside the properties in question. All right, parking was getting a nightmare everywhere, even for police cars, but . . .

For example (thought Lewis), why shouldn't Barron, like Flynn perhaps, have received his payoffs in banknotes, and kept them? No need to pay them into a bank or a building society. Why not put them in the loft? In the wardrobe? In a milk jug in the fridge? Like a few other self-employed builders, Barron might well be playing a canny little game with casual receipts, with ready-cash payments, with VAT evasions. And, if so, he would certainly not be overanxious to account for any largish sums of money regularly entrusted to some official depository.

Lewis himself had felt pretty certain that Barron was their man; Morse was absolutely convinced. And yet the evidence thus far gathered seemed to be stacking up a little bit the wrong way. Lewis knew it. He had ever been a champion of the cumulative-evidence approach to crime: a piece-by-piece aggregation against a suspect that gradually mounted into an impressively documented pile that could be forwarded to the DPP. All right! Morse's method was occasionally very different. Yet many of the murders that the pair of them had solved together had been relatively uncomplicated: no real mystery, no real cunning, no real deviousness, no carefully woven web of deceit. Domestic stuff, next-door-neighbor stuff, most of it, with the husband returning home unexpectedly from work and finding his spouse abed with postman, milk-man, gasman . . . builder?

But whichever way one looked at things, any direct evidence *against* the builder was proving surprisingly difficult to come by.

At 8:45 P.M., tired and hungry, Lewis decided that whatever further developments there were to be—and they were coming in all the time—he would have to take a break; and he drove home to Headington. But only after trying Morse's number once more. Ringing tone. No answer.

Morse came into HQ three-quarters of an hour later and rang Lewis's home number immediately. Ringing tone. Answer.

Resignedly, about to start his eggs and chips, Lewis brought Morse up to date with the information received, suggesting that it was, at this point, all a bit ambivalent and equivocal, although in truth Lewis made use of neither of these epithets himself.

Morse sounded mildly interested, giving his own verdict in somewhat pompous terms. He asserted that the character of the human condition was indeed "ambiguity," the virtually inseparable mixture of the true and the false. But in the present case such apparent contradictions could be explained so very easily—in fact in exactly the way Lewis himself had just explained them. "And," continued Morse, "you can be quite sure of one thing—no, two things: Barron murdered the pair of 'em; then somebody murdered Barron. Get that clear in your head, and we might make a bit of progress. OK? I'll see you in the morning."

"Sir! Before you ring off. We tried to get you several times earlier but there was the engaged tone all the time."

"That's funny. I only remember making the one call."

"I thought perhaps—you know, you seemed a bit whacked . . ."

"You'd be wrong, Lewis. I *nearly* spent some time in bed. Not quite, though. Goodnight."

* * *

The dramatic news came in at twenty minutes to midnight, as Morse sat at home making out a rough draft of his will. He'd no immediate relatives remaining, none at all; and therefore instructions for the postmortem dissemination of all his worldly goods should not present too much of a complication. Nor did they. And he was writing out a fairish copy of a simple second draft—when the phone rang.

"What?"

. . .

"What?"

. . .

It was two minutes later before he spoke again: "I'll be over straightaway."

Chapter Forty-eight

> We trust we are not guilty of sacrilege in suggesting that the teaching of Religious Knowledge in some schools would pose an almighty challenge even for the Almighty Himself.
> (From the Introduction to *Religious Education in Secondary Schools: 1967–87,* HMSO)

Roy Holmes, aged fifteen, was a crudely disruptive pupil at school, a truculently uncooperative son in the Witney Street house he shared with his invalid mother, and a menace wherever he walked in the wider community. He took drugs; he was an inveterate and skillful shoplifter; he regularly snapped the stems of newly planted trees striving to establish themselves; he spat disgusting gobbets of phlegm on most of the pavements in Burford. In short, Roy Holmes was an appalling specimen of humankind. He deserved to have no real friends at all in life; and he had none.

Except one.

* * *

Ms. Christine Coverley, aged twenty-seven, in her second year at Burford Secondary School, was not an impressive personage. A small, skinny, flat-chested, spotty-chinned, mousy-haired woman, she could scarcely have expected admirers anywhere—either among her fellow male members of staff, or among the motley collection of pupils, especially the boys, she was timetabled to teach. And, indeed, she had no such admirers.

Except one.

To complicate her incompetence as a teacher, she had been appointed *faute de mieux* to teach Religious Knowledge, a task wholly beyond her ability. Her classes taunted her mercilessly; and on more than one occasion such was the uproar in her classroom that teachers in adjacent rooms had barged in—only to find, with deep embarrassment, that a nominal teacher was already present there; and with even deeper embarrassment for Ms. Coverley herself, resulting in fevered nightmares and anguish of soul that was often unbearable. One class, 4 Remove (Holmes's class), was even worse than the others—a group of pagan half-wits, of both sexes, whose interest in the pronouncements of major and minor prophets alike was nil. Over the year her hebdomadal clash with these monsters had been a terrifying ordeal; and the situation was quite hopeless. But no—not quite hopeless. Each night of term she would kneel in her bedsit and beseech the Almighty to grant her some deliverance from such despair. And one day her prayer had been answered.

In the middle of the summer term, at the end of one of her spectacularly disastrous lessons with 4 Remove, her eyes smarting with tears of humiliation, she had stopped the cocky, surly Holmes as he was about to leave the room:

"Roy! I know I'm useless. I *wouldn't* be though—if I got a bit of help, but I don't get any help from anyone. I just want some help. And there's someone who *could* help me so easily if he wanted to. *You,* Roy!"

She turned away, wiped her moist cheeks, picked up her books, and left the empty classroom.

But Roy Holmes stood where he was, immobile. For the first time in his life someone had asked him for help—*him*—the despair of mother, vicar, social workers, headmaster, police; and suddenly he'd felt oddly, unprecedentedly moved, conscious somewhere deep inside himself of a compassion he'd never known and could scarcely recognize.

If, as Ms. Coverley believed, her God sometimes moved in a mysterious way, it was not quite so dramatic as the way in which Roy Holmes was soon to move. In the next RK lesson one of the boys in the back row had been particularly foul-mouthed and disruptive, whilst Holmes had remained completely silent. After school that day, the youth in question returned home with a bleeding mouth, two broken teeth, and one bruised and hugely swollen eye. No one knew who was responsible. But then no one needed to know, since everyone knew who was responsible.

The nightmares were over, and Ms. Coverley's last few weeks of the summer term were almost happy ones. Yet she knew that she was not the stuff that teachers are made of, and her resignation was received with relief by the headmaster. For the time being she decided to stay on in Burford, renewing the let on her ground-floor bedsit for a further two months.

The bell rang at 11:15 P.M. and Roy Holmes, somewhat the worse for drink or drugs or both, stood at the door when she opened it. His words were the words she had used to him, almost exactly so:

"I just want some help. And there's someone who can help me, if she wants to. You!"

It wasn't a lot he had to say; not a lot *she* had to say to the duty sergeant, half an hour later, when she rang Burford Police Station; and not a lot when *he*, in turn, rang Thames Valley HQ, almost immediately put through to the home number of the man in charge of the inquiry into the death of J. Barron, Builder.

Roy Holmes, a pupil of Burford Secondary School, aged fifteen, living at 29A Witney Street, had been riding his mountain bike along the footway on the south-

ern side of Sheep Street at approximately 10 A.M. that
Monday, August 3. By the youth's own admission he
was showing off, expectorating regularly, terrorizing
any pedestrians, riding no-handed—when he'd decided
to defy all superstition and ride beneath the ladder he
saw in front of him—when he'd badly misjudged whatever he'd misjudged—when he'd collided sharply with
the bottom of the ladder—when the whole thing had
jerked sideways—and when a man had toppled from
the top of the ladder and landed on the compacted pathway outside "Collingwood" ...

Chapter Forty-nine

> "God save thee, ancient Mariner!
> From the fiends, that plague thee thus!—
> Why look'st thou so?"—"With my cross-bow
> I shot the Albatross."
>   (Coleridge, The Rime of the Ancient Mariner)

The following morning, Morse had been early summoned to the presence, summoned to Caesar's tent.

"Won't do, will it, Morse. Just won't do! You tell us
to go and bring Barron in. And why? Because you say
he's knifed Flynn and Repp. Fine! There's three of 'em,
you say, originally involved in the cover-up over the
Harrison murder, three of 'em prepared to stick to their
stories—for a fee of course. Then suddenly we find two
of 'em murdered, and somebody—*somebody*, Morse—
thinks this'll be as good an opportunity as any to finish
off number three. So whoever this somebody is, he
decided he's been forking out way over the odds anyway, and he goes ahead with his plan. He's been living
with three albatrosses round his neck, and suddenly he
finds somebody else has cut the strings off *two* of 'em.
Too good an opportunity to be missed. All adds up,

doesn't it? Except, matey, for one thing: Barron's death turns out to be a bloody *accident*. Just some teenage lout . . ."

Strange took a breather, gulped down the last of his coffee, and stuck another chocolate biscuit in his mouth: "Fancy a coffee?"

"No."

"They'll be open in an hour, you mean?"

"Fifty minutes, actually."

Strange suddenly sounded extremely pleased with himself: "Did you actually say 'actually,' Morse?"

Oh dear.

It was Strange who broke the ensuing silence. "Where are we, in all this?" he asked softly.

"I dunno. I felt convinced that the same fellow— Barron—had murdered both of them, both Flynn and Repp. I thought the motive was a pretty familiar one— money. You know, there's nothing much worse in life than people doing the same job and getting paid at different rates. It happens in every office, in every profession in the land. Anger . . . jealousy . . . bitterness . . . usually controllable but potentially dynamite. And I thought Barron had found out he wasn't doing half so well as his partners in crime."

"And who exactly is this golden goose?"

"You know that as well as I do."

"I do?"

"Oh, yes," replied Morse quietly.

A knock at the door heralded PC Kershaw, the fast-track recruit with a First in History from Keble who'd driven Morse out to Sutton Courtenay, and whose duties for the present consisted mostly of supplying the Chief Superintendent with regular coffee and chocolate biscuits.

"Anything I can do for you, sir?"

"Yes," growled Strange. "Bugger off!" Then, turning back to Morse: "Are you making *any* progress?"

"Early days. We've not even had the final path reports yet. Life's full of surprises."

"And disappointments."

"That too, yes."

"Well if it *wasn't* Barron . . ."

"Dunno. But I'm sure the key figure in both cases is one and the same person—the man who was in bed with Yvonne Harrison the night she was murdered."

"You don't think it was Repp?"

"No. As I see it, Repp had been recceing the property, maybe for several nights. It was going to be a gift for any professional burglar like him. And he knew pretty well all that went on that night—"

"Knew the fellow who was in bed with Yvonne?"

"Yes. But I don't think it was Repp or any other burglar who disturbed the bondage session that evening. I think that was somebody else. And I think it's most likely that our lover-boy knew that someone else."

"And in your book Barron was the lover-boy?"

"Well, he was doing a job for her—hanging about the place quite a bit—strong, good-looking sort of fellow—the husband away a good deal of the time . . ."

"But I'll say it again—what if it *wasn't* Barron?"

"Plenty of other candidates, surely?"

"Oh yes?"

Morse measured his words carefully. "I think that anyone meeting Yvonne Harrison, if she turned things on a bit—anyone, including me—would have given a month's beer money—"

"A week's in your case."

"—for an hour or two between the sheets, or between the bedposts, or between anywhere else. By, er, by all accounts she was a . . . well, let's say she had the same effect on men as they tell me Viagra has on the impotent, or the victims of chronic erectile dysfunction, as they're known these days."

"Really! So for all we know, this chap could have been a client from North Wales or somewhere."

"More probably South Wales, sir."

"And much more probably, somebody local."

"Agreed."

"Any ideas?"

"Well, the only fellow I've met in that little community who's topped up with surplus testosterone is the landlord of the Maiden's Arms."

"You've interviewed him?"

"No."

"Why not?"

"Because I'm still trying to come to terms with the fact that it *wasn't* Barron. You see I still think he's the key to all this ridiculously complex business. But complex only because those involved deliberately *made* it complex."

"Barron's phone calls, you mean? No luck there?"

"No. Change of BT office, change of procedure, change of monitoring, files reclassified . . . no hope! Wouldn't help anyway. All Barron said was that he'd rung her and the number was engaged; and then rung her again and the call wasn't answered. Neat, wasn't it? No record of anything."

"He was lying, you think?"

"Yes."

"What about the burglar alarm?"

"Thunderstorm, possibly—that sets 'em off."

"There wasn't a thunderstorm that night."

"No? Probably a cat then—they set 'em off too."

"They hadn't got a cat."

"Oh."

Strange lumbered to his feet. "Look! You surely don't still think Barron's your man, do you?"

Morse smiled. *"Don't I?"*

Chapter Fifty

> I can't tell a lie—not even when I hear one.
> (John Bangs, 1862–1922)

In the world of detective fiction, alibis are frequently concocted in order to mystify the reader. In what is called the "real" world they usually provide an invalu-

able method of eliminating a few runners in an already
limited field, thereby affording the police a better
prospect of backing the likely winner. For (except in
Morse's mind) an alibi is an alibi: if someone is seen in
one place at one particular time, it seems highly improbable that this same someone may be seen in some
other place at the *same* time. Yet it is sometimes difficult
adequately to corroborate an alibi—viz, that plea of the
criminal to have been in another place at the material
time; and alibis may well be doubted, closely checked,
and indeed, on occasion, be spectacularly broken.

This in various ways.

It is highly unlikely, for example, that a well-focused
video camera will be in operation in that first particular
place; and even if it is, some smart electronic alec may
well be able to doctor the evidence. Almost always,
therefore, corroboration will depend on the testimony
of eyewitnesses who, even if honest, can be the victims
of tricks of memory over times and sightings; *or* on the
testimony of witnesses who are dishonest, and are willing to fabricate falsehoods—for friends, perhaps, or for
a fee. The alibi problem is further complicated by the
confident assertion of some mystic sects that one *can*, in
fact, be in two places simultaneously, although the
police are grateful that such bizarre beliefs are currently
not widely embraced.

Morse himself championed the view that all alibis
should probably be ignored in the first instance, on the
not illogical grounds that if just *one* of them were suspect, it was sensible to assume that all of them were . . .

Such views (with variants) Sergeant Lewis had heard
several times before, and it was therefore with some dif-
fidence that he broached the subject the following
morning.

"Don't you reckon it would be a good idea to get all
these alibis sorted out a bit clearer?"

"A bit more clearly, Lewis."

"The night Mrs. Harrison was murdered, the morning Flynn and Repp were murdered—"

"And don't forget Monday morning."

"Barron, you mean? You surely don't still think—?"

Morse held up his right hand in surrender. "You're right, perhaps. Let's make a list. Well, you make a list. Ready?"

He steepled his slim fingers in front of him and stared into the middle distance, though with little observable enthusiasm in his eyes:

"Frank Harrison
Simon Harrison
Sarah Harrison
Harry Repp
John Barron . . ."

"That's the short list?"

Morse nodded.

"OK. First I'll recheck where they all were, or where they were all supposed to be, first when Mrs. Harrison—"

"Already been done. You've read the files."

"Weren't checked very thoroughly though, some of 'em."

"Long time ago, Lewis. People forget or want to forget or pretend to forget."

"A day like that though, when she was murdered? Biggest day in village history. Everybody remembers where they were, like when Kennedy was assassinated."

"Nonsense, Lewis! People remember where they were and what they were doing at the time they *heard* of things like that. Agreed. But what else? Do you remember what you were doing for the rest of the day when Kennedy was shot? Do you?"

"No. I take your point, sir."

"Who are you thinking of particularly?"

"Well the family got away with some pretty flimsy alibis, didn't they? Especially Simon and Sarah. No one seems to have checked them much at all."

"Ye-es."

"Simon said he got home from work about a quarter past five, had a meal, then went down to the ABC cinema in George Street to see *The Full Monty*. Still had his ticket if I remember rightly."

Morse nodded and Lewis continued:

"Sarah? She was at a diabetes conference in the Radcliffe Infirmary that day—no doubt about that. And after it had finished she went over the road to the Royal Oak for a drink with a few friends—no doubt about that either—and then left for her flat in Jericho at about a quarter to seven, where she listened to *The Archers*, had a long hot bath, watched the *Nine O'Clock News*, and then had an early night."

"Making no mention in the course of her evidence that she had a phone call in the middle of the evening, as a result of which she tore down to the ABC Cinema, bought a ticket for *The Full Monty*—"

"Probably no seats left that night, sir."

"—bought a ticket and promptly tore it across the middle and then tore out of the place—"

"Sir! Not so much of this tearing about all over the shop! She'd sprained her ankle just before then and she'd probably be hobbling—"

"—she hobbled out of the cinema with a very valuable little alibi in her pretty little hand."

"Alibi for Simon, you mean?"

"Or for herself."

"You're losing me again, sir."

"I'm losing myself. Don't worry."

"What about Frank Harrison?"

"You tell *me*!"

"Well, anyone who finds the body first is usually going to be number one in your book, I know that. But there's no doubt about Paddy Flynn being on taxi shift from 8 P.M. that night. He was seen on and off by his fellow drivers as well as being contacted at regular intervals from base. No doubt either about him picking up Frank Harrison about eleven from Oxford railway station. But that's not to say—*is* it, sir?—that Harrison had just got off a train at the railway station. It would be the most natural thing in the world for anyone to *think* he had, but . . ."

Morse smiled. "Could hardly have put it better myself. But somebody paid Flynn for something. So it was probably for something that happened after eleven o'clock. And there was only one person with Flynn then: Frank Harrison. And he's the only one of the whole bunch with the sort of money to buy Flynn off."

"*And* buy Repp off, if we're right about him being there that night. Harrison must be earning, well . . ."

"A little more than you are, Lewis, yes. In fact he got a bonus—a *bonus*—of £85,000 last year. Seems he was sorting out his bank's involvement in the Nazi confiscation of Jewish assets, and his bosses were more than pleased with him."

"How on earth do you know that?"

"Aren't we supposed to be detectives?"

Lewis pursued the matter no further. "So, what do you think?"

"Waste of time as far as the children are concerned. But it might help to look at their father again."

"You think it was Harrison who murdered his wife?"

"I dunno."

"You think he murdered Flynn and Repp?"

"He had enough reason to. He couldn't go on forking out indefinitely."

"So we'd better have a careful check on wherever *he* was that Friday morning."

"Well, wherever else he was he wasn't in his London office."

"How on earth—?"

"What else can I tell you?" asked Morse wearily.

"I've just asked you. Do you think he murdered Flynn and Repp?"

"He could have done. But somehow I don't believe he did."

"So who. . . ?"

"I keep telling you, Lewis. My modest bet is still on Barron."

"Shouldn't we be looking a bit more into their backgrounds? Repp's? Flynn's? Barron's?"

"I don't think we're going to get anything more out of Debbie Richardson."

"Why do you say that?"

"Just a feeling, Lewis. Just a feeling."

"What about Flynn?"

Morse nodded. "You're right. He was being paid for something. Exactly what, though ... Yes. Leave that to me."

"What about Barron? Shall I leave that to you, as well?"

"No, no! The less I have to do with the women in this case the better. You go along. And if you can find out more about where he was or where he was supposed to be on both those days ... Yes, you do that!"

"All right. But don't you think we ought to widen the net, sir? Haven't we got any other suspects?"

"Tom Biffen, perhaps?"

Lewis's eyebrows shot up. "You mean—?"

"The landlord of the Maiden's Arms, no less. We'll go out and interview him together once we get a chance. You'll be able to buy me a pint."

"But wasn't it a Tuesday when Mrs. Harrison was murdered?"

"You're right, yes."

"Well, he always goes out fishing on Tuesdays, Biffen—dawn to dusk."

"Really? How on earth do you know that?"

"Aren't we supposed to be detectives, sir?"

Chapter Fifty-one

Once cheated, wife or husband feels the same; and where there's marriage without love, there will be love without marriage.

(Benjamin Franklin, *Poor Richard's Almanack*)

At 9:30 A.M. the following day, Mrs. Linda Barron stepped back from the threshold, nodding rather wearily as Lewis produced his ID. In the kitchen, he accepted her offer of instant coffee.

She was a brunette of medium height, slightly overweight, with a small, cupid-lipped mouth, wearing a blue-striped kitchen apron over skirt and blouse.

Lewis decided she was coping with life, just about.

The smallish kitchen was cluttered with shelves and cupboards, the floor space additionally limited by the usual appliances: cooker, dishwasher, fridge, microwave, washing machine. Lewis immediately noticed the damp patch of crumbling ceiling over the cooker. Same old story! Husband a plumber, and a tap-washer never gets fixed; husband a builder, and there's a two-year wait before a bit of replastering gets done . . . Difficult to say, offhand, whether the Barrons were better or worse off than they appeared.

From experience, Lewis had learned never to try his hand at commiseration or counseling; but when he questioned her, he did so in the kindly fashion that was his wont. He asked her tactfully about the times and places relevant to her husband's alibis; more tactfully about the family finances; most tactfully about the state of her marriage.

Alibis? On the two key dates she could be of little help. Mondays to Fridays he usually got home about 6 P.M., when she'd have a cooked meal ready for him. Between 8 and 9 P.M. he'd quite often go out for a pint or two, either down at the local or sometimes at a pub in Burford. But he wasn't a big drinker. She knew he'd rung up Mrs. Harrison on the night of her murder— something about roofing tiles—but he'd not been able to get through. Tried twice—he'd told her so; the police knew all about that, though: it had been important evidence. On the second key date, the Friday, he'd gone off to Thame in the morning, she remembered that. He'd been asked for an estimate on some work there, and he'd gone over to size up the job. She didn't know— didn't ask—what he'd done after that; but he was back home at the usual sort of time. He always was on Fridays, because it was eggs-and-chips day—his favorite meal.

Mr. J. Barron, Builder, was going up in Lewis's esteem.

Money? They were OK. For the past three years or so houses were selling fairly freely again; and mobility in the housing market always meant new owners wanting some renovation or structural changes: conservatories, extensions, garages, loft conversions, patios. Yes, the past few years had been fairly good for them: she knew that better than he did. Her part in the business, for which she took a small official salary, was to look after the books: tax returns, invoices, VAT, expenses, bad debts—everything. If he was ever in the habit of accepting cash instead of the usual check payments, she wasn't aware of it; and quite certainly neither of them was sufficiently bright in business-finance to be able to exploit any tax loopholes. She knew nothing about any regular payments in cash. ("What payments?") She'd have known if any envelopes had arrived through the post, because the mail was invariably delivered *after* he'd set off for work every morning. They had a joint account; and he had a separate private account, with an overdraft facility of £2,000.

Mr. J. Barron, Builder, Lewis decided, was hardly in the Gates or the Soros brackets.

Marriage? It was only here that Linda Barron was less than fluent in her answers.

"Would you say the pair of you had a 'tight' marriage?"

". . . Perhaps not, no."

"Was he ever unfaithful?"

"Aren't *most* men?"

"Not all of them," said Lewis quietly.

She shrugged her shoulders.

"*Was* he?"

". . . He may have been."

"Do you think he ever had an affair with Mrs. Harrison?"

". . . No."

"Would you have known?"

She smiled bleakly. "Probably."

"What about you, Mrs. Barron? Were *you* ever unfaithful?"

". . . Once or twice."

"With Harry Repp?"

"God, no! I hardly knew him."

"Tom Biffen?"

". . . Once. He called one afternoon about eighteen months ago to bring a leg of lamb Johnnie won in the raffle. And . . ."

"What happened?"

"Do I *have* to tell you, Sergeant?"

"No. No, you don't, Mrs. Barron."

Wedlock for the Barrons (Lewis agreed with Dixon) did not appear to have been a wholly idyllic affair.

As he left, Lewis noticed on the wall in the hallway a framed photograph of a strong, fine-looking man in military uniform.

"Your husband?"

She nodded; and the rust-flecked hazel eyes were filmed with tears.

Chapter Fifty-two

> With a gen'rous ol' pal who will pick up the tab
> It's always real cool in a nice taxi-cab.
> (J. Willington Spoole, *Mostly on the Dole*)

If Lewis's (Morse-initiated) interview had been a task of some fair difficulty, Morse's own (self-appointed) mission was wholly straightforward—the single problem being that of finding a parking space in a car-cluttered Warwick Street, just off the Iffley Road.

In the outer office of Radio Taxis were seated two young ladies, their telephones, keyboards, and VDUs in front of them, with maps of Oxford, Oxfordshire, and the UK pinned on the walls around. Morse was ushered through into the inner sanctum, where a six-foot, strongly built man of fifty or so, his short, dark hair greying at the temples, introduced himself:

"Jeff Measor, Company Secretary. How can I help?"

"Flynn, Paddy Flynn, he used to work for you—until you sacked him."

Yes. Measor remembered him well enough. Flynn had worked for the company for just over a year. It was generally agreed that he'd been a competent driver, but he'd never fitted very happily into the team. There'd been several complaints from clients, including the reported "Just help me get these bitches out of here!" request to the doorman at The Randolph, where three giggly and slightly unstable young ladies were attempting to alight. And, yes, a few other complaints about his less-than-sympathetic rejoinders to clients when sometimes (quite inevitably so) traffic jams had caused his cab to be late. But Flynn had been a punctual man himself, invariably clocking in on time—one of those dedicated night drivers who far preferred the 6 P.M.–2:30 A.M. shift. He'd known Oxford City and the surrounding area well—a big factor in taxi work; and there'd been no suspicion of his driving innocent clients on some roundabout route just to jump up the fare.

"Could he have fiddled a few quid here and there?"

"Not so easy these days. Everything's computerized in the cab. But I suppose . . ."

"How?"

"Well, let's say if he's cruising around the City Centre and gets a fare and doesn't clock it in. Just takes the cash and then goes back to cruising round as if he's been doing nothing else all the time . . ."

"Did he do that sort of thing?"

"Not that I know of."

Morse was looking increasingly puzzled. "He seems to have been a reasonably satisfactory sort of cabbie, then."

"Well . . ."

"So why did you sack him?"

"Two things, really. As I said, he wasn't a good advertisement for the company. We always tell our drivers about the importance of friendliness and courtesy; but he wasn't quite . . . he always seemed a bit surly, and I doubt he ever swapped a few cheerful words with any of his passengers. Man of few words, Paddy Flynn. Not always though, by all accounts."

"No?"

"No. Seems he used to do the rounds of the pubs and clubs—Oxford, Reading, and so on—with a little group. Played the clarinet himself, and introduced things with a bit of Irish blarney. Quite popular for a while, I think, 'specially in those pubs guaranteeing music being played as loud as possible."

Morse looked pained as Measor continued: "Anyway, he just didn't fit in here. No one really liked him much. Simple as that!"

"*Two* things though, you said?" prompted Morse gently.

For the first time the articulately forthright Company Secretary was somewhat hesitant:

"It's a bit difficult to explain but . . . well, he never quite seemed up to coping with the radio side of the job. Still very important, the radio side is, in spite of all this latest technology. You know the sort of thing: we'll be phoning from the office here and asking one of the drivers if he's anywhere near Headington or Abingdon Road or wherever . . . Mind you, Inspector, the radio's not all *that* easy: distortion, interference, crackle, feedback, traffic noise . . . You've certainly got to have your wits about you—and, well, he just couldn't quite cope with it well enough."

"It doesn't seem all that much of a reason for sacking him, though."

"It's not exactly like that, Inspector. You see, I don't myself employ drivers directly. They're contracted out to me. And so if I say to any owner of a taxi, or a group of taxis, 'Look, there's no more work for you here'—well, that's it. It's like sub-contracting work on a building site. If I want to sack one of my staff here though,

in the office, I'll have to give one verbal—recorded—
and two written warnings."

"No problems with Flynn, then?"

"Oh, no. And glad to see the back of him. Everybody
was. One day he was here . . ."

". . . and the next day he was gone," added Morse
slowly, as he thanked the Company Secretary—and
felt that long familiar shiver of excitement along his
shoulders.

Chapter Fifty-three

> At which period there were gentlemen and there were sea-
> men in the navy. But the seamen were not gentlemen; and
> the gentlemen were not seamen.
>
> (Macaulay, *History of England*)

For Morse, that early evening followed much the same
old pattern: same sort of bundle of ideas abounding in
his brain; same impatience to reach that final, wonderfully satisfying, penny-dropping moment of insight;
same old pessimism about the future of mankind; same
old craving for a dram of Scotch that could make the
world, at least for a while, a kindlier and a happier
place; same old chauffeur—Lewis.

It was just after 6:30 P.M. when they were shown up
a spiral flight of rickety stairs to the small office immediately above the bar of the Maiden's Arms. Around the
walls, several framed diplomas paid tribute to the landlord's expertise and the cleanliness of his kitchen,
although the untidy piles of letters and forms that lit-
tered the desk suggested a less than methodical
approach to the hostelry's paperwork.

"Quick snifter, Inspector?"

"Later, perhaps."

"Mind if I, er. . . ?" Biffen reached behind him and

poured out a liberal tot of Captain Morgan. "You make me feel nervous!" Knocking back the neat rum in a single swallow, he smacked his lips crudely: "Ahh!"

"Royal or Merchant?" asked Morse.

"Bit o' both." But Biffen seemed disinclined to discuss his earlier years at sea and came to the point immediately: "How can I help you, gentlemen?"

So Morse told him: for the moment the village seemed to be at the center of almost everything; and the pub was at the center of village life and gossip; and the landlord was always going to be at the center of the pub; so if . . .

For Lewis, Morse's subsequent interrogation seemed (indeed, was) aimless and desultory.

But Biffen had little to tell.

Of *course* the villagers had talked—still talked—talked all the time except when that media lot or the police came round. No secret, though, that the locals knew enough about Mrs. H.'s occasional and more than occasional liaisons; no secret that they listened with prurient interest to the rumors, the wilder and whackier the better, concerning Mrs. H.'s sexual predilections.

It was left to Lewis to cover the crucial questions concerning alibis.

The day of Mrs. H.'s murder? Tuesday, that was. And Tuesday was always a special day—a sacrosanct sort of day. (He'd mentioned it earlier.) His one day off in the week when he refused to have anything at all to do with cellarage, bar-tending, pub meals—fuck 'em all! Secretary of the Oxon Pike Anglers' Association, he was. Had been for the past five years. Labor of love! And every Tuesday during the fishing season he was out all day, dawn to dusk. Back late, almost always, though he couldn't say exactly when that day. No one had questioned him at the time. Why should they? He'd pretty certainly have met a few of his fellow anglers but . . . what the hell was all this about anyway? Was he suddenly on the suspect list? After all this time?

Thomas Biffen's eyes had hardened; and looking across at the brawny tattooed arms, the ex-boxer Sergeant Lewis

found himself none too anxious ever to confront the landlord in a cul-de-sac.

Biffen was a family man? Well, yes and no, really.
He'd been married—still was, in the legal sense. But his
missus had gone off four years since, taking their two
children with her: Joanna, aged three at the time, and
Daniel, aged two. He still regularly gave her some financial support; always sent his kids something for their
birthdays and Christmas. But that side of things had
never been much of a problem. She was living with this
fellow in Weston-super-Mare—fellow she'd known a
long time— the same fellow in fact she'd buggered off
with when they'd broken up.

"Whose fault was that?" asked Morse quietly.

Biffen shrugged. "Bit o' both, usually, innit?"

"She'd been seeing someone else?"

Biffen nodded.

"Had *you* been seeing someone else?"

Biffen nodded.

"Someone local."

"What's that got to do with it?"

It was Morse's turn to shrug.

"Well . . . chap's got to get his oats occasionally,
Inspector."

"Mrs. Harrison?"

Biffen shook his head. "Wouldna minded, though!"

"Mrs. Barron?"

"Linda? Huh! Not much chance there—with *him*
around? SAS man, he was. Probably slice your prick off
if he copped you mucking around with his missus."

Lewis found himself recalling the photograph of the
confident-looking young militiaman.

"Debbie Richardson?" suggested Morse.

"Most people've had a bit on the side with her."

"You called yourself occasionally? While Harry was
inside?"

"Once or twice."

"Including the day after he was murdered."

"Only to take a bottle—I told you that."

"You fancied her?"

"Who wouldn't? Once she's got the hots on . . ."

Morse appeared to have lost his way, and it was Lewis who completed the questioning: "Where were you earlier on the Friday when Flynn and Repp were murdered?"

"In the morning? Went into Oxford shopping. Not much luck, though. Tried to get a couple of birthday presents. You'd hardly credit it, but both o' my kids were born the same day—3rd o' September."

"Real coincidence."

"Depends which way you look at it, Sergeant. Others'd call it precision screwing, wouldn't they?"

It was a crude remark, and Morse's face was a study in distaste as Biffen continued: "Couldn't find anything in the shops though, could I? So I sent their mum a check instead."

Downstairs, it was far too early for any brisk activity; but three of the regulars were already foregathered there, to each of whom Biffen proffered a customary greeting.

"Evening, Mr. Bagshaw! Evening, Mr. Blewitt!"

One of the warring partners allowed himself a perfunctory nod, but the other was happily intoning a favorite passage from the cribbage litany: "Fifteen-two; fifteen-four; two's six; three's nine; and three's twelve!"

With an "Evening, Mr. Thomas!" the landlord had completed his salutations.

In response, the youth pressed the start button yet again, his eyes keenly registering the latest alignment of the symbols on the fruit machine.

"Now! What's it to be, gentlemen? On the house, of course."

"Pint of bitter," said Morse, "and an orange juice. Want some ice in it, Lewis?"

A bored-looking barmaid folded up the *Mirror* and pulled the hand-pump on the Burton Ale.

Chapter Fifty-four

> *The time you won your town the race*
> *We chaired you through the market-place;*
> *Man and boy stood cheering by,*
> *And home we brought you shoulder-high.*
>
> *To-day, the road all runners come,*
> *Shoulder-high we bring you home,*
> *And set you at your threshold down,*
> *Townsman of a stiller town.*
>
> (A. E. Housman, *A Shropshire Lad*, XIX)

It was just after 7:30 P.M. that same evening in the car park of the Maiden's Arms that Morse, after admitting to a very strange lapse of memory in missing *The Archers*, suddenly decided on a new line of inquiry that seemed to Lewis (if possible) even stranger: "Drive me round to Holmes's place in Burford."

"Why—?" began a weary Lewis.

"Get *on* with it!"

The ensuing conversation was brief. "What did you make of Biffen, sir?"

"He decided to enlist in the ranks of the liars, like the rest of 'em."

"Well, yes . . . if Mrs. Barron was telling me the truth."

"Probably not important anyway."

Lewis waited a while. "What *is* important, sir?"

"Barron! That's what's important. I'm still not absolutely sure I was on the wrong track but . . ."

". . . but it looks as if you were."

Morse nodded.

"What did you make of—?"

"Concentrate on the driving, Lewis! They're not used to Formula-One fanatics round here."

A blurred shape slowly formed through the frosted glass of the front door, its green paint peeling or already peeled, which was finally opened by a pale-faced, wispily haired woman of some fifty-plus summers.

Lewis paraded his ID. "Mrs. Holmes?"

With hardly a glance at the documentation, the woman neatly reversed her wheelchair and led her visitors through the narrow, bare-floored, virtually bare-walled passageway—for indeed there was just the one framed memento of something on the wall to the left.

"I suppose it's about Roy?" She spoke with the dispirited nasal whine of a Birmingham City supporter whose team has just been defeated.

In the living room, in a much-frayed armchair, sat a youth smoking a cigarette, drinking directly from a can of Bass, a pair of black-stringed amplifiers stuck in his ears.

He vaguely reminded Morse of someone; but that was insufficient to stop him taking an intense and instant dislike to the boy, who had made no attempt to straighten his lounging sprawl, or to miss a single lyric from the latest rap record—until he saw Morse's lips speaking directly to him.

"Wha'?" Reluctantly Roy Holmes removed one of the ear-pieces.

"Why didn't you answer the door yourself, lad, and give your mum a break?"

The youth's eyes stared back with cold hostility. "Couldn't 'ear it, could I? Not wi' this on."

No Brummy accent there; instead, the Oxfordshire burr with its curly vowels.

His mother began to explain. "It's the police, Roy—"

"Again? Bin there, 'aven't I. Made me statement. What more do they want? Accident, wonnit? I didn't try to 'ide nuthin. What the fuck?"

Morse responded quietly to the outburst. "We appreciate your cooperation. But do you know what you've

made of yourself in life so far? Shall I tell you, lad?
You're about the most uncouth and loutish fourteen-
year-old I've ever—"

"*Fifteen*-year-old," interposed Mrs. Holmes, more
anxious, it seemed, to correct her son's natal credentials
than to deny his innate crudity. "Fifteen on March the
26th. Got it wrong in the papers, didn't they?"

"Well, well! Same birthday as Housman."

Silence.

"*And*" (Morse now spoke directly to the mother)
"he'll be able to smoke in a year's time, and go to the
pub for a pint a couple of years after that—if you give
him some pocket money, Mrs. Holmes. Because I can't
see him earning anything much himself, not in his present frame of mind."

If Lewis had earlier noticed the telltale sign of drug
dependency in the boy's eyes, he now saw a wider blaze
of hatred there; and was sure that Morse was similarly
and equally aware of both, as Mrs. Holmes switched
her wheelchair abruptly around and faced Morse
aggressively:

"It was an accident—could happen to anybody—
he didn't mean no trouble—like he *said*—like he *told*
you . . . That's right, isn't it, Roy?"

"Leave me be!"

"Perhaps it wasn't you we came to Burford to see."

For a few seconds there was a look of bewilderment,
of anxiety almost, on Roy Holmes's face. Then, draining his can of beer, he got to his feet, and left the room.

Seconds later the front door slammed behind him
with potentially glass-shattering force.

"What time will he be back?" asked Lewis.

She shrugged her narrow shoulders.

"You worry about him?"

"Everybody worries about him."

"How long's he been on drugs?"

"Year—over a year."

"How does he pay for them?"

"You tell *me*."

"Not much of a son, is he?" said Morse.

She shook what once must have been a very pretty head with a gesture of desperation.

"Does he get the money from you?"

"I've got nothing to give him. He's not stupid. He knows that."

"But. . . ?" Morse pointed to the empty beer can; the empty packet of cigarettes.

"I dunno."

Morse got to his feet. Lewis too.

"How long. . . ?" Morse nodded to the wheelchair.

"Six years."

Morse stopped in front of the one framed picture in the dingy hallway. Not a picture, though. A diploma.

Oxfordshire, Buckinghamshire, Berkshire
Athletics Association

This is to certify that in the annual three-counties cross-country championships held in Cutteslowe Park, Oxford, on the 19th July, 1974, the winner of the ladies event from a field of seventy-two runners was:

ELIZABETH JANE THOMAS

Congratulations!
Signed: *Monty Hillier* (Assn. Pres.)

For the second time that day Lewis noticed a film of tears in a woman's eyes; and for the second time that day Morse felt a shudder of excitement run along his shoulders.

Before they left, Morse turned to the erstwhile athlete. "The gods haven't smiled on you much, have they?"

"Not that I've noticed."

"It's important for your son to do exactly what they've told him—with his Police Protection Order. You know that?"

"I suppose so."

"And if you want cheering up a bit, Mrs. Holmes, I'll tell you a big secret: I was about his age when I started drinking myself. A year younger, in fact."

But the confession appeared to bring little comfort to the woman maneuvering her wheelchair to the front door.

Morse gave her his card. "One last thing. If there's anything you've forgotten to tell me? Anything you've not been willing to tell me. . . ?"

As the two detectives walked along the litter-strewn path up to a wooden front gate stripped of all but two of its vertical slats, Lewis's mind puzzled itself over those last few words. But Morse seemed deep in thought; and any questions for the moment, he knew, would be wholly inopportune.

Chapter Fifty-five

> Wherefore seeing we also are compassed about with so great a cloud of witnesses, let us lay aside every prejudice and error that doth so easily beset us.
>
> (St. Paul, *Hebrews,* ch. XII, v. 1)

In his own way, Lewis was not unhappy that Morse had failed to put in his usual, comparatively early appearance the following morning. His own preferred program of alibi confirmation had earlier (as we have seen) been endorsed by Morse, albeit with muted enthusiasm; and Lewis was content to pursue such a program solo.

It now appeared that Morse's simplistic hypothesis—that of casting Barron as a double murderer—was wholly discounted. It would have been convenient, certainly, if it *had* been Barron; and if Barron in turn had been murdered by whoever was behind . . . well, behind everything, really. Frank Harrison, say. And why *not* Frank Harrison? In Lewis's betting book he was the one

runner in the field with the requisite bank balance to
fork out the regular dollops of hush money. But with
the potential collapse of global equity markets, such a
bank balance might soon not be looking so healthy. And
one of the laws of economics, as Lewis knew, was that
people with pots of money could easily *lose* pots of
money, including the person who hitherto had seen it as
a matter of self-interest to divert some proportion of
such monies to others: to Flynn, to Repp, perhaps to
Barron. Then, almost miraculously, two of them had
been crossed off the payroll; and if the third one . . .

Lewis could understand Morse's thinking perfectly
well. But it had been wrong, as the great man had (virtually) admitted the previous evening. There had been
that dramatic development in the case: Barron's death
had been an accident. And the coincidence of Barron
being knocked off a ladder *by accident* at virtually the
same time someone else had planned to murder him *by
criminal design* had clearly struck even Morse (a confirmed believer in coincidence) as quite extraordinarily
improbable.

So what was needed now was a bit of old-fashioned
procedure: some immediate phone calls; some speedy
arrangements of interviews; some urgent checking of
alibis. And so fortunate was Lewis that by 9:45 he had
written down a firm timetable:

10:15 a.m.—interview with Simon Harrison (Jordan-
              Hill)
11:15 a.m.—interview with Frank Harrison (Randolph)
12:15 p.m.—interview with Sarah Harrison (Ratcliffe
              Infirmary)

Back in HQ just after 2 P.M. (still no news from
Morse), Lewis looked down, not without some satisfaction, at the notes he had made:

SIMON H
Friday, July 24: at his desk all A.M.—lunch in

canteen—back at his desk till 4 P.M. when he took bus down to Summertown dentist (hr). Home c. 6 P.M. Plenty of witnesses on and off all day, it seems.
Monday, Aug 3: (day off work) A.M. drove via M40 → Stokenchurch hoping for siting of red kite there—tried earlier in the year at Llandudno—both trips unsuccessful (keen bird-watcher). Back for lunch in White Hart (Wytham)—witnesses would include landlord etc.

Impossible for him to have been in on the Flynn/Repp murders. *Could* have pushed Barron off the ladder, if we wanted him for that, which we don't. Deafer than I thought and lip-reads a lot. Names a big problem: Flynn OK, but Repp and Barron hard for him—its something to do with the labial consonants (so he says). Intelligent, bit too *intense*, loner (?).

FRANK H

Friday, July 24: meeting in London office 10–11:45 A.M. with four colleagues. (Check!)
Monday, Aug 3: at Randolph (booked in the day before). Breakfast 7:50–8:40 A.M. (approx) with "partner" (real honey acc. to Ailish at the bar). Car apparently not moved from Resident's garage that day.

As suspect? Same as SH (see above). Smart business exec. type, pleasant enough, bit abrupt, not short of the pennies—asked me to join him in glass of champange (£7 a go!) Thinning on top, thickening in middle. Seems used to getting what he wants in life.

SARAH H

Friday, July 24: at BDA Conference in Manchester with boss—arr 12.30 P.M. ret 9:50 p.m.—rail both ways. Forget her!
Monday, Aug 3: consultant duties at Diabetes Centre in Ratcliffe Inf. Saw ten patients. Lunch in League of Fiends cafeteria. Forget her!

Attractive, clever, but perhaps hard streek somewhere?

Yes! Lewis felt pleased with his morning's work; and even more pleased with his afternoon's work, after he'd typed up the notes, correcting four of the six misspellings and tidying up one or two of the punctuational blemishes. There remained quite a bit of checking to be done, but none of it would be particularly onerous, and most of it probably unnecessary. The general upshot was unambiguous. None of the Harrison clan had murdered Flynn or Repp. Two of the three *could* have been on the scene when Barron was killed but neither of them had murdered him, because *no one* had murdered him. That was the only thing in the whole tragic business that now seemed wholly incontrovertible.

Chapter Fifty-six

> *Have I Got News For You!*
> (TV program title)

In nowise was Lewis surprised to meet Dixon in the police canteen.

"Busy day?"

"Well, yes and no really. Morse rang me up early—"

"He *what*?" spluttered Lewis.

"Well, early for me. Wanted me to check out on a few things, didn't he?"

"Such as?"

"Well, names of those going to lipreading classes these last few years."

"Simon Harrison, you mean?"

"Didn't say, did he? No problem, though. Just got the lists photocopied, didn't I?"

"What else?"

"Well, funny really. He wanted me to find out who Flynn's dentist was—"

"He *what*?"

"Well, easy that. Then to find out something about that

Mrs. Holmes—you know, before she was married . . . before she had her accident."

Yes, Lewis could understand that.

"Then to ring that SOCO chap Andrews, the one who was out at Sutton Courtenay. Ask him to get a bit of a move on—you know, give him a kick up the arse, like, about the fingerprints. Morse got him to take Barron's, you knew that, didn't you?"

"Of course I knew that!" lied Lewis, euphoria fading fast.

"Well, there we are then. I suppose old Morse was just hoping, you know . . ."

Yes, Lewis knew exactly what Morse had been hoping.

"Has Andrews found anything?"

"Well, still working on it, isn't he? Messy old job, he said. Soon as he had any news though . . . Anyway I called round and stuck the stuff through the door. He was there, I reckon. The telly was on—"

"What?"

"Yeah, pretty certain of it. But he didn't come to the door. Odd sort of chap, isn't he?"

But the introductory "Well"s and the inquisitorial clausulae, (hallmarks of every Dixon sentence) had become too tiresome; and Lewis was glad when the canteen intercom cut across the conversation:

"Message for Chief Inspector Morse or Sergeant Lewis: Please ring Northampton SOCOs immediately. I repeat. Message for . . ."

Where are you, Dixon, in the hierarchy here? I'll tell you, mate. Nowhere—no bloody where—that's where!

Yet Lewis left such ungracious thoughts unspoken, jumping to his feet and leaving Dixon where he was, cheeks now jammed once more with a doughnut.

Two minutes later Lewis was through to an exultant Andrews, who wasted no time in breaking the dramatic news: there was a "hit"—yippee!—a match of fingerprints! In the car. Two sets—definite, distinct. The prints of J. Barron, Builder, of Lower Swinstead!

As he walked back to the canteen (Morse's phone still engaged), Lewis reflected on his brief exchange of views with Andrews. Morse had asked for any news to be communicated to him direct, and if necessary at his home number, though as both men knew there'd been little chance of that. Yet the situation was now perfectly clear; and Lewis freely conceded that Morse's early conviction that Barron had been involved in the murders seemed wholly vindicated. No room for more than three people in the cluttered stolen car, surely? And since neither Flynn nor Repp had stepped out of that car alive, the discovery of that third set of prints, Barron's, was of momentous significance: *Barron himself had been in the car.* The logic sounded pretty childish when it was put like that but . . .

Andrews's guess had been that Morse had suddenly fallen into some deep slumber after—well, after whatever; and Dixon's guess that he'd been watching TV with the volume too high. But the latter explanation seemed unlikely. Morse could (Lewis succumbed to his second unworthy thought that day) *could* have purchased some pornographic video; but would he have been able to master the operating instructions? Doubtful—especially having no children (better still, grandchildren) to explain things to him. Morse seldom watched TV anyway, or so he claimed. Just the news. Just occasionally.

Lewis finished his coffee, slowly coming to terms with the extraordinary news he'd just received: that Barron was a murderer—the second thing in the whole tragic business that now seemed wholly incontrovertible.

He rang Morse once again. If the call wasn't answered, he would drive down and see the situation for himself because he was getting a little worried.

The phone was ringing.

The call was answered.

Chapter Fifty-seven

Ah, could thy grave, at Carthage, be!
Care not for that, and lay me where I fall!
Everywhere heard will be the judgement-call:
But at God's altar, oh! remember me.

(Matthew Arnold)

Morse opened the front door. "And there's me hoping for a rest day, like they tell me they have in the middle of test matches."

But, in truth, he had not tried overhard to have much of a rest day . . .

Early that morning (as we have seen), he had rung Sergeant Dixon and given him a list of duties.

At 10 A.M. he had received a middle-aged, palely intelligent gentleman from Lloyds Bank, a guru on (inter alia) wills, dispositions, codicils, and covenants.

"From what you tell me, Mr. Morse, you're not exactly going to bequeath a large fortune, are you? And with no relatives, no immediate dependents, no unmanageable debts—well, you might just as well write down a few things on half a page of A4. Save yourself money that way. Do it now, if you like. Just write a few simple sentences—'I leave the house to blank, the bank balance to blank, the books and records to blank, the residual estate to blank.' That'll cover things for now—and you say you *do* want things covered? Just sign it, I'll witness it, and I'll see it's carried through, in case, you know . . . Then we can flesh it out a bit later."

"No problems really then?"

"No. We shall, as a bank, charge a small commission of course. But you expected that."

"Oh yes, Mr. Daniel. I'd expected that," said Morse.

At 11:15 A.M. he had taken the 2A bus down the

Banbury Road as far as Keble Road, where he alighted and walked across the Woodstock Road to the Radcliffe Infirmary, where he was directed up to an office on the first floor.

"Yes? How can I help you?" The woman behind the desk seemed to be a fairly important personage with carefully coiffured grey hair and carefully clipped diction.

"I'm thinking of leaving my body to the hospital."

"You've come to the right place."

"What's the drill?"

She took a form from a drawer. "Just fill this in."

"Is that all?"

"Make sure you tell your wife and your children and your GP. You'll avoid quite a few problems that way."

"Thank you."

"Of course, I ought to tell you we may not *want* your body. The situation does, er, fluctuate. But you'd expected that."

"Oh yes, I'd expected that," said Morse.

"And you must make sure you die somewhere fairly locally. We can't come and collect you from Canada, you know."

Perhaps it was a bleak joke.

"No, of course not."

It had been a joyless experience for Morse, who now walked slowly down St. Giles toward The Randolph. He'd thought at the very least they'd have shown a little gratitude. Instead, he felt as though they were doing *him* a favor by agreeing (provisionally!) to accept a corpse that would surely be presenting apprentice anatomists and pathologists with some appreciably interesting items: liver, kidneys, lungs, pancreas, heart . . .

In the Chapters' Bar, Ailish Hurley, his favorite barmaid, greeted him in her delightful Irish brogue; and two pints of bitter later, as he walked round into Magdalen Street and almost immediately caught a bus back up to the top of the Banbury Road, he felt that the world was a happier place than it had been half an hour earlier.

Once home, he treated himself to a small(ish) Glenfiddich, deciding that his liquid intake of calories that lunchtime would nicely balance his dosage of insulin. Yes, things were looking up, and particularly so since the phone hadn't rung all day. What a wonderful thing it would be to go back to the days pre telephone (mobile and immobile alike), pre FAX, pre e-mail!

And, to cap it all, he'd bought himself a video—in front of which, in midafternoon, he'd fallen fairly soundly asleep, though at some point half-hearing, as he thought, a slippery flop through the letter-box.

It was an hour later when he opened the envelope and read Dixon's notes on Simon Harrison; on Paddy Flynn; on Mrs. Holmes.

Interesting!

Interesting!

Interesting!

And very much as he'd thought . . .

Only one thing was worrying him slightly. Why hadn't Lewis been in touch? He didn't want Lewis to get in touch but . . . perhaps he did want Lewis to get in touch. So he rang Lewis himself only to discover that the phone was out of order. Or was it? He banged the palm of his right hand against his forehead. He'd rung Dixon early that morning from the bedroom; then he'd had to go downstairs to check an address in the phone book, finishing the call there, and forgetting to replace the receiver in the bedroom. He'd done it before. And he'd do it again. It was not a matter of any great moment. He'd ring Lewis himself—not that he had anything much to say to him; not for the minute anyway.

He was about to pick up the phone when the doorbell rang.

Chapter Fifty-eight

> It remains quite a problem to play the clarinet with false teeth, because there is great difficulty with the grip (this may even result in the plate being pulled out!). In addition there are problems with the breathing, because it is difficult to project a successful airstream.
>
> (Paul Harris, *Clarinet Basics*)

"Been trying to get you all day, sir."

"I've had other things to do, you know."

"You just said you'd wanted a rest day."

"Come in! Fancy a quick noggin?"

Lewis hesitated. "Why not?"

"Ye gods! You must have had a bad day—or was it a good day?"

"I've had a *good* day, and so have you."

Morse now listened quietly to the extraordinary news from Andrews, though without any sign of triumphalism.

Equally quietly he slowly read through Lewis's typed reports. Then read them a second time.

"Your orthography has come on enormously since they put that spell-check system into the word processor."

"Don't *you* have any problems with spellings—sometimes?"

"Only with 'proceed'."

"Where does this all leave us, sir?"

"Things are moving fast."

"We're getting near the end, you mean?"

"We were always near the end."

"So what do you think happened?"

"Shan't ever know for certain, shall we? With all three of them dead, all three of them murdered—"

"Only *two*, surely?"

"If you say so, Lewis. If you say so."

"You're not suggesting—?"

But Morse was not to be deflected:

"There were three people who had a vested interest in Yvonne Harrison's murder: Repp, Barron, and Flynn. Repp—because he'd been casing the property for a burglary; because he happened to be there on the night of the murder; and because he *knew who the murderer was*. Barron—a man with an SAS background, who'd found a woman who could gratify his sexual fantasies, and who also *knew who the murderer was*—because he was the fellow in bed with Yvonne that night. Flynn— the fellow who lied about the events that night and who, like the other two, *knew who the murderer was*. The three of them had got their clutches into the only person who could pay their price, the person who *did* pay their price: Frank Harrison. *He* was becoming a fatter and fatter cat in his banking business, so they thought—and, rightly it seems. So they were ready to up the stakes. And on the day Repp was released, they'd agreed to meet and coordinate some plan of action. But things went wrong. Pretty certainly they somehow discovered that they'd each been treated differently— *dangerously* differently; and bitterness, jealousy, rivalry, all surfaced, and there was one almighty row. I've said all this before! They'd stopped, perhaps in a lay-by along the A34—take your pick!—and Barron got his Stanley knife out and threatened Flynn, the man who'd just happened to be at the taxi-rank that night, and who was now overplaying his hand. And soon it must have occurred to the other two that half a cake is considerably better than a third of one; and Flynn was murdered and dumped at Redbridge in those black bags, the ones the owner of the car was originally going to cart off to the rubbish dump."

"Waste Disposal Centre."

"After that? Who knows? But suddenly the situation was becoming more dangerous still. If half a cake is better than a third, what about a whole cake? So the two of them must have wrangled about the best way to capitalize on Flynn's beneficial departure . . . But how and why and when and where things went on from there, I've no more idea than you have—and that's not saying much, is it?"

"No," said Lewis flatly.

Morse looked at his sergeant, and smiled wearily:

"You're annoyed, aren't you?"

"Annoyed? What about?"

"Dixon."

"Why didn't you *tell* me?"

"You'd've accused me of wasting police resources. Do you know what I got him to do today?"

"Vaguely."

"Well, let me tell you, specifically. First, I asked him to do a bit of fourth-grade clerical stuff at Oxpens, and get copies of those attending lipreading classes these last five years. And he did it. Very efficiently. He found Simon Harrison's name there, for three years; and Paddy Flynn's there, for two years—overlapping. *Very* interesting that, because they must have known each other!

"Second, I asked Dixon to find out more about Flynn. Flynn was known as an amateur entertainer round the local pubs and clubs in Oxfordshire, playing the clarinet and compering his little pop group. Till about three years ago, when things started to go wrong: he began to experience trouble with his hearing—something that later compromised his job with Radio Taxis; *and* at about the same time, according to the postmortem details, he had a lot of dental trouble which meant he had to have all his top-front teeth extracted. And that's not a good thing for a clarinet player."

"It's not?"

"Well-known fact. Louis Armstrong had the same sort of trouble."

"He was a *trumpet player*!"

"Same *sort* of thing! Then I asked Dixon to look into Mrs. Holmes's background. I had the impression when we spoke to her that she might have been a most attractive woman when she was younger; and I just wondered . . . I got Dixon to check up on her, that's all. Seems she used to live in Lower Swinstead before she moved to Burford and, well, look at things for yourself."

	Elizabeth Jane Thomas (b. 7.11.53)
1976 (Feb.)	Son b. (Alan) illeg.
1983 (March)	Son b. (Roy) illeg.
1983 (Dec.)	m. Kenneth Holmes
	(Registry Office)
1991 (Sept.)	Husband killed in pile-up on A40—same
	accident that caused all her trouble

Lewis read Dixon's notes:

"They don't call them 'illegitimate' these days, and it should be 'Register' Office."

Morse nodded. "You're missing the main point, though."

"I am?"

"Remember when we were in the village pub? Remember Biffen greeting his customers?"

Yes. Lewis remembered that "Evening, Mr. Thomas": the young fellow forever playing the fruit machine, the young fellow who had spoken to him in the car park.

"You mean they're half-brothers? Roy Holmes and Alan Thomas?"

"Why not *full* brothers—with the same father? I knew there was something familiar about young Holmes . . . Anyway, there it is. Elizabeth Thomas was an unmarried mum in the village; Alan was already seven when his younger brother was born; and everybody knew him as Alan *Thomas*. So he kept the name when his mother married a few months later, and kept it when he went along with the family to live in Burford."

"Interesting enough—but is it important?"

"I don't know," said Morse slowly. "I just don't know. But it throws up one or two new ideas."

"If you say so, sir. Aren't you going to offer me another Scotch, by the way?"

What a strange day it had been! Even stranger, perhaps, in that Morse now left his own glass unreplenished.

"Shall I tell you something else, Lewis? You'd never believe it, but I've been watching the telly this afternoon. I picked up one of those RSPB videos."

"You mean you know how to work the machine?"

"It's Strange's fault. Genuine bird-watcher, Strange! He told me the sparrow population in North Oxford's down by fifty percent these last few years; and he told me the sparrow hawks along Squitchey Lane are getting fatter. So I bought this video on birds of prey—you know, eagles, falcons, hobbies, merlins, red kites . . . did you hear me, Lewis? *Red kites*."

Lewis looked puzzled. "I'm not with you."

"Your interview with Simon Harrison. He's a phoney bird-watcher, that fellow. Said he'd been off to Llandudno to try to spot a red kite. Llandudno! He meant *Llandovery*, Lewis—that was the only home of the red kite in the UK until they introduced a few near Stokenchurch."

"I didn't know you were an expert—"

"I'm not. And nor is Simon Harrison. His alibi for Monday morning's worthless. He wouldn't know a red kite from a red cabbage."

Unaccustomedly relaxed, Lewis sipped his Glenfiddich and involuntarily repeated an earlier comment: "Interesting enough—but is it *important*?"

"I just don't know," said Morse slowly, himself now involuntarily repeating an earlier comment: "But it throws up one or two new ideas . . ."

"Perhaps they've *all* been telling us a few lies, sir . . . except Mrs. Barron, perhaps."

Morse smiled. "Don't you mean *especially* Mrs. Barron?"

Chapter Fifty-nine

> Wherever God erects a house of prayer,
> The Devil always builds a chapel there;
> And 'twill be found, upon examination,
> The latter has the largest congregation.
> (Daniel Defoe, *The True-born Englishman*)

Mrs. Linda Barron walked steadily up the aisle between the small assembly of mourners, her arm linked through that of her mother, both women dutifully dressed in bible-black suits . . .

On the whole, it hadn't been quite the ordeal she'd expected: in practical terms, the shock of it all continued to cocoon a good half of her conscious thoughts; whilst emotionally she had long since accepted that her love for her husband was as dead as the man who had been lying there in the coffin—until mercifully the curtains had closed, and the show was over. He would have enjoyed the hymn though, "He Who Would Valiant Be," for he had been valiant enough (she'd learned that from his army friends)—as well as vain and domineering and unfaithful. Yes, she'd found herself moved by the hymn; and the tears ought to have come.

But they hadn't.

Outside, in the clear sunshine, she whispered quickly into her mother's ear. "Remember what I said. The kids are fine, if anybody asks. OK?"

But the grandmother made no reply. She was the very last person in the world to let the little ones down, especially the one of them. As for Linda, she girded up her loins in readiness for the chorus of commiseration she would have to cope with.

And indeed several of the family and friends of her late husband, J. Barron, Builder, had already emerged through the chapel doors, including Thomas Biffen, Landlord, whose creased white shirt was so tight around the neck that he had been forced to unfasten the top button beneath the black tie; including the perennial opponents, Alf and Bert, who had exchanged no words in the chapel, but whose thoughts were perhaps in tune during the service as each of them must have mused on their imminent mortality, and the prospects of encountering that great cribbage player in the sky.

Including Frank Harrison.

Chief Superintendent Strange, who had been seated in the back row next to Morse, was the last but one to leave. His thoughts had roamed irreverently throughout the short service, and the superannuated minister's apparent confidence in the resurrection of the dead had filled him more with horror than with hope. He thought of his wife and of her death and experienced that familiar sense of the guilt that still remained to be expiated. The hymn was all right, although he'd gone himself for "Praise My Soul, the King of Heaven" in the Instructions for My Funeral stapled to his last will and testament. But on the whole he dreaded church services almost as much as did the man seated beside him; and he could think of nothing more detestable than a funeral.

Morse himself had been sickened by the latest version (Series Something) of the Funeral Service. Gone were those resonant cadences of the AV and the Prayer Book: those passages about corruption putting on incorruptibility and the rest of it, which as a youth he'd found so poignant and powerful. They'd even had a cheerful hymn, for heaven's sake! Where was that wonderfully sad and sentimental hymn he'd chosen for his own farewell: "O Love That Wilt Not Let Me Go"? Chosen, that is, before he'd recently decided to leave his body for medical science, although that decision itself was now in considerable doubt. In particular that little clause in sub-section 6 of Form D1 still stuck in his craw: "Should your bequest be accepted . . ."

He pointedly avoided the priest who'd presided—a

man (in Morse's view) excessively accoutred in ecclesiastical vestments, and wholly lacking in any sensitivity to the English language. But he did have a quick word of sympathy with the widow, shaking her black-gloved hand firmly before turning to her mother.

"Mrs. Stokes?" he asked quietly.

"Yes?"

Morse introduced himself. "My sergeant called to see your daughter—"

"Oh yes."

"—when you were there looking after the children, I believe. Very kind of you. Must be a bit wearisome . . . I wouldn't know, though."

"It's a pleasure really."

"Who's looking after them today?"

"Oh they're, er . . . you know, a friend, a neighbor. Won't be for long anyway."

"No."

Morse turned away, following in Strange's steps toward the car park.

She was lying, of course—Morse knew that. There was only one of the Barron children at home that day; as there had been when Lewis had called. The elder of the two, Alice, was away somewhere. That much, though very little else, Lewis himself had been able to learn from the Barrons' GP the previous day. Morse thought he knew why, and another piece of the jigsaw had slipped into place.

"Hello! Chief Inspector Morse, isn't it? My daughter tells me she saw you recently. But perhaps you don't know me."

"Let's say we've never been officially introduced, Mr. Harrison."

"Ah! You *do* know me. I know you, of course, and Sergeant Lewis has been to see me. You probably sent him."

"As a matter of fact I did."

"I realize you weren't yourself involved in my wife's murder case but, er . . ."

Harrison was by some three inches or so the taller of

the two, and Morse felt slightly uncomfortable as a pair of pale-grey eyes, hard and unsmiling, looked slightly down on him.

". . . but I'd heard about you. Yvonne spoke about you several times. She'd looked after you once when you were in hospital. Remember?"

Morse nodded.

"Quite taken by you, she was. 'A sensitive soul'—I think that's what she called you; said you were interesting to talk to and had a nice voice. Told me she was going to invite you out to one of her, er, soirées. When I was away, of course."

"I should hope so. Wouldn't have wanted any competition, would I?"

"*Did* you have any competition?"

"The only time I ever met Yvonne again was in the Maiden's Arms," said Morse gently, unblinking blue eyes now looking slightly upward into the strong, cleanshaven face of Harrison senior.

As Strange struggled to squeeze his bulk between seat and steering wheel, Morse looked back and saw that the funeral guests were almost all departed. But Linda Barron stood there still, in close conversation with Frank Harrison—both of them now stepping aside a little as another black Daimler moved smoothly into place outside the chapel, with another light-brown, lily-bedecked coffin lying lengthways inside, the polished handles glinting in the sun.

Morse found himself pondering on the funeral. "I wonder why *he* put in an appearance."

"Who? Frank Harrison? Why shouldn't he? Lived in the same village—had him in to do those house repairs—"

"Knew his wife had been in bed with him."

"Fasten your seat belt, Morse!"

"Er, before we drive off, there's something—"

"Fasten your seat belt! Know what that's an anagram of, by the way? 'Truss neatly to be safe.' Clever, eh? Somebody told me that once. You probably."

For a few seconds Morse looked slightly puzzled.

"Couldn't have been me. It's got to be 'belts.' Otherwise there's one 's' short."

"Just put the bloody thing on!"

But Morse left the bloody thing off as he looked directly ahead of him and completed his earlier sentence: "Just before we drive off, sir, there's something I ought to mention. It's about Lewis. I'm fairly sure he's beginning to get some odd ideas about my being involved in some way with Yvonne Harrison."

It was Strange's turn to look directly ahead of him.

"And you think I wasn't aware of that?" he asked quietly.

Chapter Sixty

> *Have respect unto the covenant: for the dark places of the earth are full of the habitations of cruelty.*
> (Psalm 74, v. 20)

Once in Charlton Kings, a suburb on the eastern side of Cheltenham, Sergeant Lewis had followed the map directions carefully (he loved that sort of thing), turning right from the A40 through a maze of residential streets, and finally driving the unmarked police car past the sign on the whitewashed wall beside the gateway— "Sisters of the Covenant: Preparatory Boarding School for Girls"—and along the short graveled drive that led to a large, detached Georgian house.

Destination reached; and purpose, shortly afterward, fulfilled.

With a few extra suggestions from Morse, Lewis had found it comparatively easy to fill in most of the picture. The Barrons' GP had professional and wholly proper reasons for his guarded reticence. But other sources had been considerably less cautious with their help and information: the Burford Social Services, the NSPCC, the headmistress of the village primary school, the local Catholic priest, and, last of all, the middle-aged nun, dressed in a chocolate-brown habit and white wimple, who was expecting him and who found little difficulty in answering his brief, pointed questions.

Five nuns, all of them resident, looked after the school, which was specifically dedicated to the physical and spiritual well-being of girls between the ages of four and eleven (currently eighteen of them) who for varied reasons—poverty, indifference, criminality, cruelty—had been ill-used in their family homes. In spite of a modest benefaction, the school was a place of limited resources, at least in human terms, and was appropriately designated "Private," with the majority of parents paying fees of between £1,000 and £1,500 per term.

Alice Barron, yes—now aged six—was one of the pupils there, referred to the school by her mother. She had been abused, not sexually, it seemed, but certainly physically; certainly psychologically.

No, Alice was not one of our Lord's brightest intellects; in fact she was in some ways a slow-witted child. This may have been the result of her home environment, but probably only partially so. Her younger sister (the teaching staff had learned) was as bright as the proverbial button; and such a circumstance could well have accounted to some degree for an impatient, expectant, aggressive parent to have . . .

"The father, you mean?"

"You're putting words into my mouth, Sergeant."

"But if you were a betting woman—which I know you're not, of course . . ."

"What on earth makes you think that?" Her eyes momentarily glinted with humor. "But if I *were*, I would not be putting much money on the mother, no."

"How are the accounts for each term settled?"

"I looked that up, as you asked me. I can't be quite sure, but I suspect it's been in cash."

"Isn't that unusual?"

"Yes, it is."

"Does Alice know about her father's death?"

"Not yet, no."

"Do you think this whole business is going to . . . ?"

"Difficult to tell, isn't it? She's improving, right enough. She's stopped wetting her bed, and she doesn't scream so loudly in the night."

"But if you were going to have another bet?"

"If I were a bookmaker, I'd lay you even money on it."

As he drove back up to the A40, Lewis felt fairly sure he knew only a quarter as much about horse racing (and probably about life) as Sister Benedicta.

Chapter Sixty-one

> **character** (n.) handwriting, style of writing: Shakes. *Meas. for M.* Here is the hand and seal of the Duke. You know the character, I doubt not.
> (Small's *Enlarged English Dict.*, 18th ed.)

Back at HQ Lewis found a handwritten note for his personal attention:

> Well worthwhile going to the crem. One or two interesting conversations and one or two new ideas (or is it one?). Super and I off to have a jug (or is it two?). Tell anybody who wants me that I'm out to lunch and shan't be available till tomorrow morning—no *Monday* morning. M.

It was in Morse's hand, that small, neatly formed upright script that was recognizable anywhere; as indeed, for that matter, was Strange's hand—large, spidery, with a perpetual list to starboard, and often only semilegible.

But Lewis was unconcerned. He would type up a report on his wholly satisfactory morning's work. And then he would sit back and let things slowly sink in, for it had now become clear that the Repp–Flynn–Barron mystery was solved. Completely solved now, with the knowledge that it was Linda Barron who had taken the hush money; Linda Barron who must have insisted that if her husband ever thought of siphoning some of it off for himself she would expose him for the child abuser that he was, and expose him to Social Services, to the police, to the folk in the village, to the Press. And she would have meant it, for she was past caring. My God, yes! And Barron had agreed.

Yes . . .

The big moments in the case were over; and he rang Mrs. Lewis and asked her to have the chip-pan ready half an hour earlier than usual.

Yes . . .

In a strange kind of way, his confidence in himself had grown steadily throughout the present case, in spite of a few irritations like Dixon! *And* there was that one thing that had been interesting him and troubling him, in equal measure, for some considerable time now. Very soon he'd have to face up to telling Morse of his suspicions. But not just yet. He'd need to know a bit more about the Harrison murder first; especially about the contents of that fourth green box-file which had mysteriously added itself to the documents in the case, and which now sat alongside the other three on a shelf in Morse's office. Perhaps a bit later that afternoon, since Morse was unlikely to return.

What if he did, anyway?

Yes . . .

Lewis sat back after typing his report, his thoughts dwelling on the case that to all intents and purposes had now closed. He *was* right, wasn't he? But there were just one or two tiny items he hadn't as yet checked; and he knew that his conscience would be niggling him about them. No time like the present.

But not much luck. Still, those alibis for the Monday morning didn't much matter any longer. Or rather *non*-alibis, since neither Harrison Senior nor Harrison

Junior had any alibi at all. And whilst Sarah Harrison did have an alibi, it still remained unchecked.

He rang the Diabetes Centre in the Radcliffe Infirmary, with almost immediate if unexpected success, since Professor Turner (clearly not a Monday–Friday medic) now confirmed everything that Miss Harrison herself had affirmed: "In fact, Sergeant, she had to take over some of my patients mid-morning when I was summoned by my superiors—"

"Do you have any superiors, sir?"

On reflection, Lewis was more than a little pleased with that last question: just the sort of thing Morse would have asked. Was he, Lewis, just a little—after all this time—moving gradually nearer to Morsean wavelength?

At a quarter past four he walked along the corridor to Morse's office, to cast a fresh eye (so he promised himself) on that bizarre, that puzzling, that haunting evening of Yvonne Harrison's murder—the source of so much trouble and tragedy.

Very soon he was virtually certain that he had seen none of the contents of that fourth box-file before; and had convinced himself that this was not merely a matter of some redistribution of the case documents. The file contained the sort of personal items that many women, and doubtless many men, keep in one of the locked drawers of their desks or bureaus, often with some sense of guilt.

There were all the usual things that from experience Lewis had known so well: letters, many of them in their original envelopes, some from women, most of them from men; photographs, many of them of Yvonne herself (one topless) with a variety of men friends; postcards from many a quarter of the globe, but mostly from Greece and Switzerland; three slim (unopened) bottles of perfume; various receipts for the purchase of ultraexpensive clothes and shoes. But for all the variety of material there, the box was scarcely half-full, and Lewis took his time. He looked at the photographs reasonably quickly (not quite so quickly at one of them, perhaps), before reading slowly (though not as slowly as Morse would have done) through the letters.

Then he saw it:

> that they would prefer to be ill in hospital
> and nursed by you than to be in full health
> and never see you again. I join them. You
> have monopolized my thoughts these last few
> days, ever since you promised—remember? —
> to get in touch once I was discharged. But
> no invitation, no phone call, no letter,
> nothing.
>
> If you have decided that it was all
> just a temporary infatuation, and
> if, on your part, it was nothing more
> than that—so be it. Just for a while
> longer though, let me look through my
> mail each morning in the hope

That was all. Just one small page of a longer letter. No date, no address, no salutation, no valediction, no name—nothing. And yet everything. Because the letter was written in that small, neatly formed upright script that was recognizable everywhere in the Thames Valley Police HQ.

As he reread the page, Lewis was suddenly aware of another presence in the office; and looked up to find Chief Inspector Morse standing silently in the doorway.

Chapter Sixty-two

> Don't tell me, sweet, that I'm unkind
> Each time I black your eye,
> Or raise a weal on your behind—
> I'm just a loving guy.
> We both despise the gentle touch,
> So cut out the pretence;
> You wouldn't love it half as much
> Without the violence.
>
> (Roy Dean, *Lovelace Bleeding*)

Anyone wishing to take up Morse's earlier promise of being available the following Monday morning would have been disappointed, since he had put in no appearance by lunchtime. Yet he was not idle during those morning hours; and any visitor to the bachelor flat would have found him seated at his desk for much of the time; and for a fair proportion of that time found him writing quite busily and (as we have seen) very neatly. His old typewriter (with its defective "e" and "t") sat at his elbow; but he had never mastered the keyboard skills with any real confidence, and he wrote now in longhand with a medium-blue Biro.

For Priority Consideration

Several things have happened these last few days which have prompted me to put down in writing my own thoughts on the present state of play.

First, I've been waking up every day recently, after some nightmarish nights, with a premonition that some disaster is imminent. Whether death comes into such a category, I'm not sure. I can't agree with Socrates, though, that death is a blessing devoutly to be wished, even if it is (as I hope it is, as I believe it is) one long completely dreamless sleep. For the very fact of being alive is surely the best thing that's happened to (almost) all of us.

Second, the last murder case entrusted to the pair of us has been (one or two loose ends though) satisfactorily resolved. Repp and Flynn were murdered by Barron, and the murderer himself is now dead. So any further insight into the original Harrison murder from *their* angles is wholly precluded.

Third, I'm certain that Frank Harrison has been the paymaster. It's high time we brought him into HQ for intensive questioning, either directly about the murder of his wife, or at the very least about some culpable complicity of her murder.

Fourth, I'm also convinced that Yvonne H. was murdered by one of her own family. Nothing else makes any sense at all, not to me anyway. That murder was not premeditated: few of them are. It was committed spontaneously, viciously, involuntarily perhaps, by whichever of the three it was who found Yvonne Harrison in a situation that was utterly unexpected—kinkiness, perversion, degradation, all rolled up into one.

On the face of it, the husband is the outsider of the three, so you will appreciate, Lewis, that in my book he's the favorite. It's the "why" that worries me, though. He wasn't and isn't anybody's fool, and he must have known more than enough about his wife's tastes in bondage and possibly masochism. So I just can't see blazing jealousy as his motive, especially since, as I strongly suspect, he regularly experienced the (reported) joys of extramarital sex himself.

A confession here.

Quite a few times I've found myself looking at the faces of people concerned with this case and thinking I'd seen them somewhere before. I thought it might be the result of interbreeding in a small community—no wonder some of the villagers are pretty tight-lipped! And I was right. That fruit-machine addict, for example: *Allen* Thomas. That's how you spell his name by the way, Lewis. I found it in the village-school records: Allen Alfred Thomas. Unusual these days, that spelling of "Allen." And "Alfred" belongs more to the first half of the century, doesn't it? I also found out (well, Dixon found out) that the Christian names of Elizabeth Jane Thomas's father were "Harold Alfred"; and that someone else in the village had a father with the Christian names "Joseph Allen." That someone else was Frank Harrison. And (believe me!) *he* was the father of the lad, and Elizabeth decided to give him a couple of Christian names that, at least for herself, could confer some little pretense of legitimacy of her illegitimate son. (I wonder if his father gives him a fruit-machine allowance?)

Let's turn to the Harrison children.

Either of them *could* have murdered their mother. What would be the motive, though? I just can't see Sarah suddenly turning to murder because she finds her mother abed with one of her many lovers. What does it really matter to her that her mother enjoys a bit of biting and bondage occasionally? Shocked and disgusted? Yes, she'd certainly have been both. But driven to murder? No. There's something about her, though—something that tells me that she's up to her very smooth neck in things.

What about Simon Harrison? As we know he's always been a bit of a mummy's darling: a boy disadvantaged because of early deafness; a boy always needing extra understanding and extra love, and who found it (hardly surprisingly) from his mother. I'd guess myself that for Simon this relationship had always been very precious. Sacrosanct almost. I'd also guess that he had no notion whatsoever of his mother's idiosyncratic tastes in sexual gratification. Then one night, the night of the murder, he'd driven out to see her. And why not? Just to say hello, perhaps? Like his sister, he had a key to the front door, and he entered the house and disturbed the copulat-

ing couple—copulating in the most extraordinary circumstances; and he would have been shocked and
disgusted (like his sister) but heartbroken, too, and
disillusioned and betrayed. His mother performing
those things with some plebeian local builder!

Where does all this lead us? First and foremost to
an early, long-overdue, full-scale interview with
Frank Harrison. Not too early though. Our colleagues got nowhere with him and we, Lewis, are a
pair of bloodhounds very late on the scene, with the
scent gone very cold.

Fifth, there's this business of the letter you found in
the Harrison file. As I told you, I take full responsibility for the fact that some items originally discovered at the Harrison murder scene were subsequently,
as they say, found to be missing. It was embarrassing
for me to talk to you about this and I know that you
in turn found it equally embarrassing to—

Morse laid down his pen and answered the phone:
"Lewis! What do you want?"

"You OK, sir?"

"Why shouldn't I be?"

"It's just that—well, you know that animal charity
shop on the corner of South Parade and Middle
Way . . ."

"I am *not* an animal lover, Lewis."

"Well, people leave things there, by the door, things
for the shop to sell for charity—"

"Get *on* with it!"

"Guess what one of the shop assistants found when
she got to work this morning?"

"Pair of handcuffs?"

"Pair of *something*, sir. Pair of red trainers! Almost
brand-new. This woman had read in the *Oxford Mail*
about the Burford jogger and she thought . . ."

"You know something, Lewis? That's very interesting.
Very interesting indeed. I'll be with you straightaway."

Chapter Sixty-three

> *With much talk will they tempt thee, and
> smiling upon thee will get out thy secrets.*
> (*Ecclesiasticus*, ch. XIII, v. 11)

"You know, come to think of it, Lewis, we could do all
of this now, couldn't we? Just the two of us."

"No Dixon?"

"No Dixon."

Lewis smiled outwardly and inwardly as he looked
down at the action plan. It seemed to him a sensible and
fair division of a good deal of labor. For example, he
himself had spoken only very briefly with Sarah Harrison; Morse had not as yet spoken at all with Simon
Harrison. Both matters now to be dealt with. And all
leading up to the two of them, Morse and Lewis, meeting Frank Harrison a.s.a.p. after these and a few other
checks and visits had been made. Harrison!—"the
corner-stone, the kingpin, the pivot," as Morse had
asserted, before running out of synonyms. "We've got
plenty of time for all this—well, no, perhaps we haven't.
So we can be pretty direct, but not sharp. Smile occasionally. No aggressiveness, no hostility, no belliger-
ence," Morse had asserted, before running out of
synonyms again.

It all suited Lewis nicely. If Morse's philosophy in life
was to aim high even if the target was altogether missed,
he personally preferred to aim low in the hope at least
of hitting something.

The voluntary (mornings only) help at the Oxford Animal Sanctuary Shop (Gifts Welcome) lived only a few
hundred yards away in Osberton Road: a widow, a cat
lover, an intelligent witness—Mrs. Gerrard. It was just

that, as every weekday morning, she'd walked down to South Parade to buy the *Daily Telegraph*, about 8 o'clock before opening the shop, and she'd seen this—

"Yes?" Lewis smiled.

—well, this youngish fellow—smartly dressed, suit and tie—and he put this Sainsbury's plastic bag in the doorway there. She couldn't describe him any better than that really; but she remembered his car, parked for a few seconds on the double-yellows alongside the shop. She wouldn't have noticed that either—except that it was the same make as hers, a Toyota Carina, P-Reg., a different color though: hers was a turquoisy color, his was silvery-grey. The trainers she had put carefully aside, under the counter in the shop.

No one in North Oxford with a Toyota was likely to drive unnecessarily far afield for any servicing and repairs, since there was a specialist garage in Summertown itself; and it took Lewis only a few minutes to learn that the owner of a silvery-grey P-Reg. Carina was a regular and esteemed customer of the company, a man named Simon Harrison.

Simultaneously Morse was driving himself in the Jaguar through the low range of open hills that border Oxfordshire and Gloucestershire. His old pathologist friend, Max, had once told him that two pleasures grew ever deeper with advancing age, the pleasures of the belly and the pleasures of natural beauty. And Morse found himself concurring with the latter proposition as he turned right at the roundabout and drove down into Burford.

Christine Coverley was clearly surprised to see him, and clearly not happy.

"It's all a bit untidy—"

Morse smiled. "Can I come in?"

"I haven't got long, I'm afraid."

"It won't take long, I promise."

"How can I. . . ?"

"What were you doing last Monday morning? Between, say, nine and eleven?"

"Not the faintest, have I? Nobody could remember exactly—"

"Did you go out—for a newspaper, shopping, seeing someone?"

"I don't know. Like I say—"

"Can you have a look in your diary for me?"

"That wouldn't help."

"What *would* help?"

"I don't know what you're getting at. Look, Inspector." She glanced down at her wristwatch with what appeared incipient panic. "Could we talk some other time, *please*? You see I've got—"

But it was too late.

There was the scratch of a key in the Yale lock and the front door was quickly opened and as quickly closed, and a youth entered from the narrow hallway to stand in the doorway of the single bedsit room.

With staring eyes he looked first at Morse and then at Christine Coverley: "What the fuck?"

"You haven't increased your word power much since we last—" began Morse. But Roy Holmes had disappeared even more rapidly than he'd appeared.

In the stillness that followed the crash of the front door closing, Morse sat down in one of the armchairs, and gestured the speechless schoolmistress to seat herself in the other.

"Please tell me all about it," he said, with no hint of aggressiveness or any of its synonyms. "If you don't, I'm sorry but I shall have to take you down to Police HQ."

After his twinkling Irish eyes had scrutinized Lewis's ID, Mr. Tony Marrinan, the manager of The Randolph, was wholly cooperative; and very soon the outline of Frank Harrison's recent stay was revealed. Double-room booked with, as staff recalled her, a sultrily attractive if less than attractively mannered partner—late twenties, perhaps; meals taken together quite regularly in the Spires Restaurant—details available, if Sergeant Lewis wanted to see them.

As Sergeant Lewis did.

Continental	☑	Full	☐
Date	3/8/98	Time	8.20
Table No.	7	Covers	1
Room No.	210	Waiter	C.M.
Room Charge	☑	Other	☐
Guest Name:	HARRISON		
Signature:			

The pair had breakfasted together on each morning
except the Monday, and Lewis was fairly soon looking
at that day's Good Morning Breakfast chit, its details
having been transferred immediately to the hotel's computer before being placed on a spike and then at the end
of the day transferred to the accounts department
upstairs for a limited period, as a check if any guest
should query an entry on the final bill.

Interesting! Especially the bottom half of the chit:

"Covers," as Lewis learned, signified how many had
been at the table: on the other chits it had the figure "2"
beside it. But on the Monday morning just the one of
them, and the restaurant manager remembered which
one of them: "It was the lady. I think Mr. Harrison may
have been feeling a little tired."

Before he left the hotel, Lewis had a word with the
chambermaid who had looked after Room 210, discovering that for much of the time over the period in question the DO NOT DISTURB notice had hung over the
outside door-knob.

"And the bed looked as if it had been slept in each
night?" (Lewis tried to smile knowingly.)

"Oh yes, sir. Oh yes."

Perhaps the restaurant manager was right. Perhaps
Mr. Harrison's stay in Oxford had been a busy and tir-
ing one.

For one reason or another.

Before driving back to HQ, Morse called in at the
Maiden's Arms, in the hope of finding Alf and Bert,

Lower Swinstead's answer to "Bill and Ben." The time was now just after 2:30 P.M.; and Morse expected that they would be gone by then. But he was lucky; or at least half-lucky.

Bert, it seemed, had "got the screws," and Alf was sitting alone by the window, slowly sipping the last of his beer, and readily accepting Morse's offer of "one for the road."

"Lost his nerve!" confided Alf. "Lost the last five times we've a'been playing. Lost his nerve!"

"Like me to give you a quick game? Just the one?"

Morse had determined to lose the challenge in as swift and incompetent a manner as possible. But unfortunately the gods were smiling broadly on his hands; and very soon, *malgré lui,* he had won the single encounter by the proverbial street.

Unfortunately?

Oh no. For Alf appeared to recognize in his opponent a player of supreme skills; and instead of his wonted sullen silence on such occasions, he was soon speaking with unprecedented candor about life there in the village in general, and in particular about the Harrisons—with the result that after twenty minutes Morse had learned more than any other police officer before him from any of the locals in Lower Swinstead.

"Did Frank ever come in the pub here with other women?"

"Never. In Lon'on most of his time, weren't he?"

"What about Simon?"

"He come in sometimes, but he never had no reg'lar girlfriend. Bit of a loner, Simon."

"What about Sarah?"

"Lovely, she were—not seen her though this last coupla years. In fact, last time I seen her was here in the pub—sort of guest appearance singing with a pop group. Nice voice, she had, young Sarah."

"Did she come in with any boyfriends?"

"Did she? I'll tell you summat—she did. Could've had anybody she wanted, I reckon."

"Who did she want?"

Alf chuckled. "Didn't want me—Bert neither! One or two was luckier though, mister."

The light in Alf's old eyes suddenly sparked, like the coals on a fire that were almost ready to sink back to an ashen grey; and he nodded his head—just as Bert, in his turn, would have nodded across the cribbage board.

Enviously.

With the consulting rooms all taken up with a series of interviews for diabetes students, Lewis sat with Sarah Harrison behind a curtain in the Blood-Testing Room.

"Did you see your father while he was staying at The Randolph last week?"

"I always see my father when he comes to Oxford. In fact, I had a meal with him one evening."

"So you get on well with him?"

Lewis's smile was not reciprocated, and she almost spat her reply at him: "What the hell's *that* supposed to mean?"

"I'm not sure really. It's just that I've got a list of questions here from Chief Inspector Morse—by the way, I think you know him. . . ?"

"I've met him *once.*"

"Well he's asked me to ask you—not very well phrased, that—"

"What's he want to know?"

"What the relationships were like in your family."

"I can't speak for Simon—you must ask *him.* If you mean did I have any preference? No. I loved Mum, and I loved, *love,* Dad. Some children love both their parents, you know."

"You never felt that your mother loved Simon a bit more than she loved you—you know, because he was a bit handicapped, perhaps because he needed more affection than you did?"

There was a silence before Sarah answered the question; and as Lewis looked at her he realized how attractive she must have appeared to all the men and boys in the village; how attractive she was now, and would be for many years to come, in whatever place she found herself.

"You know I've never thought of it quite like that before, but yes... I suppose you could be right, Sergeant Lewis."

After leaving the Maiden's Arms, where the fruit machine had stood unwontedly and unprofitably silent, Morse called on Allen *(sic)* Thomas at his home in Lower Swinstead. Alf had told him where to go: the lad was sure to be there. He'd not be at work, because he'd never done a hand's turn in his life.

And Alf was right.

The dingy room was untidy and undusted, with three empty cans on the top of the TV and a hugely piled ashtray on the arm of the single armchair. But Thomas (the facial resemblance between him and Roy Holmes so very obvious to him now) was a paragon of civility compared with the crudity of that sibling of his, and Morse found himself feeling more pro than anti the unshaven youth in front of him.

"How often do you keep in touch with your dad?" began Morse.

The cigarette that had been dangling from Thomas's loose mouth fell to the carpet; and although it was swiftly retrieved the damage had been done. Thomas knew it. And Morse knew it. And fairly soon the truth, or what Morse took to be half of the truth, had started to surface.

Yes, Elizabeth Holmes was his natural mother.

Yes, Roy Holmes was his stepbrother—or his real brother—he'd never really known.

Yes, he kept in touch with his natural father, and his natural father kept in touch with him: Frank Harrison, yes—he'd always known that.

No. His father had never sent him what could loosely be called a fruit-machine allowance.

No. His father had never asked him to keep him regularly informed about any developments in the inquiries into Yvonne Harrison's murder.

No. He'd had no contact whatever recently either with his father or his mother or his brother.

Morse was half-smiling to himself as finally he drove back to Oxford, knowing beyond any peradventure that the No No No was in reality a Yes Yes Yes.

In the semicoordinated strategy earlier agreed between the pair of them, Lewis's last allotted task had been some further inquiries into the balances and business activities of Mr. Frank Harrison. Somewhat trickier than anticipated though. Yet far more exciting, as Lewis discovered after depositing (as agreed) the Sainsbury's bag, with contents, in Morse's office late that same afternoon, and ringing the London offices of the Swiss Helvetia Bank.

Reaching the senior manager surprisingly speedily.

Being informed that he, Lewis, ought really to get to London immediately and urgently.

Deciding to go.

Using the siren (one of Lewis's greatest joys) if he found himself stuck, as he knew he would be, amid the capital's inevitable gridlocks.

Morse took the red trainers from the bag and placed them on Simon Harrison's desk.

"These yours?"

"Pardon? What shorts?"

The interview wasn't going to be easy, Morse conceded that. Yet already the suspicion had crossed his mind that any deaf man, and especially a canny deaf man, might occasionally pretend to mishear in order to give himself a little more time to consider an awkward question.

"Your car, Mr. Harrison? Toyota, P-Reg.?"

"It ought to be what, Inspector?"

"Llandudno? Mean anything to you?"

"Did you know, you say? Didn't know?"

"The time for playing games is over, lad," said Morse quietly. "Let's start at the beginning again, shall we?" He pointed to the trainers. "These yours?"

The truth, or what Morse took to be half of the truth, was fairly soon out.

The teenaged Simon had known Barron well enough because the builder had done a few things around the house, including a big structural job on the back patio. Frequently he'd found Barron in the kitchen having a mug of coffee with his mother, and he'd sensed that Barron fancied her. Jealous? Yes, he'd been jealous. Angry, too, because his mother had once confided in him that she found Barron a bit of a creep.

Then, so very recently, there'd been this upsurge of interest in his mother's murder, bringing with it a corresponding upsurge in his hatred of Barron.

Yes, he'd bought the trainers—£70! No, he'd not driven out to Stokenchurch that Monday morning. He'd driven out to Burford instead, where he knew that Barron was working.

Here Morse had interrupted. "How did you know that?"

"Pardon?"

Was it a genuine plea? Morse was most doubtful, but he repeated the question with what he trusted was legible enunciation, conscious as he had been throughout of Simon's eyes upon his lips.

"He told me himself. You see, I wanted the outside of my flat, er . . . you know, the windows, doors . . . they were all getting a bit . . . Anyway, I asked him if he could do it and he said he'd come round and give me an estimate after he'd finished his next job. And I don't know why but he just happened to mention where it was, that's all."

Morse nodded dubiously. Even if it wasn't the truth, it wasn't a bad answer. And Simon Harrison continued his unofficial statement:

He'd just felt—well, murderous. Simple as that. He'd always suspected that Barron was involved somehow in his mother's murder, and he was conscious of an ever-increasing hatred for the man. So he'd decided to go and see if Barron *was* there, in Sheep Street, balanced precariously (as he hoped) on the top of an extended ladder, painting the guttering or something. And he was.

Morse made a second interruption: "So why didn't you. . . ?"

Simon understood the inchoate query immediately, and for Morse his answer had the ring of truth about it:

"I wanted to make sure he *could* be pushed off. I'd noticed when he was doing Mum's roof that he used to anchor the top of his ladder to the troughing or chimney stack or something. And he'd done the same there, in Sheep Street—I could see it easily. So even if I'd had the guts to do it, the ladder wouldn't have fallen. *He* might have done, agreed, but . . . Anyway, I was a nervous wreck when I got back home; and when I read in the *Oxford Mail* that Mrs. Somebody-or-other had mentioned seeing a jogger there wearing red trainers . . . I should have put them in the dustbin. Stupid, I was! But they'd cost me— well, I told you. And I've always loved animals, so . . . well, that's it really."

Although less than convinced by what sounded a suspiciously shaky story, Morse was adequately impressed by the manner of the pleasantly spoken young man. Had he been as vain as Morse and many other mortals, he would probably have grown his hair fairly long over his temples in order to conceal his hearing aids. But Harrison's dark hair was closely cropped, framing a clean-shaven face that seemed honest. Or reasonably so.

Asking Harrison to remind him of his home address and telephone number, Morse got to his feet and prepared to leave.

"You'll have to make an official statement, of course."

"I realize that, yes."

Morse pushed the trainers an inch or two further across the desk.

"You might as well keep them now. I only wish I were as fit as you."

Was there a glint of humor in Simon's eyes as, in turn, he got to his feet?

"Fit a shoe, did you say, Inspector?"

Morse let it go. The man's hearing was very poor, little doubt of that. Which made it surprising perhaps that a mobile phone lay on the desk beside him.

On his second impulse that day, Morse drove down to North Oxford and stopped momentarily outside Simon Harrison's small property at 5 Grosvenor Street. The replacement windows with their aluminium frames had clearly been installed there fairly recently—frames whose glory (as advertised) was never to need any painting at all.

Courteously if somewhat cautiously received, Lewis listened carefully as one of the Bank's important personages spelled out the situation with (as was stressed) utter confidentiality, with appropriate delicacy, and with (for Lewis) a leavening of incomprehensible technicalities. In simple terms it amounted to this: Mr. Frank Harrison, currently on furlough, was currently also, if unofficially, on suspension from his duties with the Bank on suspicion, as yet unsubstantiated, of misappropriation of monies: viz. an unexplained black hole of some £520,000 in his department's investment portfolios.

Chapter Sixty-four

> *Refrain to-night*
> *And that shall lead a kind of easiness*
> *To the next abstinence: the next more easy;*
> *For use almost can change the stamp of nature.*
> (Shakespeare, *Hamlet*)

Sloane Square . . . Gridlock . . . Siren . . . Gridlock . . .
Siren . . .

It is not a matter for any surprise that car drivers
occasionally contract one of the minor strains of the
road-rage virus—even that patient man in the siren-
assisted police car who finally pulled over on to the hard
shoulder of the M40 and rang his chief.

"Been stuck in traffic, sir. Be with you in about an
hour."

"Lewis! Can't you hear the wireless? It's five-past
seven—bang in the middle of *The Archers*. It can wait,
surely!"

Lewis supposed it could; and would have said so. But
the phone was dead.

Wireless! Huh! Everybody called it a "radio" these
days—well, everybody except Morse and one or two of
the old 'uns, like Strange. Yes, come to think of it,
Morse and Strange were the oldest of the HQ lot, with
Strange six months the older and due for retirement that
next month.

The road was free and Lewis drove fast. It could
wait—of course it could—the news about Harrison
Senior. Perhaps it didn't matter all that much; and as
Morse frequently reminded him nothing really mattered
very much at all in the end. But he was looking forward
to a swapping of notes. There had been some interesting developments, certainly on his own side; and he

doubted not that Morse's researches that day had generated a few new ideas. Not that they needed any more high-flown ideas really, he decided, as a sudden torrential downpour called for more terrestrial concentration. He reduced his speed to 80 mph.

At 7:20 P.M. Morse was sitting back in the black-leather armchair, knowing that only a few of the pieces in the jigsaw remained to be fitted. Earlier in the case the top half of the puzzle had presented itself as a monochrome blue, like the sky earlier that evening, although of late the weather had become sultry, as though a thunderstorm were brewing. But the jigsaw's undifferentiated blue had been duly broken by a solitary seagull or two, by a piece of soft-white cloud, and later perhaps (when Lewis arrived?) by what Housman so memorably had called "the orange band of eve." He felt almost happy. There was something else, too: he would quite certainly wait until that arrival before having his first drink of the day. It was quite easy really (as he told himself) to refrain from alcohol for a limited period.

The storm reached North Oxford fifty minutes later, traveling from the southwest at a pace commensurate with Lewis's speed along the M40.

It may have had something to do with Wagner, but Morse enjoyed the intensity and the electricity of a thunderstorm, and he watched with deep pleasure the plashing rain and the dazzling flashes in the lightning-riven sky. From his viewpoint by the window of his flat, a slightly sagging telephone wire cut the leaden heavens in two; and he watched as a succession of single drops of rain ran along the wire before finally falling off, reminding him of soldiers crossing a river on rope-harness, and finally dropping off on the other side. As he had once done himself.

Crossing the river . . .

His mother would never speak of "dying": always of "crossing the river." It was a pleasing conceit; a pleasing metaphor. If he'd been a poet, he might have written a sonnet about that telephone-wire just outside. But

Morse wasn't a poet. And the storm now ceased as suddenly as it had started.

And the front-door bell was ringing.

It was after 10 P.M. when, with Lewis now gone, Morse took stock of the situation—with renewed interest, though (truth to tell) with little great surprise. Lewis had declined the offer of alcohol, and Morse had decided to prolong his own virtually unprecedented abstinence. He felt tired, and at 10:30 P.M. decided that he would be early abed. So many times had he been counseled that beer made a lumpy mattress, that spirits made a hard pillow, and that in general alcohol was the stuff that nightmares were made of. So, if that were true, he could perhaps expect to be sleeping the sleep of the just that night. It would be a new experience.

He put on the RSPB video, and once again watched the wonderful albatross gliding effortlessly across the Antarctic wastes. So relaxing . . .

At 11:15 he switched off the bedroom light and turned as ever on to his right-hand side, conscious of a clear head, a freshness of mind, and a gently slumbrous lassitude.

Wonderful.

In spite of his occasional disillusionment about being cast up on to the shores of light in the first place, it would be wholly untrue to say that Morse was over-eager to embark on that final journey to that further land. Indeed, like the majority of mortals, he was something of a hypochondriac; and that night he found himself becoming increasingly fearful about his own physical well-being. Or ill-being.

The illuminated green figures on the alarm clock showed 2:42 A.M. when he finally abandoned the unequal struggle. His mind was an uncontrollable whirligig at St. Giles Fair, and the indigestion pains in his chest and in his arms were hard and unrelenting. He got up, poured himself a glass of Alka-Seltzer, poured himself a glass of the single malt, took up his medium-blue Parker pen, and resumed the exegesis he'd been writing when Lewis had interrupted him, deciding however to cross out the last (and uncompleted) sentence:

It was embarrassing for me to talk to you about this and I know that you in turn found it equally embarrassing to—

There would be ample time to put that part of the record straight in the days ahead.

Tomorrow and tomorrow and tomorrow . . .

Chapter Sixty-five

Jealousy is that pain which a man feels from the apprehension that he is not equally beloved by the person whom he entirely loves.

(Addison, *The Spectator*)

Simon H. is not a good liar, and I dragged some of the truth out of him. He is genuinely very deaf, and the telephone must always be a nightmare for him. So what's he got a mobile for? Even people with good hearing often have trouble with one. But, remember, even someone who's stone deaf can communicate to some degree with someone on the other end, because he's always able to *speak* if not to hear.

Many people must have wanted Barron dead. And no one more so than Frank Harrison, who'd learned that Barron would soon be working up at some giddy height in a quietish street in Burford. The job had been mentioned, among other places no doubt, in the Maiden's Arms. And one person in that pub was in regular communication with Frank H.: Allen Thomas, that soon-to-be-married youth who regularly wastes his substance on the fruit machine. How come? Like so many others in this case, he's dependent on Frank H.—his father, remember!—who (rumor!) has just bought him a small flat in Bicester, and who has pretty certainly been making him a regular allowance for many years.

The plan had been a reasonably simple one—with one snag. Both the Harrisons, Senior and Junior, had some knowledge of Barron's ladder technique from the several times he had worked at the family home: specifically his habit of tying the top of his ladders to something firm up there in the heights. It would seem likely that he'd do the same again, and there'd be little point in giving the ladder one great hefty push if it wouldn't topple to the ground. Some recce was therefore required; and Simon picked up his father that Monday morning in Oxford and drove him the twenty miles to Burford, leaving the car at the western end of Sheep Street, and then jogging up and down the opposite side of the street in tracksuit and trainers, noting that Barron was moving the ladder along every twelve minutes or so, and predictably reroping the top each time. The only possibility then was to catch Barron after he'd *re*-climbed the ladder and was refixing the rope. A minute or so? Not much more. But enough. Simon's job was to phone his father, mobile to mobile, and just say "Now!" Nothing else. He hadn't the spunk he says (I believe him) to perform the deed himself; and it was his father, also in jogging kit, who would run along the pathway there and topple Barron to a death that in Simon's view was fully deserved and long overdue.

That was the plan. Something like it. So I believe.

But the countdown had been aborted because (Simon himself a witness) a bicycle, the front wheel jerked up repeatedly from the ground, was lurching its way along the path, and under the ladder, *and into* the ladder. Surplus to requirements therefore was the plan the Harrisons had plotted. Or so we are led to believe. Why such a proviso? Because I shall be surprised if any plan devised by the opportunistic Frank Harrison has ever come to a sorry nothing. Is it possible therefore that the accident of Barron's death was not quite so "accidental" after all? Already Frank Harrison had accomplished something far more complex—his manipulation of the evidence surrounding his wife's murder, when it was imperative for him to establish one crucial fact: that no other living soul was present when he went into his house that night. But three other people knew this fact was untrue; and all three of them—whichever way intercommunication was effected—were subsequently rewarded for their roles in the conspiracy of complicity and silence.

Back to my proviso.

Can it be that Frank Harrison trawled his net even wider and dragged in the cyclist who sent Barron down to his death, the boy Holmes—the brother of Harrison's son Allen?

We turn now to the Harrison clan itself.

Our researchers have given us several pointers to the relationships within that family. The marriage itself had long been loveless: he with a string of mistresses in his Pavilion Road flat in London; she with a succession of straight or kinky but always besotted bedmates, with whom she fairly regularly dallied with mutual delight. And, doubtless, profit. Of the two children, Simon was clearly the mother's favorite—a boy who had battled bravely with his disability; a boy for whom his mother had found an affection considerably deeper than that for her daughter Sarah—a young lady who was very attractive physically, very bright academically, very talented musically, who from her early years had almost everything going for her, and who (unlike her brother) needed far less of her mother's tender loving care. Both children, as well as their parents, were probably fully aware of the imbalance here; and tacitly and tactfully accepted it.

At the time of their mother's murder, both the children had left home several years earlier. Sarah had already qualified as a doctor specializing with considerable distinction in the treatment of diabetes. And Simon had landed a surprisingly good job in publishing, and was now financially independent—if not emotionally independent, because he still yearned for that unique love his mother had always shown him; a love that had meant everything to him in those long years of an ever-struggling school life in which he knew with joyous assurance that it was he—Simon!—who'd acquired the monopoly of a mother's love, more of it even than his father had ever had. He called to see her regularly, of course he did. But she probably always insisted that he ring her beforehand. No reason to ask why, surely? Simon was completely unaware of his mother's vesper-tinal divertissements.

But Frank certainly knew all about them, and they served as some sort of excuse and justification for his own adulterous liaisons. He didn't much care anyway. Perhaps he could shrug things off fairly easily. But Simon couldn't. Simon turned up unexpectedly one evening and found his mother lying on that very same bed where as a young boy (perhaps as an older boy?) he'd snuggled in beside her when his dad was away; and where he'd seen a man straddled across her on his elbows and his knees.

I doubt it had been exactly like that, though. More likely he'd seen a man bouncing down the stairs toward him, jerking up his trousers and fastening up his flies. A man he knew: Barron! Then he'd found his mother lying in the bedroom there: naked, gagged, handcuffed, with a pornographic video probably still running on the TV. Shell-shocked with disbelief and disillusionment, in the white heat of a furious jealousy—yes!—*he murdered his mother.*

Chapter Sixty-six

> We might now be stepping through a dark door with no bottom on the other side, and fall flat on our faces.
>
> (A member of the Honolulu City Council,
> quoted by the Press Corps)

Conscious that he was writing with increasing fluency, Morse poured himself another tumbler of single malt and resumed his narrative:

With regard to events immediately thereafter, we can only guess. But at some point Simon rang his father in predictable panic. He had very few people he could call on. But he *could* call on his father—and there was a special loop-system on the telephone there. And Frank H. got to the house as quickly as any man could have done that night. His BMW *was* in for servicing, that was checked; and I now believe (a bit late in the day) that the sequence of events was precisely as he claimed: taxi » Paddington; train » Oxford; Oxford (enter Flynn!) » Lower Swinstead.

Then? Probably we'll never really know. But five people, three of them now dead, *they* knew: Barron, who'd been disturbed *in medio coitu*; Flynn, the petty crook who just happened to be on hand; Repp, the burglar who'd been watching the property all evening; Frank H.; and Simon H. himself. Simon doesn't seem to me the caliber of fellow who could stay long at such a ghastly scene on his own; and I think it's more than likely that his father rang Sarah and told her to get along there posthaste, on the way buying a cinema ticket as an alibi for Simon. Certainly when I met Sarah I felt strongly that she probably knew who had murdered her mother. The trouble was that the three outsiders also knew: Repp and Barron, who were both local men—and Flynn, who'd met Simon in the lipreading classes at Oxpens, and who must have seen him there that night.

What then was the family plan of campaign?

The two (or three) of them were determined to create the maximum amount of confusion—their only hope. The murder couldn't be concealed; but the waters around it could be made so muddied that any investigation was likely to shoot off into several blind alleys. We may postulate that a gag was tied around Yvonne's mouth (as I recall the report: "no longer tight as if she had worked it looser in her desperation"); that a pair of handcuffs was snapped around her wrists; that one of the panes of the French window was smashed in from the outside. Why Yvonne's carefully folded clothes were not scattered all over the floor, I just don't know, because "attempted rape" would have seemed a wholly probable explanation of the murder.

When and how the circling vultures closed in for their shares of the kill—your guess, Lewis, is (almost) as good as mine. Some early liaison there must have been with Barron in order to establish the telephone alibi. Flynn probably just stayed around that night— a petty crook going through a bad patch, and naming his price immediately. I suspect that Repp, a real pro, held his hand for a couple of days or so before threatening to spill at least half the can of beans . . . unless he could be persuaded otherwise.

Whatever the case, financial arrangements were made, and as far as we know faithfully met. After the murder of his wife, much money was diverted from the assets of Frank H. into other channels, although I'm still surprised to learn that there may well have been some serious misappropriation of funds at the Swiss Helvetia Bank.

All of which leaves one or two (or three!) points unresolved.

First, the burglar alarm. Now on his train trip from London Frank H. must have had thoughts galore. Several times he would have phoned home from the train, and *Sarah* must surely have been there to take the calls. And it was probably from the back of the taxi that Frank had the clever idea of ringing Sarah and telling her he would be ringing again, when the taxi was only half a minute or so from home, and asking her (Flynn wouldn't have heard, would he?) to turn on the burglar alarm. It *was* a clever idea, let's agree on that. It certainly and understandably caused huge confusion in the original police inquiry. The only person not wholly confused was Strange. It was he, from the word go, who suggested that the alarm might well have been set off deliberately by the murderer himself. (Never underrate that man, Lewis!)

The time, as Morse saw, was 3:40 A.M., almost exactly one hour after he'd started writing. He was feeling pleasantly tired, and he knew he would slip into sleep so easily now. Yet he wanted to go (as Flecker had said) "always that little further"; and perhaps more immediately to the point he wanted to pour himself a further Scotch—which he did before resuming.

There is one more thing to consider, and it is of vital importance, as well as being (almost!) the only thing about which I was less than honest with you. That is, the extraordinary relationship between a drink-doped, drug-doped juvenile lout and an insignificant-looking little schoolma'am: between Roy Holmes and Christine Coverley. Something must have happened, probably at school, which had forged a wholly improbable but strangely strong bond between them—including a sexual relationship (she confessed as much). That's the reason she stayed on in Burford after the end of the summer term. Why is this important? Because we have been making one fundamental assumption

in our inquiries which thus far has been completely
unverified by any single independent witness. But
truth will out! And first, and forthwith, we shall
call in on Ms. Coverley for further questioning.
How wise it was to hold our horses before facing
Frank Harrison with a whole

(Here the narrative breaks off.)

Morse, who had been deeply asleep at his study desk,
his head pillowed on folded arms, jerked awake just
before 7:30 A.M., feeling wonderfully refreshed.
Life was a funny old business.

Chapter Sixty-seven

> To run away from trouble is a form of cowardice; and, whilst
> it is true that the suicide braves death, he does it not for some
> noble object but to escape some ill.
>
> (Aristotle, *Nicomachean Ethics*)

The following morning Lewis was pleased with himself. Before Morse arrived, he'd turned to the *Police
Gazette*'s "Puzzle Corner" and easily solved the challenge
there:

> What initially would an intelligent cyclist's
> thought be on studying the following list of
> operas by Verdi?
>
> *Tosca*
> *Aida*
> *Nabucco*
> *Don Carlos*
> *Ernani*
> *Macbeth*

"Initially"—that was the clue; and once you twigged it, the answer stared you in the face vertically.

Morse made an appearance at 9:10 A.M., looking (in Lewis's view) a little fitter than of late.

"Want to test your brain, sir?"

"Certainly not!"

Lewis pushed the puzzle across the desk, and Morse considered it, though for no more than a few seconds:

"Do *you* know the answer?"

"Easy! 'Initially,' sir—that's what you've got to think about. Just look at the first letters. Cyclist? Get it?"

"I thought the question was what would an *intelligent* cyclist's thought be."

"I don't quite follow."

"Not difficult surely, Lewis? You've just got the answer wrong, that's all. Any intelligent cyclist, any bright bus driver—anyone!—would think exactly the same thing immediately."

"They would?"

"The *question*'s phony. Based on a false premise, isn't it? Based on the assumption that the facts you've been given are true."

"You mean they're not?"

"*Tosca?* Written by *Verdi?*"

Oh dear! "You were quick to spot that."

Morse grinned. "Not really. They often ask me to submit a little brainteaser to the *Gazette*."

"You mean—?"

Morse nodded. "And talking of false premises, that's been a big part of our trouble. We've both been trying to check up on such a lot of things, haven't we? But there's *one* thing we've been prepared to accept without one ha'poth of evidence. So we'll get on to that without delay. Couple of cars we'll need. I'll just give Dixon a ring—"

Lewis got to his feet. "I can deal with all that, sir."

"Si' down, Lewis! I want to talk to you."

Through the glass-paneled door Dixon finally saw the silhouette moving toward him: a woman in a wheelchair who brusquely informed him that she knew nothing of the whereabouts of her son. He had not been home the previous evening. He had a key. He was sometimes out all night, yes. No, she didn't know where. And if it was of any interest to the police, she didn't care—didn't bloody well *care*.

There was no reply to PC Kershaw's importunate ringing and knocking. But at last he was able to locate the mildly disgruntled middle-aged woman who looked after the two "lets"; and who accompanied him back to the ground-floor flat. She appeared to have little affection for either of the two lessees, although when she opened the door she must have felt a horrified shock of sympathy for one of them.

Christine Coverley lay supine on a sheepskin rug in front of an unlit electric fire. She was wearing a summery, sleeveless, salmon-pink dress, her arms very white, hands palm-upward, with each of her wrists slashed deeply and neatly across. A black-handled kitchen knife lay beside her left shoulder.

Young Kershaw was unused to such horrors; and over the next few days the visual image was to refigure repeatedly in his nightmares. Two patches on the rug were deeply steeped in blood; and Kershaw was reminded of the Welsh hill farm where he'd once stayed and where the backs of each of the owner's sheep had been daubed with a dye of the deepest crimson.

No note was found by Kershaw; indeed no note was found by anyone afterward. It was as if Christine had left this world with a despair she'd found incommunicable to anyone: even to her parents; even to the uncouth lout who penetrated her so pleasurably now, though at first against her will; even to the rather nice police inspector who'd seemed to her to understand so much about her. Far too much . . . including (she'd known it!) the fact that she had lied. Roy could never have been cycling along Sheep Street when Barron fell to his death because at that very moment he had been in bed with her . . .

Chapter Sixty-eight

> It is not the criminal things which are hardest to confess, but
> the ridiculous and the shameful.
>
> (Rousseau, *Confessions*)

Lewis had not been surprised—no, certainly not that.
But disappointed? Yes. Oh yes! And Morse had been
aware of his reaction, clearly anticipating it, yet saying
nothing to lessen the impact of the revelation. The relationship between them would never be quite the same
again, Lewis realized that. It wasn't at all the fact that
Morse had driven out one evening (two evenings? ten
evenings?) to meet a seductively attractive woman.
Lewis had seen the sharply focused photographs of her
body stretched out on the bed that night; and it could
be no great wonder that many a man, young and old
alike, had lusted after a woman such as that. No, it was
something else. It was the out-of-character, underhand
way that Morse had allowed the dishonest subterfuge to
linger on and on from the beginning of the case.

Indeed Morse had been less than wholly forthcoming
in his confession even now, Lewis was fairly sure of it.
Yes, Morse agreed, he *had* gained access to the file containing the intimate correspondence addressed to Y H.
Yes, he *had* "appropriated" the handcuffs, police handcuffs, with a number stamped on them that could easily
be traced back to the officer issued with them, in this
case to Morse himself. And yes (he readily admitted it)
he *had* "withdrawn" the relevant sheet of the issue-
numbers kept at HQ. As far as the partial letter was
concerned (Morse accepted immediately that it was in
his own hand) Lewis had hoped, in an old-fashioned
sort of way, that Morse had in fact *never* been invited to
Lower Swinstead, in spite of his own plea for some

communication from her; in spite of that almost school-boyish business about looking through his mail every morning in the hope of finding something from her. And that was about it. Morse had wanted to cover up something of which he was rather ashamed and very embarrassed; just wanted his own name, previously his own good name, never to be associated with the life—and the death—of Yvonne Harrison. He'd been careless about leaving that single page of a longer letter but (as he asked Lewis to agree) it was hardly an incriminating piece of evidence. What Morse stoutly refused to accept was that what he had done, however cowardly and dishonest and foolish, had in any way jeopardized the course of the original inquiry, which he now had the nerve to assert had been conducted with almost unprecedented incompetence. Such arrogance was of course not all that unusual; yet in the present circumstances it seemed to Lewis quite gratuitously cheap.

Leaving all such considerations aside though, what stuck in Lewis's throat was that initial, duplicitous refusal on Morse's part to have anything to do with the original case. Agreed, once he had been drafted on to what seemed to both Lewis and Strange the second half of the *same* case, Morse had risen to his accustomed heights of logical analysis and depths of human understanding. Agreed, he had (as usual) been several furlongs ahead of the field—and, for once, on the right racecourse from the "off."

Who else but Morse could have put forward the quite extraordinary hypotheses made earlier that morning about the murder of J. Barron, Builder? The hypothesis (seemingly confirmed) that Roy Holmes—who'd do almost anything to *get* drugs and who'd do absolutely anything when he was *on* drugs—was having a sexual relationship with Christine Coverley; the hypothesis (seemingly confirmed) that the weirdly incongruous partnership had resulted from some incident or series of incidents at school; that the youth had agreed, for money, to make a statement to the police about a supposedly accidental collision with a high ladder—a statement that was wholly untrue, because Roy Holmes had been nowhere near Sheep Street that morning; the hypothesis (to *be* confirmed!) that it was Frank Harrison who had murdered Barron, and who had engineered an ingenious scheme whereby all suspicion would be diverted both from himself and from Simon— the scheme itself probably prompted by another son, by Allen Thomas, who regularly gathered a good deal of information from his vantage point in the Maiden's Arms and who regularly passed it on to his father, the man at the center of everything.

Lewis nodded to himself. No wonder Frank Harrison had gone to earth somewhere. Not for long though, surely. He had nowhere to go; nowhere to hide. Airports and seaports had been apprised of his passport number, and photographs would be on their way. Unless it was too late.

It was Morse's suggestion that the two of them together should interview Roy Holmes and Christine Coverley, with Lewis invited to do most of the talking with the youth. "I detest him, Lewis! And you're better at those sorts of things than I am." It was flattering, but it didn't work. Morse was sadly wrong if he thought he could so easily re-establish some degree of integrity in the eyes of his sergeant.

In midmorning, Lewis left the office without asking Morse if he would like a coffee. He knew that the omission would be noted; he knew that Morse would feel the hurt.

Not so.

When Lewis returned ten minutes later, he found Morse leaning back and beaming happily.

"Fetch me a coffee, will you, Lewis! No sugar—we diabetics, you know ... Something to celebrate." *The Times* was folded back in quarters in front of him, the crossword grid completely filled in. "Six and a half minutes! I've never done it quicker."

"Shouldn't that be 'more quickly'?"

"Good man! You're learning at last. You see it's a

question, as I've told you, of the comparative adjective and the comparative adverb. If you say—"

The phone rang.

Dixon.

For the moment Roy Holmes was not to be found: he wasn't at home; he wasn't anywhere. Did Morse want him to keep looking?

"What the hell do you think?" Morse had snapped at him. "You remember the old proverb? If at first you don't succeed, don't take up hang gliding."

The brief telephone conversation pleased Lewis, and for a few seconds he wondered if he was being a little unfair in his judgment on Morse. But only for a few seconds.

"Not the only one we can't find, sir."

"Frank Harrison, you mean? Ye-es. I'm a bit puzzled about him. He might be a crook—he *is* a crook—but he's not a fool. He's an experienced, hard-nosed, single-minded, rich banker, and if you're all those things you don't suddenly put your fingers in the—"

The phone rang.

Kershaw.

Morse listened, saying nothing; but the eyes that lifted to look across the desk into Lewis's face, if not wholly surprised, seemed very disappointed and very sad. Much as two hours earlier Lewis's own eyes had looked.

In midafternoon (Morse was no longer at HQ) the phone rang.

Swiss Helvetia Bank.

"Could we speak to Superintendent Lewis, please?"

"Sergeant Lewis speaking."

Chapter Sixty-nine

At 5:20 P.M. he was still standing beside his minimal hand luggage a few yards from the Euro-Class counter at Heathrow's Terminal 4, looking around him with as yet dismissable anxiety, but with gradually increasing impatience. 5:10 P.M.—that was when they'd agreed to meet, giving them ample time, once through the fast-track channel, to have some gentle relaxation together in the British Airways Lounge before boarding the 18:30 Flight 338.

Paris . . .

A long time ago he and Yvonne had gone to Paris on their honeymoon: lots of love, lots of sex, lots of sight-seeing, lots of food and wine. A whole fortnight of it, although he'd known even then that just a week of it would have been rather better. It was not difficult (he already knew it well) to get bored even in the presence of a mistress; and he'd begun to realize on that occasion that it was perfectly possible to grow just a little wea-ried even in the company of a newly wed wife. There had been one or two incidents, too, when he'd thought Yvonne was experiencing similar thoughts . . . especially that time one evening when she'd quite obviously been exchanging long looks with a moustachioed Frenchman who looked exactly like Proust. He'd called her "a flir-tatious bitch" when they got to their hotel room; and when she'd glared back at him and told him they'd make a "bloody good pair" one way or another . . .

There would be no trouble like that with Maxine: only two and a half days—just right, that! And she was a real honey, a law professor from Yale, aged forty-two, divorced, a little oversexed, a little overweight, and hugely desirable.

She finally appeared, pulling an inordinately large suitcase on wheels.

"You're late!" His tone was a combination of anger and relief; and he immediately moved forward ahead of her to the back of the short queue at the first-class counter.

"You didn't get my message, did you? I tried and tried—"

"Like I told you? On the mobile?"

"It wasn't working. I think you'd forgotten—"

"Christ!" Harrison took his mobile from an inside pocket, tapped a few digits, then another few; then repeated the blasphemy: "Christ! I'd had enough of the bloody mobile recently and—"

"And you forgot that we'd agreed—"

"Sorry! Say you'll forgive me!"

He looked down at her squarish, slightly prognathic face, her dark-brown silky hair cut short in a fringe across her broad forehead and above the quietly gentle eyes that were becoming tearful now, perhaps from her hectic rush, perhaps from the undeserved brusqueness of his greeting, but perhaps above all from the knowledge that his love for her homodyned only with the waves of that physical lust which so often excited him. Yet the brief holiday had been *her* choice, and she knew that she wouldn't regret having made it. She enjoyed being with him: he was good fun and intelligent and well read and still handsome and still excellent in bed and—yes!—he was rich.

They moved nearer the counter, neither of them too anxious to speak—a phenomenon not uncommon with persons queuing, as if their concentration were required for the transactions ahead. But she volunteered some incidental information:

"Accident there was, near Stokenchurch, and I tried to—"

Gently he ran a hand through her silken hair. "Sweetheart? Forget it!"

"It's just that we must have been stuck there half an hour and we saw—one of the other passengers pointed it out—a beautiful bird of prey there. A red kite."

"Tell me later!"

There was now just the one business-suited man in front of them.

"Where have you booked us?"

"The best."

"And the best air-tickets—?"

"Sh! Nothing but the best for you. Why not? Just think of me! No wife. No blackmailing kids. No problems at work. Nothing to spend money on for a day or two—except on you. I'm a rich man, sweetheart. I thought I'd told you."

"Tickets, please?"

The smiling young lady scrutinized the perfectly valid tickets.

"Passports, please?"

The young lady scrutinized the perfectly valid passports.

"Smoking?"

"Nonsmoking."

"Window-center? Center-aisle?"

"Center-aisle."

"Luggage?"

Frank Harrison lugged the great case on to the trackway beside the desk.

"Only the one?"

"Yes."

"You know where the club lounge is?"

"Yes."

"Enjoy your flight, sir, and enjoy your stay in Paris!"

He handed her a glass of champagne, and two glasses clinked. "Here's to a wonderful little break together. Ritz—here we come!"

He leaned across and kissed her on the soft, unlipsticked mouth—a long, yearning kiss. His eyes closed. Her eyes closed.

"Mr. Harrison?" A tap on the shoulder. "Mr. Frank Harrison?"

"What—?"

A uniformed police officer stood beside the small table: "I'm sorry, sir, but we need to speak to you. Routine check."

"Thames Valley Police, is this?"

"That's right, sir."

"What exactly—?"

"It's not *just* that. Your employers want to speak to you as well."

Harrison's eyes squinted in bewilderment.

"What the hell do *they* want? I'm on official furlough, for God's sake. They'll have to wait till I get back."

"Will you come this way, sir? Please!"

A second uniformed policeman—young, dark-haired—stood just inside the entrance to the executive lounge; was still standing there a quarter of an hour later when Maxine, after drinking the one and then the other glass of champagne, went over to speak to him.

"Do you mind telling me, Officer, by whose authority—?"

"Not mine, miss," said PC Kershaw. "Please believe me. I also am a man *under* authority."

"You haven't answered my question."

"I'm from Thames Valley—we both are."

"Who sent you here?"

"The CID."

"Who?"

"Chief Inspector Morse."

"Who's he when he's in his office?"

"He's an important man."

"Very important?"

"Oh yes!" Kershaw nodded with a reverential smile.

"You talk as if he's God Almighty."

"Some people think he is."

"Do you?"

"Not always."

"How long will you be keeping Mr. Harrison?"

"I just don't know, Mrs. Ridgway."

Maxine poured herself a further glass of champagne, and pondered as she sat alone at the small table. They knew *her* name too . . .

He wasn't a particularly lucky man to associate with, Frank Harrison. The last time she'd been with him, over a year ago, he'd had that phone call from—well, he'd never said who from—to tell him that his wife had been murdered . . .

She was tempted to get up and—well, just leave. Just get out of there. Her case was on the plane by now though—suits, dresses, lingerie, shoes—but it *could* be returned perhaps? She still had her handbag with its far more important items: cards, keys, diary, money . . .

But she felt sure the PC at the door would never let her out. That's why he was there. Why else?

An announcement over the lounge Tannoy informed her that first-class passengers for British Airways Flight 338 to Paris should now proceed to Gate 3; and a dozen or so people were draining their drinks and gathering up their hand luggage. But for Maxine Ridgway it was now a feeling of deep sadness that had overtaken those earlier minutes of indecision and despair. She was no fool. She knew by heart the role she'd been asked to play in the Ritz; and she'd accepted the bargain, because it *would* have been a bargain.

She was not even bothering to wonder what she should do next when she heard the voice behind her: "Come on, sweetheart! You heard the announcement. Gate 3."

With her mind in a mingled state of amazement and relief, she picked up her hand luggage and followed him to the exit-doors, where there was now no sign of PC Kershaw, the man who had seemed to have a greater familiarity with Holy Writ than she had herself.

"Routine check, that's all," asserted Frank Harrison. "Just like the man said."

Chapter Seventy

I cried for madder music and for stronger wine,
But when the feast is finished and the lamps expire,
Then falls thy shadow, Cynara! the night is thine;
And I am desolate and sick of an old passion,
  Yea hungry for the lips of my desire:
I have been faithful to thee, Cynara! in my fashion.
              (Dowson, *Non Sum Qualis Eram*
                    Bonae Sub Regno Cynarae)

"Let him go, Kershaw. Let him catch his flight."

"You think that's wise, sir?"

"*What?*"

"I just wondered—"

"Look, lad! If I ever have to look to you as a fount of wisdom, it'll be the day you're dry behind the ears. Is that clear?"

"Sir!"

Morse put down the phone. It was 6:10 P.M.

"Do you think that was fair, sir?" asked Lewis.

"Probably not," conceded Morse.

It had been Lewis, an hour earlier, who had received the call from the Bank: profound apology; embarrassing recantation; chagrin unspeakable! Over £500,000 indeed was still unaccountably missing; but not, *not* from Harrison's department. Inquiries subsequent to Lewis's visit had now established that any embezzlement or misappropriation of funds was most definitely not to be laid at the door of one of the Bank's most experienced, most trusted, most valued blah blah blah.

It was a call in which Morse was most interested, now repeating (with some self-congratulation) what he had earlier maintained: that Frank Harrison might well be, most likely *was*, capable of murder; but that it was quite out of character, definitely *infra dignitatem*, for him to stoop to cooking the books and fiddling the balance-and-loss ledgers.

"Do you think you may be wrong, sir?"

"Certainly not. He'll be back from Paris, believe me! There's no hiding place for him. Not from me, there isn't."

"You think he murdered his wife?"

"No. But he knows who did. *You* know who did. But we've got to get some evidence. We've been checking alibis—recent ones. But we've got to check those earlier alibis again."

"Who are you thinking of?"

"Of whom am I thinking?" (Morse recalled the suspicion he'd voiced in his earlier notes.) "I'm thinking of the only other person apart from Frank Harrison who had a sufficient motive to kill Yvonne."

"You mean—?"

"Do you ever go to the pictures?"

"They don't call it the 'pictures' any more."

"I went to the pictures a year and a bit ago to see *The Full Monty*."

"Surely not your sort of—?"

"*Exactly* my sort of thing. I laughed and I cried."

"Oh yes." (The penny had dropped.) "Simon Harrison said he'd gone—"

" 'Said,' yes."

"Said he'd gone with someone else, didn't he? A girlfriend."

"Wasn't checked though, as far as I can see."

"Understandable, isn't it? Nobody ever really thought of someone inside the family—"

"Oh yes they did. Frank Harrison was one of their first suspects."

"But with those signs of burglary, the broken window, the burglar alarm . . ."

Morse nodded. "At first almost everything pointed to an outside job. But then it slowly began to look like something else: a lover, a tryst, a sex session, a quarrel, a murder . . ."

"And now we're coming back to the family, you say."

"No one seems to have bothered to get a statement from the young lady Simon Harrison took to the pictures that evening."

"Perhaps we could still trace her, sir?"

"Yes."

"It's a long time ago though. She'd never remember—"

"Of course she would! It was all over the papers: 'Woman Murdered'—and she'd been with that same woman's son the evening when it happened. She could never forget it!"

"It's still a long time—"

"Lewis! I don't eat all that much as you know. But when I'm cooking for myself—"

(Lewis's eyebrows rose.)

"—I always make sure the plate's hot. I can't abide eating off a cold plate."

"You mean we could heat the plate up again?"

"The plate's already hot again. She's still around. She's a proud, married mum now living in Witney."

"How do you know all that?"

"You can't do *everything* yourself, Lewis."

"Dixon, you mean?"

"Good man, Dixon! So we're going to see her tonight. Just you and I."

"You think Simon murdered his mum."

"No doubt about that. Not any longer, Lewis," said Morse quietly.

"Just because he found her in bed with someone . . ."

"With Barron. I *know* that, Lewis."

Never before had Lewis been so hesitant in asking Morse a question:

"Did . . . did Mrs. Harrison ever tell *you* that she was . . . seeing Barron?"

Morse hesitated—hesitated for far too long.

"No. No, she never told me that."

Lewis waited a while, choosing his words carefully and speaking them slowly: "If she *had* told you, would *you* have been as jealous as Simon Harrison?"

Again Morse hesitated. "Jealousy is a dreadfully corrosive thing. The most powerful motive of all, in my view, for murder—more powerful than—"

The phone rang once more and Morse answered.

Kershaw.

"They'll soon be winging their way across the channel, sir. Anything more you want me to do?"

"Yes. Have a pint of beer, just the one, then bugger off home."

Morse put down the phone.

"Good man, Kershaw! Bit of an old woman though. Reminds me of my Aunt Gladys in Alnwick, my last remaining relative. Well, she was. Dead now."

"I think he'll do well, yes."

"Kershaw? Should do. He got a First in History from Keble."

"Bit more than me, sir."

"Bit more than me, Lewis."

The phone was ringing again.

Strange.

"Morse? You've let him out of the country, I hear?"

"Yes. We need a bit more time and a bit more evidence before we bring him in."

"I agree," said Strange, unexpectedly. "No good just . . ."

"He'll be back for the day of reckoning."

"You think so?"

"I know so."

"And in the interim?"

"He'll be having a beano—kisses, wine, roses. 'But when the feast is finished and the lamps expire . . .' You know the Dowson poem, sir?"

"Course I bloody do!"

"Well, I don't think he'll ever be really happy with any of these other women of his."

"This one sounds like a bit of all right though."

"I'd still like to bet he wakes up in the small hours sometimes and thinks back on the woman he loved more than any of them, feeling a bit desolate—"

"—and sick of an old passion."

"Exactly."

"Yvonne, you mean?"

"No, not Yvonne, sir. Elizabeth—Elizabeth Jane Thomas."

Chapter Seventy-one

> What more pleasant setting than the cinema for sweetly deodorized bodies to meet, unzip, and commune?
>
> (Malcolm Muggeridge, *The Most of Malcolm Muggeridge*)

Sylvia Marsden (née Prentice) was temporarily living with her mother in a pleasantly appointed semi on a housing estate at Witney. And it was her mother (Lewis had phoned earlier) who had answered the door and shown the two detectives into the lounge where the buxom Sylvia, blouse open, was breast-feeding a very new baby—not in the slightest degree disconcerted to be thus interrupted in her maternal ministrations, one hand splayed across an engorged nipple, the fingers of the other playing lovingly around the lips of the suckling infant.

An awkwardly embarrassed Morse moved slowly round the room, simulating deep interest in the tasteless bric-a-brac that cluttered every surface and shelf in the brightly decorated room; whilst Lewis stood above the mother and child, smiling quasi-paternally and drawing the back of his right index finger lightly across the cherubic cheek:

"Little treasure, isn't he? What's his name?"

"She's a she, actually—aren't you, Susie?"

"Ah yes, of course!"

Morse temporarily declined to take a seat but accepted, strangely enough, the offer of coffee, and began his questioning whilst looking through the window on to the neatly kept back garden.

"We're just having to make one or two further inquiries, Mrs. Marsden—"

"Call me Sylvia!"

"It's about one of your former boyfriends—"

"Simon, yes, I know. That Sergeant Dixon told me. Nice man, isn't he? He got on ever so well with Mum."

Morse nodded, aware of the probable reason. "It's a long time ago now, I realize . . ."

"Not really. Not for me it isn't. The night Simon's mum was murdered? Can't forget something like that, can you?"

"That's good news, Sylvia. Now that night, that evening, the 9th—"

"Oh no! You've got it wrong. It was the 8th—the night Mrs. Harrison was murdered. I'm quite sure of that. My birthday, wasn't it? Simon took me to the ABC in Oxford. Super film! All about these male strippers—"

"Did the police ever ask you about it?"

"No. Why should they?"

Sylvia rebuttoned her blouse, and as Morse turned at last to face her, Lewis could see the disappointment on his face.

Mrs. Prentice (née Jones), who had clearly been listening keenly from the adjacent kitchen, now brought in two cups of coffee. "I can remember that," she volunteered. "Like she says, that was your birthday, wasn't it, Sylv?"

"How did you find Simon, Mrs. Prentice?" asked Lewis.

"I liked him. He used to come in sometimes but I think he felt a bit . . . you know, with his hearing."

"He didn't come in that night?"

"No. I remember it well. Like Sylv says—well, not something you forget, is it? I saw him though, after he'd brought her back. And I heard the pair of 'em whispering on the doorstep. Nice boy, really. Could have done worse, couldn't you, Sylv?"

"I did *better*, Mum, OK?"

Clearly there was less than complete family agreement on the merits of baby Susie's official father and

Morse swallowed his coffee quickly and, as ever, Lewis followed his chief's lead dutifully.

In the car outside they sat for some time in silence.

"You knew it was the 8th, sir. Why—?"

"Just to test her memory."

There was another long silence.

"Looks as if we've been wrong, sir."

"Looks as if *I've* been wrong."

"Alibis don't come much better than that."

"No."

"You know when Mrs. Whatshername said she heard the pair of 'em whispering outside, she probably heard more of the conversation than Simon ever did!"

Morse nodded with a wry grin. "You don't think there's any chance that somebody bribed our Sylvia and Sylvia's mum . . . ?"

"Not the remotest. Do you?"

"No."

"Where do we go from here, sir?"

"You can drop me off at the Woodstock Arms or . . ."

"No. I meant with the *case*, sir."

". . . or perhaps the Maiden's Arms."

It seemed that Morse was hardly listening.

"I know you're disappointed, sir, but—"

"Disappointed? Nonsense!"

Some light-footed mouse had just scuttled across his scapulae; and when Lewis turned to look at him, it seemed as if someone had switched the electric current on behind his eyes.

"Yes, Lewis. Just drive me out to Lower Swinstead."

Chapter Seventy-two

> *Below me, there is the village, and looks how quiet and small!*
> *And yet bubbles o'er like a city, with gossip, scandal, and spite.*
>
> (Tennyson, *Maud*)

Unwontedly in a car, Morse was almost continuously talkative as they drove along: "Do you know that lovely line of Thomson's about villages 'embosomed soft in trees'?"

"Don't even know Thomson," mumbled Lewis.

"Remarkable things! Strange, intimate little places where there's more going on than anybody ever dreams of. You get illicit liaisons, hopeless love affairs, illegitimate offspring, wife-swapping, interbreeding, neighborly spite, class warfare—all that's for the insiders, though. If you're on the outside, they refuse to have anything to do with you. They clamp up. They present a united defensive front because they've got one thing in common, Lewis: the village itself. They're all members of the same football club. They may loathe each other's guts for most of the week, but come Saturday afternoon when they put on the same football shirts . . . Well, the next village better look out!"

"Except Lower Swinstead doesn't have a football team."

"What are you talking about? They're *all* in the football team."

Lewis drove down the Windrush Valley into Lower Swinstead.

"They don't all clamp up, anyway. Not to you, they don't. Compared with some of our lads you've squeezed a carton of juice out of 'em already."

"But there's more squeezing to do, Lewis—just a little."

Unwontedly in a pub, Morse had already taken out his wallet at the bar, and Lewis raised no objection.

"Pint of bitter—whatever's in the best nick."

"It's all in the best nick," began Biffen.

"And . . . orange or grapefruit, Lewis?"

The fruit machine stood idle and the cribbage board was slotted away behind the bar. But the place was quite busy. Most of the customers were locals; most of them people who'd earlier been questioned about the Harrison murder; most of them members of the village team.

On the pub's noticeboard at the side of the bar, underneath "Live Music Every Saturday," was an amateurishly printed yellow poster advertising the current week's entertainment:

8:30–11:30 P.M.

DON'T MISS IT

The widely acclaimed folksinger

CYNDI COOK

with the ever popular

3 R's

Randy, Ray, Rick

"Popular?" asked Morse of the landlord.

"Packed out we are, every Sat'day."

"Ever had Paddy Flynn and his group playing here?"

"Paddy who?"

"Flynn—the chap who was murdered."

"Ah yes. Read about it, o'course. But I don't think he were ever here, Inspector. You know, fifty-odd groups a year and—how many years is it I've—"

"Forget it!" snapped Morse.

"The beer OK?"

"Fine. How's Bert, by the way? Any better?"

"Worse. Quack called to see him yesterday—just after we'd opened—told Bert's boy the old man oughta go in for a few days, like—but Bert told 'em he wasn't going to die in no hospital."

For someone who knew almost nothing about some things, Thomas Biffen seemed to know an awful lot about others.

"Where does he live?" asked Morse.

It was Bert's son, a man already in his late fifties, who showed Morse up the narrow steepish steps to the bedroom where Bert himself lay, propped up against pillows, the backs of his hands, purple-veined and deeply foxed, resting on the top of the sheet.

"Missing the cribbage, I bet!" volunteered Morse.

The old face, yellowish and gaunt, lit up a little. "Alf'll be glad of a rest. Hah!" He chuckled deeply in his throat. "Lost these last five times, he has."

"You're a bit under the weather, they tell me."

"Still got me wits about me though. More'n Alf has sometimes."

"Still got a good memory, you mean?"

"Allus had a good memory since I were at school."

"Mind if I ask you a few things? About the village? You know . . . gossip, scandal . . . that sort of thing? I had a few words with Alf, but I reckon his memory's not as sharp as yours."

"Never was, was it? Just you fire away, Inspector. Pleasure!"

Lewis, who had been left in the car, leaned across and opened the passenger door.

"Another member of the local football team?"

Morse smiled sadly and shook his head. "I think he's in for a transfer."

"What exactly did he—?"

"Get me home, Lewis."

On the speedy journey back to Oxford, the pair spoke only once, and then in a fairly brief exchange:

"Listen, Lewis! We know exactly where Frank Harrison is; who's with him; how long he's booked in at his hotel; when his return flight is. So. I want you to make sure he's met at Heathrow."

"If he comes back."

"He'll be back. I want *you* to meet him. Charge him with anything you like, complicity in the murder of his missus; complicity in the murder of Barron—please yourself. Anything! But bring him back to me, all right? I've seldom looked forward—"

Morse suddenly rubbed his chest vigorously.

"You OK, sir?"

Morse made no reply immediately. But after a few miles had perked up considerably.

"Just drop me at the Woodstock Arms!"

"Do you think—?"

"And present my apologies to Mrs. Lewis. As per usual."

Lewis nodded as he turned right at the Woodstock Road roundabout.

As per usual.

In Paris, in the Ritz, later that same evening—a good deal later—Maxine Ridgway was finding it difficult to finish the lobster dish and almost impossible to drink another mouthful of the expensive white wine that looked to her exactly the color and gravity of urine. She was tired; she was more than a little tipsy; she was slightly less than breathlessly eager for another bout of sexual frolicking on their king-size bed. And Frank, too (she'd sensed it all evening), had been strangely reticent and surprisingly sober.

She braved the exchange: "You're not quite your usual self tonight, Frank."

"Why do you say that?"

"It's that business at Heathrow, isn't it?"

Frank leaned across the table and placed his right

hand on her arm. "I'll be OK soon, sweetheart. Don't worry! And I ought to tell you something: you're looking absolutely gorgeous!"

"You think so?"

"Why do you reckon all the waiters keep making detours round our table?"

"Tell me!"

"To have a look down the front of your dress."

"Don't be silly!"

"You hadn't noticed?"

"Frank! It's been a long day—and I'm just so tired . . . so tired."

"Not *too* tired, I hope? *Nicht zu müder?*"

"No, darling."

"You don't want a sweet? A coffee?"

"No."

"Well, you go up. I'll be with you soon. I've just got a couple of private phone calls to make. And I want to think for a little while—on my own, if you don't mind? And make sure you put that see-through thing on, all right? The one that'll send the garçon ga-ga when he brings our breakfast in the morning."

"You've arranged that?"

Frank Harrison nodded; and watched the backs of her legs as she left the table.

Yes, he'd arranged for breakfast in their room.

He'd arranged everything.

Almost.

Chapter Seventy-three

> When I have fears that I may cease to be
> Before my pen has glean'd my teeming brain . . .
> (Keats, *Sonnet*)

Slowly Morse walked homeward from the Woodstock Arms, disappointed (as we have seen) if not wholly surprised, that the favorite in the Harrison Stakes had fallen (like Devon Loch) within sight of the winning post. But now, at last (or so he told himself), Morse guessed the whole truth. And feeling pleasingly over-beered, he had earlier taken the unusual step of ordering a bar snack and had enjoyed his liberally horse-radished beef sandwiches. He thought he would probably sleep well enough that night. After a while. Not just for a minute though. Truth was that he felt eager to continue (to finish off?) the notes he'd already been making on the Harrison murder, just in case something happened; just in case no one would be aware of the sweetly logical solution that had formulated itself in his mind that day.

Much earlier (Morse knew it) he should have paid far more attention to the thing that had puzzled him most about the Harrison murder: *motive*. Until now, Simon had fitted that bill pretty well, since Morse was sure that the mother–son relationship had been very close; much *too* close. Good thinking, that! Then, that very afternoon, a busty lusty lass sitting with Simon in the three-and-sixpennies had innocently scuppered his carefully considered scheme of things.

Once home, Morse poured himself a modestly liberal measure of Glenfiddich, and changed into a gaudily striped pair of pajamas that blossomed in white and purple and red . . . before continuing, indeed completing, his written record.

> This evening in Lower Swinstead I spoke at quite some length with Mr. Bert Bagshaw. Why did I not follow my first instincts? Had I done so, I would have realized that any clues to that (most elusive) motivation for the murder of Yvonne Harrison would ever be likely to lie in the immediate locality itself, rather than in some external rape or alien burglary. Hardy's yokels usually knew all about the goings-on in the Wessex villages; and their role is paralleled today by the likes of the Alfs and the Berts in the Cotswold public houses. Although I now know who murdered Yvonne Harrison, it will not be easy to prove the guilt of the accused party. I am reminded of the Greek philosopher Protagoras, who found it difficult to be dogmatic about the existence of the gods, partly because of the obscurity of the subject matter, and partly because of the brevity of human life.
>
> But herewith I give my final thoughts on the murder of Yvonne Harrison, that crisply uniformed nurse who looked after me in hospital once (but once!) with such tempting, loving care . . .

He finished writing an hour later at 12:45 A.M.

Or perhaps, to be accurate, he wrote no more thereafter.

At which hour Lewis was somewhat uneasily asleep, not at all sure in his mind whether things were going well or going ill. Morse had insisted that it should be he, Lewis, who would be on hand when Frank Harrison and his lady passed through Arrivals at Heathrow. No problem there though. Still thirty-six hours to go before the scheduled British Airways flight was due to land, and Morse had been adamant that Harrison *would* be on that flight, and not flitting off to Katmandu or the Cayman Islands. Yet one thing was ever troublously disturbing Lewis's thoughts: the real nature of the puzzling and secret relationship that had clearly existed between Morse and Yvonne Harrison.

Chapter Seventy-four

> We are adhering to life now with our last muscle—the heart.
> (Djuna Barnes, *Nightwood*)

Morse awoke at 2:15 A.M., his forehead wet with sweat, an excruciating ache along the whole of his left arm running up as far as his neck and jaw, a tightly constricting corselet of pain around his chest. He managed to reach the bathroom sink where he vomited copiously. Thence, in pathetically slow degrees, he negotiated the stairs, one by one—finally reaching the ground-floor telephone, where he dialed 999, and in a remarkably steady voice selected the first of the Ambulance Fire Police options. He was seated on the lime-green carpet beside the front door, its Yale lock and bolts now opened, when the ambulance arrived six minutes later.

It all happened so quickly.

After being attached to a portable heart monitor, after a pain-killing injection, after chewing an aspirin, after having his blood pressure taken, Morse found himself lying, contentedly almost, eyes open, on a stretcher in the back of the ambulance.

Beside him a paramedic was looking down with well-disguised anxiety at the ghastly pallor of the face and the lips of a purple-blue: "We'll just get the docs to have a look at you. We'll soon be there. Don't worry."

Morse closed his eyes, conscious that life had always been a bit of a worry and seemed to have every likelihood of so continuing now . . .

He should perhaps have rung Lewis from upstairs—Lewis had a flat key—instead of ringing 999.

But then, he realized, Lewis wouldn't have had all that medical equipment, now would he?

He'd been a little disappointed that he'd heard no ambulance siren.

But then, he realized, there wouldn't be all that much traffic, even in Oxford, at such an early hour, now would there?

Soon, he knew it, they'd be asking for his "Religion."

But then, he realized, it wouldn't take too long for him (or them) to write down "None" in some appropriate box, now would it?

"Next of Kin," too. Trickier that though, because the penultimate member of the Morse clan had recently died, aged ninety-two.

But then it wouldn't take too long to write down "None" again.

And there were more cheerful things to contemplate. Perhaps Nurse Harrison would be there in the ward again to sit by his bed in the small hours . . .

But then, he realized, Yvonne Harrison was now dead.

Perhaps Sister McQueen would be on duty to pull him through again?

But then, he realized, she was away for a month in far Carlisle, tending a frail, demanding mother.

The kindly paramedic held him down gently as he tried to sit up on the stretcher.

"Lewis! I must see Sergeant Lewis."

"Of course. We'll make sure you see him as soon as they've had a quick look at you. We're nearly there."

The night nurse in the "goldfish bowl," at the right of the Emergencies Entrance watched as the automatic double doors opened and the paramedics wheeled the latest casualty through, deciding immediately that Resuscitation Room B was the place for the newcomer. Quickly she bleeped the Senior House Officer.

The next ten minutes saw swift and methodical action: blood samples were promptly dispatched somewhither; chest X rays were taken; an electrocardiograph test had firmly established that the patient had suffered a hefty anterior myocardial infarct. But it was time for

another move; and the activities of a young and kindly
nurse with a clipboard, dutifully requesting details of
medical history, next of kin, religion, and the like, were
mercifully cut short by a specialist nurse who with all
speed supervised an urgent transfer.

Morse had always delighted in sesquipedalian termi-
nology, since his education in the Classics had given him
much insight into the etymology of words more than a
foot and a half long. And now, as he lay in the Coronary
Care Unit, he listened with interest to the words being
spoken around him: thrombolysis, tachicardia, strepto-
something-something. One thing was certain: much was
happening and was happening quickly again. As if there
were little time to spare . . .

Were angels male or female? They'd started off life as
male, surely? So there must have been a sort of trans-
sexual interim when . . . Morse's mind was wondering . . . What gender was the Angel of Death then,
whom he now saw standing at the right-hand side of his
bed, with a nurse holding one gently restraining hand
on a softly feathered wing, and the other hand on his
own shoulder.

Morse awoke to full consciousness again, opened his
eyes, and found Lewis's hand on his shoulder.

"Sorry to disturb you, sir."

"You? What the 'ell are you doing here?"

"One o' the paras—knew who you were—and heard
you say, you know . . ."

Morse nodded, and smiled.

"How you doing, sir?"

"Fine! It's just a case of misidentity."

"I mustn't be long. They've told me just a coupla
minutes, you know."

"Why's that?" asked Morse wearily.

"They say you need, you know, a lot of rest."

"*Lew*-is! Why do you keep saying 'you know' all the
time?"

"Not said 'actually' yet though, have I?"

"When you go up to bring Harrison in today—"

"Tomorrow, sir."

"You sure?"

"Quite sure."

"Don't forget! *I'm* doing the interviewing."

Lewis turned to find Nurse Shelick standing behind him. "Please!" her lips mouthed, as she looked down on Morse's intermittently closing eyes.

"Shan't be a second, nurse."

He bent down and whispered: "Anything I can do, sir?"

Morse's eyes were still closed, but he seemed to regain some of his earlier coherence.

"Yes. Second drawer down on the right. There's a Carlisle number for Sister McQueen. Give her a ring. Not today though ... like you say, tomorrow. Just say I'm ..."

Lewis prepared to go. "Leave it to me, sir, and ... keep a stout heart! Promise me that!"

Morse opened his eyes briefly. "That's what my old father used to say."

"So you *will*, won't you, sir?"

Morse nodded slowly. "I'll try. I'll try ever so hard, my old friend."

Lewis was checking back the tears as he walked away from the Coronary Care Unit, and failed to hear Nurse Shelick's quiet "Good-bye."

Chapter Seventy-five

> The cart is shaken all to pieces, and the rugged road is very near its end.
>
> (Dickens, *Bleak House*)

That same day was to be the longest and almost the unhappiest in Lewis's life. At 6:30 A.M. he drove out to Police HQ and sat quietly in Morse's office, the Harrison case the last thing that concerned him. At 7 A.M. he rang the JR2 and learned that Morse's condition was "critical but stable," although he had little real idea what that might signify on the Coronary Richter Scale.

Strange, early apprised of Morse's hospitalization, came in at 8 A.M., himself immediately ringing the JR2, and impatiently asking several questions—and being given the same answer as Lewis: "Critical but stable." As much was being done as humanly possible, Strange learned, and any visit was, at present, quite out of the question. For the minute it was all tests and further treatment. The ward had the police number of Sergeant Lewis, and would ring if . . . if there was any news.

Morse was fully conscious of what was going on around him. He felt fairly sure that he was dying and pretended to himself that he would face death with at least some degree of dignity, if not with equanimity. He had been seated beside his old father when he'd died and heard him reciting the Lord's Prayer, as if it were some sort of insurance policy. And Morse wondered whether his own self-interest might possibly be served by following suit. But if by any freak of chance there *was* an Almighty, well, He'd understand anyway; and since, in Morse's view, there wasn't, he'd be wasting his really (at this time) rather precious breath. No. The long day's task was almost done, and he knew that he must sleep . . .

At 1:30 P.M. the consultant looked down on the sleeping man. There had been no positive reaction from the comprehensive tests and treatments; no success from the diuretic dosages that should have cleared the fluid that was flooding the lungs; no cause for the slightest optimism from the echocardiogram.

He sat at the desk there and wrote:

"Clinical evidence that the heart is irreparably damaged; kidney failure already apparent. Without specific request from n.o.k. in my judgment inappropriate to resuscitate."

The nurse beside him read through what he had written.

"Nothing else we can do, is there?"

The consultant shook his head. "Pray for a miracle, that's about the only hope. So if he asks for anything, let him have it."

"Even whiskey?"

"Why do you say that?"

"He's already asked for a drop."

"Something we don't stock in the pharmacy, I'm afraid."

The nurse smiled gently to herself after the consultant had left, for someone had already slipped a couple of miniature Glenfiddichs into the top of Morse's bedside table; and there'd only been the one visitor.

Seated outside a café on the Champs Elysées, Maxine Ridgway clinked her glass across the table. It had been a splendid lunch and she felt almost happy.

"Thank you! You're a terrible, two-timing fellow—you know that. But you're giving me a wonderful time. You know that, too."

"Yes, I do know. Trouble is the time's gone by so quickly."

"No chance of staying another few days? Day or two? Day?"

"No. We're back in the morning as scheduled. I've got a meeting I've agreed to attend."

"A board meeting?"

"No, no. Much more interesting. A meeting with a chief inspector of police. I've met him once before, only the once, at a funeral; and then only very briefly. But he's—well, he's a bit like me, in a way, I suppose. He'd never run away from anyone, I reckon; and I'd never forgive myself if I ran away from him."

Maxine looked over at Frank Harrison and realized

for the first time in their relationship that she was probably in love with the man. In those early heady days it had been all Daimlers and diamonds; but she would always have chosen the wine and the roses of these last forty-eight hours . . .

Suddenly she sensed that she was never going to see him again, and she yearned at that moment to be alone with him, and to give herself to him.

"Let's go back to the hotel, Frank."

"What? On a beautiful sunny afternoon like this?"

"Yes!"

Frank Harrison leaned across and placed his right hand on her bare shoulder. "Shall I tell you a secret, my darling? I was about to suggest exactly the same thing myself."

It was a happy moment.

But a moment only.

Harrison got to his feet.

"I've just got to make a phone call first."

"You can ring from the room."

"No, it's a private call."

"And you don't want me to—?"

"No, I don't."

"If he asks for anything," that's what the consultant said. And when Morse made his second request (the first already granted) the nurse rang Police HQ immediately. Lewis and Strange—Morse wanted to see them.

Perhaps she had given the two names in alphabetical order, but Lewis hoped it had been in order of preference—a hope though that had probably been unjustified, he thought, as he stood waiting at the back of the unit, since it had clearly been Strange who had been first on Morse's visiting list.

"Right old mess you've got yourself into, Morse!"

"Looks like it, I'm afraid."

"You're in the best of hands, you know that."

"I'm going to need a bit more than that."

"Look, Morse. Don't you think it would be a good thing . . . don't you think I ought—?"

But Morse was shaking his head in some agitation.

"No! Please! If you really want to help . . ."

"Course! Course, I do!"

"Can you ask Lewis . . . ?"

"Course! Just you keep hold of the hooks, old mate! And that's an order. Don't forget I'm still your superior officer."

"Lewis!" Morse spoke the name very quietly but quite clearly. His eyes were open, and his lips moved as if he were about to say something.

But if such were the case, he never said it; and Lewis decided to do what so many people have done beside a hospital bed; decided to speak a few comforting thoughts aloud:

"You've got the top load of quacks in Oxfordshire looking after you, sir. All you've got to do—promise me!—is to do what they say and . . . And what I really want to say is thank-you for . . ."

But Lewis could get no further.

And in any case Morse had closed his eyes and turned his head away to face the pure-white wall.

Just a little word from Morse would have been enough.

But it wasn't to be.

A nurse was standing beside him, testing his lipreading skills once more: "I'm afraid we must ask you to go . . ."

At 4:20 P.M. Morse seemed to rally a little and held his hand up for the nurse.

"I'm allowed a drop more Scotch?" he whispered.

She poured out the miserably small contents of the second miniature and held a jug of water over the glass.

"Yes?"

"No," said Morse.

She put her arm around his shoulders, pulled him toward her, and held the glass to his lips. But he sipped so little that she wondered whether he'd drunk a single drop; and as he coughed and spluttered she took the glass away and for a few moments held him closely to her, and felt profoundly sad as finally she eased the white head back against the pillows.

For just a little while, Morse opened his eyes and looked up at her.

"Please thank Lewis for me . . ."

But so softly spoken were the words that she wasn't quite able to catch them.

The call came through to Sergeant Lewis just after 5 P.M.

Chapter Seventy-six

> *Say, for what were hop-yards meant,*
> *Or why was Burton built on Trent?*
> *Oh many a peer of England brews*
> *Livelier liquor than the Muse,*
> *And malt does more than Milton can*
> *To justify God's ways to man.*
> (A. E. Housman, *A Shropshire Lad*)

Before leaving for Heathrow, Lewis had informed Chief Superintendent Strange that it would not be at all sensible, in fact it would be wholly inappropriate, for him to continue as a protagonist, virtually *the* protagonist, in the Harrison case: he was exhausted mentally, physically, emotionally; and, well . . . he just begged for a rest. And Strange had granted his request.

"I'm going to put someone in charge who's considerably more competent than you and Morse ever were."

"Yourself, sir?"

"That's it," smiled Strange sadly. "You have two or three days off—from tomorrow. You could take the missus to South Wales."

"I said I needed a rest, sir! And there are one of two things that Morse . . ."

"Make a few calls you mean—yes. And go through his diary and see what dates . . ."

"I don't think there'll be many of those."

"You don't?" asked Strange quietly.

"And I haven't got much of a clue how he was going to tackle Frank Harrison."

Strange lumbered round the table and placed a vast hand on Lewis's shoulder. "You've got a key?"

Lewis nodded.

"Just bring Harrison Senior straight to me. Then . . ."

Lewis nodded. He was full up to the eyes; and left without a further word.

On journeys concerned with potential criminals or criminal activity, CID personnel were never advised, and were seldom permitted, to travel alone. And the following morning Lewis was not wholly unhappy to be traveling alongside a familiar colleague, albeit alongside Sergeant Dixon. After the first few obligatory words, the pair of them had lapsed into silence.

There was never likely to be any risk of missing the returning couple at the Arrivals exit. Nor was there. And it was Lewis who read from his prepared notes, as unostentatiously as he could: "Mr. Frank Harrison, it is my duty as a police officer to inform you that I am authorized to remand you into temporary custody on two counts: first, on suspicion of the murder of Mr. John Barron of Lower Swinstead on the 3rd of August, 1998; second, on suspicion of the murder of your wife, Yvonne Harrison, on the 8th July 1997. It is also my duty to tell you—"

"Forget it, Sergeant. You told me what to expect. Just a couple of favors though, if that's all right? Won't take long."

"What have you got in mind?" In truth, Lewis had neither the energy nor the enthusiasm to initiate any determined pursuit had Frank Harrison and partner decided to make a dash for it and vault the exit barriers. But that was never going to happen. Nor did it.

"Well, it's the car, first of all. I left it—"

"All taken care of, sir. Or it will be."

"Thank you. Second thing, then. You know the one thing I really missed in Paris? A pint of real ale, preferably brewed in Burton-on-Trent. The bars are open here and . . ."

"OK."

Dixon stood beside him as Harrison ordered a pint of Bass and a large gin and tonic (and, of course, nothing else) whilst Lewis sat at a nearby table, momentarily alone with Maxine Ridgway.

"You know," she said very firmly, "you're quite wrong about one thing. I don't know too much about Frank's life, but it does just so happen I was with him the night that his wife was murdered. We were together in his London flat! I was there when the phone rang and when he ordered a taxi to Paddington—"

Frank Harrison was standing by the table now: "Why don't you learn to keep your mouth shut, woman!" But his voice was resigned rather than angered, and if he had contemplated throwing the gin and tonic in her face, it was only for a second or two.

He sat down and drank his beer.

The damage had been done.

In the back of the police car as it returned to Oxford, Lewis realized, with an added sadness, that Morse had been wholly wrong, as it now transpired, in his final analysis of the Harrison murder. Frank Harrison, if his lady friend were to be believed, just could *not* have murdered his wife that night; and the police must have been right, in the original inquiry, to cross him off their suspect list. It had all happened before, of course—many a time!—when Morse, after the revelation of some fatal flaw in his earlier reasoning, would find his mind leaping forward, suddenly, with inexplicable insight, toward the ultimate solution.

But those days had now gone.

It was not until the car was passing through the cutting in the Chilterns by Stokenchurch that Harrison spoke:

"Red kite country this is—now. Did you know that, Sergeant?"

"As a matter of fact I did, yes. I'm not into birds myself though. The wife puts some nuts out occasionally but . . ."

It may hardly be seen as a significant passage of conversation.

Harrison spoke again just after Dixon had turned off the M40 on to the A40 for Oxford.

"You know, I'm looking forward to seeing Morse again. I met him at Barron's funeral, but I don't think we got on very well . . . My daughter, Sarah, knows him though. He's one of her patients at the Radcliffe. She tells me he's a strange sort of fellow in some ways— interesting though, and *very* bright, but perhaps not taking all that good care of himself."

Lewis remained silent.

"Why didn't he come up to Heathrow himself? Wasn't that the original idea?"

"Yes, I think it was."

"Are we meeting at St. Aldate's or Kidlington?"

"He won't be meeting you anywhere, sir. Chief Inspector Morse is dead."

Chapter Seventy-seven

> Dear Sir/Madam
>
> Please note that an entry on the Register of Electors in your name has been deleted for the following reason:
>
> DEATH
>
> If you have any objections, please notify me, in writing, before the 25th November, 1998, and state the grounds for your objection.
>
> Yours faithfully
> (Communication from Carlow County Council to an erstwhile elector)

After returning to HQ Lewis gave Strange an account of the quite extraordinary evidence so innocently (as it seemed) supplied by Maxine Ridgway.

But he could do no more.

For he had nothing more to give.

Unlike Morse, who had always professed enormous faith in pills—pills of all colors, shapes, and sizes—Lewis could hardly remember the last time he'd taken anything apart from the Vitamin C tablet he was bullied to swallow each breakfast-time. It had therefore been something of a surprise to learn that Mrs. L. kept such a copious supply of assorted medicaments; and retiring to bed unprecedentedly early that evening he had swallowed two Nurofen Plus tablets and slept like the legendary log.

At 10 A.M. the following morning he drove up to the mortuary at the JR2.

The eyes were closed, but the expression on the

waxen face was hardly one of great serenity, for some hint of pain still lingered there. Like so many others contemplating a dead person, Lewis found himself pondering so many things as he thought of Morse's mind within the skull. Thought of that wonderful memory, of that sensitivity to music and literature, above all of that capacity for thinking laterally, vertically, diagonally— whateverwhichway that extraordinary brain should decide to go. But all gone now, for death had scattered that union of component atoms into the air, and Morse would never move or think or speak again.

Feeling slightly guilty, Lewis looked around him. But at least for the moment his only company was the dead. And bending down he put his lips to Morse's forehead and whispered just two final words: "Good-bye, sir."

Chapter Seventy-eight

> . . . & that I be not bury'd in consecrated ground
> & that no sexton be asked to toll the bell
> & that no murners walk behind me at my funeral
> & that no flours be planted on my grave . . .
> (Thomas Hardy, *The Mayor of Casterbridge*)

Morse had always been more closely attuned to life's adagios than its allegros; and his home reflected such a melancholic temperament. The pastel-colored walls, haunted by the music of Wagner, Bruckner, and Mahler, were decorated with somber-toned reproductions of Rembrandt, Vermeer, and Atkinson Grimshaw; and lined, in most rooms both upstairs and down, with long shelves of the poets and the novelists.

The whole place now seemed so very still as Lewis picked up two pints of semiskimmed Co-op milk from the porch, picked up four letters from the doormat, and entered.

In the study upstairs there were several signs (as Lewis already knew) of a sunnier temperament: the room was decorated in a sun-bed tan, terra-cotta, and white, with a bright Matisse hanging on the only wall free of the ubiquitous books, CDs, and cassettes. A red angle-lamp stood on the desk with, beside it, a bottle of Glenfiddich, virtually empty, and a cut-glass tumbler, completely empty. Morse had timed his exit fairly satisfactorily.

Lewis sat down and quickly looked through the letters: BT; British Diabetic Association; Lloyds Bank; Oxford Brookes University. Nothing too personal perhaps in any of them, but he left them there unopened. He fully realized there would be quite a few details to be sorted out soon by someone. Not by him though. He had but the single mission there.

In the second drawer down on the right, he found six photographs and took them out. An old black-and-white snap of a middle-aged man and woman, the man showing facial lineaments similar to Morse's. A studio portrait of a fair-haired young woman, with a written message on the back: "Like you I wish so much that things could have been different—love always—W." Another smaller photograph, with a brief sentence in Morse's own hand: "Sue Widdowson before she was arrested." A holiday shot of a young couple on a beach somewhere, the dark-headed bronzed young woman in a white bikini smiling broadly, the young man's right arm around her shoulders, and (again) some writing on the back "I only *look* happy. I miss you like crazy!!! Ellie." Clipped to a photograph of a smartly attractive woman, in the uniform of a hospital sister, was a brief letter under a Carlisle address and telephone number: "I understand. I just can't help wondering how we would have been together, that's all. *I'd* have had to sacrifice a bit of independence too you know! Always remember my love for you. J." Only the one other photograph: that of Morse and Lewis standing next to each other beside the Jaguar, with no writing on the back at all.

Lewis tried the Carlisle number; with no success.

On the floor to the right of the desk lay a buff-colored folder, its contents splayed out somewhat, as if perhaps it may have been knocked down accidentally; and he picked it up. On the front was written: "For the attn. of Lewis."

The top sheet was the printed FORM DI/D2, issued by the Department of Human Anatomy in South Parks Road, the second section duly signed by the donor; and countersigned by the same man who had witnessed the validity of the second single sheet of A4 to which Lewis now turned his attention:

MY WILL

I expressly forbid the holding of any religious service to mark my death. Nor do I wish any memorial service to be arranged thereafter. If any persons wish to remember me in any way, let it be in their thoughts.

If these handwritten paragraphs have any legal validity, as I am assured they do, my estate may be settled with little difficulty. I no longer have any direct next of kin, and even if I have, it makes no difference.

My worldly goods and chattels comprise: my flat (now clear of mortgage); its contents (including a good many rare first editions); two insurance policies; and the monies in my two accounts with Lloyds Bank. The total assets involved I take to be somewhere in the region of £150,000 at current rates and values.

It is my wish that the said estate, after appropriate charges, be divided (like Gaul) into three parts, in equal amounts (unlike Gaul) with the beneficiaries as follows:
(a) The British Diabetic Association
(b) Sister Janet McQueen (see address book)
(c) Sergeant Lewis, my colleague in the Thames Valley CID.

For several minutes, Lewis sat where he was, unmoving, but deeply moved. Why in heaven Morse should have shown such bitterness toward the Church, he couldn't know; and wouldn't know. And why on earth Morse had remembered *him* with such . . .

His thoughts still in confusion, Lewis tried the Carlisle number again; again without success.

He washed out the empty tumbler in the bathroom, and returned to the study, where he poured himself the last half-inch of Glenfiddich, sat down again, silently raised his glass, and drained it.

He looked down at the several sheets of paper remaining in the folder, marked on the first page "Notes on the Harrison Case," and all written in Morse's hand, that same small upright script that Lewis had found in the Harrison files. He'd go through it all later though. For the moment he placed the other two single sheets on the top, and was preparing to leave, when he opened the second drawer down again, took out the photograph of the Jaguar, and slipped it into the folder—on top of everything else.

And noticed something else there, pushed to the back of the drawer.

A pair of handcuffs.

Chapter Seventy-nine

> *Heaven has no rage like love to hatred turned,*
> *Nor hell a fury like a woman scorned.*
> (Congreve, *The Mourning Bride*)
> *If you're guilty, you'll have to prove it.*
> (Groucho Marx)

Lewis finished reading through the folder early that same evening. Most of it he'd known about already. It was only when he'd come to the last three sheets that he was aware of the wholly new tenor of Morse's thinking.

But herewith I give my final thoughts on the murder of Yvonne Harrison, that crisply uniformed nurse who looked after me in hospital once (but once!) with such tempting, loving care.

From the start of this case, one person stood out high above the others in firmness of purpose, daring, and clarity of mind: Frank Harrison. He was still sexually attracted to Yvonne, but she was no longer attracted to him; indeed one night in hospital she told me that she used to hook her foot over her own side of the mattress to establish a sort of no-man's-land between them. But she remained a woman obsessively interested in sex, both as practicing participant and addicted voyeur. (She had mentioned to me some Amsterdam videos. But although I looked quite carefully through the scores of videos there, I could find nothing. I suspect they were innocently disguised under such labels as *The Jungle Book* or *Cooking with Herbs*.)

Now clearly Frank Harrison was—is—someone with a very strong sexual drive, and doubtless he claimed his marital rights on his spasmodic periods at home. But inevitably, when they were away from each other, Yvonne knew what he was up to, just as he knew what she was up to. And for that reason, I can find no compelling motive for Frank Harrison to have murdered his wife. There *might* have been the opportunity, for all we know. But his alibi was uncontested, since there seemed no reason to suspect the firm and explicit evidence of the man Flynn, who claimed to have picked him up from Oxford Station and driven him out to his home to Lower Swinstead.

It is now my view (I look forward to interviewing Frank H. on the matter) that Flynn was not in fact paid for fixing his taxi times for the purpose of Harrison's alibi. He was paid for something different.

Until so very recently I thought that Simon must have murdered his mother. He had ample motive if he found his beloved mum in bed with the local

builder—God help us! And the other facts fitted that
hypothesis neatly: he was known to Repp, the local
shady character familiar to everyone around, as well
as being a regular at the Maiden's Arms; known to
Barron, of course; and also known to Flynn, because
the pair of them had attended lipreading classes
together.

As you know, I was wrong.

But there was someone else who had an even more
compelling motive, with the other facts fitting equally
convincingly: Sarah Harrison. What motive could *she*
have had? Simply this: that she and Barron had been
secret lovers for a year or so before Yvonne's murder.
I learned something about this from two most
unlikely witnesses—from Alf and Bert, denizens of
the Maiden's Arms. Particularly from Bert, who had
seen the two of them together, both at the Three
Pigeons in Witney and at the White Hart in Wolver-
cote, when he was playing away in the cribbage
league. I've little doubt that others in Lower Swinstead knew about it too, but they all kept their
mouths shut. On that fateful evening, Sarah called
home unexpectedly, and found her secret lover in bed
with her mother—God help us! She was already
known to Repp, as well as to Barron, of course. But
where does that opportunistic fellow Flynn fit into
the picture this time? There is now ample proof that
he knew Sarah fairly well, because in the years before
the murder the pair of them had performed in a pop
group together in several pubs and clubs in West
Oxfordshire (some details are known) although never
as it happens at the Maiden's Arms.

And that's almost it, Lewis.

There remains just the one final matter to
settle. The murder weapon was never found. But the
path report, as you'll recall, gave some indication of
the type of weapon used. There were perhaps two
blows only to Yvonne's head. The first rendered the
right cheekbone shattered and the bridge of the nose
broken. The second, the more vicious and it seems the

fatal blow, crashed across the base of the skull, doubtless as Yvonne tried to turn her head away in desperate self-defense. The suggestion made was that some sort of "tubular metal rod" was in all probability the cause of such injuries.

An arm crutch!

How do I know this? I don't. But I shall be inordinately surprised if I am not very close indeed to the truth. And—how many times this has happened?—it was you, Lewis, who did the trick for me again! Remember? You were reining back some fanciful notions of mine about Sarah tearing down to the cinema to buy a ticket, and you said that she wasn't going to be tearing about anywhere that night, because she'd sprained her ankle rather badly; and that if she were doing anything it would be *hobbling* about. Yes. Hobbling about on one of those metal arm crutches they'd probably issued her with from the Physiotherapy Department. (Will you find out, Lewis, if and when the arm crutch was returned?)

I realize that it won't be easy to establish Sarah's guilt, but we've got the long-awaited interview with her father to look forward to. He'll be a worthy opponent, I know that, but I'm beginning to suspect that even *he* has almost had enough by now. If I'm overoptimistic about such an outcome, there'll still be Sarah herself. It will be a surprise if the pair of them haven't been in close touch in recent days and weeks, and I've got a feeling that like her father she's almost ready herself to emerge from the hell she must have been going through for so long. Quite apart from judicial convictions and punishments, guilt brings its own moral retribution. We all know that.

One thing is certain. This will be—has been—my last case. I am now determined to retire and to take life a little more gently and sensibly. We've tackled so many cases together, old friend, and I'm very happy and very proud to have worked with you for so long.

That's it. The time is now 12:45 A.M., and suddenly I feel so very weary.

All the manuscript notes were with Strange within the half-hour.

And Lewis had nothing further to do with the investigation.

Chapter Eighty

I am retired. I am to be met with in trim gardens. I am already come to be known by my vacant face and careless gesture, perambulating at no fixed pace nor with any settled purpose. I walk about; not to and from.

(Charles Lamb, *Last Essays of Elia*)

It seemed there was little to cloud the bright evening at the end of August, that same year, when Strange held his retirement party. The Chief Constable (no less!) had toasted his farewell from the Force, paying a fulsome tribute to his colleague's many years of distinguished service in the Thames Valley CID, crowned, as it had been, with yet another significant triumph in the Yvonne Harrison murder case.

For his part, Strange had spoken reasonably wittily and blessedly briefly and had included a personal tribute to Chief Inspector Morse:

"I don't think we're going to see his like again in a hurry, and people of lesser intellect like me should be grateful for that. And it's good to have with us here his faithful friend and, er, drinking companion" (muted amusement) "Sergeant Lewis" (Hear-Hear! all round). "Morse had no funeral service and no memorial service, just as he wished; but I make no apology for remembering him here this evening because, quite simply, he had the most brilliant mind I ever encountered in the whole of my police career . . . Well now. All that remains for me is to thank you for coming along to see me off; to say thank you for the lawn mower and the book" (he held aloft a copy of Sir David Attenborough's *The Life of Birds*) "and to remind you there's a splendid buffet next door, including a special plate of doughnuts for one of our number." (Much laughter, and much subsequent applause.)

Lewis had clapped as much as the rest of them, but he had no wish to stay too long amid the backslapping and the reminiscences; and soon made his way upstairs to the deserted canteen where he sat in a corner drinking an orange juice, wishing to be alone with his thoughts for a while . . .

The conclusion to the Harrison case had proved pretty much, though far from exactly, as Morse had predicted. Two hours after her father had been taken to HQ for questioning, Sarah Harrison (refusing to see her father) had presented herself voluntarily and made a full confession to the murder of her mother, making absolutely no apology for anything—except for causing her father (she knew it!) all that pain and agony of spirit. What would happen to her now, she said, would not really amount to imprisonment at all; but, in a curious sort of way, to a kind of liberation.

And perhaps it had been much the same, albeit rather later, for Frank Harrison himself, who (less eloquently than his daughter) had by degrees unburdened himself of his manifold sins and wickednesses, including the subsequent murder of his wife's lover, John Barron . . .

His actions, after receiving his daughter's frantic, frenetic phone call on the night of Yvonne's murder, had been straightforward. Train to Oxford; then taxi to Lower Swinstead, whence Barron had long since fled; and where Repp, though still around, remained unseen. Harrison had paid off Flynn, expecting him to drive away forthwith; thereafter very quickly dispatching his distraught daughter home. Coolly and ruthlessly he'd taken over. Confusion!—that was the only hope; and the only plan. Yvonne was already handcuffed, presumably for some bizarre bondage session, and what a blessing that had been! He'd tied a gag lightly around her mouth; gone on to the patio and smashed in the glass of the French window from the outside before unlocking it; he'd turned the lights on, every one of them, and yanked out the TV and the telephone leads, both upstairs and down; and finally, with illogical desperation, he'd decided to activate the burglar alarm, since even if no one heard it, it would be recorded (so he believed).

He'd done enough. Almost enough. Just the police now. He *had* to ring the police, immediately; and suddenly he realized he *couldn't* ring them—he'd just made sure of that himself. But there was his mobile, the mobile on which he'd already rung Sarah several times from the train and once from Flynn's taxi. He could always *lose* it though: and the longer he waited to ring for help, the better the chances for that confusion he'd tried so hard to effect. In detective stories he'd often read of the difficulties pathologists encountered in establishing the time parameters for any murder. Yes! He'd just go up to the main road and walk (run!) the half-mile or so to the next house. Which indeed he was doing when he heard the voice at the gate that led to the drive. He remembered Flynn's words exactly:

"I t'ink you moight be needin' a little help, sorr?" . . .

Epilogue

> Certainly the gods are ironical: they always punish one for one's virtues rather than for one's sins.
>
> (Ernest Dowson, *Letters*)

"Didn't you want any food?"

"No thank you, sir. I've got a meal waiting at home."

"Ah yes. Of course."

"And I didn't particularly want to watch Dixon eating doughnuts."

"No, I understand." Strange lowered himself rather gingerly on to the inappropriately small chair opposite. "Talking of eating, Lewis, what the hell's eating *you*, pray?"

As he'd requested (and as we have seen) Lewis had nothing further to do with the Harrison case. He had tried, and with some considerable success, to distance himself from the whole affair, even from thinking about it. There was just that one persistent, niggling worry that tugged away at his mind like some overindulged infant tugging away at its mother's skirts in a supermarket: the knowledge that Morse, on his own admission, and for the first time in their collaboration, had acted dishonestly and dishonorably.

He looked up at Strange.

"What makes you think something's eating me?"

"Come *on*, Lewis! I wasn't born yesterday."

So Lewis told him.

Told him of the unease he'd felt from the beginning of the case: that Morse had known far too little about it, and then again far too much; that Morse had originally voiced such vehement opposition to taking on the case, and yet had spent the last days of his life doing little else than trying to fathom its complexity.

"And that's all that's been bothering you?"

"*All?*"

"Look! Tell me! What's the very *worst* thing you think he could have done? There's this attractive nurse pulling him through a serious illness in hospital—a place where patients can get a bit low, and a bit vulnerable. Nurses, too, for that matter. And she fell for him a bit—"

"How do you know that?"

"She told me so. She told me one night in hospital when she was looking after *me*! Morse fell for *her* a bit, too—anybody would!—and after he's discharged he writes and asks her why she's not been in touch with him. But she doesn't write back, although she keeps his letter. Know why, Lewis? Because she doesn't really know how to cope with being in love herself."

"How do you know *that?*"

"Does it matter? When she was murdered—well, you know the rest. Morse was on another case at the time—you were on it *with* him, for God's sake! And he said it was too much for the pair of you to take on another."

"Only after he'd found his own letter."

"Lewis!"

"Only after he'd recognized the handcuffs."

"*Lewis!* Listen! Nothing Morse did then—*nothing*—affected that inquiry in the slightest way. Yvonne had kept some letters from her men friends, the kinkies and the straights alike. She certainly didn't keep any from Barron. Maybe because he never wrote any, I dunno. Maybe because she just didn't want to."

"Just the ones from her favorite clients."

"You know that. You've seen them."

"Some of them," said Lewis slowly.

"Well I saw *all* the bloody letters!"

"Including the one from Morse."

"Not a crime you know, writing a letter. It was immaterial anyway, as I keep trying to tell you." Strange looked exasperated. "It's just that it would have been awkward, wouldn't it? Bloody awkward! I wanted to protect the silly sod. You never thought he was a *saint*, did you?"

Lewis was silent for a while. No. He'd never thought of Morse as a possible candidate for sanctification.

But there was something wrong about what he'd just heard.

"So *you* saw the letter before *Morse* saw it, is that what you're saying?"

"Morse *never* saw the letter, not till you showed him that page of it. You see, Lewis, *I* took it—not Morse."

"And you didn't check—"

"Couldn't have done, could I? It was a longish letter. But I didn't read it, so I wouldn't have spotted if there was any gap."

"So it was you who kept some of the evidence separate?"

"Afraid so, yes. I was scared stiff one of *my* letters might be there, if you want the truth. And as things turned out it just became impossible for me to put that stuff back in the folder while the original inquiry was still going on."

"So you got a new box-file when the case was reopened . . ."

Strange nodded. "Always felt guilty about it but—"

"Why didn't Morse spot the page you'd missed?"

"Perhaps he didn't look all that carefully. Not his way usually, was it? Perhaps he wasn't too interested in the literary shortcomings of her other admirers. Not very fond of spelling mistakes, now was he . . . ? or perhaps he just felt the letters were too private, like he'd hoped his own letter would be. How do *I* know? What I do know is that he wasn't looking for a list of lovers who might have been in bed with Yvonne that night. Somehow he was convinced he *knew* who the man was. He told me who it was; and he told you who it was. And he was right."

Lewis nodded.

But the supermarket brat was giving a final tug.

"Plenty of letters and none of them any help, I agree, sir. But just the one pair of handcuffs! And Morse realized there'd be no problem in tracing them, so he destroyed the issue list. And we both know why, don't we, sir? *Because they were his.*"

"Come off it, Lewis! There's a hundred and one worse things in life than him giving some bloody cuffs he'd never used once in his life to some woman who'd asked him for them—whatever the reason."

Slowly shaking his head, Lewis stared down at the canteen carpet disconsolately.

"It's just that he seems not quite the man . . ."

"And you can't forgive him for that."

"Course I can forgive him! Just a bit of a jolt, that's all. Can't you understand that? After all those years we were together?"

"That's what's *really* eating you, isn't it? Be honest! It's just that you don't think as much of old Morse as you used to."

"Not quite as much, no."

Strange struggled to his feet. "Must be off. Good to talk. I'd better get back downstairs."

Lewis got to his feet. "Mrs. Lewis sends her very best wishes, sir."

The two policemen shook hands, and the interesting exchange was apparently over.

But not so.

Halfway to the canteen exit, Strange suddenly turned round and came back to the table.

"Do you remember those issue lists for handcuffs, Lewis?"

"It's a long time ago . . ."

"Well, they're just handwritten lists, kept up to date in a series of columns: date, name, rank, serial number. Just like this." Strange took a folded sheet of A4 from an inside pocket. "But you remember the serial number on the pair you found in Morse's drawer?"

"Nine-two-two."

He handed the sheet to Lewis. "You've got a good memory!"

"Where did you get this?"

"Someone took it from HQ, Lewis. Morse did!"

Lewis looked down at the list, but could find no mention of Morse's name. Could see another name though—at the seventh entry down, along with the other details in the neatly ruled lines:

3 June '68	Strange	PC	734	922

"You mean . . . ?"

"I *mean*, Lewis, that Morse knew I was having an affair with Yvonne Harrison. I don't know how he knew, but he always tended to know things, didn't he? He pinched that form, and he kept it till after the wife's funeral. Then he gave it to me. Said it would be useless without the cuffs, which he said *he* was going to keep anyway, just in case I ever did anything bloody stupid. And he said exactly what I said to you a few minutes ago: nothing—*nothing*—that happened then had affected the inquiry in the slightest way. Is that clear, Lewis?"

Yes it *was* clear. "You're saying that all Morse did was to save you . . . and save Mrs. Strange . . ."

"It would have broken her to pieces," said Strange very quietly. "And me. Would have broken both of us to pieces."

"She never knew?"

"Never had the faintest idea. Thanks to Morse."

Lewis was silent.

"Just like you, eh? About lots of things. You never had the faintest idea, for example, that I re-opened the Harrison case on the basis of a couple of bogus telephone calls, now did you?"

"You mean—?"

"I mean there *were* no telephone calls. I made 'em up myself. Both of 'em."

"I just didn't realize . . ."

"Nobody did, except Morse of course. He guessed straightaway. But I'd like to bet he never told you! He just didn't want to let me down, that's all."

"Why didn't he tell me all this though? It would have made such a lot of difference . . . at the end . . ."

"I dunno. Always an independent sod, wasn't he? And always had that great big streak of loyalty and integrity somewhere deep inside him. But you don't need me to tell you that. So he was never worried too much about what people thought of him. He certainly didn't give two monkeys what *I* thought of him, at least most of the time. In fact the only person he did want to think well of him was *you*, Lewis. So let me tell you something else. It's one helluva job having to live with guilt, as I've done. Almost everybody discovers the same, you know that. Frank Harrison did, didn't he? Sarah Harrison, too. It's something I hope you'll never have to go through yourself. Not that you ever will. Nor did Morse though. He once told me that the guiltiest he ever felt in his life was when a couple of the lads saw him flicking through a girlie magazine in the Summertown newsagent's. So . . . So just keep thinking well of him, Lewis—that's all I ask."

The former Chief Superintendent lumbered across the still-deserted canteen to join the jollifications below.

But Lewis sat where he was.

Apart from the middle-aged woman at the counter reading the *Sun,* there seemed there no one else there. And after looking around him as guiltily as Morse must have done in the Summertown newsagent's, for a little while, in his desolation, he wept silently.

Masterful suspense...

DEATH IS NOW MY NEIGHBOR

by Gold Dagger Award winner

Colin Dexter

◆

Published by Ivy Books.
Available at bookstores everywhere.

Did you enjoy this
Inspector Morse novel?

Then why not go back
to the beginning . . .

LAST BUS TO
WOODSTOCK

The first Inspector Morse
mystery

by Colin Dexter

And the series continues with . . .

LAST SEEN WEARING

**THE SILENT WORLD OF
NICHOLAS QUINN**

SERVICE OF ALL THE DEAD

THE DEAD OF JERICHO

**THE RIDDLE OF THE
THIRD MILE**

THE SECRET OF ANNEXE 3

THE WENCH IS DEAD

THE JEWEL THAT WAS OURS

**THE WAY THROUGH
THE WOODS**

THE DAUGHTERS OF CAIN

DEATH IS NOW MY NEIGHBOR

MORSE'S GREATEST MYSTERY
and Other Stories

Published by Ivy Books.
Available at bookstores everywhere.

Investigate another
Inspector Morse mystery.

THE WAY THROUGH
THE WOODS

by Colin Dexter

Somewhere north of Oxford a young woman disappears
. . . twelve months later the case remains unsolved.

Chief Inspector Morse insists it is murder but without a
body how can he prove it? Then an anonymous letter
arrives at Thames Valley Police headquarters and the letter
contains a cryptic poem that the writer claims is the key to
the mystery. Morse reads news of the letter in the paper
and begins an investigation that will become the most
astonishing even of Morse's career.

Published by Ivy Books.
Available at bookstores everywhere.

*Don't miss this thrilling
Inspector Morse mystery!*

THE DAUGHTERS
OF CAIN

by Colin Dexter

It was the chief superintendent's opinion that too little
progress in the past had been made by the Thames Valley
Police since the discovery of a corpse in a North Oxford
flat. Inspector Morse and Dectective Sergeant Lewis take
over the case and uncover startling new information about
the life and death of the victim.

Yet another body is discovered and suddenly Morse finds
himself with too many suspects and he receives a letter—
a letter containing a declaration of love. . .

Published by Ivy Books.
Available at bookstores everywhere.